In memory of my parents,
Vasile and Aurelia Hâncu

A memento to the exquisite dancing of my dear friend
Sonia Dumitrescu

This is a work of fiction. Names, characters, places, and incidents are either the product of author's imagination or are used fictitiously. Any resemblance to actual events or locales or persons, living or dead, is entirely coincidental.

Copyright © 2010 by Marius Hancu

All rights reserved. No part of this publication can be reproduced or transmitted in any form or by any means, electronic or mechanical, without permission in writing from the author.

The quotation on "Body and Soul" from W.H. Auden is from *The English Auden: Poems, essays and dramatic writings*, ed. Edward Mendelson © 1977. Used by permission of Curtis Brown Ltd.

Our Lives as Kites

1 - Introduction, 1952-

The takeoff, the start of things — that's what Yvonne would always have the most trouble with in all her endeavors. How difficult it was to separate herself from human inertia, from the death of the spirit, as she would, in more critical-language-filled moments, reveal and resent. It was as though roots known and unknown negated her liftoff, as though everything, family, personal history, known tunes, would wage an all-out war — dysentery-filled trenches and poison gas, old Berthas and bayonets — to keep her in place and unchanged but for the effects of age, which were always on the cards and guaranteed and allowed to everyone and everything living.

"Why would an amazingly beautiful girl like you be playing with kites?" some people were asking. "This is like going to the university, even worse, in, say, engineering. Girls like you don't need and don't do things like these, not if their heads are properly screwed on and their eyes are wide open. For centuries, life comes to them carried on a golden plate and, in much finer terms, awash in more resonant music and glorious wines, without all this groping around and wasting of time. And, by the way, now that we're here — your ballet also is too much work. Galley work. But at least it keeps you trim and shapely."

Kites, kites, kites.

Sometimes, that was all Yvonne wanted around her. When she looked at her life, both as in a movie of the past and as in a glass bowl showing the future, time past was an archipelago of islands, strewn everywhere, while the present and the future showed up as a constant, uninterrupted, massive wall in front of her, still to come and be overcome. On each of these islands of the past, she had, at one time or another, in timidity or in daring, raised a *cerf-volant* of experience, just to feel and sound off, fathom, the pull or the balking of Father Time, to find out how his winds were blowing at that particular instant, with or against her, or just to irritate him, as children sometimes do to their grandparents.

Many times, those were real kites she would fly, real *cerf-volants* — the French name seemed to her so beautiful, suggestive of wonderful and strange happenings, in which, she would say so later, as in Chagall, things and people were equally allowed, willing, and purpose-filled to fly in the sky, vertically, horizontally, upside down, the direction didn't really matter, once the take off had somehow been miraculously achieved.

Of the sky, there were hallways and highways, labyrinths and hide-and-seek corners, tunnels and fountains, that her kites would try to navigate and to float, to penetrate and to skim over, to diffuse and to indiscreetly peek through.

The pull on the string, its nervousness and sheer zip, the direction of the yanking, its rhythm, would tell her the story of advancement her messengers were supposed to report back to her from the domain of wind and light, the domain of what people, indiscriminately to her, called weather. And, many times, she took this message and carried it over to her day-to-day messy tangle of facts, with the hope and sometime the bare conviction that some sense detected in far-away, high nature could be read, would translate, as premonitions of the travails, intrigue and yellowness, energy and lassitude, high purpose and don't-give-a-damnness of the living around her.

She didn't go far enough with this so as to report this serious hobby of hers, such messages and their possible readings, to others around her, as she confidently knew, even as a child, that they wouldn't understand her, but instead they'd even expose her to their and others' put-downs. And a sect, as some would perhaps have called it, she didn't want to establish, though enough of such doings were contemporarily reported as having success, and what is meant here by it is first and foremost financial success, in the world at large. Only her father really knew about it all, as he had been at the source of it.

Then, there was another source for her, a source of felt judgments, of thinking at its most intuitive and irrationally emotional, which came forth from deep within, from the territory for dreams and the edge of the consciousness, the awareness of the domain. There, classified as in a hidden library, there, close to her touch, sat large books from the time of incunabula on huge oak shelves bent under their weight, books to be read with the inner eyes in the secret of sleep and dreams.

The keys to the domain were under her bed cushions, close to the reach of her hands but invisible, on one condition only, to want it, the opening. On going to bed, it wasn't seldom that she launched inner kites and balloons to have the domain explored for her during her detachment and floating of dreaming, just as she was doing during days and hours spent in the outdoors in the company of the sky, clouds and winds. It was as though means and purposes fit for the air outside were equally capable to deal with this depth within; it was as though combinations were still in order in order to bring to fruition those sharp essences required for the day-to-day experience of a girl in wonder of the world.

The bridge in all this multi-layered architecture of her own living and thinking she always looked at with the amazement of the newcomer, of one of the novitiates, was what the fresh, blood-dropping flesh of reality brought to her in sharp shots of the sweet, the sour, the happy, the loneliness, the pungent taste of and in the social world, the taste of school, the taste and with it the high excitement of ballet, her highest obsession, the clamoring words of the parents in agitation about her, and last, but somehow not least, the men in her life, the roses and the pains they gave her in indiscriminate attention or awful neglect.

This bridge, it seemed to her, was the whole purpose of her presence about in the world, so it was there, in crossing it, from one level to another, in being stationed temporarily on it between rushes of motion, of plain living, that she took it in, the life, where everything came together, premonitions and ideas, perceptions lost and revived by dreams, the thoughts that moved her along toward her own horizon.

The business of kites had all started off with her father, Gilbert Fillon, a former officer in the French navy, born in 1920 or thereabouts — she had never been able to have a peek at his *certificat de baptême* as it seemed to have been lost in tupsy-turvy times, possibly allowing him to make himself forever younger by two or even three years — in Saint-Malo, who had graduated there from the *lycée* and *l'École de Marine* as luck would have it right during the years before WWII, and had become a second navigator under commandant l'Herminier on one of the French submarines, *Casabianca*, which managed to escape to Allied-controlled Africa at the end of 1942, immediately after the whole French fleet had been scuttled in Toulon when the Germans were only hours away from getting their hands on the it all. After arrival in Algiers, *Casabianca* was only one of the few French warships thus able to fight with the Allies, being used as patrol ship and on several secret reconnaissance and espionage missions. Unfortunately, in May 1944 a British plane hit her by mistake and she was forced to stay in Philadelphia in the US until the March of 1945 for repairs.

During the stay in Philadelphia, Gilbert Fillon, Yvonne's father, managed to get in touch with the Canadians and, right before the Casabianca was set to sail back for Europe, left for Canada on land to work in Montreal as a navy liaison officer on behalf of France. However, immediately after the VJ day, he asked the French for permission to retire from the military side of the navy and the Canadians for the right to stay in Canada, and, after a quite wobbly and tense wait of about two years, both requests were satisfactorily dealt with by the powers-that-were of the time. He then continued to work in the Montreal harbor, as a civilian navy officer in the administration of the port, and, following that, as a pilot on the St. Lawrence Seaway to the ocean.

A bony, still wide-shouldered, tall man, called the "Italian" by other sailors for his dark good looks, he had met Eliza Littlejohn in Toronto, on the CNE grounds, in 1950, while attending a military air show with what was to be, several years later, the Canadian Snowbirds, in a lineup for ice cream. So, Yvonne held it for a true fairy tale as a small child, "it was ice cream that had made our family and, not much later, would somehow make myself." The ice cream was as such revered in the family, and the end-of-the-week occasions when Papa Fillon would bring home a large plastic tub full of it in rainbowed, creamy, colors were awaited with trepidation by her and her mother and the cutlery and plates were sure to be washed afresh to avoid any undesirable interference with the flavor.

    As a young boy in France, Gilbert had very much been into vaudeville, cinema, theatre, *les chansons*. At one time, as many other youths, he had followed with fascination the stories about the love between Gabin and Dietrich, the demigods who, in those years, were splashed all over the white screens. Gabin who, her father said, had been the oldest armored car commander in the Free French Forces, ending up the war fully white-haired. Later on still, Gilbert would follow the movies of Gérard Philipe, and *Le Rouge et le Noir* and *Fanfan la Tulipe* were to be some of his preferred. He could watch for hours Fanfan outdueling the mustachioed soldiers who were after him in mountains of hay and still get a fresh laugh out of the pursuits and feints of sabre.

On the other side, the business of dreams had started with herself entering life, in her early years, with her awareness of a child — blooming unobserved by her parents and of course by herself. And she hadn't needed any initiation, she navigated from the word go through them as on automatic pilot, extending, as it were, from under her pillow, a hand there, another, sometime later, here, to pick up unseen from the library the dream of interest to her then and there as scribes would pick up for the pharaoh in times immemorial the scrolls with day's proclamations and sublime thoughts in the patient shadow of the Sphinx, as, she would later see it, from a Saint-John Perse poem of high noon.

2 - Saint-Malo, 1979

Les cerfs-volants de Saint-Malo, so storied to her during childhood by her father, were at rendezvous, with five or six children or thereabouts, the latter counted not better than she could separate them from afar in the other corner of the *remparts*, pulling at their tethers and releasing them, trying to guide their flimsy kites stubbornly on and against the winds present in the air right about them and the ones impossible to fully perceive, and thus much trickier, up in the sky.

Yet they didn't let them fly too high, out of sight, or behind some clouds, for then the faces of the kites and the large smiles painted on some of them would become unseen and lost to a Circe lying in ambush up there in the immensities of the air, ready to tangle with and break the fine sails or the lines.

The tide was high, lapping the skirt of the citadel in salvos of unrepentant waves, a gray disquiet in their colors to mirror the sky of the day.

On account of her own history, it wasn't surprising then that she had nursed for quite some time this idea of a ballet with four male dancers agitatedly roaming the ground trying to control their out-of-view kites, fighting and dealing with adversity in their lines, reeling them in and reeling them out, trying to avoid tangling their own tethers with the rest of the group out on a picnic, attempting to impose their will on the wind — the lost and mad proposition. Suddenly then, two women, not of the party, would come in and would try to comprehend what these thin and athletic men were so busily up to and what they were playing for, as the lines of the kites wouldn't be visible or would plainly be absent, poking questions and irony at them. The answer, mimed back to the women, would be *we're playing for the pleasure of speculation*, and at this point signs of heavy abstraction, abstruse symbols, would show up around the background. Then one would gradually discover that there were two worlds at play out there on the stage: one, of the reality around the characters and of the thinking of it, anchored and rooted in the ground; the other, to which each of them was tethered as to *cerfs-volants*, of the unconscious, constantly and pitilessly pulling at them with no respect and no warning, and those worlds would be as different from each other as the sky was from *terra firma*.

She had faced polite, still quite stiff, opposition from Mr. B when trying to suggest a piece along these lines for the New York City Ballet repertory. "There's too much miming involved in it, and I'm not Marcel Marceau. How does one dance *speculation*? Plainly speaking, it's not *dansable*" George Balanchine morosely and hopelessly asserted, pulling at his thin western bow tie with his fingers, plopping one of this preferred French words right at the end, perhaps also a bit tired on that day, and in his late seventies.

Now, back in St-Malo, faced with those children playing with the very toy she had had in mind, she confronted again her own idea as one looks upon children born out of wedlock, with some guilt for their stubborn, obnoxious existence, and the thought popped up that it might be worthwhile to have a stab at choreography for herself. This way, she wouldn't need anyone's permission to put out and even stage her ideas, just their money. Creating strange, original choreographies would be her duty by fiat, the first article of her professional constitution. Thus went her song about herself then.

Her father's passion for things American had been incited by 'Gone with the Wind,' which he had seen on a weeklong leave to Paris. A half-rogue who hush-hushed his romantic bent for the sake of his macho-ism and would quiet down after the marriage, he liked having his suits in blue — "as a sailor should," he said — and burgundy ties — "which show and allow character, you know, the color of dried blood." Years later, Yvonne would talk about him in his youth as of an Erik Bruhn lookalike, distinguished, cool, intelligent, slim, lacking only blondness.

Yvonne's mother, Eliza Littlejohn, was Canadian, of English ancestry, born in 1926 in scenic Banff, Alberta, out in the Rockies,

Yvonne's grandparents working there at the time in the hotel industry. Her grandfather, after having started on some lowly rungs of the ladder, would in time get to a managerial position, while her mother, initially a chamber maid, was at the time of Yvonne's birth a clerk in accounting in the same hotel. She was small, blond, spindly, with nicely rounded breasts, treats that would be passed on to her daughter, who would inherit her height from her father, though.

Having gone into accounting mostly under the pressure of her own mother, and hating it and the chair-anchored life it brought along with a vengeance, Eliza thought she wanted something brighter for her daughter, and decided that Yvonne should dabble in ballet, just in case she might like it. The fact that by that time the Fillons had moved to Winnipeg, out on the Canadian prairie, where the Royal Winnipeg Ballet had been established right before WWII by two ladies, Gweneth Lloyd and Betty Farrally, and brought to some prominence by Albert Spohr and others, was not unrelated to this decision.

To assuage the boredom brought on by accounting, Eliza liked to read a lot, and had Yeats, Auden and D.H. Lawrence — with *Sons and Lovers* her preferred novel — most of the time on her bed table. Bored or not bored, she was an excellent accountant, with an omnipresent fear of being poor, well-injected by her own parents, and knew how to properly manage the family's money, which Gilbert let her, in his considerable wisdom, do.

She had always wanted a Frenchman — "They are more ebullient than us. We, the English, we're too bland," she had used to say in her teenage years to her girlfriends — so this was, as it happened, a match made in heaven.

At the time of Yvonne's visiting St-Malo on this occasion, her mother, a widow by now, lived in Calgary, Yvonne having decided she didn't want her on her own ballet vagaries as a chaperon, one similar to what the Black Queen a.k.a. Hilda Hookham, Margot Fonteyn's famous mother, had been decades before that — one has to say to an out-and-out success.

"Now, most of the time," her father had told her, "your *cerf-volant* won't interfere with anyone else's, as in this world we're quite alone. If you're lucky, as I was with your mother, you'd have someone for a longer time around you, and, God forbid, they would support you, not run interference and jealousy, as some people I know did and went far into it, to the troubled waters of divorce. Still, this goes outside the family, I'm telling you just so you wouldn't take it the wrong way. At your place of work, you might find yourself associated with people you wouldn't like to be around you, but they are there and you'd have to carefully guide your kite so it wouldn't interfere with theirs or jam into it. No, I don't mean to be servile or anything like that, and I don't mean not being competitive either — which you should be — just avoid tangling with each other in stupid ways — the small envy, the petty jealousy. Especially avoid tangles where both of you look bad in the eyes of a third.

"I remember a time right before the war where both myself and a fellow Jacques Vuarnet, while students in the navy, worked summers on a merchant ship going back and forth to the Levant — Alexandria, Tripoli, places like that. So, on one night, the whole crew went ashore on a leave and as luck would have it, had bumped into each other in a seedy bar for foreigners in downtown Cairo. One thing led to another and I was lucky to click with this girl from the British Embassy, clerk, typist, something like that. Now, the Vuarnet fellow caught sight of her too, but that was only after I was already clinking glasses with her. No, he didn't come over and try to steal the girl from me — he was not man enough for it — however, for months afterward, on the ship, he threw bad words and tried to compromise me in front of my captain — I and Jacques being both chief of the watch on that ship. Matters were really bad, as I was supposed to enter watch after him most of the time — there being only three of us in this position — so he had to report to me the events that had occured during his shift out there at sea, U-boats appearing on the prowl or some such. After this happened, he simply avoided passing me the report on those moves around us, as though he wanted to get me into trouble. Well, the war came, and we were both assigned to military duty, but finally on different ships of *Les Forces Françaises Libres*, and he was torpedoed and sunk in the freezing waters of the Atlantic with his whole crew. So, you see, only in the heavens — if we both reach it — is going to be another opportunity for us two to get over these bad feelings, and it's a pity, as this was such a minor issue.

"So, to come back to *cerf-volants*, ride yours as high and proud as you want, just be aware that others might watch you with envy even for doing that; try to avoid their runaway kites, otherwise you might lose precious time and have sour feelings on both sides.

"Your out-and-out enemies are only those who want to steal your *cerf-volant* or cut your line, as they mean to leave you with no tools for your trade, and that's the worst, not being able to earn your living or exist as an independent person. These fellows deserve your hate, still, to my mind, it's more worthwhile of your time and energy to avoid them, if you can. If you can't, fight them to the bitter end, as they won't leave you in peace."

Two *cerf-volants* that both belonged to Yvonne and she had to keep them from interfering with each other, and to some extent, out of the public eye, were her concomitant on-and-off trysts with Patrick Donovan and George Granath. In its stubbornness, fate had insisted that they both should start at about the same time, and that had been three years before the visit at St. Malo already mentioned, thus in 1976.

Why she had kept both of them on her leash and in her retinue is something better left to the indeterminacies of life and morals and to the inexpressible but unerring difficulty of really making up her mind about her own preferences in terms of men and about what they engendered in her being in all its facets — sexual, spiritual or of another nature — as well, and this had to be the deciding factor, to the fact that neither of the two men had ever trodden, not even in the most tentative manner, the hollow ground of proposing to her in one manner or another. On the other side, not able to fathom in herself something that could have been associated, in these cases, with the lofty notions of love and dedication, she played the two men to the extent they allowed themselves to be played with and to the extent to which temporary inclinations moved her sails toward one or the other of their shores.

Lying in her hotel-room bed in St. Malo, she was trying to segregate the two men then present in her intimate life, leaving aside on this day, to avoid complications and unwanted headaches, everything but the physical and the sexual.

Patrick was six-foot tall, slim as a Yogin, only about one hundred and sixty pounds, even though quite bony. With his dancer's flexibility, most of the positions depicted in any Kama Sutra book could have been attempted with relative comfort for both of them. There was this feeling of hard, scarce flesh, tout skin bumping against hers, the impact on the very surface of her body was more felt, sharper, as though a battering ram in plain polished oak wood would concuss and press her.

He was fully depilated, so the skin-to-skin friction was pure and she could feel her own and his beads of sweat sliding translucently and trickling between their bodies, as the extra whitish solution slides around a soap bubble and accumulates at the bottom of it, emerging from the tip of a tube with which a child plays on a relaxed afternoon on his parents' veranda. When revved up, his voice, pouring out here and there a sputter of dirty words, was thin and squeaky, in content perverted, but difficult to be taken seriously at its worth in decorticated, weightless words, as though an out-of-body vaudeville actress would have been on loan to say them, the excitement to Yvonne residing a lot in this out-of-time manner in which those words rolled out during their act.

His phallus was terribly small — so he wasn't comfortable with her cupping it, gripping it, as though there was a fear of it disappearing in a ridiculous trick in her hands, as in the hands of a magician — but firm, rebel and agitated, so her pleasure came and was accentuated in the rhythm of its punctuations and enterings.

Still, the nature of those words, the dirtiness, was enough to spike her keenness or maintain her on the crest of a wave and carry her away to territories and islands remote from which she usually didn't want to come back until paying a heavy toll to the shadowy merchants of pleasure and frenzy.

His teeth were sharp and liked to cling and grab at the flesh of her shoulders and munch at her pudendum, but he was careful to just initiate pangs, but not pursue them to pain. At those times she liked to grab his long blond hair, never clammed or clogged by sweat, in her fretting fingers and pull it toward her in the rhythm of the coupling.

Both of them were low-perspiring, and their sex needed jellies, creams and other help to avoid becoming dry and sore affairs for either or both of them.

George was an altogether different sexual being, animal and partner at six-feet two and two hundred and sixty pounds, his muscular contours having been modulated by natural bodybuilding and conditioning. At contact, his skin felt rougher, for he had never considered even remotely depilating himself, his veins were prominent and skin-blueish in the arms, calves or neck, and a richness of hair ornated his chest, arms and shoulders in a ursine manner. His sebaceous glands seemed to be always in overdrive, he sweated profusely, especially during sex, and Yvonne had to make sure to have clean sheets at hand for changing two or three times per night, if she didn't want them to live in a pool of perspiration. His being so big and heavy meant Yvonne preferred being herself the one on top, and this could only help in terms of limiting penetration to the range of the pleasurable, as his main argument was off-the-scale, as much as Yvonne could tell based on her not extensive knowledge of the subject. Things being this way, she didn't want to be bored and pinned down by such a sexual implement, even though in a happy contrast it reached points which no man had ever explored in her inner sexual neighborhoods. The play with George was much slower and careful than the one with Patrick; she enjoyed his massivity, his opening her as a large shell on a sacrifice table, in not-speedy salvos of passion.

She liked to lie herself prone on top of him, her breasts orange-squashed and widened on what one could only describe as mountainous pectorals, running in thick fibers across his torso, bathing in his sweat and other profuse secretions, which most of the time made any artificial lubricants totally unnecessary at the intimate interfaces.

3 - Her shells

Remote times, now, she found it more and more. And it was in those remote times that she had grown her shells on, one above and around the others, a tortoise grandly residing in her soul.

The first shell, the innermost and the source for all others — for anyone trying to get in touch, on some level or another, with her — the remote and untouchable star around which everything turned, was, for her, the ballet.

She must have been four when her mother started to take her in busses and trams to an elderly lady located somewhere in the Beaches, who had a small studio for children. The lady had been a corps dancer with the *Les Ballets Russes* in her youth in Paris and recalled the later reincarnation, *Les Ballets Russes de Monte Carlo* led by Colonel de Basil, touring the States in transcontinental trains during World War Two in search of an audience.

With too many robberies around her neighborhood, the old lady had bought two huskies. Castor and Pollux they were, one patrolling the outside and one the inside of her average-size house — built while her husband, a bank clerk, still lived, and took care of the material interests of the household. With their massive, thickly-furred, unfriendly presence, they instilled a fear of dogs, especially large ones, in the young Yvonne that would stay with her for all her life, to the benefit of domesticated felines. That was her second shell, as it were, at least for the dog lovers who might have wanted to get closer to her and never did. Never would Gilbert, her father, be able to rid her of this fright, with all their going together, to playing areas for the dogs in the city, just for the sake of convincing his daughter that not all canines wanted to shred you to pieces the moment they got sight of you.

The old teacher — she was by then in her seventies, still showing a ramrod back — would shoo away the dogs the moment visitors were in, to tether them in a backyard closed-in by sparse wire fence, as she had figured that lights and the movement of people inside would keep away robbers for the duration of the visits. Also, she didn't want dogs running amok through her classes, bumping into students at those times, or worse. She would always wear corduroy pants for classes, which suited well her slim carriage, of which she was proud. The large living room of the house was used as a small dance studio, with a *barre* on a side, the rest of the room being parqueted with no rugs and the little furniture there was being carried away to the walls, wide windows generously letting light in at any time of the year — the teacher hating having people dance in the dark, as, she complained, it caused her headaches, too dire a sight to contemplate, she said, dance is Apollonian, thus protected by the light of the sun and should stay so. In one corner, she had an upright piano on which she played the music to which the pupils were supposed to dance or drill, with authoritarian fingers punch-stressing the rhythm so that the young dancers would know what and when to emphasize in their *pliés, arabesques* or *pointes tendus*, with her right hand suspended up in the air toward them whenever she felt that a fluttering of fingers or a flight of an arm would help their suggestion and imagery, their butter-melting to the music.

Presiding above the whole room was this huge elk head, decapitated and stuffed by a taxidermist after a hunting exhibition in the North by her late husband. "He's Jowls; don't mind him too much; he's very placid these days, " she laughed, sometimes, on her good-humored days, adding perniciously, "he's retired from everything, from stud too," sotto voce to the adults bringing in their children to her lessons, who sometimes stayed for the duration.

Placed against a side wall rested a bench on which all students would sit to adjust their ballet slippers, tie them up tighter or simply retire for a short while when too tired, or in tears from some of the comments received from the old lady, the old hag to them in those times, which were both harsh and encouraging at the same time. It certainly was the "bench of tears," as it had seen them at their worst, after hours of drills and rehearsals that apparently didn't seem to produce anything. "Ars longa, vita brevis," the teacher told them.

The bunch who assembled here was a good one, many of the children going on to the National Ballet's school and some of them — true, very few of them — even to dance with the Ballet, and the parents didn't skimp or scrounge paying the pretty penny involved in order to get there, as Mrs. Johnson's hours weren't cheap by any means. Thus, this is where Yvonne made many life-long acquaintances, friends and rivals, all in the same bowl, for in this art, as in others, you can have all of them in the same person.

Also, this is where another shell gradually grew on her, her own body, steeled to pain in toes and foot arches, in ankles and knees, the body of someone who had to be ready to respond the cry of "the show must go on" and to hold the flag high. She recalled how flexibility came gradually as a gift of the long drills, how a split which wasn't available before became second-nature, drawing wows from the children in her neighborhood who didn't know anything of ballet or gymnastics and couldn't compete with such apparently awesome feats. And the other girls would touch her thighs and wonder "Your muscles are getting as hard as a boy's; there's no softness to them any more; aren't you worried?" but the shells were already on her, so such questions were readily dismissed.

So, when after innumerable *adagios* with *rondes de jambes a terre* at the *barre*, she went back limping to Mrs. Johnson's bench, and had to wonder also if her beauty wouldn't be affected by what she had just done, the beauty as seen by boys — who were the people who really counted, the ultimate arbiters of femininity, as told in those years by her mother — she needed all the moral reinforcement that came through other channels, and most powerfully from Mrs. Johnson, who told them all the time, in her voice made hoarse by classes, "Girls and boys, we're dancing for the ineffable, to voice our inner yearnings, not for any profit or worldly pleasure. In fact, we're dancing beyond all this, in that space in which poets and singers tread, and even past that, as our tool, our body, is the most flimsy, the most temporary and perishable, and nothing is left, except in ether, and even there there are only few and puny drops of our dances. Except for those of us lucky enough to be taped for TV, and this only recently. And by the way, the door is open for those who don't enjoy the view; I don't want any of you or of your parents to come over to complain that you weren't warned. But, I'm asking, is there anything more beautiful than a well-timed *développé*?" And Yvonne, she didn't know that space in which poets and singers treaded, as she wasn't reading too much anyway in those years, except for school, overwhelmed by ballet classes and the time and energy that went to them as in a black hole, as seen by her father. "Why shouldn't she focus on medicine, law or even fashion?" he quizzically asked. "Well, *you* told her about *cerf-volants*, this is one of them, isn't it?" her mother replied in the marital bed at night. For the benefit of any curious and doubtful outside observer, a case in point for her having already developed pretty hard shells, if nothing else, already by that age: at ten, she competed for entrance in the National Ballet School in Toronto, only days after the doctors had diagnosed a fracture line in her foot. The only way to go through it was novocaine injections meant to freeze the area, which she immediately and doggedly asked for, when advised by the doctors, until she got them. So entered she the school with flying colors, years before a Béla Károlyi and a certain Kerry Strug would make recourse to the same medical stunt for a famous vault at the Atlanta Olympics.

***

What I liked first in ballet was the tutus, the tights, the slippers and the pointes, for I didn't know any other place with them, the girls being so light, so without those heavy dresses and long coats that we have here in winter, that looked like other girls, not themselves, more like flowers in a garden, but now that I am used to it for perhaps five years, I still think the same, those are perhaps the things which I like most and the music, this music which flows on and on and tells you how to move with it, so that it comes from within ourselves, as Mrs. Johnson was saying, the steps are so easy, you just relax and let go, lift the arms as in a *développé* and the legs will move of themselves, I don't feel any strain, and I don't have to push myself to do things as I sometimes need to do in my studies, even the pointes come naturally now, not that I don't feel them afterward in my poor feet, but at the time it's just the pleasure of being taller and moving delicately on them, in small points to the ground here and there, as a woodpecker pecking the ground, just touching it, so I feel more in the air than on the ground, and so it is in the pirouettes too, you just feel the ground just in that single point, that you are not of it, you're mostly above and detached of it, or in the *grands battements* one feels like a large insect, spreading thin legs in the air and kicking it away, and then I like that in class, being four or five at the *barre* and doing those *battements* or *pliés* all at the same time, it's like sharing the music with the others, girls and boys at the *barre*, as though each of us makes a small part and all the parts are put together and there's that feeling of one movement going over, through and over all of us, it's like we're more friendly to each other, and I think the same about those *pas de trois* or *pas de quatre* from *Swan Lake* in which you feel those oh so beautiful swans moving and stepping and light kicking together, arms going from one to the other and linked as molten together so nicely either in front or at the back of them, and how difficult that is to do without one of them tripping and falling and bringing the whole line of them down to the ground with her, which would be an awful thing to happen but it certainly has happened more than once since it was danced first all over the world, and imagine the embarrassement of the young ladies falling flat either on their behinds or on their noses, imagine that in a show, not at a rehearsal, and the focus they must have to avoid that of all things, but let's talk of something else now, how strange some people are not to know ballet or, even more, not to like it, when to me it shows everything beautiful, and you don't need words for it, just a body in good shape, or willing to move, and arms and feet that would of their own go ahead and do a pirouette, 'coz I guess this is just natural to all of us, this wish to move and rotate, and feel how you're getting dizzy but pleasantly dizzy while doing it, and all and everything disappears around you and-and the only thing counting is the music and your body and that desire to link music and body with no words, and the bends and the rotations come to you easily if you like it and after a time you don't need teachers to show you what and how to dance, but the music will enter your body and move all by

Marius Hancu

itself, and I feel a whoosh around me, and I know it is the air and my tutu running around in it, and if you don't believe it give me your hand even if you're older than I and you may not like this music I have on now, because will show you the steps which come naturally with it and will rotate, and step and advance and move back and you'll feel what I feel, perhaps not so clear as you haven't learned how to dance like I did, but still it will be with you this feeling of trying to step out of your body and move away in the room, leave your body in a corner if it won't follow, and follow me just with your mind and will and that will be enough, you will be dancing even so, the tra-tra-tra and pram-pram-pram, and skip, and skip, and round, and round, and nothing will be easier to you then if you try it, it's so easy, believe me, and even though you're saying this is for kids and not for grown-ups like you, I still know everyone can dance, this is what I know from my first days at Mrs. Johnson, when she told us that the dance is not only for ballet dancers, but for everybody who wants to feel how their bodies really feel and are, and I was probably five or six then, but I got the idea, things are not so difficult as people around us try to make them, but they become easier if one just tries them and steps into it, steps into a dance, and even if OK you look ridiculous that's only to you, others may not feel it because they don't think the way you may think about dance, as a difficult thing, but they are willing to try it, or at least to imitate someone who likes to do and-and you can see it on their faces that it's there, in their smiles, and in their eyes and mouths open, and if they're too old or sick, they'll still watch you and move with you in their minds, raising hands as Zorba did in the movie, you know it, no? of course you do, Anthony Quinn was the actor, what a dancer, see that wasn't ballet, but everyone is moved by it, and how could anyone not move or shake and make a gesture with their hands when they see that dance and hear that music, and Mrs. Johnson always tells us, I still go to her, even though I'm with the National's school now, for my parents think that a master is a master and I should continue working with her while I still can, Mrs. Johnson she tells us, the older children with her, that we're like the tulips, ready to bloom, and we better be aware that that's going to be a short time in our lives, and to enjoy and do what we can to have our dancing as pure and perfect as we can while the sun is high above us, for the season is short for everyone in this art, and like the teacher said, ballet is a life unto itself, unto, she said, you have to eat for it, you have to sleep for it, you have to even think for it, think about yourself being light and ethereal, that is too say lighter than air or anything around us on earth, all those fatty foods around us are a no-no, but now that I'm here after five, six years, it's like my body already rejects them, before even temptation starts, she even told me, you, Yvonne, you may be too athletic for classical ballet, I mean being a soloist in one, as you're too rounded, now, of course in a beautiful, but perhaps too muscular, way, so in time you may want to think to move into modern ballet, there the form is less thin and streamlined as indeed they are and need indeed to be the swans, and your closely-cropped curly hair, which you keep page-like also fits better with modern things and fashions, so I listen, better to be prepared when the time comes to take a decision, as my father told me once, the prepared make the choices, the unprepared take the leftovers, now, you'll excuse me, as I need to practice this piece, and you ask what music this is, the teachers at school told us this is Bach and it's difficult to dance, because it has a slow movement, and it has what the older people call *gravitas*, which would be earnestness and seriousness, measure in what you do, so I need to time it very well and not rush through it, because Bach wrote the *Well-tempered Clavier*, so it must of course be well-controlled as a metronome, and calm but firm like it, so my mind must be emptied of everything that would bring excitement in deportment, as the teachers call it, and I must move cleanly through the motions as I am a clock myself, a well-running, patient clock, whose only job is to keep the time and to respect it, and you see I'm alone doing it, there's no one in this room or outside it who can help me holding the pattern when I start it, I must have it in myself, and stick to it, and this is when the loneliness in ballet comes in, you really have to stick to yourself if you want to manage to be true to others, Mrs. Johnson told us, so many times I feel that in our neighborhood, we're now in Scarborough, I don't meet too many of the other kids anymore, perhaps they feel I'm a high-nose already from too many ballet classes, but it's the same with those of them who are into swimming

Marius Hancu

or hockey, all day long chauffeured by their parents to training sessions at five in the morning or until midnight, depending when the pools or skating rinks are open for them, but it's true in Canada, at least for boys, hockey's an understood craziness, but probably not the same we can say about ballet, isn't it, and at times I'm concerned, as some of the kids, boys mostly but also girls, and even at the National school, say that from ballet you don't get as a girl to grow too much of a breast, as you are too awfully slim, and then the boys might not like it when the time would come to choose a sweetie,

, and this is just for me, last night I went to the bathroom, perhaps about midnight as I don't like to watch the clocks, someone told me if you do, I mean watch them, the time of your life will pass quicker for you and it's better to leave it alone, couldn't sleep too well, was too full, so, when I came back I heard Mom and Pop kind of arguing, but it was mostly Mom, asking for something, not everything came out through their door to the corridor where I was walking back with no slippers, it's faster to get into bed this way, I know, mother tells me it's not hygienic to walk shoeless anywhere, and that is at home too, and the whispering went harder from my parents sleeping room, and she, Mom, said, could you please me with the small machine too, Gilbert, I'd like you to do it to me with it too, and my father was like mumbling, like he didn't quite want to do it, and mother said, oh, you French, you are old world and old-fashioned, we're married, aren't we, we should try this too, and this is where I went inside my room 'coz I had been if anything for too long on the hallway half-listening to it, and then their talk was shut out from me, and then I was left wondering about the *it* I had just heard, and then I remember the girls at the ballet school talking during breaks about Elvis and his hip movements and how in some of their churches this was spoken of badly on Sundays, and why, was the question, because that movement is very similar to when making babies, you stupid, was the answer from another of the girls, and the one asking was full red by now, and I remember that another day, some other girl mentioned discovering a huge penis, you know, a large willie, she explained for those of us who'd made inquiring faces, in one of the drawers in the night table beside her mom's bed, and when she pressed a button, the thing started to move and buzz, and it showed veins and a round cap at the top, and-and, was the question, did you try it, what do you mean by trying, did you put it down there in you, you dummy, and then we all ran inside the classroom, 'coz the bell had rung and the French hour was coming, taught by that Quebecoise lady, who some of the girls said has in fact a bad French accent, not like the one spoken in France, that is, and the giggling on that thing stopped then, but the little machine that had been then mentioned stayed on my mind, and now I think it may well be just what was whispered about last night by my parents, it's just I don't have the courage to rummage in my parents' room, and I don't think that would be right either, this I know about it myself, and yes, lately Mom isn't coming every Sunday with us anymore at the church, we go to a Catholic one, even though her parents were Anglicans, 'coz this is what my father is, Catholic, she tells us she's busy and she's making the rounds in the kitchen, but when we're coming back the radio is on and loud and lots of rock music fills the house, she seems the only Mom in our Scarborough neighborhood interested in it, I don't hear the music coming out from their houses, but what do I know, we really don't visit with the neighbors, there are some Greek and Italian families around here, and I know the Greeks are Christian too, but different from the Catholics or the Anglicans, the Italians should be OK, they show up, many of them, at the church we're going to, however my parents aren't too much into knowing the neighbors, just hello, how are you, that's it, so perhaps this much music helps my Mom get away from it all, as she says, from time to time, especially with her work in accounting, which she never liked, as she's always been telling us at dinner, which is boring, as she

4 - 1966-67

Dancing. Lucien Chu is having a bad day and is bringing me down with him, hopefully not literally, though. Could he have learned in Montreal this gift of spoiling another's day, I'm trying to mischievously inquire of him under my breath while still dancing together, with that remotest of hopes that anger might wake him up to a better incarnation of himself. Coz he's definitely only a shadow of his better days; anyone in the audience could tell *that*, for sure, even though he's just fourteen, just like me. Glad he hasn't changed the black in his tights, white on him would be laughable in this more modern piece, making him swanny, as it were. His square jaw is set today, as though he has something to prove to everybody around and protruding it would be the best business under the circumstances. His knees and hips still seem low to my taste, I couldn't quite tell why, though I know I like their contours, within which the muscles are becoming more clear in form and firmer these days.

The luck is, the audience this morning, at the National Ballet's school in Toronto, is only other students — a dozen, perhaps more, but not by much — as well as Mme Alyutina, our teacher for the morning class and rehearsals. However, the history of other mornings shows only that familiarity brings out the harshest critics, not necessarily in the open, but guaranteed out there in the rumor pipeline at work.

So when I'll be showing up at the residence for the out-of-town girls, later in the day, a place I am sure to visit for what I'd call social flip-flopping, I am, guaranteed, going to be bombarded with idiot questions, say 'Wonder what's going on with your *pointes*, Yvonne? Soon they gonna be as flat as a plate for a lunch with no soup in it. Did you hear what I said, girls? A plate for a lunch with no soup it.' And another is going to take over, 'Yes, I heard, but I know something which is really boss. As flat as a C flat!' 'Oh, no,' another is going to play and counterpoint along the same tack, 'as flat as Mme Alyutina's rear! No, I'm way off, mind you, she has no front nor back!'

And howling and yawping should of course start in short order. Bet you two bucks on that, no questions asked.

Or the milling would let itself be sidetracked by just a whisper of a line, 'Hey, girls, Yvonne's getting stronger than poor thing Lucien. Now, that's manliness at its best. Look at those arms of hers and look at the thighs, in three years you won't find room for them in her tights.'

And hee, and ha, and hee hee hee, all over again.

'What do you mean, too many boys in those tights of her? Latest research doesn't show any hope for that. Even Lucien and, who's that white boy, oh yes, I remember now, Vince Pearson it is, might leave the field in total disarray after finding what they'd find.'

'Like what, what'd they find?'

'Muscles and bones in considerable stock, girls, that's what they would find. Clear enough for you, Sharon?' So Tabitha Clark would identify for all to know the latest concerns over the so-called over-development of my body, which is doing just fine, thank you very much.

Tabitha Clark, of all. Think about that. Holy Beatles! As if it weren't she who had with zero chance of joining the National after getting the paper. Read that? Zero. I mean, she's double the stage for a dancer. I mean she's panoramic, face-wise and body-wise, and for heavens' sakes, we're only fourteen, most of us, add or subtract one year, in our class. Seems to be some Alberta hotel property in the family, angelling her here, playing the lady bountiful on her behalf. I mean, 'the school needs generous donors, no doubt, arts are expensive,' as my mom says, 'let it pass, girl.' So I let it pass, that's part of my code, 'The dogs bark, the caravan passes on.' Why feed the rumor mill, there are enough out there who pour into it, and Tabitha's the best, or the worst, depending on how you look at it. 'One cannot pay for dignity, nor for honor,' my father says, but with less spunk these days, even though I'm occasionally trying to man his barricades for him.

Lucien, Lucien, what is going on with you? What is it, one year since you started to partner me? It must be about that. Coming from Montreal. Rare birds, the Chinese in Montreal, still; many more in Toronto, I'd say. Recently arrived, the family, so he doesn't sound too great in neither of our two great official languages, French and English, and it pains him, you can look at his face while the gang is poking fun at his speech, it gets long, long, and disappointed, but doesn't answer back, and this is something where we two are alike.

His body isn't getting too tall, and this may be one of his pet peeves these days. Most of the boys are growing up quickly, and it seems he's slower in this respect. There's always growth to be done until one is out of one's teens, Mme Alyutina and the other coaches tell us each other day, trying to smother concerns some of us, such as Lucien, have, but we all know there aren't any written guarantees, and by looking at some of our parents, the questions won't disappear overnight, on the contrary. I'm lucky with my father, six feet two, as my mom isn't any taller than five five, and that on a good day, as some would say. 'I must have missed all the rainy days in school, but you, Gilbert, you must have been out in St. Malo with your sweeties in torrential rain, I guess, each and every time *l'opportunité* showed up,' she's still cranking it to my father. 'Oh, *ma chère,* this only shows you really know me, and the glorious workings of your imagination, and if you must assume that, I can't deny you the pleasure, especially as I am showcased in such a, mmm, favorable, I'd say, light in front of our dear daughter.' My father laughs back at her, leaves for the kitchen, if we're in the living room, and continues to laugh sonorously from there, taking in large gulps of air in between guffaws, and I love it — it just tells me how big and strong he still is at forty-six or thereabouts. Caveat to the curious: I still haven't seen, at this point in time, the birth certificates of my parents, so who's to say they told me the truth about their ages; many people are running carefully designed circles around the issue, *that* I know for sure.

Lucien has been on tenterhooks since he learned about my intentions to continue with him as a partner only for the modern, I mean not for the classical stuff. Everyone was shocked to learn —

that must have been two months ago — that I went to Mme Alyutina and I asked to have two partners.

The coach was quite on pins and needles that day, which was visible even in her broken English. This was September, quite warm outside, still she had to lug, coiled around herself, the silver-fox collar that could tell her at any time of the year from half a mile, no doubt, her and her needle-ish frame, apparently prone to fall over under any faint breeze from the Lake, still so sturdy and well-balanced when it came to showing something in class. She was holding her handkerchief hidden in the left cuff of her dress, as usual, ready to dab any sweat that might appear on her pale, dignified, but sucked-in face, which told me Father Time might well have spun tales of need on her. Her dress was always ankle-length, today a beige gabardine, and she was known to despise the mini and those carrying it, of which Twiggy was one of the banner carriers in her sights.

'Who you are, mademoiselle, fourteen, to ask for two partners? What's wrong with Lucien for everything? You been wiz him for one year and half now. What the problem is?'

'Well, Mme Alyutina, it's that he's a bit too stiff for classical dancing and it bothers me that we can't have a good style together. I've nothing to complain about him in modern pieces, and I want to stay with him for that.'

'Well, well, getting bit too specialized already here. Sometimes soon, I might myself come, to you, Mademoiselle Yvonne, and tell your body build is going less favorable to classical dancing and a better fit for modern ballet. What are you going to do zen? Must your partners reject you because of that? Think a bit. This is school, not ballet company, difficult to put people sideways just on your own taste. Concern is first and foremost everybody enrolled here has a chance to become a dancer, educate people. Pruning out, I think you call zat in English, is part of, but I don't think we teachers should allow students to do that job themselves. Young people just don't have a long-terms experience.'

'OK, could you, please, talk to other teachers and find a solution for me? I don't want to embarrass Lucien with observations all the time, it's not fair.'

'Well, I will try see. But, mademoiselle, do you in a moment ask yourself who is going to dance with Lucien classical parts if is found in fact you rejected him? He talented dancer, he might not best be, perhaps, his niche, in classical ballet, but he was accepted in school on his merit, has been progressed quite well from admission, so I don't see problem for him to success in another area of ballet or dancing, or even classical. You young people, growing and changing a lot, bodies, as well minds, and perhaps the holy ghost — or someone else, I know you young don't like us to talk religion any more, but this is how things are — will help him in this dancing kind too. You a bit egoistic taking it this way this early, you know, no? Many people are possible to get strong miffed at you.'

Just three weeks ago, Mme Alyutina took all of us from the School and its studio on Maitland Street, with those cathedral-tall windows and ceiling, to a television studio downtown to show us a four-year-old recording of Nureyev, the great star we haven't seen here in Canada yet. It was made, the technicians told us, by an American network, in the Bell series. It was Nureyev, only twenty-four then, dancing with Maria Tallchief, the great ballerina that seems to also partner Erik Bruhn from time to time — who, to me, seemed quite wide-hipped, sorry. The piece was the *pas de deux* in the 'Flower Festival in Genzano.' We were all shocked to see Mr. Nureyev so young and sporting such a short haircut, he who's known for his great flowing hair. Mme Alyutina told us stupid American television executives forced 'Rudi' — this is how she calls him, as though he's family to her, which of course he isn't — to go through the terrible put-down of having had to cut his hair, just to get on air in *'Free Amerika,'* this how she put it, and there was like vinegar in her words. 'I mean, even if he was their replacement for Mr. Bruhn, still he is ze great Nureyev, but they know nothing, some of ze Americans, from culture, so Puritan and so forth. Haircut, as army, GI, pfft. He ran death from KGB, now stupid Americans instead. Life. But girls and boys, look at him, open your eyes and look.'

And he was indeed, something to behold, so light in his jumps and staying up-up-up there as though forever; light-blue knee-length breeches with laces on the sides of the knees, white thin hoses on his ankles and white shirt, a navy-blue neckerchief, a thin smile, and sending to us with a small irony under his lips, 'Look how easy and nice the ballet is,' but I knew already then and there that I might not ever see something like it in *legèrité et panache*, and that it takes something soh-soh rare to have those super-light jumps, the height of which never ended, those quick-as-mercury *entrechats*, those high *raccourcis* and *tours*, those cat-always-falls-on-his-paws-like landings.

'Zis is style Bournonville at best, boys and girls. Do not forget, choreography, redone by Mr. Bruhn, Danish person too, like Bournonville, closely works with Mr. Nureyev,' happily Mme Alyutina sang away, and we, young teens still, started to look at each other, as even we had got a whiff of the nature of the relationship between the two great men of the ballet of this time. Not that we know or understand too well the details.

***

On two nights during that week, I had dreams about Mr. Nureyev. At times he was being nice and even wanted to dance with me, but had to get away, still telling me, and I respected him for sticking to manners and protocol, before leaving airily through some exits in a barely distinguishable stage 'But, you know, Yvonne — this is your name, no? — I have to dance with Miss Tallchief and Mr. Bruhn tonight and I plan to do some of those *double sissonnés* and *double jetés* that I know you like to see me do in the *Flower Festival*. Perhaps other time, when you get bigger and older,' or 'You like me dancing, Yvonne? You should then see Yuri Soloviev from the Kirov Ballet; unfortunately, he doesn't come too frequently to the West.' Other times, he was terribly angry at me, telling me 'You'll never amount to anything in ballet, Yvonne. I know, Mme Alyutina has told me already, you haven't been able to dance even with Lucien Chu, what is zat?' and his accent was terribly thick and Russian-like, just like Mme Alyutina's, but he was more bossy, as I imagined great men should be. Not that I had met any of the kind, my acquaintances having been, I was starting sorrily to realize, terribly normal and ordinary people, and that had to start, unfortunately, with my parents, their kindness and all. Even though I was willing to issue a special dispensation to my father, for his introducing the kites to me and teaching me how to deal with them and use them in day-to-day life, which still seemed to me terribly neat, and for thinking and imagining together with me what could happen when of a day one would launch and fly and drive them around in the sky and its clouds. My father has always been so sweet he can give you cavities if you don't really take care.

When I was a child, I liked to take cutouts from my ballet books with me in the bathtub during bathing and to make the greats of the art swim in my bath, until slowly, sloshed and heavy with water, they went to the bottom, to my utter dismay. Why were they so lazy as not to want to swim and stay longer at the surface? I asked myself. Mother hated this, as it was she who had to clean the tub of all those smudged and ink-leaking pieces of paper, before they managed to clog the pipes, which entailed more expense, to bring in the seemingly ever-expensive plumbers. I was learning to consider some crafts and professions, as the word was told me, as rather to avoid, if one was desirous — 'desirous,' I like this word I read in old books — of having an easy life. That included doctors, of course, lawyers, plumbers and electricians. 'One should marry some of them, if one becomes interested,' said my mother, suddenly worrying about some abstract circumstance that was never thought about before, 'but not to have them wait on you, or you wait on them.'

Two days ago, I met Lucien Chu on the stairs leading to the School's studio. He caught up with me coming from behind, in fact, both of us on the way to change in tights and shorts for the morning class. He had a lost look in his eyes, as though part of it was going past me, toward another part of the world, I don't know how to put it. There was no smile on it and to me he felt tense, not in the regular joking mood he usually has or sometimes even parades for me.

'So we won't be dancing together tomorrow, will we?' he continued.

'What do you mean? I said.

'Come on, you know, Mme Alyutina told me already.' A

prominent vein on his forehead pulses.

'What did she tell you?'

'That we won't dance together any more in the classical.'

I was caught short, as I didn't know what else Mme A. had told him about my own wishes starting it all. So I decided to let him continue. Just listening.

'I think it was you who asked for it, wasn't it?'

I suddenly realized that things weren't as bad as they could've been. It seemed to me that Mme Alyutina didn't tell him about me asking for it. Good thinking on her part, thank God!

'Asked for what?' I continued to play the innocent's part, and I realized I was doing it for the first time in my life for the benefit, if that was a benefit, of someone outside our family. This play was usually enacted in front of my parents — whenever there is no other escape, play possum.

'At least we're going to remain together for the modern part.' He looked at me more directly this time, as though sounding off the truth of this sentence.

'We are?' I continued trying to remain poker-faced as hard as I could.

Again, that bumblebee or whatever it was caught his sight and he looked past me, suddenly older and sadder.

'OK, let's get changed, today is the modern class, so we'll dance together.'

'OK, let's,' I agreed, mouse-like, to let his eventual anger pass. I knew from my mom that many men 'have a short fuse' — what that really meant I never asked — and one just has to wait for it to blow and the smoke to be fanned away.

Somehow, the girls in the locker room knew already about the change.

'Ah, look who's here, Yvonne, all decked out. Is it true that you won't be partnered anymore by Lucien Chu, oh, sorry, the Buddha Head, in the classics? So finally you've decided you don't like anymore his copping a feel at you?' Tabitha had been lurking in wait.

'What? Where did you hear that?'

'I won't tell you that, but I know it from sources better than yours, you dirty little schemer, you.' Thinking she'd just chopped me, she pulled a face at me, while taking off her street clothes, our uniform of Scots design, then getting her class stuff from her locker.

Once again, she seemed to have one up on me, better posted than I was about the goings of the teachers and of the board. 'Small wonder,' said I to myself, and I'm sure my mother would have been in full agreement with me on this issue.

Today's morning class, after *barre*, was modern, as I've said. We all know this isn't Mme Alyutina's cup of tea, for even when showing a simple pose, she strikes it in a very showy way, as though standing on the edge of a pedestal, close to tumbling down in some undefined ravine there available as if by chance for the use of the unlucky dancers, as in old Sparta on Mt. Taygetos. Still, each of us was seriously putting themselves through the motions, which today were tap dancing as Fred and Ginger in 'Dancing cheek to cheek' of 'Top Hat.' The boys had to bring yard-long sticks, which had to do for his cane — which, by the way, he didn't carry in that piece — and some borrowed mixed choice of hats, all purporting to be his top hat, all, as expected, too big for their heads, so needing some improvised filling arranged on the spot from crumpled newspaper, disused bad-smelling cafeteria rags or other stuff.

There was something extra in the air between Lucien and I during that time today. I felt somehow it pushing me to be nice and smiling, as he most definitely looked tense after the latest news. The weight of the overall showing of our couple had suddenly been flushed onto me, as if the lights of an imaginary stage had been focused just on me, something which I found it not to my liking at all, but then I had to be a trouper under the most dire circumstances. This, I knew already, came part and parcel with being a performer, something that had been so much drilled into us by now, and probably successfully, at least in part, in my case, that I didn't feel shaky at all, not today.

We had to do a small bit of the final dance between Ginger and Fred that takes place on the columnated terrace in the movie, the part where they tap separately but in that total sync, each of them with both their hands raised for balance and advancing in a line together to and from the edge of the stage, while their feet tap, tap, and the main of their bodies shifts to the left, then to the right, in an undulating controlled wobble on alternating support legs. The most difficult part, of course, was where we had to tap a three hundred and sixty degree turn, each around our own axis at the time, still in a perfect replica of the partner's.

5 - December 1968

I have known Tony Rendall for several months now — having danced with him in 'Don Quixote' for the National. I mean, to remain honest and not boast on fumes, or perfumes, as it were, he didn't partner me, he danced Basilio, the athletic — just think of the jumps, *grand pas de chat, attitude sauté en tournant, coupé jeté en tournant, cabriole*, he has to do in the entrance scene — barber in love with Kitri, while I was the Queen of Dryads showing up ethereally in Don Quixote's love dream in several performances, and that only because the ballerina originally dancing her broke her ankle getting out of a taxi in a pair of high-heels on some cobblestones and I knew the part from a gala the School had put on for sponsors and parents the previous summer to collect funding. Imagine, if that is possible, even more dumb luck in store for me: all the ballerinas knowing the part gone to other companies on sabbaticals or exchanges. He's older, of course, a principal already at twenty-five or so; I was then a sweet sixteen, still in school. However, when I danced it with the School, I rhymed with the part a lot and I think I was good enough in it to spark and store up some memories for the powers to be at the Ballet, so when the accident happened, they called *me* up. Quite a roulette, isn't it? And the ball was mine this time. I mean the party, not the *roulette* ball, hee, hee.

I was at the school *costumière* and tailoress, Mrs. Schwadowski, the Austrian lady — *Lederhosen*, we nicknamed her; of course, not to her serious, obfuscating face — had borrowed a needle and pinkish thread and on a low stool, was darning away at my pointe shoes, ungracefully the largest in my class, when the call came in from the National Ballet and it was Mme Alyutina who asked me to come to her office 'right away' to take the most important call I had ever taken in my life. 'They seem to want you there, dahling,' she said, 'perhaps it's something temporary in the corps. Listen careful, don't open your mouth until asked. Careful what you're saying, dear,' she said, one palm covering the receiver, after the messenger, a smaller girl, had closed the office door behind her on tiptoes. I later realized, thinking back to that scene, that she had been enough in the trenches, Mme Alyutina, to recognize something in the air and, like a race horse, to shake with expectation and to carry a pair of eyes ready to pop out from their sockets when she handed over the phone to me for the call which I had to take standing, for there were no chairs whatsoever on that day in front of her dull brown-lacquered wooden desk.

'Miss Fillon?' The male voice came over wires haphazardly crisscrossing Toronto and I knew that this must be a native English-speaker, as the accent had come on the first syllable of my family name.

'Yes, please, it is I.' I had crammed enough for my grammar exams to know that in the most formal of the occasions, one must not use 'me.' Most definitely, I wasn't talking to the Queen, still something similar could be in the works, and I thought I had better make the right impression from the get go. Mme Alyutina, watching my lips, nodded in relief on my issuing the 'please,' as though centuries of etiquette were exhaling in sync with myself through it.

'Miss Fillon,' the voice continued, 'it's George Faraday calling. I'm the casting director for "Don Quixote" at the National Ballet. We've heard you seem to have some experience in this wonderful piece of our repertory.' The voice reverberated, and I imagined someone with a three-hundred pound frame generated those waves coming to me unabated, someone that simply *had* to be an exact replica of Orson Welles in Falstaff.

'Yes, sir,' I said, blundering away at my words, 'indeed I have, however my experience is limited to dancing the Street Dancer and the Queen of Dryads,' and I knew, right then and there, that the conversation would most probably end after this, as this double is really the second most important female part of "Don Quixote" as staged by Petipa and later by Gorsky at the imperial theaters in

Moscow and St. Petersburg. But I was ready to take on even the most modest role of a member of the Gypsy camp, no questions asked. On my 'limited,' Mme Alyutina telegraphed 'No, no, this isn't good,' and her face lost consistency as a balloon piqued by a needle.

'Well, Miss Fillon, I think we have a wonderful surprise for you: we would like to invite you to audition with us for this exact double role, and very soon. Some of us here have glowing reminders of your performance with the school.'

Glowing reminders? I asked myself as though wanting to pinch myself. 'If you don't mind, sir, how soon would you like it to be?' Mme Alyutina looked lost here.

'We need to have it tomorrow at ten AM. Could you, say, come at eight thirty, take the company class with us, warm yourself up properly and be ready for the audition at ten sharp? Our schedule is very pressing and we've had an accident with one of our principals. And, by the way, you may want to bring the School's tape, so you wouldn't be handicapped by not being quite familiar with our music and slash or its pace. You may also want to bring the costume you had on that occasion, but that's only if you want it. We'll see through it anyway. Should you decide to come, please tell me forthwith, so I can arrange for your leave from school tomorrow.'

'We'll see it through it.' Wow, that was a bit cold to me. I felt some serious gulps of air were immediately in order as I put my left hand on the edge of Mme Alyutina's desk, just in case I might faint. Took me a short while, but I was able to breathe back a 'Well, I think I'll manage all that, sir; as well, thank you for your invitation.'

'You're most welcome. I and the other people in charge with the production look forward to seeing your dancing tomorrow.' The line went eerily dead as though some other world has just become again disconnected, the way it ever had been.

'They want me to audition for the Street Dancer in "Don Quixote."' I told Mme Alyutina, whose eyes were at their limit of poppingness, as she probably hadn't breathed for like five minutes.

'But that comes together with the Queen of the Dryads, it's tradition,' she went, inquiringly.

'Oh, yes, it's for both, sorry. They, I mean some of them, must have seen me with the School in that,' I kind of reluctantly apologized. 'Also, they seem to have had an accident.'

'Honey, what can I tell you, this is great! This is why we teach here, moments like this!' She really seemed happy for me, Mme Alyutina, so whatever misgivings I might have ever had about her went away in smoke.

Right away, I kindly asked Mrs. Schwadowski to find my old costume for the part, which she quickly found under 'Mercedes,' the name of the Street Dancer, on one of her wooden shelves climbing to the ceiling. It was a burgundy fluffy knee-length skirt, with vertical black stripes to its bare-necked and bare-armed top only. She didn't find my tutu for the Queen of the Dryads part, 'it must be in here, mademoiselle, but my pile's too big and I know you don't have time,' but she said to take any white tutu that might fit me and to ask during the audition for a short intermission for costume change going from the Street Dancer to the Queen where I would just swap the skirt for the tutu and be done. 'I think that's enough to suggest the Queen character; let's not complicate things further. In auditions, you don't want under any circumstances to keep them waiting, there might be several others in the lineup.'

Several others? Then I realized that I had been quite a fool not to ask if there were others involved in the whole thing.

'Forget it, mademoiselle, only need to know yourself and your performance. Even if others, think yourself and your dancing, that's where world and focus needs to be,' Mme Alyutina coached me, then left for the sound library, a windowless room crowded with carboard boxes, to look for the school's cassette tape for 'Don Quixote,' which she found at the end of what, to me, seemed an interminable quarter of an hour, as she normally didn't find her way to there, it being the fiefdom of Mrs. Corwin, the School's pianist and accompanist.

'All ready now,' she told me, 'Now go home, take hot shower, relax muscles, then good night sleep et *voilà.*' She obviously didn't want to pack in more advice, in order to avoid confusing me even more at such a time.

I went home by subway and tram, as usual, arrived there by five. My mother was already back in from grocery shopping. I told her, 'I want to eat and go to sleep immediately. I've got an audition tomorrow with the National and I don't want to talk about it.'

'Audition with the National?' she retreated a step toward the window of the kitchen, did a double take, in a new, different way, at me, as though I'd just gained new rights to something important, perhaps the Grail, then asked 'What would you like then to talk about, then?'

'Tell me how you've spent your day, or tell me about what recipe you've used for these dishes. Silence would help. Anything but *that*.'

'Silence would be fine with me too then.' She didn't seem upset by my request, I mean, what, we had had by then nine or so years of ballet together as a family. She milled around the table, set it up with me just sitting there on one of the kitchen chairs as a neutral witness. My father would arrive home from work in about two hours time, so she set the table for him also.

We finished eating, my mom and I, and I immediately took a hot shower and went to bed. It couldn't have been later than six forty-five in the evening, but I knew that in case of need, I was able to sleep even twelve hours non-stop, and there and then I was in dire need of extra energy. The alarm clock was dutifully set for six the next morning, enough to give me time to fully wake up to the new day and be in it and of it.

During the hot shower, I looked at my body with the acute realization that the next day it had to be at its best and I told it as much under my breath, 'You should take good care of yourself and of me tomorrow.' I soaped and rinsed myself profusely, as though in cleanliness there was a secret hidden, as though I was trying to absurdly thin out my skin and remove any obstacles and impurities so as to easier radiate my inner power to those attending the audition and judging me. 'And, God, save them from the ill of their arrogance of even attempting that!' I laughed to myself.

***

The whole night Mercedes the Street Dancer was on the streets of

Barcelona, streets in full fiesta swing now, preening for the attentions of Espada and the other toreros, running from one small orchestra to the other, poking her curious nose in here, asking for still hotter music there, getting dirty looks and snorts from jealous fully decked old matrons, from young married women and from her line rivals alike, as well as jeers from the street kids.

She was dark-haired, tall, beautiful, daring and cheeky, ranting and raving when piqued, but most of all dancing like a young Bagheera, prancing and jumping and twisting and stepping daringly into your face and challenging you to love, her or anyone else; she didn't care, just open your heart, she asked, carry it on your sleeve, don't back off like a coward.

In the other world in which Yvonne travelled at the same time as though she had two incarnations each on its own white cloud on an Mediterranean sky, the Queen of Dryads was there for Don Quixote, to allay his fears that chivalry might be at its end, that Dulcineas were being left with no defenders, to tell him that calm was calm, that sweetness and love and Cupid were still brought by the breeze around him for support to his lance, that ideals were there to live on even when nothing carnal was involved and present any more in life, that it was still all right to roam the world to fight and annihilate monsters of any kind, power and face.

***

The next day was a December day, so I had on me a whole lot of heavy stuff against the razor-like-slashing wind of settled winter coming from the Lake: my long sheepskin coat with its tall collar raised for the occasion sideways and back of my face that was already obscured by a scarf wrapped around the lower part of it and of my neck, the knee-length black boots cleaned and polished — I assumed by my father in the bathroom during the night — as well a tall bomber fur hat, drawn deep down to my eyebrows, as though to hide unspeakable shame of which I was not yet aware of in my insensitivity.

So arrived I at the National, decked in and overloaded. I knew where the ladies main dressing room was — the one assigned to everyone in the corps, yet not to the principals, who had their own — so I went to it, anxious to get rid of my winter outerwear and to put on my tights and top for the morning company class that must have already started, as I heard the accompanist's piano going with high notes at a slow tempo through the first motions of the warming up routine. Right at the entrance in the dressing room there was a small adjacent room used now, in winter time, for wardrobe purposes, and this is where I unloaded some of my most weighty stuff. At the porter's desk — now, that was an imposing white-moustached man if I ever saw one — I had been already handed in, when I asked if there was anything for instructions to my name, an unsigned nattily typewritten message on a small white-yellowish lustrous piece of paper, telling me to kindly show up at ten, after company class, in one of the rehearsal rooms, for the audition.

I soon found the metal lockers and put some of my other stuff in one of them, while I changed — a feverish rush now upon me — into slightly luscious light-blue ballet tights with a narrow pink thin scarf-belt, ordinary rundown pointe shoes that had become part of my skin as I was using them for class every day, and a matte black top that I liked for its contrast with the tights, all topped, naturally, by the short blond curls I had at the time.

There were *barres* everywhere, all of the white walls eyeing with cathedral-like windows as though in amazement the sparseness and drabness of the winter light coming from outside through those very eyes transparently into the large room. The class was given by Madame Annette Michaud, the main ballet mistress of the National Ballet, whom I recognized, even though only as a famous relative several times removed, from pictures of some of our graduates prominently displayed on the hallways of the School, and with whom I had never worked before.

Her voice was intentionally paced, as masters do during the class, to tether us anew gradually and painlessly to the old soul of ballet's Gulliver, anew bringing and washing past and future steps and motions through our veins, as Big Muddy running through America.

It took me a while to untie and unleash my muscles, to have them go into the *pliées, ronds de jambe, battements*, all those oh-sohabitual warming up motions. As though knowing what was expected from them on that morning, they held their fire, to be able to truly release it later in the day. Not an unfamiliar feeling: *Somnambula*, this is how my mother called me on occasion for this slowness of a morning. That, not uncoincidentally, there was an opera with that name didn't make me feel any better, I'll tell you that. On that day, there was something pinching in my lower back, I might have slept twisted to a side, so I treaded ahead carefully, waiting for the moment when it would disappear, warm body and all, and I could let go and fly into my steps and motions.

I had placed myself at one of the less crowded *barres*. Later on in the routine, when I started to really sense the people around me, their doings and moves, I became aware that there weren't any looks directed my way, as though I didn't exist or was in a black hole. Yet, at one time I happened to intercept, or so it seemed to me, as a reality check, a side nodding of a head toward me as though in a question, 'Who's that over there?' answered with a shrugging of shoulders by another woman dancer two *barres* away on the adjacent side of the room in that corner, both of them still going on ahead through the motions of the class without looking at me not even for a blink, so I thought, in the end, that it must have been my inflated imagination or sense of my self-importance.

Soon though, such thoughts gave way to the nuts and bolts of the warm up, to my separating from everybody else as though a wall of crystalline water had flushed and erected itself high around me to let me see all of them but to be of me only and so was I able to let my thoughts be only with my dancing to later come in the day.

The *grands battements* part of the *barre* exercises were on now. The working leg was moving high, fluttering, from the hip, laterally or at the back, with no impediments now, whatever tension I might have had at the beginning of the practice faded away. Feeling all fluid and firm in movement, my confidence on the rise.

'Yvonne, Rachel and Diane, to center practice now please,' the mistress suddenly asked when the *barre* routine was completed. I looked around, then at her, saw her looking back a bit peremptorily and inquiringly at me and finally realized from the other two dancers already moving into the center area of the room that I was the only

Yvonne around, the one to go into that part of the practice.

'*Attitudes,*' '*arabesques,*' "and *pirouettes* now' off went her commands, after other introductory ones, spaced enough to allow us to do several of each and to let us breath a bit, enough to give us the feeling of controlling the exercises and to well recover from each of them; and so we progressed through all these motions and others, and I felt good all the way through, and a hush was around us, which I knew was a sign that we, I included, of course, were doing well.

'Thank you, please take your places and commence your cooldown.'

I looked at the large clock on a side on one of the walls, and I realized I had another twenty minutes to freshen myself a bit, change into the costume I brought with me for the audition, and get into the proper mood to be first the hot Mercedes of a plaza in full fiesta, then the delicate, dignified and remote Queen of the Dryads fit for a dream. I wasn't too experienced in auditions, still, thinking in my bed the previous night I had already realized that just flipping the switch between them with such a short break as the one normally allowed in auditions was going to be tough. However, I felt strong, the rush of energy had been there whenever I had asked for it during the exercises, and I thought up to the challenge.

6 – Yvonne as Mercedes, 1968

They call me Mercedes in this 'hood down in Barcelona. By rights, I be Maria Dolores Amyanta de los Llobos, but nay, even my parents, whoever they was before leaving me on the steps of the cathedral, forgive them, Father in the high, wouldn't know it, as they didn't came back for my dropping in the saintly water with holy chrism, as they sure had bigger troubles 'an my crying and hopefully bigger fish to fry.

So I know it, 'name that is, from the white-aproned sisters that took to their heads to make a good girl out of myself and got done nothing of it. Not that I would let them to have a good go at it. Seventeen times, if this poor wretched mind of mine tells well, is numbers I ran away from their huge house, slitty narrow windows, dark as hell and all.

Twenty-two, that I am now, and that's, I dare guess, much less 'an the number of men who've had a trip along Besós or whatever river, with myself in the boat.

Still, my greatest trick is dancing, not anything you verily have in your dirty minds over there. Can't be stopped by no one, once the fiesta's around, bands hot with music, air banged by drums, and strummed by guitars — then I get going moving and twirling, stepping and flinging knees legs up in the air, pushing hips as though doing you know what at you all, and only on toes I goes around, as on water.

So today I'm out in the plaza, burgundish fluffish skirt, blackish strips to boot to go with on the top, arms and neck fully showing, 'coz I have what to, darned the oglers be.

The oglers are there anyway and they sit as judges banging their staffs on the cobblestones in front of their seats, and I cry to them

'Your honors, looky' and they just bang away to the music, 'coz wifery is around, ogling them in their turn, they can't get away for the soul of them, so they just go with the music, but doing that they encourage me none the less, 'coz they want for the living out of them, they want it, to get those rumps of theirs hot and jiggling and what better show to have for that than Mercedes dancing to the crowd, no ifs and buts. Buts, hee-hee.

Jacinto's my barker, hump wobbling left-right-left-right on top of him as usual, what with him coming in a rush from over the cathedral, not to lose a whit of my dancing, begging all the way through also left and right and nipping you too if you don't open your eyes to what he does in truth with his sleigh-of-hands. He's dumped himself some way from me, he knows I doesn't want him to ruin the wonderfulness of me sight. He's whooping now and then, so any sleepy crowd be waked to attention and look at dear me. He knows well, coins jingling in my hat will, though in small part, as suckers I can't suffer, switch hands, after everything is over and he'd come shuffling to me.

The dames peeking into your future also know they'd get their due. Sitting as they are in the corners of the plaza, they now and then mumble though their litanies of feats coming to you truth words like 'Ah, and, *Senor, Senora*, don't you forget to help Mercedes, you might just help yourself by doing that. Drop something in her hat when the time comes and she walks around with the hat. Someone high up may look well upon your doing that. *They* just may, 'coz she keeps the spirits high, and high spirits becalm the waters of life in storms and enable you to behold the luck that might just be around the corner, with you unawares.'

So the *senores* and *senoras* and even the riff-raff don't think twice about it and put in their more or less hard-earned dough when the time comes, or add to it if they was already doing it, hearts even softer now and touched and melting. And this is good, 'coz winter's just several months away, and then one like me can only do the small *hostales* and the gathered and the gathering, or the other way round, are both smaller.

I be on and off these days with Espada, the matador, as he's moving all the time around Catalonia and even Spain with his *corridas*, so hanging on to him isn't small feat, no, sir, as dames are out there all over the place to curry favor with him. Crooked legs has he, but then he's hot in other parts, and so much so in his heart and soul as they burn you as a butterfly in a flame if you get too close when a bullfight is around, or men to fight over a woman like me, a woman, says he, the dahling, quick as quicksilver. Manliness aside, and not to play that down a whit, it's same bizniz with him too: you bring light on me, I bring light on you, and it all ends as everybody's face is brighter when you look or feel at your own pockets or satchels or backpacks at the end of the day.

He's with his kind of caravan, and me with mine. Only thing, mine moves just around Barcelona, whereas he needs to go where's place enough for the bulls to romp and tromp around, jerk and hack with their horns at the guts and legs of *picadores'* horses and at *matadores* themselves to make them butcher's raw. Me, I be more into engagements, weddings, baptisms, smaller crowds, and the catch of the net's likewise. I means to say up until the fiesta for the corrida, the big thing, year in year out, for all of us living on crowds and their sweetness to us. Then, on a good fiesta's day, I makes enough to pay off my butcher, my *hostaléros* — 'coz I have many of them *hostaléros* here, the way I move around a lot — and my dress maker and shoe-maker, just enough to keep the barge afloat and buy some new stuff, some of it gifted by Espada, I tells this to tell yous I be grateful, some by older men who I takes up with on the sly with when he's not around or not looking, sugar-daddies or some such, who put my bean-counter's ledger — as though I had one, he, he, he — in better shape, so to say.

He's not fiendish to girls other than me, Espada, he sure isn't, and never methought that in far away places he might not get sweetness and succor pouring out from other corners over his poor soul, and worse, body, in distress. So this helps even out the bargain amongst us.

'You, *senorita*, you take care of yourself,' he always tells me when leaving for a trip. And sure this I takes to mean 'and don't mess up with others,' but I just replies in kind, 'And you take care of yourself, Espada; don't you worry about the fire in this home, 'coz is going to stay burning hot and lively for you. Just come back in good health; your bulls make me carry bad dreams and wake up at night or morning-wise all in a cold sweat, turmoiling about you.' Still, I gather, he's one of the few calling me *senorita*, others just call me *chica*, and I clue this one to some respect and it gets stacked onto my feelings about him. Sure as God made little green apples, there's something about him, his ramrod-straight carriage and manners, that's giving him more honor than whatever that is that he does in the bullring, though myself fully knows many times this is just hot air learned in their trade, how to behave with crowds and people in eye-to-eye to hold their name high and some such nonsense. Still, it gets to me and makes the tethering worse. Worse, as I thinks that, the best dancer to see in Barcelona's fiestas, I deserves something steadier, though handsomer I don't need, he's a big chunk of a man enough for myself in that way, so much so when he's got on him his fighting attire and trimmings, *el Traje de Luces*, all tight on him to pitch that thinness of hips, calves tapering nervy and sharp above the black *zapatillas*, wide toward the knees and pushy under white knee-length *medias*, thighs nigh blowing out from under his *taleguilla*, *chaquetilla* short in front over bumping chest, showing the frilled-up oh-so-white *camisa*, and the black *montera* on his head. He's all to the good to me on those days.

He isn't so good on days when he's back in town but doesn't show up at my haunts and I hears it from Mamá Damiana or Mamá Melchora, that's he's drawn to the shore in other places and raises hell as a seven-headed dragon without caring a bit it could all trickle to me, as though I've never before been of this world.

On those days, if I has time, and I always finds some for a thrashing like that, I packs a wide belt for horses with me in a bag, show up at the place he's set up quarters, throws open the doors of the room where he's in, and if any women chance to be there, wearing or not wearing anything on them dear skin, I be known to lash at them with that belt all around the place, up and down the stairs, and so until they find the way to get out of town well before dark sundown.

Yet, not those days are the worst for me. The worst is when he's brought back gored by one of those bulls and he lays for weeks at at time in a sad hospital room with doctors and sisters from convents nearby tending to his open gashes, not of this world at times, and hanging by a thread to it. Then I know my earnings are gonna go to a naught for quite a while, as I sit with him most of the days and nights, on a chair or stool beside his bed, losing my thought and repose, as though I was his sisters or mother, none of which I sees around. So only then you see he's somehow a lonely man and what is left of crowds and making a noise in the world. And none of those dames comes in, as they surely know I be around, or better 'coz they don't care a darn iota about him when he's down and low and not making any *duros*.

'Carmencita, where are you, Carmencita?' I hears one such time, slipping out of his lips that are hot with the heat of the sickness, and it's having the props knocked from under myself, that he had in mind someone who wasn't around, and who could she be, this one? And he cries about her for days, and I be more and more out of my joints with it. So finally he gets out of it all, he's back with us and well, and he tells me this was his small sister, lost when he was seven, and that he has now and then this dream with the two of them going in a long garden with trees in blossom, leaping and skipping around and somehow by the end of the way, she's lost from sight as fading in the air of that garden. So I tells him, it can only mean you saw yourself with her in heavens, and be at peace now, you'll see her there, but don't rush time, 'coz you need a life to yourself, time's to use as you have it, as twice it doesn't come to you, as much as you might pray, and our time's not for knowing, as much we want to peer into it.

But enough of this talking! Two hours from now we have on the streets first the bulls running to the bullring in the *encierro*, then the grand parade with all the matadors with their *cuadrillas*, while in the plaza in front of the cathedral we're gonna have the loudest music and dancing waiting for their passing through and this is where I'll show up, strutting my stuff.

***

It's high noon now, all the street bands, the *murgas* — and they might well be five, they might be ten, as they suddenly shoot into action as cannons hidden in battle or mushrooms after a rain, from one place or another, some hidden in the shadows of an inn or under the awnings of a store, others sitting right there laid back and carefree under the blazing down sun — all the bands then are pitching their songs to crowds around them and riding their music high and proud. There are guitars, drums, cymbals, lutes, all sharply pitched, all hitting their paces. And the words of the *trovadores* and *cantaores* are sung with pain as though cut to their quick, as they tell about toreros, courage, love and death, wine and frollic, about losing your sweetie and fighting for her and getting her back again, about being down and lost and poor, about cruel Father Time running roughshod over us and turning the young into old and the fresh into withered and making glorious, live, powerful places, be just white sand in dry deserts.

Gone from the gates are the bulls and the oxen! They are coming, coming, coming! Here in the plaza, we all learn this now from the blast of the guns telling all and sundry to take care of their limbs and hold on to dear life if caught by the bulls, from the cries of the spindly youth, that worked themselves into a tizzy, still, hidden behind the barricades of stones and logs, some of them youth wanting to run in front of the beasts, as, they say, it's done in Pamplona, carrying red neckerchiefs and red cummerbunds to bring the devils after them. The fools, I says, the fools of them!

Jacinto's as running a high fever. He done no sleeping the whole night, so eyes show reddish on his unshaven face. He's jumping all over the place, like taken out of the mothballs, slamming and banging and pealing with an iron piece the small bell stolen from the deaconry years ago, a thing of his that no one else has that he keeps for days like this, so no one can take after him and he be it.

'You, Jacinto, you stay away from me and quiet while I dance, I don't want that pealing to throw me off of my steps!' I tells him, but there's no hope in the heavens with his child's mind he's gonna listen all the time, though he doesn't wanna get shorted on his payoff to come from me. But the devil's surely caught in his thinking and will between his own gathering an' nipping an' begging from folks and the part coming from me, and perhaps deems this rootin'-tootin' an' jumping a way to put peoples' sights on him the more.

Look!

There they come, the matadors, at the end of the narrow street coming into the plaza, each with his suite, the *cuadrilla*. Two of them are to fight later today in the corrida, and one of them is my Espada, God keep him in his heavenly sights! I knows there's gonna be no dancing with him right now, as he's grim-faced and tight, and I surely knows he wants to keep his head together for the fight. But we're gonna dance thereafter, merry-go-round all night, if God keeps him untouched by the beasts.

Back straight as a ramrod, walking with measured steps, still he shows with a short nod of a head and a dart of his eyes toward me that he knows I be here and dancing for him, in truth for all of them passing in their parade, to be caught (by the beasts) we've just seen bolting an' galloping heavy an' awful threatening in front of us.

Espada sure tries to keep away from his thinking right now the awful thing that happened to him just two years ago to the day, here in Barcelona too, when the huge Diura bull Xerfes, who felt not nor looked not behaving as any bull like all others on that day, stomping his front feet on the ground, raising his tail against the air and lashing with it in all ways as you thought it was Beelzebub's own, eying evewhere with eyes blind with fury, charging at the *picadores'* horses and killing two of them in a row an' leaving their entrails on the ground, running at the barricades in the streets an' the ones in the bullring, took into his beast's mind to charge on him right before the time of the *estocada*.

Just as he as matador trimm'd himself to end the days of the beast, so the monster had unbeknowst to Espada bethought itself to end the days of his closest foe. It didn't think of all and sundry around him cryin' an' shoutin' an' askin' for his demise, but thought only about the bein' movin' in front of him, and fluttering and rounding in ways that to it seemed to call for fury and revenge that red drape of the *muleta*.

The bull seemed to watch him for the time to have a leaf fall to the ground in heavy rain, an' seemed to follow the cape, and willing to do as asked, stand in place, an' seemed taken in and under spell, but suddenly as the matador wheeled himself just a quarter of a turn to his left, it bounded ahead with two huge steps and with a jerk of his right horn caught Espada in his right thigh, the one more to the fore, lifted him in the air up and over itself and threw him to a side as a doll with no life nor will to it. Luck made it that the Espada's toreros were close by, and came in rushing to help, with more capes to take beast's muddied sight and mind from the hurt man. Taking courage, helpers rushed in, took Espada in their arms and carried him past the barricades and into the small chapel of the bullring and tied his wide injuries with clean rags until the chirurgeon tromping heavily came in from his abode nearby.

It took Espada two full-moon's passing before he was anew in strength enough to lift himself with my help from his bed and move around the room in dark with narrow windows at the Benedictine sisters' convent, who had been so good to allow him in for healing and took care of him, with the chirurgeon.

Yet, so often was he cursin' and shoutin' at himself with anger, for havin' lost the beast for a blink of an eye from his sight.

Done all that, I sure knows I could all be anew here just for a play of luck in the stars and that no tellers could say if it would ever happen again and how not to go through it, as it's so much his craft that brings all that with it, part and parcel. And bringing Espada an' his craft apart is so much out of this realm of truth as bringing apart me from my dancing is. For no doubt, as long bodies are healthy with us, we would just go on, the both of us, 'coz ardor, fire of soul an' courage an' love fare with him an' the enticement of music and dance an' the flame of them fare with me.

7 – Yvonne as The Queen of Dryads, 1968

Then the gods gave the trees to us, the Dryads, one to each, and told us that as long green and leaves in flutter stay with them, we too we'll live and not any longer. So immortal we're not. Then, as one could have foretold, there was an awful fight among us all as to who would take over the oaks, the sequoias and the baobabs, the trees of sublimely long life that one is bound to find in place centuries later still, and who were to master the apple and the cherry trees, the humbler this way, which grow old terribly faster.

There was still this catch at hand in our favor: should we be in a place with many trees in kind, say a forest or an orchard, should one of the home trees die, we would be allowed to move on and refresh our own lives and souls with and within a new tree just coming up to the air from its roots. This is how it happens that many of us go through several lives, should the rain and the glebe of the place be giving enough to help the new crop of trees withstand their first time out.

Demeter the fruitful with the mellifluous golden locks, the goddess of bountiful crops and animal husbandry, loved us no end and spent time of no number in our company, and even more so after taking into her head to leave Mount Olympus when she learned that Hades, the god of darkness and the host of those lost from this world, Demeter's and Zeus's own brother, had stolen Persephone, she of the beautiful and fleeting ankles, her beloved daughter with Zeus, to be his, Hades's, wife and queen of the world under, and — something that Demeter could not believe until Helios, who saw everything from his wonderful carriage drawn by galloping solar steeds over the skies of mortals and the divine aether alike, lighted the truth for her — indeed all had been done at the urging and with the heavenly help of Zeus. Thus, treason upon treason upon treason, this is what divinely fruitful Demeter thought about it for a time longer than we can count.

Aeons later, in Spain, when lady Dulcinea del Toboso took in valiant Don Quixote's asseveration of love and eternal service to her, she turned to the forests to glean quiet for his soul tried to the raw, at loggerheads with the world around him. Here, she found us still tending with our lives to the green, the lush, the sap — no timeless ichor, this — thusly, in the end, to the very life of trees and to the souls of those seeking peace herein amongst them.

***

Cupid the child god was with me, the Queen of Dryads, to pacify Don Quixote and to reward him with good feelings and with the presaging of love to come from Dulcinea in return for his own.

Guided by the vision of Dulcinea he came, Don Quixote, soul troubled by vast and unending questions about the ills of the world, never doubting that he was fated to right them straightaway and determined to fight injustice with his words and his chivalrous lance and sword until his body would help him to do so.

The green around us in the woods is an ocean with waves of leaves, of pine needles, all turned over or around by unquietness in the air, the winds of change in the day or in the seasons, and we live in it as the Nereids live in the oceans of water. And as the water seas seem to disappear close to shores under heavy winter ice or under giant islands of ice travelling over them and bumping into and breaking apart the unlucky ships, so our cold seasons bring dryness, barren branches, and surrender and loneliness to the soul.

So it was that Dulcinea wanted to bring Don Quixote to us in the full glory of summer, when his eyes would marvel at the sights around him, of freshness and vegetal power, when the birds would roam and flutter about at the highest of their liveliness and sprightness and would not have left for warmer places to show us deserted or have hidden out of the seeing world in accommodating holes in trees or dugouts under the snow. She showed us to him in the tremor of the leaves under the warm breeze of summer slow as a breath in repose, branches rising proud and holding up, pushed by fresh and lukewarm sap, in the shadow still entire, in the grass crushing rich with water under the foot and springing back lively when the passing burden left it, in the streams forever dodging and running away from one place to another and sprinkling up and awry nippy drops when meeting shores or boulders or the unwonted face — be it man or beast — drinking from them unsatiatedly in the sharp heat of the afternoon.

All is unnamed, and above some meadow, a lark would use the lift provided by the hot air to even higher work on its towers of pushing high, while deer hidden in the shadow of an old oak would wait for the good time to cross the water in front of them, careful and straining at any pale hint of motion within their range.

Now and then, I shuttle around on wings of wind, of bees or of owl, to all the sisters into treedom, who never can leave their outpost while their very home, the tree itself, is alive and well, the happenings around their own part of the earthly world, this time of Don Quixote coming soon to visit to find and to gather himself and his dreams in this wood, also to oh so very shyly to perhaps anew glimpse, in the greater quiet allowed us outside of the beavering and the hustle of man, a better view of his inamorata Lady Dulcinea — who weightless and aetherial leads him to us — to boost his chivalrous strength and loving ardor.

It is again that time of the day for the breeze to come down cool from the mountains above us, rolling in featherly. The air it brings is fresher and sharper, and gives us more life, as though going straight into the vessels of sap passing up and down through our home-bodies from the roots to the touch and the gentle, lost, edge of the air around each branch.

8 - Toronto, 1968

The clock over one of the side plain-whitewashed walls having pointedly and reproachfully told me I had only twenty minutes until ten a.m. and the start of the audition, I suddenly spun into overdrive and left the room assigned for company class, to make sure I'd be on time at the most important appointment I might ever have in my entire life. Quickly toweling off in the ladies dressing room, I changed to the costume I had for Mercedes from school days, the not-a-fig-of-brilliance-to-it modest combo — a burgundy layered tulle skirt plus matte black stripes over burgundy top. There were only two other women in the dressing room, a younger one, still seemingly older than myself, and one that could have been even in her twenties, in my then-so-unreliable estimation, both looking, or perhaps even ogling, at me through the mirrors in the room, not directly, with some mix of surprise and, if I cut it fine, being miffed, however, not saying anything to myself or to each other. I guess everybody else was still in company class, which had to be in the cool-down part by now. Much later after the audition, I was to learn that they were Shelley Anderson and Jean Benoît, my very rivals for the double role. For the time being, as I had been made hyper by the situation, I didn't notice them too much, fighting as I was to get into my dress without, God forbid, tearing it while at it, as I knew full well how flimsy those fabrics were that my parents had been able to buy me for the school gala. "I wish that school would once start budgeting for such on-the-spur-of-the-moment costumes," Mother had said somewhat hotly at dinner, continuing in a lower tone "It's good they'll at least do the tailoring this one time."

    A lot of light blasted the rehearsal room reserved for the audition, a lot of it coming from outside, as though there was something special about that December day, but they also had the inside lights on. This I liked, even though it dazed me to some extent at the very beginning, until I got used to it. Later, I thought it might have been me coming from our school, and it scrimping a bit on electricity.

***

"Come in, come in please, you must be Miss Fillon." With his booming, welcoming voice and a frame that had to tip the scales at over three hundred pounds, he couldn't have been anyone else but George Faraday, the casting director, who had called Yvonne at School. He was fully bearded and had a large mane of hair around his head — so much so that Yvonne thought Walt Whitman himself and not just Orson Welles had come farther in time to make her feel better. Waves of benevolence radiated from his voice and his open, easy-to-read face, and Yvonne thought that lucky were the dancers that met him in such strenuous moments as those of an audience.

"Let me introduce you to the other gang members, or, I should say, the other members of the casting committee. Oh, come on, George, you can do better, that's too veddy-veddy proper. Too bad, because here they are," he laughed, defenseless, as he and Yvonne were in front of the table behind which sat two other men and two ladies.

"Yvonne Fillon. John Ash. John, in case you happen to have lived on another planet," he blasted a laugh, "and then we're sorry for you, Yvonne, as he is the director of our wonderful production of 'Don Quixote.'" Yvonne knew a bit about him — in his fifties, American, a former dancer said to have worked with Balanchine and Serge Lifar in France, an avid surfer. Tall, slim, he seemed the more casual one from the whole bunch, in blue jeans, a white open-necked long-sleeved cotton shirt, and a suede jacket with a front zipper, open now to show a flat chest. He greeted her with a "Hello," proffered with a firm handshake and a direct look. A faint smile on a face that looked complicated, endowed with many creaks and marks, what one could have termed well-weathered, and for a moment she wondered if this was the effect of his surfing.

"Yvonne Fillon. Bette Finlayson. You certainly must have heard of Bette — the first lady of the Canadian ballet, our honored board chair." Mr. Faraday didn't seem inclined to make any jokes about the woman in front of them, and she had an imposing manner. Slim, petite, she offered the appearance of someone used to mastering people and situations by a force of will that was all-too-easily betrayed by a pair of firm gray eyes, corseted in dominating eyebrows that seemed to have been never corrected by any tweezers. If there was a glimmer in those eyes, it remained undetected to Yvonne. "It's nice to meet, Miss Fillon. We've heard good things about you" on a neutral, unenthusiastic voice, sounded good enough for the time being, as Yvonne had decided the previous night not to look too much to any of them and not to let herself be impressed or swayed one way or another until everything would be said and done and the decision, whatever it was to be, final. She had two roles to dance and that was where her focus had to be — her thin but firm inner voice kept coming back to this.

"Yvonne. Nikos Andreatis. Nikos, our brilliant set and costume design director, creating rich environments for our ballets — and not inexpensive, I might say, may I not, Bette?" he joked, directing his affable smiles to both the subject of his new introduction and at the board chairperson, neither of whom smiled back quite in kind, as they perhaps felt budget figures is mined territory, better left alone for stormy board discussions. Nick was then forty-two, well-travelled and employed all over the world, by Ninette Valois at the Royal Ballet in Britain, the Vienna ballet, the Stuttgart ballet, l'Opéra de Paris, to name just a few, Yvonne would later learn. He wore a proper green pair of pants — not blue jeans for him, it seems, not in the exercise of his profession — ironed out to perfection to show how flared they were, which the beige wide-lapelled jacket matched perfectly, all this to push forward the bright red of his shirt, from under the collar of which a black string tie snaked out only to drop resignedly down in old- and new-world charm. He extended a friendly vigorous shake and said something to the effect of being all hyped up by the occasion of seeing new dancers at work. Yvonne was made a bit more comfortable by the statement, she certainly was "new," and said to herself "he certainly seems easy to work with."

"Mila, this is Yvonne. Mila Bergmann is our trusted ballet mistress, the one in charge of the nuts and bolts of our ballet dancing, the *barre* work and class, your, sorry, *the*, everyday technique and so on and so forth. She would be the person most responsible for teaching these roles, until, that is, you fall under the sharp eye of John, and he wants you to do something totally different." George Faraday completed the introductions with a huge guffaw. John Ash, at which Yvonne was looking right now, seemed to have taken it all in good-naturedly.

"If I remember well, I kindly asked you to bring your own tape, if you'd like to. Do you have it?"

"Yes, here you are," Yvonne meekly answered, a bit red-faced after this meeting of new people, all quite much older than herself.

He took it and majestically and unhurriedly went to the tape recorder on the edge of the jury's table, changed the spool, then went back to his seat at the table, where the others were already seated, a bit away from each other, each with a note pad in front of them. His secretary, a tall, slim woman, was left sitting with the recorder to handle the playback at their instructions.

He bent forward, looked around at everybody at the table, then declared, "We're ready when you're ready."

"Just a moment, please." She went to a corner of the room behind them, and left on the wooden floor her bag and above it the robe she had brought with her against eventual chilliness in the hallways. She then went to another somewhat remote place in the room, from where she was to start Mercedes' routine in the plaza with the daring steps required by the role, and took the initial fifth stance, chin lifted, eyes fired up challenging everything and everybody, as Mercedes had to be in her book most of the time.

"I'm ready now" she said, and Ludwig Minkus's music started in an instant to flow in the large rehearsal room from the two loudspeakers in the corners in front of the jury.

***

"Easy for you, Jean, to beat the breeze that I don't care a fig about you and that I didn't raise a finger for you to get this role." John Ash was at home in his apartment; as a matter of fact as of this less-than-happy moment of his existence he was in his kitchen, a well-appointed one, with heavily-chromed appliances, preparing a steak — it had to be well-done, or otherwise he couldn't eat it — and talking in a voice loud enough to supposedly get to the bedroom and even to the persons therein. "What would you have wanted me to do? When it came to vote, there were two for Yvonne from Nikos and Mila, one for Sherry Anderson from Bette, and the other one from me for yourself. And then even that poor balance, if you want to call it that way, went down the drain when George Faraday, late as usual in his *bonhomie*, voted for Yvonne too."

"Why didn't you talk to any of the others in advance? Why didn't you prepare things a bit?" a high-pitched female voice resounded in response. "You always tend to ad-lib. Well, in life one should also plan things in advance."

"Funny who tells me that," John said. "You, Jean, who never do a backgrounder on your roles, and never read one even when given for free, as though you're supposed to naturally fall, or should I say splash, into them, with no regard for what all they're about and how others have dealt with them."

The feminine repartee wasn't long in coming. "And kindly tell me what was so great about that girl? Are you all, the great casting committee, going for a virgin in that role or what? Had I known, I'd've gone to a cherry doctor to do something about mine. You know how dedicated to my art I am. Proof: look where I am right now."

"Where?" John Ash's baritone inquired, laughing.

"In your bed, sir, that's where, and don't play the naïve with me."

"Well, but it's the first time you're telling me I'm offered a homage to Terpsichore each time when sleeping together. Had I known, I'd have been more careful with your mythology playing, or play-acting."

"Go to hell, do you hear me?" came the high-pitched answer and a pillow was heard being sent in accompaniment on a failed orbit through the door of the bedroom. "And don't come here when you're finished in the kitchen. Yes, sir, sleep on the sofa in the living-room tonight. This might just teach you to have something on your head beside your hat when strategizing, not to use dirty words like scheming."

* * *

"Shirley, could you have Shirley Anderson come to me? When? Within a quarter of an hour, please, you know I'm fully scheduled later today." That acid "please" and that "I" came imperiously from the lips of Bette Finlayson, as most everything, especially of a morning, when she wanted to put her Rock-of-Gibraltar stamp over the day's developments.

"Hi, Shirley, glad to see you." The dark-haired girl was corps, all nineteen of her, small and thin. Intelligent, now fearful, eyes. "I just want to give you more, shall we say, tidings as to the reasons why you didn't get the role in 'Don Quixote,' even though you had my endorsement, as promised when I suggested going for it. First, you don't have any experience in the role, and for that matter, in 'Don Quixote.' Showing bits and pieces of your other roles is OK, but not quite enough when the competition comes up having been in that exact role and dancing it, I'd say, reasonably well, in a pressure-packed situation when we need to provide a replacement within days. Yes, that new girl from the School had the double role learned for one of their galas." *And she danced it quite damn well, I'd say, but there's no reason to upset this poor girl even more — losing a part is tough enough. I know it, even though* they *assume it couldn't be true, as it's usually I who has to dispense the news.* "Third, and this is what I'd like you to work on, you really seemed a bit fazed by the occasion. Do something about it, hire a professional shrink, sorry, a mental toughness coach, I think this is what they're termed these days, read some books — check the self-improvement area in your favorite bookstore, whatever, you need to get a better hold of

Marius Hancu

yourself, to show more attitude, to give off more confidence. In our business, this is vastly important, you know. You may also ask Mila Bergmann for some private classes to widen your repertory. You don't need to be perfect in those roles, nor to know them in full — that comes with dancing them in full shows, just some reasonably long snippets would be enough to be ready for such auditions. OK, that's enough for today." *Hm, I really wonder if Shirley has what it takes. The new girl, Yvonne, skipped around like it all was nothing, and as though none of us five were around. Time to go with the new. I need to call Mila to tell her to lay some stress on Yvonne's* developpés, *especially the* jetés into developpés à la seconde, *which she has to do at the beginning as The Queen of Dryads. With those long round legs of hers she certainly could get a kick out of the audience for these steps if she slows them down just a tiny bit while hanging them high in the air. Perhaps some flexibility work at the* barre *could help,* grand battements, *and so on and so forth, with that. Also those* piques de côté *could be sharper in attack, the public wants the ballerinas to visibly kill their pointes today. Too bad for the girls. She did them fine as Mercedes though. There was no point in fighting against her. She was better than I remembered her from that gala or whatever it was, she's grown nicely into that body of hers, and those short blond curls won't do any damage with the public either. Mind you, she will need to wear a wig in Mercedes, still that's what all the ladies do today in it. For a change, her natural hair would be more than enough in the Queen of Dryads and, with Cupid around, there would be a nice gentle touch, enough to perhaps and hopefully bring down the house, at least on our more enthusiastic nights, along with those* pas de ciseaux *in Mercedes in front of the aligned toreros, challenging them, at which she's quite good already.*

* * *

"Sergio, dearest, your main man Nikos calling." Listening for a

Our Lives as Kites

matter of two minutes. "Grumbling, are we? Why would that be? Haven't called recently? Didn't I tell you we're in a big doo-doo with 'Don Quixote' at the National, a rushed update to the cast, the second most important female part? Didn't I? Then why all this bitching? The sack here's missing you and you know who. Do I have something in the fridge? Of course I have, and for more than a snack. When did I *ever* leave you hanging around hungry? Many times? You must be funnin'. Anyway, here's what: fridge's full with lobster. This is not baiting anyone nor batting eyes at anyone. Want to come, fine. Don't want, fine too. Sounds interesting? Certainly is. You know how good I am at cooking lobster. Who won? The new girl, Yvonne Fillon, that's who. Sweet sixteen. How about that? How is she, you're asking? We might have a very good dancer in two years' time, and she manages, at least in this part, quite well even here and now. Wow, I'll tell you, she had quite an entrance in Mercedes, you know, the girl selling flowers, dancing on the streets for meager pesetas and having for a main squeeze one of the matadors in Barcelona, who meanwhile's leading others up the garden path, even though the costume on her was nothing to write home about. Trouble is, I'll have to mend things with both the director, that's John Ash, and the boss-lady of the board, Bette — now that I didn't vote for the favorite horse of either of them. But the things were obvious, at least to me — best prepared and freshest wins. The other two girls didn't have too much of a chance, not to my attention, as they put on the table other parts to prop them up, which I didn't find quite kosher under the circumstances. If she's good looking? She certaintly is, but you know my cup of tea, don't you? She might still grow, problem in the offing for *les danseurs nobles* to lift her up. However, there's not much lifting in this double. What double? Sorry not to have told you: the part is first the dancer in the plaza, then it moves in a fairy queen, no bad jokes here, no, sir, she is a Queen of Dryads, a mental attraction, vision or prop, not in any order, if you will, for Don Quixote himself, a share of his dreaming things up. What Dryads? Fairies to Greeks and Romans, that's what, not fairies which you might have in mind, you dirty fairy you."

Marius Hancu

* * *

"Come here, where are you going, Tommy darling?" Mila Bergmann asked with a high voice. "Didn't I tell you I want to tell you everything about it, right after it all shakes out? So, here we are, I can tell you what transpired at that meeting, call it audition if you so want, of ours. Yvonne, the new girl in town, won, if you can imagine, and I'm proud to be one to have voted for her. How John and Bette had to moxie to vote for the other two, I don't know, but something wasn't right in their heads. 'Coz it was so damn clear how the wind was blowing from the word go, from the time when she did those *pas de ciseaux* with so much verve, panache, power, aplomb or any other that you may want to use here, that any man in any Barcelona would have had eyes only for her and her long legs and nifty bee-like midsection. She pretty much knows both roles, so the only thing I'll have to do with John should be around harmonizing and sync-ing her with our music, to our tempo, and to the way the others in the ensemble are moving around the stage at one time or another. Oh, yes, she needs more *métier*, but this is why I am there. She needs more extension, more calm and sweetness in the *port de bras*, more stability in the *arabesques* and the planting of legs, in getting her to move faster in her pirouettes, but the main things are already there. As for pride and deportment, those are outstanding, she displays them naturally, so no one — or not many anyway, 'coz you know how people and envy meet each other — can pretend she's grandstanding or can think she's doesn't deserve her place. There will be some who might carry the green-eyed monster in their souls for her or feel that a monkey wrench has been thrown their way, especially in the corps or second-tier soloists, but, hey, this is life. Still, talent should be happy to rise as oil to the surface as it happened in this particular occasion. And come here into my arms, Tommy," she said and the cat didn't have any difficulty in being accommodating."

* * *

"You may find mirth in what this young woman told me, Father. After the audition and when everything was settled in her favor, she asked me if there were any places close by where she could go to raise some kites. This being around two in the afternoon, and the day being full of your splendor, even of a winter, the idea didn't in itself seem strange to me, still, I opined that going to the wide place in front of the Convocation Hall at the University, on King's College Circle, might be a better idea, as that is less cluttered with buildings and all in all a much more unimpeded place.

"Only then did I observe, Almighty, that she had brought a large bag with her, and that the ends of what I now recognized to be sails of one sort or another protruded from it.

"To my question as to why she would be doing it, she answered simply, with a serious face, 'Because I have to. I have been doing it since my childhood. Was taught by my father first how to launch them, then, much later, how to explore the high currents in the air in maneuvering them around in the sky.'

"'Do you attach any special meaning to it, Miss Fillon?' I then asked.

"'No, not more than exploring my fate, seeing how its large currents are working for me at the time.'

"'Are you religious?' I said, a bit embarrassed.

"'Somehow, yes, perhaps. My father insisted that I become a Catholic, which I am, though I'm not really feeling like one, not these days.'

"'What do you mean by "these days"?' I asked.

"'You most probably know that already, Mr. Faraday: most people my age don't show up at services much, so I feel embarrassed if I go with my father.'

"'But I see you somehow concerned with fate, the way her strange winds blow about.'

"'Yes, but this doesn't have anything to do with being a Catholic, not the way I see it; it's more like a feeling out of the world, not my fate, if you know what I mean.'

"This is why, Father, I am here in front of you today, trying to represent to you how today's people think. Perhaps my humble words will help you help them better, especially this young lady who seems to still believe in something."

Five minutes later, after lighting up two whitish candles for his parents, George Faraday exited from his Toronto church, head still bent in humility.

He was about to go to Mila Bergmann's place, but this was something that no one knew about in those days, something not having been reported even in his confessions yet.

9 - April 1969

The kite was a large one, an orange and red bulbously-eyed dragon bought from Chinatown for ten dollars or so, which was a lot those days, and Yvonne had been anxious about its making good on the promise from the seller — "it goes very high," he had boasted. When she yerked, as her mother used to say, down on the string, it tended to drop its tail and to raise its flattened head as a bucking and rearing steed would, and she liked that. It showed some spunk and cheek in dealing with the winds and the small drafts — the flutterings of air, she termed those — around it, so it was easy to jockey to make it ascend.

"What's going on with you today, dragon?" she talked to it, at the same time dreamlike and disappointed, leaving alone for home from the large circle of grass, the start of bright lush green, at the Convocation Hall, the place where she was going with her kites lately. On that day, it had felt difficult to maneuver and preferring lower altitudes, a ribald troubadour versing away at his own pleasure, with no control from seigneurs who fed him. Still, there were winds of trouble and change in herself; she felt as though she were hedged in, by what exactly she couldn't quite tell yet. And she had started to recognize that as the ultimate source of her scrapes with the kite. "Inattentive hands can't be responsive and firm enough," her father had always proclaimed in his temperate bass voice.

It had been Aloysia Breckenridge — what a name, she thought, Breckenridge, sounds like a line regiment colonel's daughter, and Aloysia, of all, one of Mozart's loves — giving her two months before that, in one of the breaks at ballet school, copies of pages from *Human Sexual Response* — "got out only two years ago, you know" — that had raised more question marks, caused broodings and wonderings, than let her focus on her work. Now that she was, even "but temporarily, Miss Fillon, you surely understand" as she had been duly warned by the direction, a soloist with the National in *Don Quixote*, continuing her schooling at the same time brought about quite a tough schedule for her, what with rehearsals scattered among classes. In some strange way she felt upset at Alo, as they called her, for having given the excerpts to her in the first place, although she had read them line after line after line with no respite.

Alo was gabby, friendly, but, Yvonne surmised, not a scent more experienced then herself in the matters discussed with clinical detail by Dr. Masters and Ms. Johnson, playing the informed girl just to net-and-squeeze more attention and perhaps with the remote hope of becoming popular, if that was ever truly possible among such a competitive bunch of teens. At least Alo wasn't Tabitha Clark of Alberta hotel fame. No, Alo didn't have anyone famously rich in her family, she wasn't on a warpath to such elevated rungs, nor was she, for that matter, great looking, carrying around a pale, delicately dappled face lacking significant passion in the eyes or in the mouth, and, as she was saying, she would have to dance honest to do something with her life, which she already did, being most of the time the first to arrive to ballet class and the last to leave. So it happened that she was known as the one to most frequently change ballet slippers, and not because she was heavyset — she was not so at all. There was help to her cause, and it came in the guise of a pair of very quick-to-learn legs, nicely shaped, even though a touch on the dry, muscular side, with fibers in clear relief and display even through some of the thicker tights. Clever too, she was, one of the earliest to have learned self-massage, from another book again, to send off — as on a breeze, she asseverated — at the end of a long day, part of the piled up stress.

Yvonne getting to dance that soloist part in *Don Quixote* had taken most of the other girls, as well as some of the teachers, by a swell of surprise if not shock — the closest know or understand the least, it seemed, at least at times. Her presence at various parties was now sought as a desirable prize, thought to possibly bring hope that others would be successful as well in identical or similar endeavors.

It possessed the good and bad markers that success always carries among people, from pure and sincere elation to straight and green envy. One looked at her with more care, trying to find the quick recipe for the hole in one. One also tried to hope that there's an uncertain, undefined level in the domain of person–to-person communication, where success wafts or oozes over as the agents of a benign contagious disease do through some secret channels. Stories were duly invented and she was held by some to have been the lover of more people all throughout Toronto, and in, as it were, all allegedly freemasonic spheres of influence that could even tangentially be touching on ballet, than she had ever known, relinquishing herself and her morals in the process, all in a stew, on the altar of fame. The tree of knowledge, or a copy of it worthy of consideration, seemed to many to have been now re-planted — you know, temporarily, dear, can't last — in her courtyard, and no small numbers of them wanted to share in the forbidden fruit or in an imitation thereof. Just as well, to the same or others still, she seemed to be the gully-gully woman having mastered the cobra.

***

On this day, Tony Rendall had finished practicing his *temps de fléche, attitudes sauté en tournant* and *pas de chats* for Basilio, and sat now lazily on a small stool in a rehearsal room in a pair of wasted-blue tights, fluffy legwarmers and a worn-out black cotton top, attempting to keep warm in a shaggy bathrobe, wrapped and belted around him, kept for such occasions in his locker. His aim was to just relax and to look at his partner in Kitri, Jean Sears, the other principal around, going by herself — still, supervised by Mila Bergmann, as always on barricades — in the center area through some pirouettes, waiting to begin rehearsing together several of their *pas de deux* for *Don Quixote*. Jean was thin and compact, a light dream for her *porteurs*, a sensitive dark-haired bravura ballerina up and ready for all challenges, and Tony enjoyed dancing with her in this third year of their being paired up. He was looking forward to passing her several of his observations, which she always wanted from him, even though she was two years older than his twenty-five — "I always need an extra eye and yours are special, Tony, so please, do." It seemed to him her *port de bras* were a bit negligent on that day, and he wouldn't shrink from telling her so. "Arms going in all directions, you know, Jean, keep everything under tight control, fingers, elbows, that's what I think."

Yvonne had watched him from the sides during his series at the center, while she was doing light *barre* close to one wall, for flexibility, in a prelude to her own turn with the toughest sequences in her part. There was no hesitation in his attacks, which fell as calm and as ineluctably timed as drops of water in a cave. Tall and finely-boned rather than muscular, angular chin held high, back a bit arched past the vertical, shoulders drawn back, everything was adding to her eyes to what a critic would have called an overall impression of dignity. *Wow, that's it.* When she also looked at his straight-lined legs, long in their main segments joined by tight knees, at the narrow midsection, she thought she saw a perfect silhouette going through the routine with what really was scary geometrical precision and lots of panache. And, to cap it all, there was the long red hair flowing freely from under a tennis bandanna, lashing the air while hot green eyes were burning it and everything in their light path. *Now, that's intensity for you.*

A silhouette on a distant screen, that again is what he had then seemed to her, still with the will to do more than what the projectionist lost behind in the grand smoke of time, Petipa, or was it Gorsky, and his choreography, dictated. He, Tony, could hold the tempi, make the orchestra wait for and with him, delay a jump, turn a *tour* faster, he could hold himself in the air for a split second longer at his whim, and most of all, his face was always alive and passion-full, it was red-hotly his, not detached, but in it all — and telling you you were there too with him, not lonely, godforsaken on an island — as though a harvest was there to be collected in happiness and the way to do it was by dancing, and all that was simple, simple, nothing to be afraid of, that drop of water going down from too much gravity.

However, it started to develop, to grow into awareness of it, of it in herself. It was not only words, maleness, sexuality, and sentences in the book fluttering and floating at the back of her mind, the story-like or biblical devil throwing dry coals into the fire just to make it burn faster and higher. It was his, Tony's, reality in another space that was tantalizingly tempting to explore and a door so close at hand, perhaps already ajar.

The male in him was so barefaced, that centerpiece bumping within the shorter slips Nureyev and others had lately introduced that you had to be blind not to observe it, the same Nureyev of the frontal nudity fame in Avedon portraits that circulated then and later among those in the know, as well among those in the mixed-bag businesses of bareness or of sex — in the case of the latter, on both sides of a divide that is never neutral. The rumor among girls at the National, trickling down even to the School, was that in Tony's, no less than in Nureyev's, case you'd better be a witness to believe it. Still, Tony being Tony, which is to say a reputedly reserved Englishman hailing from Manchester, few ever got to him in any shape and form outside the dancing itself, rehearsals and shows. There was this other rumor that the tenant, or, more probably, taking into account his nature, the mistress of his love or plain interest at the time was a mature, some said staid, sculptor, built in the lavish size, in her thirties, who was supposed to also use him in more modest, but finally more public in exposure, capacities for modeling purposes. They were said to have been seen together at various parties around Toronto, without too many outward signs of heat between them. But who knows what happens behind the august doors of privacy.

Yvonne took a stool for herself and sat beside him.

"Hello again."

"Oh, hi, Yvonne. How are you? Great dancing two days ago. You really made them eat out of your palm in the plaza scene. Something's telling me you've got more confidence and spunk now, after four months in *DQ*."

"Well, wasn't a bad show for yourself either. I notice they really jump up each time they see you with that *pas de chat* at the beginning. Now that I remember to ask you: sorry, for how long are you in Basilio? I'm not sure if I ever heard you or someone else mentioning it."

"Nothing to be sorry about," he said, "but better to ask me, others

Marius Hancu

might have a shorter memory of my performances, and more so the ballet critics at some newspapers," unpresuming but with the edge of a sarcastic smile. "Two years, that's it, two years, young lady. I'm not reluctant to mention it — that is, not yet reluctant, let's talk again in ten years from now." He laughed, carefully, with the hand to the mouth, as not to disturb the others. Yvonne saw for the first time how high his eyebrows went at their outside ends when laughing, as he were himself surprised at his going for it.

Yvonne looked into his eyes and whispered as though padding on thin shoes not to be heard by others around them, "We never seem to have much time to talk here. Do you, the regulars, sorry, the full-timers, ever talk to each other outside work?" Those eyes were more green than grayish, she discovered only now, and seemed to have opened themselves wider, just a bit, and the hair lashed or fluttered just a short dice throw.

He looked back at her, but found that there had not been any singsong to her speech. At least that. These girls, you never know what they want or where and how far they're taking you. So, he deadpanned.

"Really, it depends, if one is comfortable with the other persons." Careful to use the oh so neutralizing plural. "Dancers aren't exceptions in this, but I guess I'm not giving you any news by saying this."

"Could, er ... would you ... ever have some time to talk? " — she had wanted to say 'together,' but didn't. The question was obviously well rehearsed, perhaps even in front of the mirror, still, she didn't seem to find it any easier, but kept her cool nonetheless in looking at him. Thinking at the same time with having both feet in a bath of ice definitely helps.

It was he who grunted in apparent surprise, inhaled once louder and had his skin reddening to the roots of the hair, as though he were the sixteen-year old, not she, but the man in him found the repartee soon enough not to create an embarrassment.

"Anytime. Over a coffee, perhaps?"

She didn't miss a step, as just opening a roll of music in front of her and falling into song at first sight. Proof of forethought. "Sure. How about Thursday, after the rehearsal?" That would have to be in two days, both of them realized. Time enough for any moves to accommodate or dismiss, defuse the situation — the date, as this is what it would have reasonably seemed to any young red-blooded males and females out there.

He avoided an immediate answer, and this told her that thoughts both pro and con were churning away, and she dithered for a moment, but then he said "Good idea. Why not on Thursday, sure. It's done." Then, he apologized and took a break to have a walk to the men's, where he would be looking shortly at himself in the mirror in both some mild surprise and satisfaction, glad no one else was around to sputter curiosity toward something in view right then on his face that could be read as a dash of buoyancy.

***

Thursday came. Rehearsal — from two to four o'clock. Right during the beginning of the warm-up, he came up unobserved by her and, sotto voce, en passant, while slightly bending sideways, but not really turning, told her in one rapid yet calm volley "Five p.m., in front of the ROM, please." When she turned toward him from her *barre*, where she was alone for the time being, stretching, he had already wafted himself to another corner of the room and wasn't even looking her way, volubly now talking to Jean, his partner. Five minutes later, mental wheels whirring feverishly, she suddenly realized that discretion, the better side of valor, the adult territory she was then first stepping on, was at play and didn't approach him during the whole rehearsal, the point having been made to her that he had somehow thought better about it all, and this was his preference, for one reason or another that she would hopefully learn about in due time, and that she should play accordingly if she didn't want to shoot down the thin glider of hope. That he had been calm and casual during his short address made her calm too and suspended things in an idle state, which for lack of a better term she had to call patience.

When they met at the Royal Ontario Museum, she realized that, most probably, just like her, Tony had taken only the briefest of showers after the rehearsal and had come straight by subway and walking, as both of them were a full quarter of an hour in advance, and they laughed at the rush.

"Sorry about relocating our coffee talk over here," he opened, terse and earnest for a moment, then switching to smiling, which made her instantly relax. "The rumor mill, you know — something better to avoid."

"I think I understand," she said. "Fine with me."

"Where should we go? Ah, I think I know several small places on Bloor. Would that be OK with you?"

"Yes, just not purely-drinking places, please. You know — the age. Coffee spots would be best."

"Yes, the age. Thought about that too, somehow. What are you in fact, sixteen, seventeen?"

"Seventeen in two months."

"I'm twenty-five, senior citizen for you guys, I can imagine."

She laughed. "Thanks for sharing the info, and no, not in the least."

They were walking west on Bloor for just several minutes, when Tony pointed out a place, just across from the Royal Conservatory of Music. "Coffee. Tea. Cakes. All hours," said the advertisement hanging in the window, nicely-calligraphed large red letters on a white rectangular piece of cardboard. Neon sign above, not lit yet, "Crissie's Coffee." Thin, short, semitransparent-white, gauzy curtains, upper edge chest high, screening the tables a bit from the street, low enough to allow a look at the counter and the chest-high, aluminum-framed, glass display cases inside. They crossed the street — surprisingly low traffic for that time of the day. It had to be rush hour already.

"Look, they have a window table. I love that, especially on Bloor, people walking by, cars. I love to look out at them," she unexpectedly raved for one moment, and the teen in her was out in the open this time.

"And they would kindly reciprocate and look back at us," Tony murmured.

"Yes, indeed," she said. No reason for being too much on guard, things could always be invented if someone saw us together this far from the National.

As if he had had the same thought, he continued, "OK, let's get in and check the offering from the closest of ranges. That doesn't mean getting in the kitchen," and he laughed.

Inside by now, he was a bit behind her at the glass display case, only sparsely populated with house offerings, and she turned toward him, raising slightly her head to the side to look at him and ask as in a guessing game "Cherry cheesecake for me. How about yourself?" and the short crown of blond curls was page-like as though with soft turned-in cactus spikes, the smile open and artless that he had to connect to the light-blue eyes aglimmer as though with something unsaid that made him wonder, eyes enlarged in asking in truth about what he wanted. He could see the pinkish skin on the nape of her neck, and wondered at the marble hues in it that disappeared when his gaze went on to her face, now radiating as in what must have been her best hours of the day, fully awakened to her surroundings, pale-pink throughout, with no variation over its expanse in the heat coming from within. Her time to spell life.

At the table, sooner or later he had to ask "How is it that you've decided to talk to me?"

She thought for a short while, sipped from the glass of water, then replied, looking straight at him, no sign of shyness in the temperature of her checks, issuing the words in a sweet rhythmical sequence as they were put to simple, clear, music and she didn't want to be sidetracked out of that simplicity, "I was pleased with the idea. Is this a good enough answer to you?"

"As good as any, probably better. I like 'idea' and its use in the circumstances," he deadpanned, a benign, slightly cheeky, smile on his face.

She thought to herself how just hours before that, she had stood in front of the full-sized bathroom mirror at home, only in bra and panties, asking herself, and lightly, ridiculously, but perceivably, hyperventilating while at it, the same question, so she would be prepared for exactly what he had just now inquired. She hadn't been able then, of a morning, to come up with any fully-defensible or - reasonable answers, certainly she can't give out the store or be girlish and say lilting the words "Because I like you and my eyes follow you around with what I myself think it may be desire and I want to find the truth." She had simply decided to react on the spot — especially, again, Yvonne, especially without pushing things, as you don't even know how to do that with real men — should the time come and should the question be popped up, which it had been. Now the question wasn't anymore balloon-in-a-cartoon-ish, it having materialized with some trepidation for what she liked to think was both sides, just as he was real in front of her and she needed to recover her wits a bit at the impact of it all. And the answer had come out, as he himself had said it, and who could have been a better judge, just right for the circumstances.

10 - Toronto, May 1969

It was May now and the scattered magnolia trees were in bloom throughout Toronto. The university was mostly already in summer recess, at least the students definitely were, except for the odd research assistant passing now and then in front of Hart House or of roundish Convocation Hall that just days before resounded with the joys of graduation, parents reveling in their progeny, progeny enjoying the presence of each other, before what for some could mean life-long separation. Even the remaining studious seemed to be at ease in the light breeze that promised summer.

It was also just one month since Tony and Yvonne's first date and they had been in this place or in similar ones, coffee shops, tea shops, cake shops, ethnic eateries, all along Bloor or Spadina, or in the dining hall of Hart House at the university. Always going to places somewhat removed from the "headquarters," as he liked to call the location of the National.

This particular English-fare place had large ceiling fans rotating very high at ease as large birds preparing for take-off to distant lands, only these never took off. The late spring light of an afternoon was bursting in via large clean windows in recent wooden frames, and wiped out in one sweep the old age of the place, which one could tell from the heavy tables with mastodontic legs, barely hidden by the corners of the heavily starched thick table cloths, or from the massive counter which looked as though dislodged in one piece off a baobab tree.

Tony looked across the table and there she was, faintly smiling at him that smile which seemed benign yet contained a challenge. "In fairness to us both, can you deal with me?" seemed to him to be the message.

Momentarily skipping the potential challenge he said, "Yesterday I looked closer at your feet — I mean your feet action," he corrected himself with a smile she could take for an apology if she wanted. "You prefer springing into your pointes, right?"

"Yes," she said, "it's like this works better for me than the gradual thing, the rolling up thing. It gives me more pop into it, also perhaps less strain on the ball of the foot. Or it's me just being more familiar with it. Other school, isn't it?"

"Guess not, depends more on the occasion and the comfort you want to achieve for yourself, also on your training and physical shape. All methods, Cecchetti, the French, the Russian, Vaganova that is, have several ways to go around doing them.

"Also, when you enter your pirouettes, have you ever thought of using a bit of a *fondu* for more oomph into them? I mean, have the rear foot straighter and more toward the back before the attack?"

"Well, that's Balanchine, I guess. I'm not sure I want to do that in the classical things. Seems to me too athletic-looking, taking too wide of a base, like I'm a plane and I'm ready to take off to some other place." She laughed. "In Balanchine's modern bits, that might not be a problem, I mean, they're athletic already, some of them, but in the classical pieces, I'd rather not do that, they demand more of a daintiness in appearance. Probably prejudice, but I wouldn't do it. Not, say, in *Le Corsaire* or in *Swan Lake*, no. Others would, I'm sure."

The wooden-box loudspeaker in the upper corner at the entrance of the place, right above the cashier's register, filtered out of its inner profundities the end of *Proud Mary*, then switched to Neil Diamond's *Sweet Caroline*, without losing time even for a passing consideration to congruity.

He smiled. "I know what you mean; different, what they call them, aesthetics. If that's not too fancy a word to you."

"No, it's not, don't be too concerned about that, I take whatever's thrown at me, but words don't mean much once I'm catching, to some extent, your drift — dancing's the thing. Bet the same's true for you. Say you're a choreographer or director, I don't care what words you're using to describe what I have to be doing. Still, I much more like to be shown. Don't you?"

He said, "I rather do, yes. I think John, he's quite good at that, isn't he? Do you know he's worked with Balanchine and Serge Lifar?"

"Heard that. Good for him — and for us."

"But did you know Serge Lifar's Russian, I mean Ukrainian?"

"That I didn't. I heard about him and Yvette Chauviré dancing together, so, with the name, I thought French," she said with apparent surprise.

"No, Ukrainian. First dancer in *Prodigal Son*. At l'Opéra, Paris, I mean, he gave us more power."

"Us? Who, us?" she inquired.

The Beatles' *Hey Jude* was rolling out.

"Why it, of all songs?" Tony wondered. "Any signs to it? Should I take care of anything?" Then, loud, "Us, the men, of course. More leading roles for us."

"Oh, you, the men, you never have enough power," she said, pouting, but her eyes were not angry.

"But it's true. Ballet's always been like that, since La Taglioni, you ladies first, largest and choicest pieces of the cake, so you can't quite complain, can you? I mean, look around in your school, how many boys are there? I'd wager not many." He raised his hands, palms opened, fingers stretched, to the sides, and laughed. "And he gave power not only to men. Lifar, I mean. He said that ballet can live without music, or independently of it, or thereabouts. Wanted music made to his choreography, not the other way round."

"More power to him, I'd say. That's the way." She applauded lightly, jumping a bit in the chair, so some people at the neighboring tables turned around or peeked to the sides to see the source of the hubbub.

"Relax, please," Tony told to a pair, smiling, "right now, she's just enthusiastic about some things ballet," the last word of which made them look away and concentrate on their food. Definitely not their cup of tea.

"Look what you've done, cut their appetite." She laughed under her breath to him.

"Still, back to our muttons and Lifar," he continued, "I heard from other immigrants there whom he had talked to he wasn't happy in France. Perhaps once an immigrant, always an immigrant, some warmth remains forever in the cockles of the heart for the old country."

"Aren't you yourself an immigrant?"

"I guess you're right. I should be counting myself as first generation. I'm not sure where I'd be otherwise. Canada's been good to me. Good country, many are saying, especially now, running away from the 'Nam war to come from the States here, or from all those Eastern-European countries to escape the Russian yoke," he said with some heat at the end.

"Russian yoke? Uh-huh, you must really have a serious bone to pick with them."

"Oh, yes. Hate them. I've learned more about them after Stalin's death, as Khrushchev started crowing a bit, for a change, about the truth, labor camps, gulags. Read *One Day in the Life of Ivan Denisovich*, I think that's the title, by Solzhenitsyn, if you ever want to learn about that, and what with many Soviet spies being caught — or not quite caught, and running with the goods to Moscow — in Britain or in the US, Kim Philby, the Rosenbergs, Profumo affair, even Lee Oswald he was in Moscow too at a time, and so on and so forth, you maybe don't know about it all. They truly are evil, the Soviets."

"No, I don't know about those in Britain, but I think I remember my father mentioning the Gouzenko, I think this was the name, affair, here in Canada. My father was upset that King, our PM at the time, never really wanted to help then, in order not to bother the Russians."

"Also, the other way round, and surely the thing for what we both are doing, we've had, of course, Nureyev, now for, what, seven, eight years, I think, with Margot and the Royal Ballet, after getting away from under the clutches of KGB thugs in France, at the airport. Literally walking to the French police minutes before taking off to Moscow."

"Sorry, I'll have to call home to tell them, I mean, Mother, that I'll be a bit late today. She likes to know that. No curfew time, don't worry." And she went to a chromed wall phone close to the entrance, past a wood-and-glass partition. Heads turned after streamlined roundly muscular ankles, ramrod back, ballerina's step *en évidence* and short curly halo. He felt pride by association. Was it a pang of jealousy there too? He didn't want to delve into it all. Just sipping his water.

Using Yvonne's absence, a blushing gangly teenager of perhaps the same age as her, sneaked in close by in clomping Dutch-like wooden clogs from another table, asking Tony, "Mr. Rendall, I presume?" as though they were in some Livingstone-Stanley reenactment, and upon having that confirmed, mumbled for and kindly got an autograph, in the possession of which she returned triumphant at her own table, where the others in the group started to whisper for several minutes, looking with curiosity toward him.

When Yvonne returned, blue-glazed eyes suddenly brighter under tacitly questioning eyebrows — as in what was happening here? — on seeing him again — and he saw that — back from the short walk and temporary change in view, she continued, "I've seen him, Nureyev I mean, only on TV, in that series with Erik Bruhn and others, guess Maria Tallchief, Sonya Arova and so on. Looked great in the *Flower Festival in Genzano*, didn't he?" The delicately transparent face, peach-like in consistency and hue, now truly radiated that event of past pleasure and he enjoyed looking at the way its reflexions had come up flooding ungated to the surface, as from a submarine stream, initially more powerful than the whole of water around it for a time, then submitting to its fluid massivity after a short duel.

And there you are, *Mrs. Robinson* now in the air. Let the elderly and DiMaggio be concerned about it for now, he thought.

"In that series, I think I liked him more in *Le Corsaire,* yet , should you mean freshness, you may well be right about the *Flower Festival*, young lady," he smiled at her, feeling inside a mature Gavroche. "Back home in England, saw him and Margot, in both *Giselle* and *Swan Lake*. Big time success, which is a 'bomb' in Britain, don't be surprised, over twenty curtains with the royals in the house, the works. Think rock stars. Though I heard he's very hard on her, dropping her sometimes from lifts on the floor like a sack of flour right at the exit from the stage when angry at her, sending her to, sorry, her motherly origin as well, in Russian, no questions asked, if you know what I mean."

"That can't be true, come on," countered Yvonne, rolling her head slowly from left to right in disbelief, in a very long "come."

"As true as you're seeing me now. From other fellows at the Royal Ballet, people who give it to you straight, no extra muck or grapevine. You know, I was with them, before getting the offer here in Toronto. We are all, I mean, people, the same flesh and blood, aren't we? So, why be surprised?"

"But he's such a great artist, isn't he?"

"Probably, at least I think he is. Many times these things don't fit together as nice as in a jigsaw puzzle, I mean on one side your behavior, your style, in the end your life, and what, on the other side, what you blast out, what you fashion or put out in your art. Those wobblies of his — oh, sorry for my Briticism, I think the pondial version is conniption fits — might be just the thing he needs to clean out some of the juice, sorry, energy channels in himself and to start afresh. New batteries so to say and so on."

"It takes all sorts to make a world, doesn't it?" she asked. "Now, I've got a big question for you: do you think the mind, or the body, or the heart, is the thing in dancing? For me, it's mostly and mainly as it were mind over body, yet I feel I'm truly dancing only when I forget about thinking and let my muscles, the physical me, go into my steps as though on automatic pilot. Thinking constricts me. I need to do it in order to learn the piece, to, as we call it these days, visualize it, to understand it, but gradually I'm trying to unload it, to free myself of it. If my head is heavy with thoughts, even all related to the piece, all my body feels heavy too, as though pressing down upon my shoulders. It's ridiculous" — It's not, Tony signaled by nodding his head sideways — "but true. And I'm dancing well only if my heart, call it passion, is into it. Also, body-wise, I think I need to reach a certain temperature to do things really well. I need a rush going on through me."

"To each his own, but I don't think I'm too far from all that either."

"Glad to hear that I'm not that strange; not glad to see I'm not original," she said and laughed.

" Let's not forget," Tony continued, "one gets to that automatic firing point and pilot after fumbling through tens of going-overs only. Those patterns have already visited deep into your mind and have left their traces there, clean or ragged as they might be, especially in what they call, if I remember rightly, central motor control and coordination, some of the doctors and psychologists I've talked to told me. Let's not forget the sweat paid in the wrong moves."

"Listen to this," she said, taking his hand in both of hers. "Shh," she then, half-serious half-keep-laughing motion with a finger at her lips, demanded to those around them. Otis Redding had already started his *Sitting in the morning sun.*

"Let's buy this record. Could we?" she asked and he duly observed the plural.

"To do what exactly with it?"

"Oh, I'd like to dance on it with you, could we, Tony? I mean like regular dancing, not ballet." She lisped her words a little, tempting, and turning her shoulders a bit, back and forth, in a suggestion of slow dancing.

"Where to dance?"

She thought for a moment, perhaps more about the manner in which to put it to him than about the very contents, then said looking straight at him, and there was no drama in her lineaments or eyes, "Your place, for example. You do have a record player, don't you? Would you mind?"

"You realize that you're underage and I'm twenty five? I don't want to be seen as corrupting young ingenues."

"Who's to know that we went to your place — I mean, to dance? Do we have to report to anyone? Police, parents?" She looked ironically at him.

He felt that the man in him had to rise to the challenge, at least in part, he couldn't just back away and still look strong, even to himself. *Man, these new girls, they are really something. I mean, squealing like hell to the Beatles or to Elvis, now this.*

"You do realize what would happen if this thing transpires at the National with the brass: I'd be cooked. I mean, you're still underage. Dancing with an unchaperoned underage girl in a compromising setting. You swear you won't tell to anyone, including your girl pals?"

There was no hesitation in the way she threw the dice.

"If this makes you more comfortable, I swear. Here you have it. Good enough?"

He drank slowly some water and took time as though to think again about it all. And while he felt his face and his eyes were under her eyes all the way through, they never went away as in looking into her dish or out the window.

"OK, I'll buy it myself, a single should do, don't have to buy the whole album, and tell you two days in advance?"

"Why not buy the whole album? Are you afraid to dance with me? Oh-oh, my, my." She laughed at him. "Why not go together right after this to the Sam the Record Man store on Yonge, it's just five streets from here, and get it? So, we could set up even today the day for the dancing, you know, wouldn't have to like hide in bushes, I mean this, of course, figuratively, not anything in the props, he, he, at the National, to talk over it. Voilà." She put the goods on the table as though with a magic wand while approving of her own good idea with a nod and a bit of a jeer, all said benignly, visibly and carefully not to appear or be mean.

Tony lowered his voice, made sure that no one around watched them too closely.

"Well, you know it's impossible to talk such stuff there, do you? Any allusion, any sniff that they get, and I'll get in trouble and you might too. There's too much at risk, careers even. I know how a bad construction can be put to any small boo-boo and how this can snowball. I guarantee you there are always some people willing to get promotion, over me or even over you, by talking to the powers-to-be, or just by slipping in the mail the odd anonymous letter. As effective as a grenade and fast, no complications for the talented letter-writer. You're probably too young to know how prissily people can act sometime. We need to keep appearances and distance."

"Fine, fine, if you take it this way, I'll trust your *savoir-faire*, whatever that might be, sir." She openly laughed at him.

11 - May 1969

I had on the kaleidoscopic-flowered-but-mostly-blue-with-sunflower-patterns silk dress I had bought just three weeks before in a shop near Eaton's on Yonge, caught in a thin red leather belt, fully-skirted it was, but thin-thin, I didn't really feel it on me. "Wow, what and whom are we having in here!" twinkled Jon Posada, seeing me climbing down the stairs at the National after the rehearsal, all-in-a-rap going down and taking and jumping steps two at a time as I was in rush, which I really was, as I had only half an hour max to get to Eglinton, to meet Tony there, if I didn't want to be late, which I hated.

Out after a heavy rain that had fallen between ten and noonish, the sun made me feel great about myself and the world, at least the world around me, which I guess is all what the great majority of us want, fully pepped up as I had just listened to the *The Age of Aquarius* and *Let the Sunshine In* on the radio. They were right at the top in the rankings on that Canadian station and most everywhere else in North America, we were being told.

The previous night we had a gala showing with *Don Quixote* at the National that reminded me that not even a year before I'd had another, naturally, much smaller, gala with the School, and how well everything turned out for me, getting to dance it now with the big boys and girls and being able to bring home to Mom and Dad flowers from the public, whether given to me directly or shared with the company after the show. It was nice to have my parents in boxes for some of the shows and for them to see the curtain calls I was getting, the 'wows' and 'bravos,' especially those from the gallery, which everybody knows are the toughest to get, the most precious and most sincere, whether you're at Bayreuth or at *La Scala* or any small place in the world. I knew this was especially true for my mom, as she had had some, although not many, hopes about dancing herself back in Winnipeg when she was young, hopes that hadn't amounted to much, as the ballet there took off too late for her parents to be aware of the art and so on. Not to speak of the fact that I think, but I've never told her — what would've been the point? — that my ballet genes and especially my long legs obviously came from my father, the taller side of the family — truly a Daddy-Long-Legs! — and also perhaps the more dreaming-like. But the nerve and edge, perhaps what we call the *attack*, then, I prolly have it from her. And it's a mean one, if I listen to John, our director for *Don Quixote*, when he's on a good day. So there you have it, my short genealogy like.

Also, appearance fees were not something to sneer at, and allowed me to think about going during the upcoming summer to Europe, or somewhere else, if I so wished.

Tony had borrowed a car for that afternoon from one of his friends and was supposed to wait for me right at the exit from the Eglinton subway station, which he timely and honorably did. He drove a small red Fiat 600, I think. Much better, he said, to go this way to him, less people would be able to get an eyeful of us or, worse, peg us in the subway or on the street going to his place. Not that I'd have minded it, but he did, so I said, fine, your call and pet project.

Now, in the car, I realized he liked to rock out; the loudspeakers would, in fact, be blasting with The Beatles' *Lady Madonna* the whole way to him.

"What do you make of it?" I asked.

"Of what? Don't quite get it."

I tapped on the car radio. "This, the lyrics. Do you make anything out of them?"

"Ah, that, *The Beatles*, the words? Who knows, some say a prostitute changing tricks, sorry, customers, every day; some say a Mother Teresa taking care of street children; others still, a mother with many real kids of her own; all, and that's the point, barely making ends meet. Not an open-and-shut case, as you might imagine."

"Wow. You, sir, should've been a grammarian or whatever ah ah a librettist or a lyrics writer. You might even be able to kindly illuminate me on 'Surry down' in 'Aquarius,' I mean 'The Age of Aquarius,' if you don't mind."

"Oh, it's *Fifth Dimension* now? That's easy. 'Surrey down,' plainly speaking, has, no wonder, an 'e' in there, in other words, take a horse-drawn pleasure carriage or whatever romantic vehicular implement, to speak NASA jargon, to whatever interstellar station you might want to consider for your next life — *or whatever*. Get it?" he turned laughing at me, releasing busy eyes after carefully turning right at an intersection.

"Whatever. Roger you," and both of us shook with a short peal of laughter.

The small car was coughing and choo-choo-ing along and I thought about Louis Jordan's *Choo choo ch'boogie*. I recalled how much my mother liked the song, as it reminded her of her youth in the forties. She even had an old black vinyl record with it, which in time had acquired a mean set of scratches from being called too much into action, which made its playing unbearable to me.

It was four in the afternoon, the streets around Eglinton suspended in an inexplicable and I could bet temporary and random privation of traffic, so Tony quickly found his place. It was in a four-story apartment building, stolid apparent red brick for the façade but confidence inspiring, visible now even through the small windshield of the Fiat while driving up to the visitors' parking in front of it, as he didn't have the proper sticker for the residents' place, not having his own car.

"Facing the street?" I asked.

"No, there's a small park at the back. No matter, the light is better, in fact, for that side, most of the day. Still, I haven't been on my balcony in ages; it's good not to have my own flowers, I'd totally neglect them. I'm a bad flower keeper."

"A park? Then, nature in bloom for you at this time, isn't it?"

"You don't know how right you are. One of the magnolias, and, funny, a quite ragged one, still has some flowers on. Thick petals, that one."

"Mind taking me to it right now? I kind of miss each year the right time and this spring I haven't been close to one of them."

So we excitedly — at least I felt excited — sashayed our way through a small darkish, round-vaulted in its ceiling, tunnel, built in the center of the ground-level of the building leading to the park behind, several apple trees and this magnolia in a corner of the pebble-covered patch which proffered itself in its middle. The magnolia seemed quite old and its bark had crags and crevices no end in it, still the flowers were finger-like large, fleshy, white throughout and pinkish on the petal edges and didn't show in any way the effects of old age, as though they had been suspended in the air, with no connection whatsoever to the tried and tired tree which just happened to be close to them. I slowly, carefully, put my hands on some of the flowers and felt the solid consistency of the petals to my fingers. We, mostly myself that is, walked around the tree for several minutes, peering at it, with no words between us. In the end I said, "Farewell for a year now." I took one flower with me — the thought to have it in one of Tony's glasses while we danced. Right around us, Father Time had already dropped ravished sisters of the ones I had touched, and the fallen ones had captured the sun and didn't gain any power, but only the brown hue and touch of passing away and putrefaction.

Tony didn't say a word during the whole trip in the small park, as though he wanted to let me be, also to have a closer look at the real me to see what happened when he did that. And I thought it OK for him to do that. "Are you the deep, silent, type and I didn't know?" I asked him showing some teeth, as happy and careless as a lark, while climbing up the narrow staircase toward his fourth-floor flat. "Perhaps, it happens from time to time. Hope you don't mind," he said, slightly lost or absent voice, both in volume and stress put to some of the words, and I realized he was thinking, but I didn't want to press the issue by asking what or whom it was all about. It seemed to me men wanted more time before starting to speak out on something or another than us women needed, even when they were older than you. Or were they more secretive? The elevator passed up and down twice while we were still making our way up, people seemed to prefer faster ways of delivering themselves to their honeycomb cells at the end of the workday; on the contrary, we seemed to be taking our time.

The apartment building wasn't that new, still in good shape though. "I like the tall windows you have in here," I told Tony, who at this time was frantically trying to find the keys somewhere in the many pockets of his sports shoulder bag. He rejoined, "Yes, tall everything, you mean, especially the ceilings. Definitely better than in some of the latest buildings, the cubicalized ones, isn't it?" At last, he found the keys and went in first, switched on the light in the small square entrance hall, a walled-in closet visible already in it from the outside, then held the tall door for me to get in.

After closing the entrance door, he went toward the living-room balcony, opened wide the door leading to it, drew the curtain aside and snapped it to the wall with a small retaining band, to let the fresh air come in.

Large living-room, white on white — furniture, walls — color seeping in from covers of armchairs and sofa and from several tall paintings, some of them in harsh hues and thick, aggressive lines and washes, partly abstract. Nothing too metallicky, mostly dark-reddish-wood, furniture-wise.

First things first: I asked Tony for a small deep plate with water in it and placed the magnolia flower in it.

"Are these French or Canadian?" I asked, pointing to some of the paintings.

"Mexican, in fact. 1940s. Friends, thereabouts, of Frieda Kahlo and Rivera. They themselves are too expensive already, unfortunately."

Modern simple candelabrum — a circular thing, white again, in wood, flush with the ceiling, long fluorescent tubes hanging down from it, several sizes, stalagtite-like.

"Like to drink something?"

"Such as?"

"Red wine, white wine, vodka, whiskey, orange juice, mineral water, your pick and choose, but limited to the above, I'm sorry."

"Orange juice for the time being. Don't you forget I'm a minor". Slight smile on my part. Same in reply from him.

"Oh, I think we know *that*. But don't you ever drink wine with your parents? Easter-time-wise, turkey-time-wise? Your father, if I remember well from what you've been telling me, is French, and I haven't heard of many French people not enjoying their siestas and their red wine."

"What can I say? Definitely not wrong on the French, but I rarely drink. Perhaps while we dance, if I'm getting thirsty."

"OK, we'll sip of bit of it then. Orange juice for now?"

"Fine, thanks. Large glass, please, I feel a bit dehydrated after the rehearsal today."

He went to the fridge and brought to the table a two-liter tropically-colored plastified-paper container with orange juice, opened it skewedly at one corner at the top, then fetched two large tumblers from the kitchen and filled them up. "Here you are. Prosit."

"Your health and cheers." Clinked glasses. I looked at him. He looked at me. He looked relaxed and sharp, red hair in a bit of disorderly conduct. "Invitation still standing?" I asked.

"To dancing? Having any doubts? We're on, what would you think?" And I was able to see his face opening in a smile, in a touch of keenness — wasn't just neutral or indifferent, which I would have hated to see.

"Then you have it? I mean, the recording?"

"I most certainly do, young lady." He closed the door to the balcony, released the curtain from the grip of its belt and closed it over the door window. My wristwatch told me we were getting close to five now.

"Turntable ready. Record on, in position. Apollo 11 ready for takeoff to the Moon. We only take two astronauts today," he joked. "Now, if you don't mind, I'm going to go put on another shirt, this one could be fresher right now, after a whole day."

"May I use your bathroom?"

"Be my guest, I'll go in the bedroom and change my shirt there. I'll let your 'Aquarius' in continuous mode for now," and within two shakes the apartment was full of the five psychedelic voices, twisting and resonating around each other sidereally. "That's where the bathroom is. Yes, don't ask: I've got fresh towels." He laughed. "By the way, kindly — no television today, 'hope we have a deal on this — it spoils everything," he said, went to the entrance door, locked it, leaving the key in the security lock, muttering in explication, looking straight at me "You know, I don't want anyone crashing our little party!" and disappeared in what I supposed to be his bedroom.

I went to the bathroom, a tall clean mirror to the side showing me to same appealing enough not to get too concerned; showed teeth at myself: A-OK, having brushed them already at the National after my lunch; unzipped, unbuttoned and put aside, carefully carefully, my flowery silk dress; then in a rush slipped off the white bra and the panties, remaining in the buff in mid-heel shoes. I freshened up with cold water all the sensitive parts, brushing them to temporary redness with Tony's clean towels, a bit on the fluffy side for my taste, snapped my mini perfume spray out of the squarish handbag I had with me, sprayed and dabbed with my finger around my ears, neck and underarms, as well as the breast. Very light scent, very thin, transparent-like, I never liked the gussied up things, this must come from my mom. Back into my things — all of five minutes.

Tony was already back in the living room, humming a song and making a bit of order, or making himself look busy, serious and preoccupied, or none of the above, on the table where he had placed a tray with sandwiches and one with drinks, labels of red Californian wine and Scotch whisky. He had on a dark blue, patterned shirt, psychedelic flames of bright yellow, orange, red reaching up and licking each other, long sleeved, cuffs rolled up just under his elbows, medium-wide lapels, dropping a bit to the front, curved corners. The shirt harmonizing well with his red hair, long now, à la Jim Morrison — perhaps — cut, or not cut, but definitely trimmed a bit; fussy about appearance, he sure was that. The thinness of the middle section tightly caught by a pair of flared white cotton pants, breezy-light in texture.

He raised eyes, smiled smart from under the red halo of his and came slowly closer around the table to face me, away at several steps, face skin a bit red. "You look great. Would you care to dance, milady?" he said with the small flourished arc of a cheeky imitation reverence.

"Thank you. Likewise. And — but of course, gentle sir."

"Then let's have *Sitting on the Dock of the Bay* up 'n runnin' in

Marius Hancu

no-oh ti-ime on that turnta-able the-ere,"he said, drawling vowels in the Southern or Black manner.

"Can you make it run in that 'continuous' thingy you mentioned, to listen to it several times?'

"Consider it done." Otis Redding was in the air and the most important part of it was having Tony come up to me, his raised left arm inviting and taking my right, his right feather-like around me, my left pressing gently around his upper arm and shoulder in a Tango grip, both starting to move around in a slow mo that wasn't really a Tango. We stepped and weaved, found our way amidst and around pieces of furniture on the clacky parquet, he lead me with very light finger touches, and the piano I was by then responded easily and pushed back alive. At times, I felt swooning with joy and sweet-yearning, as though my heart not I myself were being carried around the room by him in his arms and I were having difficulty of staying in touch.

The song had carried, with no mechanical devices behind its airy existence, had traversed and had taken us through spaces of music and feel, having gone around itself two times or so by now, and then at this sweet moment in our whirling around and pausing for turns in direction, he gently signaled he wanted a change of style and grip and closeness with a light twisting and detaching away of his left-hand fingers from my fingers, moved both his palms to my hips and I complied and moved in myself closer and placed my palms and fingers around his neck, locking him, the side of my head against his neck, my hair, firm as it is, feeling as touching his face and brushing against his own hair from underneath. It was the first time I had a true man in my arms this close and he had me likewise — those before having really been just boys; sorry, guys.

The sun was setting. The weak light of the late afternoon getting past the curtains felt lost by degrees. I closed my eyes, and I let me feel this man in my arms without pushing more than just an idea on his body, faithful extra-corporeal antennae fiddling to snuggle in position, as though by straining myself to become more feeling than by any obdurate and obvious pressure of and by my body to sense him, as on a day of summer and unbearable heat when you simply open the windows to let the fresh air in and flop in an armchair to

Our Lives as Kites

catch and feel the breeze, fully knowing it'd be mindless to make anything forceful.

We let the music take us along, closer together than we were just minutes ago. He walked-touched-passed several times the tops of my hips with his fingers when taking a slow turn and I knew it was intentional, yet I enjoyed it and reared up a tiny bit on the balls of my shoes, tensing back my spine in response.

Images stored in the eyes of my mind told me his neck was on the side of thick for his being thin overall, and the distances and the sensation of my fingers confirmed it, its fibers telling themselves hard under his skin. I felt my left breast eager to crush itself more against something that could be only his sternum, where already it was.

I felt so carried away, and, with the thought to witness to it somehow, without speaking, I snuggled my face into the side of his neck. Then, I felt it — it had to be him kissing my hair only a bit from above — he was only one, at most two, inches taller. I turned my face even more in against his neck and just in gliding over kissed his neck which felt very hot under lips even for what had to have been just a tiny fraction of a second. Two or three seconds passed. No-oh. I raised my head and, still with closed eyes, asked cattily "Do I need to file a special request to be kissed, Tony?"

He murmured with the music, continuing to lead me and gently take me into turns, "Wa-asting ti-ime — 'You sure, Yvonne dear?"

I opened my eyes, turned them up and tuned them into his, and answered as easily, yet as earnestly as I could make it, "I really am."

He slowly raised his right hand, its fingers touching now against the back of my bra, I felt the only ring he had, gold-squarish I recalled it later to be, in re-projecting this to myself, moved his left hand behind my head to better support it, gently inserting and pushing his fingers as a huge live comb through the short hair I had at the time and always had, and in holding me this way, bent down his head and kissed me on the lips, slowly moving his slightly open lips around, pressing and releasing the pressure on my back and moving his hands around with some uncorked unpatience and hunger. He had great lips, a bit thick or fleshy, call your word, and nicely bow-contoured, and I hook-locked lips and teeth on them and gently bit them back and forth and pulled at them as at an open, raw, plumpy fruit, then dipped and plunged myself again in other, deeper kisses. His mouth felt wine-ish, felt sweet and sour, felt wet like a bitten peach or watermelon. A wall of heat was around us and it came to me first though his touches, then though the air, and in between the kisses I kept hearing both of us like moaning low and deeply breathing in, nose and mouth, in odd gulps.

12 - Tony's story, May 1969

While kissing, next thing I know, hurried fingers are about to unbutton my shirt starting at the neck, they get inside it while the work is only half-done and start caressing my nipples and pecs, thin as they are, and sneak to my back to feel it, whereby my skin prickles and tenses under their touch, story of being hot in other ways, a dermatologist told me the level of my superficial innervation, that's how he said it, seems higher than in many others, that is closer to the surface, so the skin, the carrier of that innervation, can't but respond, which it is doing gloriously — drop that: like a doozy — now, while the same fingers take my right hand and place it awkwardly on her left breast, not to feel discriminated against, I'd like to reciprocate, if you know what I mean, but I need to ask permission in this day and age, could I take your shirt off too, don't ask, she says, just go ahead, but do you feel like it, and she asks me, don't you see it, and she bounces up lightly in excitement on her toes and laughs like small cascades of water out-flowing from an inundated apartment, and I say, even if I see it, I need to be told, what with you being a minor and I not being one and so forth, proceeding here with no agreement is a serious matter, so she says, if you say so, perhaps, but you have my quote unquote invitation if you make all this sound this way, and I say, that is, you want it? that's right, she says — I want it, come on, it's cold here, hold me in your arms, cold, I wonder, this is only May, well it may be May but it's the end of the day, all right, here you are, so I hold her, and I touch-caress just under her ribs and on her round-throughout hip and I unzip the side of her botanically-flowered dress to be able to slip the dress up and down on her body depending on inspiration, so now the guess is up and I feel her thigh with the fingers of my right hand, matter of grasping the hem of the dress and not only, the muscles are tensing under my touch, she's very round, silky as the moon there, but firm as well as only ballerinas are, in my experience, but my experience is not something one could boast about, and the while my left hand bungles several attempts to unbutton the top of it under her neck, let me do it myself, and she takes my hand away and gets done with those small finicky buttons indeed made for hands of a woman, not those of a blundering man who doesn't want, in politeness, to tear apart the dress, but perhaps they want them, the dresses, torn apart, except for the financial remorse, the women, perhaps they want it to be taken violently as in those forties movies, ravished is the word, so now she's only in her bra and slip and I in my pants, and the sun is out, and this is confirmed inside here as an irrefutable fact of life, as much as it trickles through the medium-thick curtain, when it goes inside the room and it stores itself in corners from which reincarnates himself again as our personal god of light on the next sunny day, but not on dark ones, in the same room, helped by his twin brother, always more powerful, living outdoors, and reconstitutes for me the same environment of screens on whitewashed walls on which I can project my simple life as in magic-lantern shows, sunny day by sunny day, and on the dark days what is reincarnated is a gloom in which everything must come from inside, the power to wake up, to move around, to start going out to one's work, as from a battery which one needs well to recharge on lucky days in order to do anything with on the less fortunate days, and so the sun has set, and when we take each other in arms, as we do now, there's also between us, between skin and skin, a sandwich of layers of darkness, so before I'm getting to her physical self I need, in a gradient, to penetrate-go layer of layer of darkness, and I know that where there is no darkness anymore and I feel the heat, it is where she dwells, in her castle of skin and muscles, ready to caress me, and we envelop each other in arms that tremble, but mostly with desire, that desire which is lone in one's experiences, when you meet someone in the real flesh for the first time, which is so poignant and can't be recovered by later rendezvous, perhaps improved in intensity, confidence, trust, but never in the feeling of new vistas, new terras incognitas suddenly opening, the good thing about this

Our Lives as Kites

darkness being that it shuts out everything, it makes us, of necessity, reach for the other more in tactile feel, with no turning away, the tactile having now the security in which to grow and propel toward our minds its reports, as a watering pipe sneaking and distending itself slowly and revealing its water to dry mouths, as anatomy discovered pierces the mental centers much more readily now than in the presence of light, when everything is embroidered around us in other presences, presences of objects which we don't feel at this time, except in their silences, as our feet feel each other as there's no show to forbid contact, and they tread lightly on each other, at play, don't do that, stay away from my feet, do you listen, you, ugly dragon, ah, so, I'll give it back to you, you, ugly dragoness, but suddenly this feetly commotion stops as I have my toes over both of her feet and I clamp them down and immobilize her in tight cooperation with the ground in carpetty disguise, and she does this statue-rootedness for one moment, and I sneak my hands behind her back, get under her bra with my fingers, all the way fumbling through the dark, and this was easy, unclasp the bra and throw it away from her in obscurity so she can't reclaim it, and she glues herself to me, her breasts come a-calling, and it comes down now to rawness, skin and nerves, no nothing in between for masking, I'm feeling them, they are so globular and up-ending that I instantly know this is one of the things I'm going to sharply, intensely and definitely like about her, and I let my fingers and hands play and bring them to heat, moving in serpentine rolls around their tips, and both of them so sweet-quivering and firm to the touch at the same time, as I lower myself and bring them one at a time into my mouth and caress and suck them in small and large gulps of fresh young flesh from which I help myself jump-sucking from the left to the right, your flesh your flesh, and licking the firmness at the top and no less the side, softness and roundness emerging as wonders on the bone of the breast, and moving to kisses on the neck and bottom lobe of the ears, biting at them perniciously while she moans and presses as well as she can to stay close in with my skin and my lips, but, hey, there's news, hands gripping now my pant belt, fighting with it until finding the clasp and overruling it, to unfasten the belt and tug at the pants, until I decide to help in the process and unbutton and fight out of them and kick them to the side, and while doing this we get unglued from each other, and confused in the dark, until, hesitating, we find each other again with hands and she presses hips against me, hands on my buttocks, as she wants me really close to her, and plays with my slip as though, she wants it off, and I say, OK, both at the same time, no otherwise, OK, she says, and both of us crouch and get down the slips to the ground in one single motion, and we laugh, and she comes in close, finds me in the dark, and tells me in my ear, I want, you know, I want for you to show it to me, what do you mean, I'm saying, you know what, she says, your ah ah, and I go to her ear and ask her, my member? and change voice to a deep bass, my huge memba'? and she laughs at it and nods twice and I feel her face nodding on mine that has gotten raspier from not shaving since this morning, so, I say, you want more light, we'll give you more light, but only in a corner, so we wouldn't mess the charm of all this, so I take her, my hand on her back just above her buttocks, slowly caressing each of them in turn at the beginning of their curving down, I take her where I know there must be a corner table, and with care, so I don't draw the curtain beside open by any chance so we would be seen from outside at that hour which is early evening, I switch on the light, and I pull her back so as not to have quite all the stage lights on the most living part of me, which shows gloriously, at least in what precedents as I know them are concerned, erect past the horizontal, bulbous at the top, and curved a bit to a side, such as its wont is, and she says, first time, you mean, first time you see it, she says, first time everything, she touches it, but in no way such a thing would be caught by any experienced girl, but as she would take something extraterrestrial fallen upon as a meteorite for examination between her fingers, checking its resilience to compression, so she presses on the middle part of it, then flexes her knees and touches it with her breasts, this time much better as she closes her eyes and touchbrushes on it, and I barely keep everything under control, like being on the edge of the huge crevasse with nothing to support you but your mind, and she stands erect now and comes back again to my ear and asks, do you have any ah prot--ection? and I'm saying, no, didn't expect us to get to this, I mean not quite, OK, she says, I have some, but have heard you men are fussy, so I bought several, wait, and lo and behold gets to her handbag and brings over five, I mean five packs, all differently ribbed and flavored, you know, the whole market choice, and I start laughing, and laugh, and she switches off the light, comes over and asks me, why are you laughing I feel embarrassed as though I did something ridiculous, and I take her round the shoulder and we sit naked on the sofa, and tell her to her ear, you know, I, first of all wasn't so sure at all you might want it to, I mean, go all the way, then, I totally neglected in my stupidity to take care of the, what do you call that, logistics of the situation, no, she says, I've always thought you looked great, especially in close ballet slips, so the way things showed up, I was curious and thought starting this way with you might be a great idea, so I organized myself, aha, I say, so I'm asking, are you still of the same mind about it all, and she says, if you want me, I want you, if you don't want me, I don't want you either, so let's ask each other, so I take her hand and put it where it has been earlier, and tell her, take care of little Will, then I position myself, push open her thighs and get down there and she obviously is already prepared, but I go in and do my best for several minutes while she does the same on me while I guide her hand from time to time, and we already are there, so I guess we know, don't we, I tell her, we're up to it, so lemme have it, the things that you brought, and I look among the small boxes, select a plain one, never liked anything to interfere with my feeling, even this is too much for my taste, so I go to the light and put it on gently and carefully but I am so anxious now, ready to shudder, so containment is an issue, come back to her and tell her, hop on, and I take her in my arms and carry through the door and plop her nicely on my bed in my bedroom, on her back, I fight a bit with the bedspread and the top sheet, I take them away from under her, holding her up under her back with one hand and working with the other, then, when all this is out of the way, I snake above her, and make sure she is still on and ready, which I know as she grasps at my neck, muzzling and biting in and biting off one of my ears now, and I enter her, and I feel her tight in pleasurable and pleasuring geometry, and she first lets a huge gasp and moan then, can't be sure if it was pain or pleasure, so I just start to slowly travel the long way, and to feel all the walls, knock at all doors, trace and retrace all alleys, gently or more aggressively,

Marius Hancu

listening in and tuning in with my ears and my skin as her breathing and temperature, and squirmings and moanings go, which are on this occasion nothing whatsoever to what they are to become during our following dates, matter of habit I guess

13 - Yvonne

In the algebra of things, it had to be her father losing an old friend to colon cancer that had started all this outpouring from him. Taking her aside to share an impromptu thought, or writing, or calling, when they weren't in the same city, seemed now to have upstaged everything in his life, as though there was an invisible albatross that had become important and ponderous, as if the flowers in his garden had been invaded by weeds that had to be dealt with urgently and as though he were out there with a machete to accomplish it.

The lightning flashes crossed each other in the sky. She thought of Lorca, and his señores passing through high corridors and their sky coursing through her mind made her ask herself what would be the next move of nature on this day. Perhaps those señores were right then and there rambling and rumbling through the air up high, treading a cumulus nimbus after another in the altitudes where Francis Gary Powers had been shot down above Sverdlovsk in Russia over a decade before.

With Lorca in her mind, it was still mostly what her father had tried to impress on her in writing or talking that took center stage. "Your body, most of the time, won't be able to get there up high where the kites go or higher," he wrote, "as you're not a pilot of planes or of *montgolfières*, yet your soul can definitely soar in those places. There's no limit for it, only tethers, chains and manacles you might have yourself fastened onto your dreams. Or, God forbid, we, the family around you, might have, even with the best of intentions — intentions do not make for reality. Touch around with your hands, with your fingers, watch for any limiting ties and cut them early." This time face to face to her, he took up the earlier thought

"Snip they go, and you're free like a children's balloon," he said, while lifting his hands up toward the sky in showing the notion and likeness of a balloon taking off. "Up you go!"

She was writing and talking back. "Father, even if God himself were to watch over me and wait for me up there — which the latter, I hope, isn't in the cards for quite a while, as I plan to have a long life — I'm young, I can't forget about my flesh and blood. That's what my dancing is all about."

"You may well think that way now, and there's nothing wrong to it, that's the truth, to a large extent, but in time you'll see how much every step and turn you care to put into a ballet or dance — be it rising on your toes in a *relevé* or stepping proud or taking an *attitude*, or launching yourself in your very jumps, *jetés*, whatever, you know better the terms than I do, and, most of all, accumulating courage and energy for them — comes, as from a spring, from your soul. I'm sure your teachers have stressed that to you, so somehow I'm befuddled by your somewhat one-handed take to it. For with no courage, you can't dance, not in any significant manner, can you, Yvonne?

"There'll also be the time, for it comes for all of us, alas, when the physical fire to fight, what your body will be able to put on the table, as it were, will, to some extent, be diminished, and what will remain to support your pleasure to live against boredom and repetition, against that now-and-then lack of energy, will mainly be a sharp mind and a fighting spirit, should you take care to keep them up. And if so, you may be able to reinvent yourself, say as a creator of dances. But you'll need to leverage yourself rightly in the transition, pick and choose those talents that could best serve you then and there. You'll have to cultivate yourself, and that should be starting right now, if you haven't done it yet, as more of a thinking and creative person, as opposed to just being a dancer and performer, even a great one."

She said, "Ah, but I'm not sure I want to do that, it's so much pushing the others to do the job, as opposed to enjoying it done by myself. I'm not sure I can stay in dance when the physicality of it is gone for me."

"You'd better start considering your options and preferences now, *mademoiselle*, for, I'm going to tell you, you won't be able to change yourself overnight, no one can. That's going to ask for a radically new angle to the dance at large and to your everyday work, to cutting the roses." He had ended with one of his preferred touches on flowers and that pleased him. And she liked seeing him pleased, pleased as punch.

"Well, Father, this may come as a surprise to you, but I don't see myself as just bodily, corporeally, driven in my dancing. I think I carry around with me a lot of thinking in doing it, and some have accused me at times of being too cerebral. What gives?"

"Right, cerebral. Still, thinking about things is one thing, and imagining things, forward-going, anticipating and growing them from scratch by yourself is another. And that's not to say anything about the ethereal part of it all. You need detachment from the world to be able to talk in any new fashion, in any way that breaks the mold, about it. Just describing it from inside would not work, to my mind. And my kites are just a minor thing to take you out in those ethereal domains, to that detachment, to those other flows.

"As well, being cerebral and thinking, to my mind, doesn't equal soul. Other ranges at play."

14 - George, 1982

George Granath was, at thirty-four, still on the Canadian discus throwing team. Not that he could have competed with the great Al Oerter in terms of success or longevity, which was saying something, after entering the team — at twenty-six, thus late already — mostly by default, when the entrenched members of the team were dismissed on confirmed steroid charges and the coach had to go on a national search for able-bodied males eager to take on the challenge. Still a metal foundry worker at an auto parts factory close to Toronto, he'd never considered going full hog into sports, too much the well-anchored man not to keep the idea at a long pole's distance.

Losing your mother at seven in a driving-under-the-influence frontal hit-and-run does that to you — especially when you were the oldest, and when Christina, at five, and John Jr., at two, named after their father, were too young to even grasp what had come over them and had refused for weeks to even get up from their beds, asking for their mother to come back from wherever strange place she had gone to.

In ninth grade, young George had decided by himself there were more pressing issues than completing high school, and entered the factory, not even sixteen, to help provide for the family. A large body, for his age, had helped him found a place in the shipping department, notwithstanding any reservations the hiring manager might have had, and by eighteen, already the largest man in the place, the switch to the foundry itself had been only a natural move to the best paid location in the factory, that is to say for blue-collar workers, and the most taxing on one's body and energy, a place and a move he had targeted from his first day at work.

Our Lives as Kites

On his way to becoming the six-feet two, two-hundred-and-sixty-pounder of his mature years, he was strong enough already that in hand-to-hand competitions during the breaks he was soon a sure winner. So it was that betting against him, and not for him, became the preferred choice on the underground network well and alive in the factory, the pay-out for such unforeseen circumstances as his losing going through the roof, with the only drawback that you had to wait months at a time and you needed to get him on a very bad day to see your money.

Rumors then started to transpire from the communal showers and the locker rooms that his endowment was full and complete in all respects, so that on his birthdays, gangs of his co-workers put money in improvised collection caps and hard hats in order to present him with a mail-a-telegram call-girl loquacious enough to be able to tell them afterward of his unnatural exploits in ample and colored detail, of course for a fee, just to confirm them in their belief that from their ranks someone nigh other-worldly had come forward in legendary fashion, even though finding a generous or even prolific father like Thespius, willing to offer his forty-nine daughters for validation of heroic feats, was not something to contemplate in our modern, birth-controlled times.

He and Yvonne had met each other by chance in downtown Toronto, on Yonge, at Eaton's flagship department store, when she was twenty-four, he four years older, both of them absorbed in searching for toys to give their nephews and nieces. On one of the aisles of the huge store, she was suddenly faced with this mountain of a man with a dark, short, curly hair, blocking passage, still nevertheless seemingly polite enough to realize the bottleneck he produced in the traffic, and squeezing himself into one of the shelves to let her pass.

"I'm sorry," he mumbled, and made a red, guilty face, dropping at the same time one of the packages he held.

"There's nothing to be sorry about." She hurried to oblige, fascinated by the veins in relief on this huge neck, and bending at the same time with him to pick up the box.

"Sorry to inconvenience you," he said, and at that low level, in crouching, and close proximity, ready to bump heads, she recognized in his eyes the gray waters of discomfort at the same time with an opening in their inner contours that conveyed to her already extended antennae the message of recognition of beauty, the message of lost surrender, which any woman would any day pay to receive.

They stood up as embarrassed children caught in the act, both red-faced by emotion and by the act of crouching itself, and she, with that sixth sense women have, recognized him as the introvert and taciturn type, not one to push for advantage in front of women, and decided to take initiative.

"Hi," she said, "I see you too are into buying toys. Family?"

"Yes, *my brother*'s children." He had recovered his composure just enough to stress 'my brother' and to flash what she thought was a nice, sincere smile at her, coming from quite up high, the heights of poplars and quite tall men, she felt.

She laughed. "I'm Yvonne, buying for a friend's children."

"Oh, sorry, I'm George. My brother is John. Do you often shop at Eaton's?"

"Whenever I need a good bargain for my money." She goofy-smiled. "I'm cheap most of the time, but with gifts one needs to be more circumspect."

She looked back at the heights of poplars and he nodded.

"Right, one can't quite lose face, especially to children. Face being one of the few things still left to each of us."

"That's a poignant observation, but appropriate for our times." She giggled just a bit. "What do you do for a living?" She looked at him, a bit worried about the reaction — as many times those days people had to answer, "You know, I'm *currently* looking for a job."

"Metal, I'm melting and pouring metal, if you know what I mean." His face was calm and unconcerned, for a line of work she didn't come into contact with every day.

"No, as a matter of fact I don't, would you mind telling me more?"

"I work in a foundry, shaping metal at high temperatures. Sound any better?" Clearly he was comfortable with it, and perhaps even a bit proud, so she felt, why should she be fussy about it? Men came in all shapes and sizes, as well as many professions. She didn't care too much, as long there was pleasure on their own part in what they were doing.

"Which metals, if you don't mind?"

"Not at all. Mainly aluminum and steel. Think about auto parts and you'll know where the final products fit in."

"Couldn't be in Toronto, could it?"

"You're right, it's something like twenty miles from here."

"Ah, so we should consider ourselves lucky to get you among us?"

"If you want to take it that way. I don't. Not that I don't consider myself lucky to have met such a lady in this of all places." His teeth showed up and the smile was just a bit sarcastic, but to her it seemed not more than comfortable, or a bit on the confident side. "So, and only if you don't mind, it's my turn to ask what you're doing yourself for a living."

"I don't mind at all, in fact I think it's only natural to reciprocate in kind. I'm a dancer, but not an exotic one, if you know what *I* mean," she said, with a similar turn of phrase to the one just minutes before having come forth from him.

"Should I have thought first about an exotic dancer? Why would that be?"

"Well, men like to go for such assumptions, or perhaps *you* don't? No, I'm a classical dancer, or less limiting, a ballet dancer. Less limiting, because these days I'm dancing both modern and classical pieces, and I'm into choreography for modern stuff too. If that doesn't sound too pretentious of me."

"No, but I'd like to see you at work, to get the whole notion of all this." He drilled a conquering smile sideways to her.

"Oh, so you want a free ticket?"

"Didn't say that, nothing of the kind." He sounded a bit hurt. "Seing you in rehearsals would do, too."

"Oh, then we can arrange it. This is a Wednesday. Are you still in Toronto tomorrow at 11AM?"

"Lucky me, I still am. I took three days off and I am here for training at the Varsity Stadium."

"Training? What for? Hopefully not for your job, tough as it sounds."

"Nah, I have a training session with the other guys on the national discus team there."

She measured him once more, realizing in more detail the physical accoutrements of this outsized human specimen, the super-wide shoulders, visibly padded in natural stuff, the biceps growing unimpeded from under the short-sleeved shirt.

"So, tomorrow at 11AM, you're coming to see me at a rehearsal with the National?"

"National, as in Ballet? I think I can manage, I mean I can manage it for someone like you." And she felt the courtesy and the slight flattery of his words, paid with a smile direct and warm.

So the second day it was. For him, seated on a bench on the edge of the proscenium of the rehearsal hall, on which the group of dancers were polishing their pieces, this was an opening of eyes in a quite unexpected way as to what athletes from other sport — as he saw it to a large extent, and he knew it must have been simple-minded to reduce it to that, to the physical exertion, to the flexibility and strength involved in it all, but this is what he had been used to — were trying to do, but there was also this feeling that the form was more important in this — art as they most visibly saw it — than in the sports, the expression was more searched for under the microscope, as the director was continuously going for it in small detail of hand or head positions, for him a bit of overdoing it. With no education in this field new for him, just several ballet shows glimpsed in part on the TV, he still realized that while in his own sports event, the discus throw, where there was also so much stress put on the form, the spectators were not looking at it, in the very end, but at the results, the lengths of his throws, while here everything was done in order to digest and enjoy at length the development of form in a thin air of feeling that had to envelop everything and was much more graduated, as the various pieces required, than the raw effort put into a throw.

And this was what he liked, this graduation, the fine nuances. So much so as his whole life he had been taught by need to go for the direct result, like a cobra he had once seen in a movie, be it the money helping his family, the repetitive but evermore risky moves in the foundry, those of carrying or handling the hot molten metal lava ready to maim or kill you upon the first wrong move, or the explosion and the huge exhalations and roars into the discus throws.

He recalled, and laughed under his breath at it, the two unbelievably large and woolly St. Bernards of the national team coach, Janos Kiss, starting to bark whenever George was commencing triple or double pirouettes in preparation to throwing, and howling to the wide-open sky while watching the discus fly to the other end of the stadium, slightly wobbling and slashing through the air, a reason for them not to be brought around on meet days, or the whole stadium would have focused with hilarity — a case made many times in training, so as to remove any doubts — on them and their desperate barking in duet, instead of watching the athletes.

Yvonne passed in front of him at that very moment, in full motion at the center of the stage, practicing with her partner several *grands jetés* and other jumps and throws. He could grasp from her face, from her half-opened mouth, the dilated eyes, the joy she had in doing it, her body in long thin lines, but with something very special in terms of roundness to it, piercing and slashing through the air and mounting up from the ground in what they wanted to make appear effortless, lifting for that very short while that humans are allowed to break free from gravity. She had powerful thin lines, again, rounded rather than sharp and edged, more athletic than classical, still everything was compact on her, and there also was the pink skin wet with perspiration on her neck under the short cap of curly blonde hair, the tongue flashing here and there to flick the beads of perspiration off her lips and to keep them wet at the same time, something which in itself was a challenge.

He had been let in just by mentioning her name to the porter, simple formalities here, he had thought at the time, but he arrived a bit too late for them to meet before the rehearsal. However, she recognized him and nodded a brief greeting during one of the short breaks, radiant from effort, but with no obvious smiles, some professional blankness to it. Later on, during one of the main pauses, while other dancers went on to the dressing rooms, she come over to him, excusing herself for having to use a towel at times, and they conversed fragmentedly for several minutes, interrupted now and then by quips from other dancers passing by.

He wondered, "So this is how you start your days, at 11AM? Ni-ice."

"Wrong, sir," she said, laughing back at him. "For your information, we started all at nine, with class, ballet class. That's warm-up for you people in sports. A large part of it is at the *barre*, our own rack for torture. One hour, one hour and a half, meant to thoroughly wake you up and re-build you afresh. Flexible and warm enough in body and soul now to be able to perform. Voilà! By the end of it, we are as good as circus performers; and by that I mean contorsionists, able to bend our bodies in every way known to man. In what I think are the words of your work, it's like having been between the anvil and the hammer for close to two hours. So, don't envy us, please don't."

"I won't then," he agreed, decidedly amused. "Also, we have other words in our trade, say, 'being taken to the rollers,' just in case you need more."

"I'll write them down, don't worry. By the way, for how longer can you be around? Or do you have to leave soon perhaps for your training?"

"As I matter of fact, yes, we start training at Varsity Stadium at two o'clock, so I'd better grab something serious to eat. Today is general conditioning, it leaves you flat dead if you haven't had a good meal in advance, and it might already be too late for me to get the food down into my system. But could I call you tonight?"

"Yes, that'd be very nice, say six thirty. This is my phone number."

"Thank you, and this is the number for this student residence where the federation keeps us during these three days. Ask for room 412, please, at the reception, and they'll connect you."

"Student residence? Couldn't be too large a room, I imagine?"

"You bet it isn't. Still, it's on Bloor, close to St. George, and so near to Varsity Stadium. Matter of fact, within walking distance."

"OK, talk to you tonight, I need to leave now for the dressing room. Need a bit of — OK, let's call it dress or equipment adjustments. Bye, I'm flying."

"Good bye."

15 - Patrick the Star, 1986

Patrick Vyacheslav (Slava) Donovin — with the considerably more Anglo-Saxon Donovan used for local color in terms of *nom de scène* — could be described in rough terms as made for dance, and only for dance, as a serious vocation. He *was*, in fact, described as such, at least by some in the favorable camp of the ballet critics. Still, there was a sidebar. The gracious sidebar was: and he's also destined for but a small number of transient, still satisfying, activities, such as voracious sex. However, this was added only among friends, as in this world of ours a suit for libel is always a concern. A concern, indeed, even outside of what they and others — whose name was legion — considered the all-out legal circus pertaining to the USA.

With both parents White Russians who entertained a cult for Vaganova's school in the former St. Petersburg — Leningrad at the time of this story — and who had some connections with Diaghilev's Ballet Russes, holding on to their heritage in post-WWII England, as well with a large share of luck in terms of genes, the boy seemed destined for great things sooner rather than later.

Manchester, which he boasted as his native city, having been born there in 1954, didn't learn too much about him during his childhood years. His parents, once convinced early on — he must have been four or five at that critical, but, for him, auspicious juncture in his life — that there really was physical *materiel* in him in terms of a future professional ballet dancer, moved immediately to London. The move was designed to get access for Slava to the best the metropolis could offer, of course for a pretty fee, in terms of teachers (many of them Russians themselves, not a small advantage in his mother and father's eyes) and ballet schools. Slava, they still called him. Contrary to his wishes, that was, as he was afraid of being branded again, and mistakenly, as son of Russian Communists, as some of the neighborhood boys had called him, which had lead to fights. Those were awful years, after Churchill's Fulton speech, with Soviet spies popping up everywhere, real or unreal — if one thinks just about the Rosenbergs and Kim Philby.

His children are spread over the world, and aren't recognized by him as his own. Four of them, that is, they are. What is that, the list of places where his genes have been generously offered for match? Madrid, Barcelona, Rome and – and an unknown place in Japan, that particular lady having gone underground. "Shame's too big in Japan, they should do something about it, perhaps the Shinto god might ask the emperor to give a decree, then everybody would definitely listen," or so he thinks. The ones in Spain – boys; the remaining two – girls. All sharing his deep, troubling, green eyes. As God wanted it, the ladies are not one and the same, nor do they know about each other or their varied offspring. Not that each of them wouldn't assume there's someone else in his life outside herself. Oh, this they know too well.

In other worlds, they'd be called groupies. Perhaps not in ballet. Well, each of them is what one calls a very distinguished woman, no doubt, as society goes today – who otherwise could afford showing up at these after-show galas? – however, getting a star dancer in one's bed after a gala party isn't very different from what groupies do, no, sir. Not to him, this he knows, so he could care less about them months – What? Days! – later.

His nature hasn't exactly been a hurdle to this end, on the contrary. Extrovert, very talkative – boastful even, some would say – he wouldn't put unnatural barriers between him and his fans, even the hotter ones. And why should he?

Mind you, Patrick is smart enough to bait and scope them from the start of the acquaintance. He's looking for the submissive ones. As such, good results may thankfully be reported in that direction: no alimony to speak of as it is, and no claims at the horizon. What more could a modern man ask for?

Take the one in Barcelona, Manuela, the Catalan. She took him to Gaudi's Temple Expiatori de la Sagrada Família, and he found an appropriate corner for a longish intimacy, somewhere under one of those great spires. Well, *that* boy should be around in 2026 to see the cathedral finished. Now then, could one's inspiration come more directly from God than in such circumstances? Seemingly not. Wonder if she would go to confession to the same spot? Probably not, for some there would be too much mix-up of feelings. Not for him. The one in Madrid took him to Prado. No, that place would have been too much for you know what; too much traffic to speak of.

But with Manuela, it was natural. She surprised him with showing up, after one of National Ballet's shows, with two pictures of the Sagrada Familia and asking him straight, "You still have a day here, in Barcelona, haven't you? Would you like to see *this* tomorrow?" There was something violet in her eyes, something deep and serious that troubled him for a beat, however, within the same flash, pulled him to her. She was very tall, taller than himself, she may have been six feet one or so, thin, but not mannequinish, her shoulders well drawn back by a very straight spine, so her breasts were in your face whatever you did about it. On that night, her hair was pulled up in a complicated coif that she would later tell him was her own concoction. The hair heavy, dark-brown, long, the tresses braided, then rolled up in that high affair, which implied what Nefertiti must have worn under that Egyption crown in that bust of hers, Patrick forgot the name of the Berlin museum. Her face was large boned, still delicately finished, with a rich although very finely oiled dark skin, standing on a thin, long, pulled-back neck, which just accentuated the way the spine was exposing the front of the body from the hips up. A raspy voice, most probably inherited, as she didn't speak too loudly, never shouted – well, never got angry, for that matter – and didn't like hard alcohol either, all of which, to his mind, when he thought about it, were things which could have lent such a rough surface to her speech.

He took the pictures from her right hand, snapped a look at them, then extended his own hand and shook hands with her, pressing her palm a bit with his middle finger in the process for a discrete sign of extra attention and sympathy. There was a flashing change of color in her cheeks for a passing moment, or so it seemed to him. "Some women respond to that, especially when they show up with pictures looking for you," he said to himself. "Could we make it tomorrow at one?" he suggested. "We have a short rehearsal at ten in the morning, it probably takes until noon, and I need a massage and a shower after that." "Fine, I'll be waiting for you at the artists' door of the theatre, tomorrow at one."

The next day, on the way out, he grabbed three red tulips from the dancers' dressing room, there are always flowers around when visiting places and having success, as they had.

She had on a light, knee-length, fluffy yellow skirt, gauze-like and apparently multi-layered as he couldn't quite detect the contours of her thighs and hips through them, the skirt standing up around her as supported by the hoops of yesteryear. It was moved to and fro by the drafts of air, so at times it looked as though she would take off, carried away by it toward unknown ethereal regions.

Tulips. Red, red, open lips. She's pushing them to his face as in a movie, perhaps made by Warhol, so striking the colors are, so contrasting, lapping various surfaces. She hangs an arm through one of his, swaying of an open, fully-rendered satisfaction, perhaps the one of being together, he can't tell. She looks like a flower herself, long legs showing up as a stem on which the corolla of the skirt balances and swings this way or another, a corolla that takes now the whole screen. Indiscreet cameraman.

***

The tall tower of the Sagrada Familia under construction, stone everywhere, carved or pinched, I can't tell, it's all stone, chiseled, penetrated, removed, carved, acted upon by perhaps hundreds of invisible hands.

I have the feeling of going up, as the images coming in on the screen are of the houses getting smaller by degree, remoter by the step. She's in front, and the contours of the backs of her full, round thighs work like scissors in the image, scissors nicely articulated in a round junction.

My hand is showed pushing forward and going from behind those thighs to in between them and touching them on a lustrous surface, which seems to be directly on her skin, so it must have been it. Moving around, is the hand.

Next, there's her head so closely to the screen, as though touching it, going toward me, as are her upper hands and shoulders. This is all the screen entertains now, head and shoulders going toward the front, around something, as though hanging her off a support.

There's some hesitation, a jolt upward and the image starts to yank up and down, her eyes are closed now, the mouth is widely open now and visibly the air is heaved out through it in large gulps.

***

[The abstract part of his ego going at it.] There's that and there's that. Then, the principle being. I wouldn't like. Gone are the days. Streaming right through. Abstract, abstract. Concretize. Ever more concrete. The contours are well-defined. Moral list of don'ts. Feminine. Sex. Grabbing a concept. Touching a point. View the contours. Detecting shape. Detecting intention.

***

Strapped in his hang glider, contrary to what his voluminous personal insurance contract as a star ballet dancer expressly stipulates, his huge, carefully depilated thighs and calves pumping away as he ran, Patrick is at this time trying to take off from a tricky ledge close to Kitzbuehel in Austria. Tricky, as it is darn slippery, also covered with a bit of dust, again reducing the traction of the soles of his high basketball shoes, the best, he thinks, in terms of preventing ankle injuries at an eventual land out. The wind is appropriately directed, just a bit too slow. His effort has to compensate for that, to avoid any drop of altitude at this critical stage in his flight. He knows the ledge lies just above a tall vertical stone face that had no grass covering at all, so any contact with it would cost an arm and a leg.

His shoulder-long, blond hair is well caught in his helmet, only a small ponytail shows up at the back, no flowing effects here. He knows that would be risky. Catching it in some of the ailerons of the frame at some unfortunate moment could mean even strangulation – no Isadora Duncan again, please, he's asking the celestial director, in case he's around and available to accommodate a short prayer. A pair of ski goggles protects his eyes against the wind and the sun which could make you, with an unexpected beaming shot through the clouds, lose your bearings for a moment, quite enough to sway you out of balance. In other circumstances, you would be able to detect the tricky, deep greenness of those eyes, which can close just barely to a threatening gleam. When he does that, a sharp furrow shows up between the two brows and the nostrils swell, and his rivals would swear his eyes dash yellow from their depths.

The torso, the upper arms and legs are covered by a dense elastic material that makes him impersonate, in case one throws Patrick's physique in the balance for a good measure, a gladiator of the air. At this time, he himself is less concerned with such comparisons and more with the nuts and bolts of the navigation.

He's done all this perhaps fifty times, however this is tricky high-altitude manoeuvering and you don't want to take unwarranted risks. A snap of the quirky winds at this height can tumble you around as a fly through the air and then you really need some acrobatics to find your way to ground safely.

The initial push of the foot-launch has been effective; he's already up in the air, away from the huge face of the mountain at a distance large enough to feel a bit more relaxed, and that's probably a half-length of a football field already.

The wind is helping for the time being, pushing him upwards, he feels hot currents driving up in virtual chimneys from the ground. These must be thermals. "We have lift-off, man, we have lift-off, we're soaring, let's call it God's Wind, Kamikaze, yeah!" words fizz in his mind.

The wings are tense over the metallic tubulature of the frame. He feels their sharing in the effort. through his harness they tell him they're nervous – racing horses launched in pursuit. The time is about 11.30AM. "Visibility perfect for the time being, A-OK, knock on wood", he tells himself.

He doesn't have radio comm on this flight, just a variometer to check the vertical speed, so no ground references nor directions are coming his way. This is his next step in getting independent, "As a bird, as a bird, man!" he told his instructor back in the French Alps, who's taking him on challenging duo flights, but who didn't feel quite comfortable with this much risk for Patrick. "You don't need that to get your kicks, Patrick, the gliding is just as good, for heaven's sake, the link is just for support in case that!" However, one just doesn't say "No" to Patrick, or he will do the opposite as a matter of course. The only concession was hiring a chopper – quite an expensive item, but "what the heck, we're Principal Dancers!" – to take him high up. That was to a platform close to the take-off area, something like two hundred meters off, so he wouldn't have to use too much energy climbing, in order to stay fresh for what mattered, the flight per se.

***

The valley opens wide in front of me right now. There's this chain of mountains on the port side, from where I took off, with the tall horn on one of its faces, still throwing a long shadow on the ground even at this late time of the morning, with sun this high. On the starboard, I make out the lower camel-back of the other chain. It's middle of the day, the sun starting to burn down on my face – normal in June – whenever I am trying to look up, around and underneath those goggles. Looks like a good idea to have bought them, just in time. The dominant color underneath me is a light, dusty brown peppered by large boulders, reduced to just points from up here.

Suspended horizontally in the harness, I'm swaying under the wings, with the sun getting to me through them now, which should mean it's closing to noon, so we're all on schedule. Indeed, time's confirmed on my chronometer on my right wrist – right, I'm a lefty. At this time, the arms are for all terms and purposes those parts of the body most involved in guiding this strange ship, or leaf, whatever, through the air, pulling on the support bars, while I'm swinging my weight around for good measure.

Feeling a thermal ascending from behind me on the starboard: it probably goes upwards at about twenty degrees with the horizontal. I'm bumming a ride on it. Why fight Mother Nature when you can use her, staying higher for just a bit longer for the same or even for less work? Sooner or later gravity will make a hash of your dignity. The valley becomes forested now, pines, firs, whatever – heck, I can't tell them apart not even when close by, the city boy rages in me – mostly dark green, dense; bald, but grassy meadows here and there.

I'm shifting my weight and pulling heavily toward port as the land rolls with more variety over there and so I like to watch it. 'Variety' is a password with me. I feel the strain in my upper left arm and my rotator cuff. Still, this is something totally different from having to heave a ballerina who has means, cheek, and access to come to rib you for your performance afterward in the dressing room. This, while you're just trying to get rid of the maquillage, of your foot and ankle taping, of your dance belt (not to call it jockstrap), and cool down. As much as I enjoy my repute of flashy and elegant porteur, this, my back tells me, isn't something that I miss right now.

Thump! What the heck is this? Thump! Thump! I'm looking up toward the frame of the wings, where the sound is coming from, and what I see is the damnedest thing ever to catch my eyes. A huge eagle, so huge it looks like the bloody Austrian-Hungarian imperial bird – that, just between us, had most probably ever existed only in the sick imagination of some heraldic painters, but I'm willy-nilly in Austria – has landed on the frame. On the frame, and right above me, also two feet toward the port from the centerline. He got a solid grab at the aircraft aluminum tubes with his enormously and frightful talons, and now is pecking down aggressively at my wing sails, all while I'm trying to gain altitude in this cloud street, just the right kind of cumuluses I need to stay up the longest.

His beak has already cut a gash of half a foot in length, right perpendicular on the frame, and the wild bird fanatically tries to perfect its damage. I'm trying to shoo him away, but this is no puny chicken to listen to measly threats. He continues his devilish work, and I don't have any damn means to reach to him.

This isn't without effect for the flight, the air gets in though the hole and we're losing altitude much faster than I expected for the current flying conditions, which were quite remarkable, before the damn imperial bird settled on the wing. I'm looking at the altimeter, and I think we're something like three hundred meters above the ground. Still forests underneath me, no habitation. As though I could call out for help. Idiot me. The tops of the trees seem much closer by the moment. I'm trying to unbalance the glider, to wobble it from side to side to make the aggressor take off; I'm putting all my weight and power into it. It's like nothing for the bird. It quickly becomes obvious, if ever there were any doubts that its stability is much better in troublesome flying conditions than mine combined with the glider's, any bloody day.

I'm trying to get into a vertical loop, perhaps the bird will be forced to detach himself, however my current speed isn't enough for that, mind you I've never really achieved it in a glider. And the bird is still perched up there and punching away at my glider, my maneuvers no matter.

I'm thinking now it'd be best to cut my straps, fall away from the glider and then open my parachute. However, I'm already too close to the ground to guarantee the time needed to safely open the chute, as well I've invested several thousand dollars in this machine and I love the way it performs with no imperial eagles attached to it. So I decide I'll stay on no matter what, if worst comes to worst, I hope to manage a reasonable crash landing.

The air swooshes in up through the hole, as we go lower and lower. I'm still shaking the whole thing, trying to get rid of the critter who's still there clasping the frame with his talons and pecking with beak against fine sailing. Ferociously, from time to time, he sneaks a peek and makes sure I'm still a prisoner in harness, as thought he'd been sent over to liquidate me, no more nor less.

Wow, the guy wants to kill me, not just get us aground. He's started to fly around me and peck toward my face, so, with no thick gloves to speak about, I need to fling about my shots at him, trying to get him go away. He just continues to make rounds around me, closing in, now reaching for me with his talons, now pecking at my face. Suddenly, he realizes my back is practically defenseless, as I am prisoner of the harness. So, he starts pecking at the back of my legs, and gets through the nylon layers to my skin and flesh, tearing out small bits. I am shouting and crying out, twirling around, as much as the harness allows, in order to push him away.

Going down, only one hundred meters up above the ground, under me I have tall pines, perhaps thirty meters tall, quite dense. Wonder if I can get through them to the ground somehow, cut a passage among the trees, or I'll hang out up in there. I'm making sure the goggles are well fastened over my eyes, as I wouldn't like to be blinded by pine needles.

The ground and the trees come rushing toward us. We impact against the trunk of a pine, perhaps ten feet above ground, straight on. One thing I know, the eagle stays with the glider up until the very moment, unblinking eyes on me until the frontal hit takes me out.

***

It took him three months in an Austrian hospital to recover from that accident.

16 - Monte Carlo, 1984

This is me in Monte Carlo. The seat of Colonel Basil and René Blum and of their companies, going for plurality when they decided to divorce in business and to compete with each other head on. The roots of modern ballet. White Russians spreading Petipa's and Vaganova's work from St. Petersburg to the whole world. Balanchine lost for Danilova, one of the *prima ballerinas* of the time. Massine, that is to say Myasin, putting great symphonies by Tchaikovsky and Berlioz in ballet.

However, Balanchine has passed to the ethereal up-there now, "Les Ballets Russes de Monte Carlo" closed shop three decades ago, my short years with Baryshnikov and others at the New York City Ballet under the great Georgian — over and done with; all of which leaves me where exactly?

I might as well start trying to deal the cards myself. Europe is already full of great dancing companies, Béjart in Belgium and Switzerland, Petit in Paris, Nureyev in London, now in Paris, Bruhn in Denmark, they all took care of that; to enter those hollow grounds one needs a great name; add to that some local roots and contacts to get the grants or the state feed even if you're Nureyev; even then, you'll be sabotaged by the locals smiling back at you in the process.

Going back to Montreal would mean going back to my roots, although in terms of contacts that'd be more of a stretch, with my leaving over ten years ago for the Big Apple and my ballet schooling done in Toronto. I may not be the most popular face in town, assuming some still remember me.

I'm staying nights in Nice. Monte Carlo would otherwise leave me hanging by the skin of my teeth, financially speaking. Whenever

I come to Monaco, I pack sandwiches into my shoulder bag. "No useless purchases in this here, dangerous territory" — this is my banner around the place. Still, I'm coming over quite frequently, not as much for the Casino, but for the view of the Mediterranean on a dry day enjoyed from the *grand falaise* bordering the Oceanographic Museum. I like to take in this quasi-infinite azure from up above, as it rises gradually toward the horizon in limpid quietude, spots of sails dabbing it here and there for short flashes of time, made presently to disappear by the water, the sun, by the unknown particles hanging up in the air, at the ready, to absorb the intruders as any good immune system would in similar circumstances.

It's not only that I love the sea; by now, I've managed to make friendly arrangements to take class with the local *Ballet de l'Opéra de Monaco* every morning, even though it's summer. Common friends from the New York City Ballet have fixed that for me. For someone at the *barre* everyday since you were four or five, and not retired yet, it's pretty much part of a routine which helps you stay functional, though not necessarily at the level where your resident ballet master or mistress would bring you, when done on a regular basis and at the fine edge of your ambition. Even though I'm not at that fine edge any more; I'm still on vacation overseas, and I think I need to allow myself a bit of a glad respite. However, caveat, Yvonne: not having your daily grand battements could seriously fray your foundations and your confidence.

I still remember the classes in NYC with Madame Danilova, Balanchine's former flame in the twenties in Monte Carlo, which could set her sights on shaking your system everyday, should you dare to step into her class. Story goes she was lucky to have met Mr. B again in the sixties somewhere on a New York street, in dire financial difficulty, and that he immediately hired her as a teacher. Former prima ballerinas should always deserve such breaks from fate, don't you think? She went on and survived the Georgian, dying in her nineties. Love and life pass you just like that. Ninety years. If you're lucky.

It doesn't happen frequently, but sometimes the social part of us superb animals takes over and one or another of the locals comes up to you at the *barre* as the grapevine has by now established for everyone who you once were, who you still hopefully are, all your epaulets duly applied for recognition, soloist here, corps there; they would know your greatest highs and lows, if they really care about you, the stray cat with visiting rights.

Also, keeping such contacts alive can help you find the numbers of the local masseur or masseuse who can be trusted for a reasonable fee to bring your time-tired joints to working order and your muscles to flexibility, where an acupuncturist can be found for your pains, and even where the local craftsmen are, those wonder costume makers able to adjust your tutu, if it happens you need to show up in anything like dancing togs or if your ballet slippers need some darning that you can't manage to do yourself or you don't have the materiel.

It's not just the sea and the dancing. I love *la Condamine*, the crowded streets toward the mountain, and at times, I wondered where Bjorn Borg may have lived in the times when freedom from taxes might have been a concern for him.

Of course, old habits of observation still strike now and then. I am looking at their turns, I mean the turns performed by the *Ballet de l'Opéra* dancers. Why do I find that they are more outwardly oriented, open, chest-exposed and offered in the turn, shoulder back, while I tend to favor in my stuff now the inner turns, shoulders in the turn, back coming over the chest in rotation, arm leading not following the body in the rotation? Could it mean age, reserve, on my part? I have this image of leaves turning upon themselves at the beginning of the autumn. It's like they exhibit and I cover and hide, they gloriously and unabashedly flashy, I reservedly discrete. Not that I am looking for this effect. It just comes out naturally, of its own.

Also, it is as though I am looking for a feel of a more circuitous motion, as though the frontal, direct approach to it is ever so fake in its appearance. And in circuitous, I mean both rotation around the own axis and the dancer roving on the stage.

Right on the same subject of curves and rotations, the last trip to St. Paul de Vence still stays with me, the narrow serpentines, medievalish roads here and there flashing almost indecently by, the modern pools of fancy villas suspended over huge slopes and ravines, hinged on new concrete projecting structures, not on anything preexisting in the natural relief. The Maeght foundation there — amazing books from the fifties with lithographies by the greats, Chagall, Picasso, Matisse, the limited editions on generous expanses of fine paper, the books — works of art in themselves.

Jacques shows up at the porter at la *porte des artistes* of the *Opéra* and sends me, through a dancer sneaking in late, a message to the class, the class having a respite at eleven. The porter is as self-important as though he were guarding the entrance to the "Loews" on the sea strip and the Grand Prix track here, and would not relinquish for the world his place to come over himself into the class to look for me and present me with the semi-crumpled piece of paper from Jacques that says only "I'm here at the entrance. 10.45AM, Jacques," which under most circumstances would make me slip out of the class during the recess to see him and share with him two of the sandwiches I brought in. Luckily for my tennis and my tan, he's well-connected enough in the principality to secure slots to play at the Monte Carlo Country Club, on the same red clay courts where Borg lost only two years or so ago to Yannick Noah. Great courts, gorgeous sight on one side overlooking the Mediterranean, the grand sea serene as ever.

I'm seeing more of Jacques for one year now, and him coming over to look for me it's a good sign, nights don't seem enough for his ardor any more, he seems to need some afternoons too, which I can't complain too much about, as he's built like an ephebus and has the passion of a satyr, yet with no any links with dancing. So much the better these days, with this new disease around seemingly getting a harsh grip on some of the male dancers.

Jacques is an accountant. Not many would guess that. When first seeing him in short-sleeved polos and shorts, muscles bulging out at 100,000 Volts as Bécaud would have said, you'd certainly believe him at least a gymnast or an athlete. The funny thing is, he doesn't do an iota of calisthenics, still keeps in that great shape. Now, that's having some genes, I would say.

We met in Cherbourg perhaps eight years ago, the transatlantic ship coming to anchor. We had started rolling out of its guts on its passerelle to the quay to what we knew was sweet France; I found myself pulling after me this huge trunk you could as well think it was from Noah's time with my whole ballet stuff, shoes, slippers, leotards, tutus, creams, not to speak about books. This was all at that time in my career when Paris wanted me in a neoclassical piece by Serge Audreuil, who'd seen me in New York in a piece prepared with the Julliard. I must have had an awfully lost look, 'coz this young French guy (he's still young today) started laughing in guffaws at me, in a group of men — I was later to find — fully prepared to play on the naïveté of American tourist women in Europe — that some others would call gigolos, and not with the gentlemanly manner of Richard Gere.

I was all sweating by then, so I started cursing them full steam — the one satisfaction presumably left to me was in casting a heavy stone at their memories — no doubt, enough for them to ever regret the moment their mothers ever thought of bringing them to a world in which damn American bitches spouted their all with enough virulence to think Sodom and Gomorrah.

Fully brought up to date on the latest New York repertory of the kind, they recoiled for a moment yet there must have been something attractive and animalistic enough in my gutsy performance to make this young Frenchman step forward and advance the idea of help in terms of a conveyance to a hotel nearby or to the train to Paris — my choice. My boiling over not entirely irrational, I relented and took him on this offer and that hotel must never have had more penetrating squealing on romantic nights, he later told me.

I should call Carla up in Paris.

***

Once in Paris, Yvonne had, on that occasion several years ago, called Carla Verdis. They had earlier met at the New York City Ballet. Since Carla was dark-haired, there was no type competition between them, what with Yvonne being blonde, as well as Yvonne being more the dynamo and Carla more the classicist, so their casting with the corps usually called for temperamentally different pieces, and most frequently even for different music.

"So, how does it happen you're in France? I'd've thought you'd go back to Canada. I mean, Toronto or Montreal, perhaps even Winnipeg?" Carla had then wondered over the phone.

"Winnipeg? Too much prairie for my taste, I'd not survive long there, I don't think. Even more, *la douce France* made me *un clin d'oeil*, so I winked in response," Yvonne had laughed.

"Where do you stay in Paris?" The voice at the other end of the line had seemed seriously concerned, and Yvonne had felt a rush of sympathy just for that reason only. "*Hôtel*? How many days around? *Tu sais*, I wouldn't mind having you star-guesting my modest apartment close to the Madeleine."

Carla's voice had come then as from afar, moving up and down, as a tide getting in and out of a deep cave. She may have kept the handset too far from her mouth, or may have been using a hands-free set while navigating through the house, popping back here and there back on the line. She seemed alone though, the noise from her apartment came uninterrupted, not as it was when she had sometime placed her hand over the set, to discreetly continue on the side some local dialogue. Also, the fact that she replied at all was a flag in the same direction. Yvonne detected a samba, probably sounding on the large expanses of red in her flat. Lots of red there, she would later find, so much so that the imagined cave had its cold walls in it too.

"That must be very central, if I remember well?" *Église de la Madeleine*, the tall colonnades, yes, she well remembered the place. More like a Roman or Greek temple, light-brown, a bit dusty, the facade, that's how her memory brought it up to the surface, its width so large it was as though her imagination had to go wide-screen and everything had become so close and clear that she could have broken with her hand through that what looked like a glass window and scavenged through her own imagination.

"It is central, and downright expensive, but it's me paying the rent, or Gérald, as it were, so why don't you pop in for a while?"

"Are you serious? What would Gérald say? I hope you two aren't into any *ménage à trois*?"

Yvonne had known for some time, even when they were both in New York, about Gérald, a well-heeled advertising executive, who "sponsored" Carla; she didn't want to play the game of not remembering from the very beginning who he was, just for the sake of serving the appearances, especially with Carla. Saving the appearances was that something which Carla felt as the strange concern that others had in their lives, but nothing of the kind for her, she'd say. That was something that people like Gérald himself or his wife may have felt constricted to keep or stick to, something that people entrenched in their lives, not someone like she, whose image of herself was that of a busy bee — or wasp, she didn't mind the connotations — flitting in onto a nice flower and the rich pollen there, then pulling out freely, unconcernedly and delicately for all involved. So no false escutcheons here, please.

"Oh, get out of here! First, he's down in Italy for a month. Second, he lacks energy even for me — work is taxing him too much. And certainly, being so tired couldn't mean his wife; I know what she looks like!"

Yvonne knew by then too, as Carla had already duly informed her. Built straight like a thimble, Mme Gérald — Yvonne never got to learn the family name — was plain, and truly indiferrent to things that Gérald might have considered as "daring," or "adventurous." She would say to Gérald, the thimble, and he reported, "What are you talking about, 'adventures,' it's just dames that you are dealing with, it's not like you're crossing the Atlantic solo on an inflatable boat like Alain Bombard in the fifties. Do what you feel like, but not come back boasting to me, as if you had gone after the Golden Fleece. Fleece yes, but not golden."

"With men, you never know, perhaps bad taste is back in fashion with him," Yvonne had cautiously countered.

"It can't be that bad. That would mean I'd have to reconsider any good opinions I still keep in store about him. That would be a costly proposition, so the pits."

Carla's apartment was modest, in an old building. However, being so close to the core of Paris, with an intrusive and ugly concierge — "aren't they all?" asked Yvonne several days later — over-compensated for any perceived disadvantages it might have had in the eyes of any short-term visitor. The green and red, Clara's colors, were amply in evidence in her tights, whether for dance or for outings, as well in the drapes, choice of kitchen ceramics, in the flowers Gérald seemed to bring her. Pictures of both of them were freely displayed throughout the flat, on the imitation mantelpiece or above the small kitchen counter.

Here they were, Gérald, of a somewhat portly inclination, with a large head carrying around the large expanse of a face, smart French eyes over a crooked nose à la Bourvil, whom Yvonne still remembered from her childhood, Clara contrasting with a small face, body visibly so filiform irrespective of what she was wearing, still with a marked well-rounded bust, in fact not very beautiful, her face, features crowded around the nose, not too much space spent on a forehead or over the cheekbones, green eyes flashing under well-contoured brows; perhaps a bit belaboured from a jokingly cosmetic point of view, those brows were still on the point of joining each other above the less-than-patrician, pointed nose, which showed a small moon in the profile of its narrow ridge, the whole attraction of that face residing most definitely in the eyes-nose triad.

On another occasion, Yvonne looked again at the pictures in that flat — Gérald must have been at that time in his fifties, Carla, in her twenties. This was a relationship ostensibly made for all the wrong reasons that still worked — everybody harboring open, wide smiles, in all appearance an air that could not lead one to believe anything but short moments of happiness, if not more. Were the pictures better than life? Perhaps so, said Yvonne to herself, but it seemed that, if anything, it was more than just a flash-in-the-pan thing.

The strange thing was the absence of *any* reference to ballet, as thought the woman of the couple didn't want to mix, not in the least, her purest exertions with those which could be seen as more questionable ones.

"Do you ever talk about ballet with Gérald?" Yvonne had once asked.

"No, from the word go he didn't want any shop-talk, not in this place. If we ever go somewhere else, say in the Alps, then there he can take it in. There, he likes me to show him pictures from my shows, talk about them, talk *Opéra* small palaver with him and so on. He just probably doesn't want to be crowded with too many things in Paris itself."

"OK, no shop talk. What are you two talking about, then? Kama-Sutra?" laughed Yvonne.

"Don't laugh. I think we both draw some considerable pleasure from talking sex. Not a boring subject, he'd definitely tell you, and I think I'd agree with him here."

"Boring, no. Still, I for one don't like to talk about it, not with my men. I'm afraid they might become too self-conscious and I might end up messing the whole thing. A woman seems enough of a risky proposition by herself for them these days, I mean just getting up to the challenge. Add talking about it and you may end up with a *bouillabaisse* they might not be willing to consider for dinner."

17 - Monte Carlo, 1984

I thought about myself last night, while alone in bed, in the dark, and I suddenly realized how astonishingly *physical* everything has been with me since I've started ballet, close to twenty years ago. All about how the — my — body looked and reacted. As though I had been dropped into a lake or river in a baptism of a kind and felt only the swish of fluid folds in it coldly moving about my skin, its flowing pressure, its transparence, muddier or lighter.

Even my loves or, as it were, urges, had been, still were, it seemed now, mostly of and for the body, of and for its nervous endings and muscles, glands and secretions, fluids and ligaments, its vibration of bones. Of a name called 'instinct.'

There must have been something that I've missed or barely touched upon, ricocheted from taking it all in this way, having been led on this particular path into the magic garden, having led myself into it.

And now that the body starts not to be what it had been, as it moves into things that it can't do any more with the same fluidity, flexibility, spring or jump, or with just, plainly, the same zest to it, there seems to be around a check, a tether, a frustration and a desire for something else, for other, unexplored sources or pathways to still live. To live otherwise, to still feel it, to feel the burning, now.

So I find myself suddenly and, sometimes, maddeningly out there hunting for the not-obvious and the structured, for the cerebral and the character, the consideration. Were they always of the journey? Sometimes, I really doubt it. It's as though another cape is taken for the wearing from the coat check and it hasn't been with us until this day of the parade, or of the modest preparation for it.

18 - Monte Carlo, 1984

I feel it in my guts as an ulcer: I need to go away at sea for a day or so. It's as though the days on dry land, among certain white and cream-colored buildings of Monte Carlo, through the asphalt veins and arteries of *autoroutes*, in closed rooms, even when they are eyed with generous windows, even when we are surrounded on the outside by palms and their thick, healthy fronds, even when these are mentally associated with the perks of having my sleeping base in Nice and those long walks along the *Promenade des Anglais*, these days, I'm saying, have crept up and accumulated on me on the sly, without notice, and suddenly they seem too many in their crowd to be borne on any longer on my head as water jugs brought from the forest fount by aborigine women, these days with no breaks to their sequence. It's also as though the sea is asking for its due time and attention, as though telling me I can't face it any longer without being on it, in it or of it.

***

This was full-blown June, the Mediterranean coast crowding with boats of all kinds, packed as sardines in the docks, much less at anchor now than other times of the year, freeing themselves to the winds and the water for the pleasure of the seafaring species. Thus, she didn't have any problems in engaging a small boat for two days. She just went, in Monte Carlo, to *La Condamine*, passed several great yachts in repose in their white shells and sails and headed for a place where, in oil-dirty overalls, several sailors or mechanics were working on the bridge of one of them over an opened-up engine.

"Local men always know best, let's see if this still holds currency," she said to herself.

"Bonjour! Do any of you gentlemen know someone from whom I could get a rental boat for two days?"

"Bonjour, madame. You may want to talk to Jean over there at the office. He certainly has better connections than we have."

So she went to the rental and administration office, set up in a spacious white wooden cabin on the edge of the docking area, and found straight away a fifty-or-so-year-old man hidden behind a large, streaked white beard, who promised her a light wooden boat for five people or so, two pairs of oars available just in case, also offering to tug her out at sea in the morning and to bring her back at the end of each day with his own motorboat, to spare her tedious rowing to and from the designated area, which she wanted to be something like a mile out in front of the Oceanographic Museum. The only thing he kindly asked on his side was to have his ten-year-old daughter — a real sailor, so he said — on the boat at all times, in order to call him via the on-board radio to pull them back into the harbor in emergencies or before the evening fell, as this was indeed his personal boat and didn't want anything to happen to it and, this went without saying, to her, his customer, who, it seemed to him, wasn't experienced in those waters.

"If you don't mind, madame, what would you like to do out there on the sea?"

"Fishing, kite flying and most of all, relaxing."

"Kite flying? Wouldn't you need some pretty heavy winds to lift them up? You know, at this time of the year, and especially during the day, you could be in a bind waiting for any sensible breeze. The air and the sea are *very* calm. Doldrums."

"Any suggestions, then?"

"I've one, heard from a monsieur from Reims: we should perhaps try using the speed of the motorboat to lift the kite to a reasonable height where, once caught in the air, you can rely on more powerful vertical currents, if any, to pull it up even when switching to the quasi-stationary boat. I think you intend to keep pretty much the same position for most of the day, don't you?"

"*Mais bien sur*, I don't want to move around. I'm taking with me a book, a line with a reel and some sinkers, some bait for fishing, my kite and a big umbrella against the sun. So you can imagine my activities for the day. Mostly enjoying being out there."

"Then all this should be *faisable*. I'll call Gabrielle, my daughter, right away, to make sure she's available on Thursday, which would be your first day out, I think."

"Indeed, that's what I wanted."

***

Everything materialized just fine in due time on the appointed day, and by now it was already close to nine in the morning, the boat in position, moving and wobbling around slightly, as pushed by an irregular, absent-minded breeze and by the currents engendered by it right under the skin surface of the sea. She could make out in the distance the high *falaise* of the Museum on the shoreline.

The kite was up, its line knotted, just in case, around one of the oarlocks, her handling it and giving it more slack now, as it wanted to push higher, it seemed. It was the Elephant, a large, square, gray kite, carrying on its face the head of an elephant with a raised, rough in the creased surface of its skin, threatening trump, which she had bought in Paris from an Indian shop close to the *Marché aux voleurs*, that place where one might get back one's snatched passport, if lucky, for a generous ransom.

It was in French that she spoke to the young olive-skinned, wide-eyed, Gabrielle, who had already expressed her desire to play with the aerial device. *"Quand ça vous conviendrait, madame, assurément."*

"Just curious: you seem very eager. Don't you have one yourself?"

"Not this. I'm rowing, kayaking and surfing, also doings lots of *planche à voiles,* but not this, even though everything with the wind I like and comes easy to me, having grown here with Papa."

"Your Mom, she doesn't live with you? Sorry for asking."

"Oh, no trouble, madame. No, she left us when I was only two. She may be in England now, with a *monsieur*, a sailor, not sure."

She lifted her thin shoulders, as though pointing them — needles into uncertainty. "Perhaps Papa knows, but he doesn't tell me stuff like this and I don't want to know it either, for she never came back to see me again, nor did she write me," she told her as though avoiding to face her saying all this, while lithely sneaking by her on all fours for balance from one end of the boat, which was a dinghy, in fact, to the other, making it wobble and roll a bit.

Now with her back to Yvonne, she asked, "Do you still have both your parents, madame?"

"No, my father passed away six years ago from cancer, back in Canada. But he's the one who introduced me to the kites, so what you're seeing now is somehow a bit of what he showed me whenever he had the time."

"Is it difficult?"

"Oh, no; on the contrary, it's very pleasant. You just need to be responsive."

"Responsive? I'm not sure I know the word."

"Well, attentive and fast, doing things immediately when needed, you know. Quick on the uptake on what the winds are asking from you."

"Then I don't think I should have any problems with it: I'm good at sports. Better than many boys, they say in my school."

Yvonne liked the youthful braggadocio of the girl and that she had somehow been able to get her out of the darker story on her mother, especially as she didn't like to have on her conscience the bad moods of others.

"Do you know how to swim, madame?"

"Course I do. Do you think I'd be otherwise in the middle of a sea, well, I mean far enough from the shore, even as beautiful a sea as the Mediterranean, even under your kind mermaid-like protection, if I didn't?" She laughed at her. "Forget about this splendid azure sky. Even though we can easily see the shore from out here, one wrong move and we're really in deep water. Now then, as far as I know, there aren't any sharks here, are there?"

"Nooo, *nothing* like that, don't worry, madame. No *Jaws* here."

"Ah, you know the movie?"

"Sure, I saw it, brrr." She shook her copper-toned elbows and shoulders, shivering with faked fear. "Ah, I wanted to ask you this, madame. *Mon papa* told me you're a ballerina. 'That true?"

"Well, I'm more or less a former ballerina now. But how did he learn about it? I sure didn't tell *ton papa* any such thing, and he didn't ask."

"He told me that's easy to tell from your turned-out walk and straight back. Like a *grande poupée* walking, he said."

"He said that, did he?" Yvonne released a wry smile. "Then, he must have good eyes, your father. Yes, after years of practice, we're probably getting those things, they become part and parcel of us, and they cling to us as sticky tape, whether we like it or not. But I can't lie to you, we usually like it. It's trained in us to like it. Some ballet teachers think it's part of our *noblesse oblige*, you know."

"D'you mean, dancing princes and princesses should make you walk like them, stiff-like?"

"Let me see, Gabrielle. I haven't known well a lot of the *beau monde* in my life, even though surely I've met many, but those that I know, though they may be pompous at times in dress or words or haughty in manner, they certainly don't walk like that. *Quand même*, perhaps they did it once, or perhaps it's just something introduced in ballet by *Louis XIV, le grand roi*, who loved to dance and, I'm sure, didn't want to lose anything of his dignity when doing it. So he might have changed the lines the body was supposed to have while dancing, what we call now in classical ballet the proper attitudes, stances and so forth, to be more like what he liked, or wanted to do or to see. Being a king makes it easy to have your decrees out in the open and heeded, I think you can imagine that," Yvonne went on, laughing a bit.

"So, why don't you dance any more?"

"Ballet's for younger people, I mean in body, Gabrielle, and I'm getting into my — quote wiser and mellower unquote — years now. Do you know what 'quote unquote' means?"

"Something like 'perhaps?'"

"Not quite, but not too far from it. Good enough. But closer to 'so called,' that is, calling something as something else, even though we're not quite sure they are the same.

"Je crois que j'ai compris maintenant, madame."

"OK, then.

"Anyway, it's a rough art that way, I mean rough on the soul, just when you *think* you're getting the whiff of enjoying it all, getting really better at it, even getting to make out the sharp edge of mastery at the horizon, just then it's yanked from you in a flash."

"Ça veut dire, ça a été vraiment dur pour vous, cesser de danser?'

"Not rough on the body, this break, though, as by now you must've had all imaginable pains and bruises, broken bones, ligaments, surgeries, months spent in rehab, the whole shebang, all paid for with your ten years out on the stage, under the lights, even in the corps, if you've been lucky. *Donc*, in some respects, you've been looking forward to a respite. Only problem is, when the break comes, it's pretty much forever; you just don't know it, many times, for quite a while. So, when you're going back, your place is taken, as in a bad movie or dream, and you're the only surprised party.

"I'd like to take a dip in the water, just here, around the boat, so I'll need you to man my kite. Want to do that?" she asked the girl.

"Very much so. What do I have to do?"

"Not much for the time being, as the winds are steady and it seems to be in control up there where it is." Yvonne had a pair of thin beige suede gloves on to protect her skin from abrasion. "Just put on my gloves, here they are, so you won't get your skin peeled off by mistake if winds suddenly yank at him. Now, using both hands, one above the other, give it a bit of line, then pull it back. Nothing too fast. OK, let's go, I'm going to double you up on the lower part of the line coming off your hands, just in case. Even more, it's fixed on the boat, so even if you lose it from your hands for just a moment, it's still anchored somewhere and we'll get it to listen again.

"Come on, easy does it. Tha-aat's right." The girl was giving some rein off to the Elephant, and it popped just a whiff higher.

"Yes, I see, it really climbs a bit," the girl said, laughing with enjoyment.

"Course it does. There are climbing currents at work right now, I felt them earlier. OK, keep steady, I'll get into the water for just ten minutes or so, just around here, within your sight, so we can shout at each other. I need to limber out a bit and feel these small waves beat on me. In emergencies, you know what to do? Call your father on the radio, as we discussed this morning, remember? Hopefully nothing happens to us three, I mean the kite and us two, while I'm enjoying the sea."

Five minutes later, she splashed head first into the waves. The feeling of buoyancy and suspension, how one cannot have that on dry land! The water all around her, the *velouté* feel, it swishing noiselessly between and around her legs, over her breasts and chest enjoying its sweet warmth of summer, underneath around her extended back when in backstroke. The precious salty water sharing her nose and her mouth during dips and swings of the head and inhalations, sputtered away in the giving back of the air to the whole space of where she was. And, whenever she was on her back, the sky so terrifically blue just above, as a very large plate serving up everything, her existence at that, as though more than half the world was there at those times and the other half was underneath her in unfathomable depths. The high of moving for herself, of tending to her own muscular pleasures, of having no one peeking at her save for the girl and of having most of herself masked from any keen spectators by the mass of water.

Now and then, spoiling herself in floating with practically no swimming strokes on her back, her line of sight went up high above to the kite, to that neighborhood of it from where, slightly colored and point-like, it radiated its presence back to her, the feelings of altitude, of winds and natural attendance, sky, clouds, sun, illuminated and transparent air, all up there around it, of another space that conjoined her most direct one, the sensuous one, and that of her dreams, those deep beneath her — just like the sea, in unfathomable depth extending the physical near. The trinity was there and she had just to extend her mind to accept it, to let herself be imbued by it and its radiance, its deep meaning.

The top layer of the immense water, the one in which transparence still had its place under her sight in her short plunges from the surface level, was blue from the sky and the sun and from the blue blackness underneath. It was there that shadows, silhouettes, lighted contours, flowing motions of unidentified things, concerts of the fluids of water and air, showed up and

Marius Hancu

dizzyingly ran their courses past her, in and out of her mind too. Yet it was as though in this age and season she was more aware of them than in times past, the eyes of her mind hungrier for them and catching their flashes more readily now.

***

She was back onboard now and, in another quarter of an hour, the girl's curiosity was still at it, unabated.

"Alors, qu'est-ce que vous voulez faire maintenant dans votre vie?"

"Wow, what a serious question for a girl just ten! What I'm going to do now? Guess this is just what I myself am trying to find out!" Yvonne said to herself but she didn't utter anything for a couple of minutes, just playing with the line of the kite, mainly freeing it to go up. "Good vertical draft again" she said louder at the end of this lull in the conversation. "These kids must learn to wait for their answers like all of us have done before them and that many a time there are simply no answers. Laying an egg takes time too, not to speak about a beautiful one."

"Me, I just want to enjoy myself," the girl said, jumping to other things. "I can't sit cooped up in the house to study, I like much more being out in the free air."

"But did you try to study outdoors? Like taking a book out to a park?"

"Well, that probably works if it's a book of stories or adventures, even though I am not doing it too much, but I can't imagine taking out my books on arithmetic. Many children would laugh at me, they surely would. Like, Gabrielle, she's cramming all the time."

"Somehow, you'll have to learn to live for your own pleasure and not for the opinions of others. It that's a book of math that you want or need to have with you at that particular moment, take it and laugh back at the idiots."

"Now, that's surely won't make me popular, and girls must try to be popular, isn't it?"

"Never felt that need."

"But you are so beautiful, you must've been hugely popular in school, weren't you?"

"Thank you for the compliments, young lady." She affected a prim smile and slight bow at her. "I don't think I ever was that way; reason is, I think, I never curried the favors of others, be they teachers or guys or girls in my class, and, looking back I believe some may have resented it."

"Neither do I. They call me *sauvage Gabrielle*. They tell me I barely climbed down from the tree, like Tarzan."

"Tarzan's good company to be in, don't be embarrassed."

"I'm not, but then I'm not getting too many invites to children's parties, people say I'm trouble. Yet, I'm not sure what they mean and not knowing bothers me."

"Not knowing rankles you? This is, some believe, the sign of a discoverer. You may be one of them, God willing. Where, I don't know; ah, where your curiosity should prove highest *à la longue*, that's where."

"God willing? Are you are believer, madame? I'm not sure I've been one since I lost my mother, or she lost me."

"I probably am, but then I must be a negligent and a lazy one, as I haven't been in a church in months, and the last time I was for someone else."

"For someone else?"

"Ah, sorry, for another ballerina, a friend. On her wedding."

"Was it beautiful? Many people?"

"Many people, yes. Beautiful? They, the couple, were beautiful. The church, nothing special, one in Toronto. The party was simple. Now you have all the adjectives."

"Adjectives! That's trouble for me, the grammar."

"Shouldn't be. Nothing too fancy. Just keep reading books and it'll visit your mind willy-nilly."

"Visit my mind — I like the sound of it. Travel and discovery books, that I sure like to read. Livingstone and Stanley, Jacques Cartier and so on."

"Ah, you know Cartier? My father was born in St-Malo, Cartier's hometown.

"What you just said. Whenever you know what you like,

consider yourself happy, as if you've just won a fight. A fight with that tiny demon of uncertainty that's never too far from any of us. Or with yourself too, if you're not a believer."

"Oh, I certainly believe there's demons." And, a bit later, "Sorry to ask, madame. Have you ever been married?"

Yvonne looked at her carefully for what to the girl appeared to be quite a while. *She's asking the tough questions.* "Just between you and me, not even close. It never was on my mind. I may want children though, even if they're the trouble that you're rumored to be." She cracked out a laugh.

19 - Denmark, Sweden, 1984

She would like to know this, as it's come to a head in her mind.

***

Any real principles to me — call on the big word, Yvonne, now you did it — things to which I agree, in full awareness of them, or that I've discovered myself, and not because they were handed down to me, as in a testament covered by starchy-dry but bloodied covers, by school, church, parents? Am I really *responsible*? What's *that*, for that matter, how does it color, and why should *I*, in fact, be that way? Should I carry this yoke? Why not live and let live, including myself?

I'm writing a story, and the worst thing about it is the prologue was written by others, my parents, as it were, and I started to come in upon the scene to write it by my own mind and hand only after lots of pages were already done and over with and sometimes smeared in such a thick, heavy ink that I may not easily straighten things out around here to my liking. Trying to fix and re-draw a rough Van Gogh with super-fine pointillistic touches when the sun is hot high up in your own life, not only in Van Gogh's out in Arles, and you don't see any hideouts from it, and when it's as though you have better items on the agenda, that would give one an idea about this enterprise — now, that's dicey, to say the least.

High up on the edge of a ledge I am, and any reckless move would send me dropping as a hurtful word down into the chasm opening underneath.

***

She was thirty-two then, and, to her, a thin skeet clay disk up in the air, time was starting to shoot too close for comfort and that wasn't her only fight. She felt at times as though two great rivers came to a boil against each other in her, a watershed in her own body and soul, and she was a prisoner of the show, unable to take her eyes off it, fascinated — to the loss of herself. There was this place for her, and another one for others; then, in this parallel domain, still in her, there was this place of seeing and this other place, of action, and there were deep crevasses all over between these places, making them into islands.

She would see things around her to which she wanted to or had to react, would make up her mind about them, and only minutes later, her actions wouldn't fit at all with her inner decisions, as if a broken watch mechanism had taken on its own on a strange journey and was pressing buttons and pulling levers left and right to which she replied in compliance, with no real power to stop it or to redirect this rush. Her actions seemed at such times to be inspired by some cochlear implant or pacemaker working in her and implementing programs set up in them by unknown others, and not by feelings of her own about the immediate world in touch with her.

Just two days ago, she couldn't sleep for half of the night, and she had decided that from the three men off and on in her life, Patrick, George and Jacques, she would need to choose the good and upstanding — what a word — man, whatever that would mean to her at that point in time, and stick with him; and by most of the measures and accounts, including those of her own, that had to be George. Still, only two hours later, she had called Jacques in Paris and scheduled a rendezvous with him the next week. Worst of all, during the entire call, there was no attempted backtracking, no doubts, as though she was on automatic pilot.

Guided by what? Solitude, overwhelming need for sex, George being over the Pond and Jacques close by in Europe, or going for the more readily available umbrella in the stall at the entrance, even though the less satisfactory when out again in the open under the rain of the critical side of her mind? Was there any intellectual discernment left to her, and if there was, was there any will to follow up on its proclamations or, to say it again in milder, more concessive words, recommendations?

Things being what they were, after she had, during the call, spilled a full cup of Turkish coffee over the writing desk of the friend in Denmark, a former assistant of Erik Bruhn's, there had been no impulse in her to clean up the mess; she'd let the pool, coldly and calmly, looking at it, spill even more around on the mahogany surface. *Lucky no one else was around at the time, to watch.* Only after the call ended, she had found it necessary to bring in some towels from the bathroom to restore apparent order; and, looking back, she realized there hadn't been any rush to make those corrections, no agitation. *Am I becoming indifferent?*

She walked inside herself as in a museum. Here, she came upon a Winged Victory of Samothrace, there, on some Elgin Marbles, and many a time, it was as though those exhibits had been brought in by unknown others, looting other countries or the fiefdoms of others only to enrich her, and she didn't want to carry the burden, she just wanted away, free of conditioning and prejudices, free of tether, be it historical or personal.

But many times, these were things collected by her own hands, only that now, or at other times of remorse or doubt, she didn't feel connected with what it had been to be her at that suspended and flimsy moment in time in the past, as though someone else had been involved, active participant and actress, and she didn't quite know whether to trust that person any more or just pull back or even rear up like an angry stallion.

Take this one at fifteen, at the National's school.

***

In ballet class, it happened at times that students from different years were put together, simply because there weren't enough ballet mistresses and those available had to take on more than one would normally see, even in a junior class as that. For quite some time, she had noticed this younger boy, probably twelve, definitely smaller in height than herself, who couldn't take his eyes off her. Streamlined as a match or a feather, collarbones prominent above a flat box-like chest with no pectorals to speak of, huge blue eyes searching for her from under bushy eyebrows that ridiculously at his age occupied most of his pale-pink face, so bushy that one could say they were his over-painted feature. He always wore a white tank top, showing pointy shoulders and the vertebrae when he turned. So he was very thin, all-bones pushing the skin as for evidence in some kind of trial of life in which he was being involved.

His regard, moist as a deer's, locked on her each time she entered the class. She could tell — or she imagined, and that was one of her issues she had to deal with, she *now* thought — from his always being early that either he liked to work hard, and in this was more conscientious than she, a difficult thing for boys at that age, or just that he wanted to make sure he could watch her make her own entrance.

On days when she was late to enter her usual class, too full already, and had to switch to a parallel one, she could see from the door his desperate look watching her departing. Still, he never had shown the courage to break ranks and come after her in the other hall, to continue his own class in the same shared space.

One day, she went to him in a beeline after class and told the stunned boy, "I'm Yvonne and I'd like to show you something."

He went gaga, not having spoken to her ever before, except most definitely in his ardent imagination, but followed her down the corridors of the school, she striding forward without looking back even for a glimpse, as though on a mission, confident of him being there, tethered in her wake.

So in a corner of the building she knocked on a door, and when no one answered pushed it in and yanked the boy in after her by one of his arms.

It was the janitor's room, populated by mops, buckets empty of water but still covered with the silt of many a washing done in any remote or distasteful place of the building, smelling of disinfectants and perhaps worse, of human waste, she thought in a flash of senses.

She hadn't used a lot of introduction.

"I know you want to see me, you know how. I'll do that for you, but only if you show me first. Come on, fast, there's not much time!" She pointed to his mid-section.

"You want me to – undress?" he babbled softly, lost.

"Of course, you dummy. Is there anything else to see?"

He didn't have much on him on the occasion. The top tank, started with it first, put it on a chair, then took off his ballet slippers, then slowly rolled down the tights to the ankles and lifted one leg, then another, to get out from them.

The skin was pale throughout, streaked by the thin blue veins of the adolescence, the face now injected with blood to the rafters. He was left only with the compact ballet slip.

"Want to take off this one too?"

"What do you think, Casanova?"

The pubis was covered by just a shade of hair, tribute to the age. The member was cold, and the temperature in the room didn't help.

"OK, fair enough, I see you're sleepy. Now me, as promised."

This was a young woman's body already. She was watching him throughout the disrobing, touching a smile on her lips, business-like, but not rushing, letting him know he was being observed. There was no tutu, as for class, so this part was simple. The tank top was burgundy, she took it over her head, with long arms and thin fingers pulling it up, the round shoulders heaving lightly. Then came the black sports bra, which showed two small but definite globes pushing. The points were looking up, and you could see there was no fat there, everything very firm and darting. There was a lull in the proceedings, as she unfastened with a jerking motion the clip at the back of the thin belt of the tights, long to the ankle. The pink thighs were round, not like those tight, long ones of the many of the other girls, her muscles encased in more rotundness. Very compact knees, then again, roundness in her calves. Nothing sharp. A skin which wasn't translucent, as though deeper, or more consistent, thicker, which couldn't be, of course, but it didn't give away anything behind it. Opaque.

She was left in a very narrow triangular slip, not much larger than a bikini. Parts of her, the shoulders, the upper sides of her breasts, were pink with excitement, the lips had opened up, the head jutting a bit backwards, challenging.

He moved back, as though to have a better angle, all eyes, not even breathing.

She casually pulled a bit sideways the slip and lowered it with two hands, with some procrastination to it all, but did not let it drop. She knew the floor was dirty. She put it on the same chair where his things were.

She made a turn of a pirouette, hands above her head in a V, "Voilà!" and looking at his now much firmer parts, proclaimed, with a point of her chin, "That's much better."

Then, with not much of a pause, "End of the show. You go out first."

***

This, in a way, was just the beginning of her troubles, she was telling Lena Braasch, her Danish friend. Lena was now a housewife in the countryside; still, just several years before, she had worked as an assistant for Erik Bruhn.

She took a long side look at her, smiled mischievously, and asked, "What do you mean by troubles?"

"Well, obviously, the boy, as shy as he was, still had a tongue, even more, still had buddies. The buddies having to be informed, the tongue worked and, discreetly but unavoidably, the news spread."

"That you had been seen in the buff?"

"Not only that, but willingly so; and the speculation grew that, perhaps, I might be interested in more. So lots of teenage boys in that school started to approach me, trying to show off their own stuff and of course, trying to go further. Not all of them were naïve, many of them full-grown young men of seventeen or so, itching to step out in the world or on the scene, after the graduation from the ballet school.

"The story never got to the teachers, thank God, or I'd have been shown the way out of the school. This just tells you how close the kids are sometimes to each other, and how far their doings are from whatever the adults think about them.

"The result was that among the boys I got more famous, without really doing *it,* except quite occasionally, than many of the girls who were putting it about with no real shame. It just tells you that a touch of titillation goes further than a ton of the real thing."

"'You talking about *Persona*?" asked Lena, and both laughed, as they had watched Bergman's movie together just days before, a private screening at Lena and Lars's home, on a night when Lars, Lena's husband, a cameraman, had been out for drinks somewhere in Jutland with the boys of his film company. "Somehow, I don't think he expects us girls to watch *Hamlet*, not tonight, even though we *are* in Denmark," Lena had, with a devilish snicker, said at the time, inserting the video cassette in the Philips VT.

20 - Denmark, 1984

Her *port du bras* went up. Arms issued muscular, nicely padded, from the shoulders, growing thin and long quickly toward the elbows and the wrists, up above her head, going slowly to one-eighth down, everything from the shoulders, nothing from the elbows, measured, tempered. Her dear old arms, as Mrs. Johnson would have said, but Yvonne wasn't inclined to any self-complaisance on this day.

Thirty-two, still at it, and with all the pleasure and fanaticism of old. Question was, "For how long?" She had started to yank from the air and digest uncomfortably rumors among the corps that her days as a ballerina might be numbered, and she knew within herself she couldn't offer any guarantees of the contrary. She still felt great, flexible, full of young animal energy. However, the main point was, how others would go about it, the powers that be. Not everyone gets to dance for as long as Martha Graham or Alicia Alonso had done. In New York City, they hadn't been too kind about it, giving her walking papers, nice of course, accompanied by the greatest and the glowing of recommendations, but the point of not quite wanting her any more had been scored with her and, worst of all, with others in the community at large.

What would come after that? Well, it would be what Mrs. Johnson herself had once been doing, teaching the newcomers, the upstarts, the new generations of boys and girls knocking more or less aggressively, as was their wont, at the gates of the empire, what the great art was all about, the tiny details — which still took years to learn or perfect even if you had the talent and the *je ne sais quoi* in gigantic heaps — that made you accomplished at it, perhaps even magical at times while showing it on a stage, even in a tiny lost corner of the world, so people would pay for it and be thankful for being able to share a bit of it with you.

Through Lena and her contacts, Yvonne had arranged to take class with the Royal Danish Ballet while in Denmark.

She took the bus every day of the week from Lyngby to Copenhagen. Clean, not crowded, coming-on-the minute busses. She was delighted to see the bike tracks on the side of the road — there's a real sign of civilization, she thought.

She had a difficulty these days with the travelling on pointes to the sides, the whole of her foot caught in a nasty swelling, the pain hitting now and then, as an express freighter coming unexpectedly out of a tunnel, with you right in the middle of the tracks, out for a pleasure walk. She had iced it in the bathtub at Lena's, but it hadn't receded, not nearly enough. Those pictures of Nureyev's legs by Avedon, heavily swollen veins and all, did justice to the grueling task of a dancer, she quipped to herself. In bed, several times she had drawn the feet close underneath her, to massage them deep to the bone with two hands. Not much effect, she'd found in the morning. She had to see a physio in the afternoon. There were many in the Danish capital, she just had to pick one and act on it. She castigated herself many a time that she had carried pains within herself for too long without taking care of them, and she didn't want to play Mother Theresa on herself.

She was seated on the right side of the bus. Right in front of her sat a white-haired older woman, perhaps a grandmother going to Copenhagen to buy gifts for her grandchildren's anniversary or just to visit again the Tivoli or the Christianborg Castle or shop on Strøget.

Yvonne had noticed her when the lady had climbed with some effort the steep stairs in front of the bus, a little bit overweight, and huffing and puffing from the short exertion. She was quite tall and wide for a Dane, and looked out the window frequently, as though she hadn't known the area for years. Suddenly, she turned to Yvonne and asked her in perfect English:

"Excuse me, madam, would you know what time it is? I have left my watch at home."

"It's eight-thirty, madam. By the way, I'm surprised you knew I spoke English."

Marius Hancu

"Oh, I've no difficulty identifying you Americans. I was married to one of you for forty years, until my Jeremy passed away two summers ago from a stroke. We met each other in England during the war. One year ago — loneliness, you know, striking again — I married a Danish old timer and moved over here. And of course, you Americans dress more conservatively than we do over here."

"You must be going into Copenhagen?"

"Yes," Yvonne replied. "In fact, I'm a Canadian. I have a ballet class to attend at nine."

"Don't tell me you're a ballerina! But of course, I should have realized that, your pretty face and short-cropped hair should have given you away. Still, my senses aren't what they used to be, my eyes, especially, so I'm missing things that years ago I'd've caught right away."

The woman was by now half-turned toward Yvonne, something that Yvonne thought would not have been forthcoming from a regular Danish person under most circumstances. Forty years with an American sometimes has that effect on you, she thought.

Then, in an apparent desire to be more discreet, the woman suddenly turned toward the bus window to her right and started to talk over her shoulder to Yvonne, right behind her, while facing the glass, in a low, personal tone.

"Would you care to play a game of chess with me?"

"Chess? Well, in fact, I haven't played it in ten years, my father was my regular partner and he passed away two years ago, unfortunately. Still, where would we be able to do that?"

"Well, of course, on a bench in Tivoli, or in the Langelinie park close to the 'Little Mermaid.' It's quite nice there on the edge of the water, you can hear the chess pieces shuffling on the table, it's so quiet. Of course, that'd be later, in the afternoon, after your class."

"I'm not sure, but I think I can make it for one o'clock, to allow for lunch." She had felt the challenge and the strangeness of it, but she felt up to it.

"Oh, but we can have lunch together in one of the nice restaurants right in front of the Tivoli, or inside."

Yvonne didn't say anything to this, but this didn't resonate well with her, as she had been keeping the purse-strings tied tightly lately;

with no certain job to speak of to generate income there was a strain. So she tried to avoid unnecessary expenses.

Also, this whole conversation, while the bus was moving over the Danish plains, had a strange air to Yvonne, so she pulled back a little into her chair. The old dame, feeling that, stopped her flow, after telling her in a short whisper, "OK then, at one, in front of Tivoli. See you there, dear."

They got off at different stations within Copenhagen, the old woman first, waving a short good-bye from the door of the bus, then Yvonne, two stops later.

Her class was uneventful and by the appointed time, she was in front of Tivoli, wondering what her new acquaintance may be about. There was this feeling of unease in her of having jumped into something without thinking too much ahead. Old people can sometimes be strange, who knew what kook she was supposed to meet over lunch?

The only thing she had with her on that day was a bright-red duffel bag, but this made her conspicuous enough, together with her short curly hair, so her acquaintance, when she arrived ten minutes late, had no problems in locating her.

"Let's get in this restaurant, they always have great salads, and I've no doubt you like them," she expansively exclaimed.

"Well, fine, however I need to warn you I can't eat anything too fattening."

"I'd imagined you'd say so. Coming from a ballerina, I get it. Much more than from half of my girlfriends, all like me, in their sixties or seventies, still fussy about their silhouettes. As though eligible marriage partners would wait at each street corner for them or they'd be invited to, sorry, Jesus's second coming. Phooey!"

They went in and sat at a corner table, in a room with tall windows starting at the floor, the light of a late summer coming in at a relaxed flutter, and the first thing the old lady did, before even getting a look at the menu list, was to take out a small chess set in alabaster and ivory from her small travel bag and open it on the corner of the table between them.

"Ready to play?" she asked with anxiety.

"Shouldn't we order first?" Yvonne asked, not wanting to irritate the waiter corps.

"Oh, nonsense, don't look at them, they're gonna show up here anyway, don't you worry."

Yvonne was more than aware this was lunch time, with tables at a premium, and wanted for heavy, multiple-course orders. Lucky for them perhaps, this wasn't a very busy day, so the waiter in that section let them settle themselves comfortably to start their chess game, and only then showed up, and with extreme politeness asked, "Good afternoon. Would you like to order something?"

"I think we'll be ready to order in five minutes. We need to scope out the menu first," the old lady said to him, to which he retired in the corner, continuing to observe with Nordic calm the developments around the hall.

"Black or White?" the Danish lady asked Yvonne, to which she recoiled a bit under so much ineluctable insistence, then recovered, "Black would be fine."

"OK, so you let me take the initiative. Don't worry, will do. But let's grant these Danish boys a favor and think for just a moment about our orders. I'm going for salmon and eggs salad. How about yourself?"

"Just salmon for me would be fine. I'll also order some orange juice, can't eat too well without some liquid, I feel dehydrated." Yvonne felt the need to apologize.

"Feel welcome to do exactly what you feel like doing," her partner said nonchalantly, with a flat, indifferent voice, at the limit of politeness, putting aside the menu cards and making a discrete sign to the waiter, meaning he would be accepted in the environs to show up and take the order, something that was done quite expeditiously and discreetely, almost furtively, one could have said, by the young man. Then the old woman plunged into considering an opening for her game, and advancing her right center pawn for two squares seemed to suit her mood just fine.

Yvonne detached herself from the game at hand for the flash of a moment and thought about the black and the white — in any medium. They did, to her mind at the time, so much break into a contrast, absorbing all colors, on a side, and reflecting all of them, on the other, that she thought she'd just found something that could flow into a ballet. Two opposing camps having a go at it with simulated, however absent, medieval armor and weapons, nothing real, something like the final scene in *Blow-Up* by Antonioni, until no one was really left alive on the chequered battlefield. Kings would order simple-minded pawns into trenches, bishops would be dropped into the heat of the battle, as paratroopers are, into the most critical areas of the battle from ropes anchored high up above the stage, queens would hide themselves behind rooks to deliver killing blows right and left and diagonally.

"You look absent-minded, dear," the old lady cut into her dreaming. "Your move."

So Yvonne, surprised *in flagrante,* moved the opposite pawn for an equal advance, but didn't lose her composure — that would have meant an unusual turn of events for her, no doubt.

The old lady was well-engrossed in the competition or, rather, fight, should the observer have taken an unbiased look at the proceedings. So much so, that she didn't utter a grand total of more than five words by the time the game ended not less than an hour later. Her blood pressure must have gone considerably higher toward the end, as the color of her face turned blood-red, her mouth went gaping, while her breathing became audibly harder, only to preface a "Gosh, I can't really believe this!" just after Yvonne checkmated her. The old lady's salad was left untouched and she seemed to have lost her appetite.

"You must be playing chess quite frequently," she said.

"As a matter of fact, I haven't played since my father passed away, and it's several years since, as I've told you." Yvonne had to disappoint her — something too pushy in her partner's attitude was upsetting her. "Your husband must have been a New Yorker?" she casually asked.

"Indeed! How would you know that?"

"Just a feeling," Yvonne replied, not willing to enter the mined terrain of how the inhabitants of the great city inclined in behavior, one way or another, or to be openly seen as advancing generalizations from her personal experience, something which she herself didn't find ingratiating in others.

The old lady had in one fashion or another completed her

mourning for the lost game and was presently contemplating better futures, developments and outcomes in upcoming ones, so in the end she switched to food and more worldly passions. Her salad thusly became a thing of the past and, of better humor already, she rummaged through her dark red handbag and took out triumphantly a dog-eared notebook, "This is my — what do you young people call it these days — ah, I know, my black book."

"You mean, the addresses of your gentleman friends in *those* years?" Yvonne asked, not wanting to add, "of your youth?" so as not to wither the feelings of the golden-age flower.

"You bet." Mischievously the other laughed with a just-between-you-and-me tone that edged on the strange that made Yvonne more curious as to what the old dame wanted to put forward as tokens of past glorious significance in this world.

"Look at him, Johnnie Sandhauser, he was one of Ike's aide-de-camps, a major, three kids back in Texas, buxom lady, if I were to believe the pics he showed me of the conjugal camp. We met at the end of '43, and believe it or not, he told me the date of D-Day two weeks in advance."

"Sorry, but how could that be? My father told me the weather was so bad at the time, that Ike himself didn't know what was going to be."

"Well, you do what you want to do," the woman told her, acting hurt, but I'll tell you that between sheets many things transpire between a man and a woman. Lucky for them, I was on the right side. Not a Mata Hari, me. Yes, he was a fine tall thin man, à la Jimmy Stewart, Johnnie was. He came to me with chocolates and nice French wine — you'd wonder where they got such stuff during a world war, but this is why they called him *aide-de-camp*, the Frenchies, I guess — but I'd have taken him anyway," she giggled like a teenager.

"Were you already engaged to your husband by then?" Yvonne cheekily inserted.

"Oh, no, I'm not that bad of a sort, you know, we were only on and off, no firm ties yet, both of us still playing the field, we were, that point in time. We married each other late in '45, after the VJ day. Me, I would never have married *anyone* during the war. Not for me the worries, no sir, I mean, no, madam."

"And where exactly did you live during the war? Was it London?"

"I was an RAF driver and secretary, most of the time. Can't complain, most of them dashing fellows, shorter lives though, that was the pain in that service, seeing them coming from training and going to unknown horizons never to be seen back again.

"By the way, just in case we may become friends, my name's Jessica. Kathy Parker, after my Johnnie, née Stevens. High-school in Wales, war mostly around Birmingham — you've just asked about it — and you may know how tested we were there."

"Glad to have met you, Mrs. Parker. I'm Yvonne Fillon."

"Then, you might be a Canadian, and not an American as I wrongly assumed all the time. How stupid of me."

"Indeed, a Canadian, but don't worry too much about the confusion. People are the same regardless of the passport, aren't they, Mrs. Parker?"

"I'm not so sure about that, I, for one, am still more comfortable with my own Anglo-Saxon, even WASP-ish, stock. I understand them easier, or I think I do. Rough necks or dandies they may be, I allow, still, they take the same compass I am familiar with, as one said in the RAF, about doing things. Not that I mind other people, say the French — and I apologize, as you've just told me your Pa was French — or the Germans, but at least I know how we say we like people or things, and how we say we don't like them, there are no ifs and buts or a mental torticollis about it, if you catch my whiff."

Something started to run and spin in Yvonne's mind, something playing on sameness and compatibility, how people limit and filter out contacts and interactions following their own prejudices. It looked a bit like "West Side Story," with rival camps, though in her putative ballet things weren't defined as specifically as in the musical, but mostly reflecting an abstract sort of belonging. The camps were shown by color, color of skin, color of dress, and the costumes were to reflect that. And with the immediate suggestions of chess, she would have at the time said the black and white would have been a good choice, no doubt. Each camp would endeavor to encircle and immobilize the other's king. Circles and spirals would be run and webbed around them. Loyalty, personal history, were to be abstracted in colors and would be, just as in chess, automatic, no questions asked.

Yvonne had tried to extract from the old lady what might have pushed her to speak to her, with not much success though, except for what she considered to be generalities. "You know, just the old thing," Mrs. Parker put forward, "a chess player feeling there's another one in front of him, ready or willing to perhaps take up a challenge, just as you, in fact, did. The feeling of foreignness, of a North-American in saddle around me, definitely spurred on my curiosity. Not insignficant, dear, is the fact that after a certain age you can't talk to anyone known on this world, with most, if not all, acquaintances gone over. So one must open up to new faces or people in one's life, or the doors of the grave will be above you sooner than expected, if not in body, in spirit. And when your partner of a lifetime leaves you alone on this world, as it happened to me, then you feel the need of company, you really do."

Yvonne mentally contemplated a chess table in black and white on the floor of the stage, that legendary sprung dance floor made from wood flexible enough so as not to hurt the dancers in their jumps and landings. The first part of this piece would follow the rules of engagement of chess, while the second part would be a general mêlée, with dancers in anguish from a general catastrophe, running around in total disorientation, asking for directions from each other and not getting them or getting them too jumbled for anyone to make any sense of them. Imagine the aftermath of a tsunami, she thought, everybody looking for someone, families dispersed and stranded, the nature roused to its worst, leaves the only thing left from once glorious trees, houses flattened or pulverized, disaster, and the words, the communication at its most primitive, not being able to say enough or to have saved them through warning. There would be the rigid societal order of the first part, in demonic contrast with the disarray of the second, defined trajectories versus flutter in going around lost and with no grace or order. The death by man against the death by nature. Imagine the first played by samurai and the second by subservient peasants in an imaginary Japan, she thought to herself.

"I think you lost me." The older woman laughed at Yvonne's obvious dreaming up of stories in some ether or other. "Feel free to, I'm just a hag anchored in times long past."

"Sorry to be absentminded at times, it's part of my work. I need to think about some new work, and am seemingly doing it at the most inopportune of times, I mean for my company."

"Focus is, to a large extent, a property of young people, thus lose yourself in it, if you can afford it. Is this something you yourself are going to dance?"

"That's a tough question. Most probably not. I might be out of the direct part of dancing by the time this comes about on some stage somewhere out in the world. I'm old enough — hope you appreciate I'm not saying anything about maturity — to realize that I can't dance everything I might want in this short a dancer's career."

The lady looked at her as though to a strange appearance in her sight, baffled, but didn't say anything. "Your garden is infinite, God." This she seemed to have related to her recent chess rival, with some limited pity, as you can't quite comfortably say something like that, not if you wanted to remain unpunished by those hidden gods of chess.

21 - Monte Carlo, 1985

There hadn't been much that went her way during the latest month, mostly indifference in spades was what she had found wherever she had tried to open new doors, for the old ones seemed to have been already knocked at to no avail.

***

I went to Nice on one of those days and on that terrific spring afternoon I saw most of the flowers in bloom on the *Promenades des Anglais.* Only that somehow they weren't exactly what I had expected in the torrid hours of my waiting for news on my new job or for, just between us, news from self, some ideas to follow, some energy to spare, but just a comical replica that wouldn't have been accepted as decoration even on some of the most desperate TV talk shows around — or so the flowers looked to me at the time, which was perhaps a fair measure of the foul mood I was in. So I deflected my path to a museum showing Chagall on huge panels and glass panes, pastel colors flowing through and from the skies in buckets and loads, and that, toward the end of the day, brought me to calmer waters. I thought that if someone else had juggled this stuff in advanced old age, while moving others and waking them to live again with some imagination alit under their bottoms in the process, there could still be a glimmer of light in the tunnel for me too, I not having reached even middle course, hopefully.

To be able to talk to myself in this journal is encouraging fact. Silence isn't pleasant to bear, especially when locked in with the dangerous animal of 'I' in the cramped cell of loneliness.

This morning, there was a feeling of something new arriving from the unknown, something that had to be good in nature and promising, enough to move me to see the upcoming day in a better light.

A ball was coming within a week or so and I had to be prepared for it. I'd made a promise to Carla Verdis who was visiting friends in Monte Carlo at the time, something that brought us together in a stroke of fortune.

"You know," she had told me, "this is the only time I can go out in the world with Gérald. In Paris that would be an absolute faux-pas with his wife patrolling *comme un aigle* everything in sight in the society there. So, if you want to bask in our glory as a couple, come on the 17th of July at the *Marius and Cosette*, the new mansion up on the hill, owned by the duc de Gendronnes, or, says I, by his Russian-American painter-cum-*amante*-cum-financier, Gala-Zoë. By the way, don't you feel one 'cum' is enough? There will be at least the two of us, Gérald and myself, as old-timers, to welcome you to the ball. Usually it's quite a zoo on party days, if you ask me."

"What would I be showing as? I mean, in what capacity, what role am I cast or should I be casting myself into? No one has even heard of me in Monte Carlo, except the people at the Ballet, and they might be already fed up with me for crashing the morning class."

"OK, so you agree this lack of visibility of yours is something which needs correcting. Just by this, great progress has been recorded on your part — tongue-in-cheek, dear, hope you've realized that already. Well, things being as they are, the best way to right things with the toffs here is to show up in full splendor and regalia, and most importantly of all, in great *nonchalance*, when a ball given by one of the *top twenty* opens up its invitation list. And they've opened it for you, as you already have the glossy invitation, haven't you, you little devil you?"

"Yes, I have it, and appreciate that. I know that much that without your barging in on my behalf they would never have taken me in." I laughed ironically at her.

"Don't mention it, my dear, you're treading mined ground. If *I* mention it, you're really in trouble, it means I need something in return. Also, as you darn well know, I don't go for the small things, the knickknacks, but am" — she laughed again — "shooting for the stars.

"Now, getting back to *nos moutons*," Carla continued, "Do you need a gentleman to escort you to the party and keep you company there? Say just a word; I can easily put the memory of my own black book at your disposal, and *le choix* will be yours. I won't force-feed you any of my former *amis de coeur,* don't worry, promise."

"Carla dear, I am convinced your former boyfriends are eminently workable, as it were, to use a word a bit on the raw side for my taste, but no, thanks," I said.

This conversation taking place in the café at 'Loews,' there was just the time and place to go out together to do some last-minute shopping for the occasion. So we jumped in her Citroën 2cv and we were over in Nice within the hour. I like to shop where I can afford, and Monaco just isn't that way, broke dancer with no sugar daddies that I am.

I bought several silk scarves — men always tell me my long neck looks good — that is, even longer — in them. So be it, I'll accede to their kind, but interested, pointers: I should consider the other fishes in the pond, even though some of them might be piranhas. One of the scarves is shimmering white, just the tone to wear with my dark velvet décolletée dress. Décolletée in both front but also at the back, plunging pretty close to the waist.

I brought over shoes — high stiletto heels, no less — from America. Mind you, they're in the end Italian, so one could say, and Carla does exactly that, defending the interests of the Old Continent, that Europe is all over me in fashion terms.

The party is supposed to start at six in the evening, however Carla warns me not, repeat not, under any circumstances, to show up before nine, as this should be a long affair, well into the wee hours of the morning, and the hosts, while being the *crème de la crème* of politeness, don't want to be stuck with you in their sights for too long.

"But don't worry," she says, "the expanse of the place is such that you'd be hard pressed to see anyone, not just the hosts, twice on that night. The main point of attraction, one should think, would be that this being a bal masqué, you aren't supposed to know to whom you're talking anyway at a given point in time, or at least that is the part you're supposed to play. And they have this underground-under-the-mountain under the Mont Agel slopes tunnel which is a huge maze where the main party is going to take place, so chance is you won't meet many faces — or, as a matter of fact, masks — twice for the whole duration of the night."

"Tunnel? This sounds already awfully claustrophobic to me. I'd've hoped to be able to take a peek at the blue — sorry, night — sky and breathe the whiff of some fresh breeze off the Mediterranean now and then, party or not, you know."

"Nothing claustrophobic to it," Carla said. "Pretty wide lighting shafts have been bored here and there in the very mountain, so the sunlight or the outside darkness stream in unimpeded, true, only in some places, however, one needs to allow for the extremely tight place in Monte Carlo, with real estate at a premium, so you can't ask for too much."

"When was all this built, or bored? Fifties?"

"Nah, Gala-Zoë is much more recent in the *duc*'s life, also she's too young, relatively speaking, to have been involved in anything that remote. No, it was seventies, probably their middle part, the real estate here experienced a boom then and the *duc* seems to have been a sharp operator during all that time. But, yes, it was Gala-Zoë who convinced him to expand and build inside the mountain. 'Why not have a Sesam of your own?' she says she asked the duc at the time."

***

Three days later, she got a call from Carla.

"Listen, *le duc* wants to have a dancing part with classical music, something like a period dance, baroque perhaps, on a menuet or a gavotte, all those willing to dance it dressed in their regular party dresses and masks, nothing special, a small parade to open it and then everyone going through the slow motions of it, or, something that would bring around the pomp and dignity of old, he says. He wants the thing to have some authenticity to it and thinks that nothing would work better than your coaching some of the people which are to be in attendance to the required steps and moves, 'course only if you don't mind, eventually in advance, again, if you are willing and they get enough interested party-heads to show up for a non-dress rehearsal."

"OK, so in short I'm here to preclude any embarrassments, am I? And did you say non-dress rehearsal?"

"Well, if you want to put it this way — to preclude — fine, but a bit of fizz would be appreciated, especially as the press will be around. Also, non-dress, right. Anyway, you don't imagine anyone would be able or even willing to show up in advance for the rehearsal in the last-minute improvised togs in which they'll crash the real party. But if they do, so much the better."

One week later, I was in that rehearsal with a gaggle of twenty or so couples.

This rehearsal took place not in any tunnel — I understood those nether regions had been reserved for the real event — but in the grand salon of the ducal residence on ground level, all windows to the small garden open, as was my express recommendation, in order to discretely dissipate sweat by letting in some sea breeze, and to ruffle the feathers of everybody present to that degree of disturbance which is variously called being 'excited,' 'aware' and 'on the edge.'

This was, if there ever was one, a messy event. Even though fully informed of being scheduled for eleven a clock in the morning, most of the people showed up in fact only by noon time, so I really had to redo the whole introduction of the *courante* as the motif dance for the great day, showing the basic steps and the floor paths to be followed. The dance itself had been chosen in concert with *le duc*, who knew that *Le Grand Monarque* himself, a presumptive, but contested, I later learned from other sources, ancestor, had been the expert of his time in it. Still, the host had misgivings. "*Trop mélancolique,* we need to inject some *énergie,*" he said, so a *bourrée* — chosen after a bit of scrapping à trois with him and Gala-Zoë, who needed to be shown the moves for every dance twice, a darn slow learner, if you ever ask me — usually of a faster tempo, appeared the normal thing to top the suite of dances for that 'period' part of the party.

Carla didn't come to the rehearsal, and consequently neither was Gérald of the attendance, which was more than OK with me, as I didn't have to ingratiate myself with them, play polite, and thus risk cutting into my effectiveness as a taskmaster for the dancing part.

The *courante* was plangent all right, the one that they had on their tape recorder, and sounded well in their sound system, a Bang & Oluffsen I recognized from my New York time, this is where I agreed with the *duc*, but I for myself thought that all *malinconia* in it could be made to bring desire and mellowness to the crowd, not acid sadness, as he seems to have been afraid, and to drive the sexes toward each other in a decent, measured, aristocratic-for-our-time way.

"Like a good appetizer," said the *duc*.

"Why not," I replied, "isn't this, Your Highness, what you want to achieve with your party, bring or at least put people together, socializing?"

"I'd rather have you drop formality, Yvonne."

"Consider it done, Your Highness." I laughed back at him.

"*Très bien, alors,* what I'd really like to have is nothing, as you and I know, like what will happen. It's like a cocktail, mix everything and pray that the results aren't too shocking. I'm convinced your profession offers you plenty of the same surprises. Just think, let's say you have too prima donnas, sorry, prima ballerinas, placed in the same ballet, you'd probably agree, you never know what the concoction will look like if they have never played together and even then. Or would you say I am wrong?"

"I guess not, indeed, but you realize during the rehearsals what the chances for a mishap or even failure are."

"That's why we have one today."

"With one significant difference, if I may: many of our protagonists won't show up today. Being paid makes a lot of difference, I can assure you. Even prima donnas or prima ballerina assolutas can't neglect that, even though they might pretend they do."

Each of the dancers wore on their wrists small scarf-like bands of silk, a rainbow in their combination of colors, which I brought over on the same morning, borrowed from the Ballet de Monte Carlo's costumiers. I thought this would bring some unity to the ensemble, what with the mishmash everyone would be expected to show up in on the night of the party.

For the *courante*, I instructed them to show large, slow, and especially composed wafts in the air, their arms well away from the body, staying steady and level during their feet delicately landing on the ground or taking off from it in small increments — "crucify your arms, and land only on the balls of your feet, please, never on the heels, please, everyone" — and taking off lightly again. "You should dance it with the dignity and the poise of a king, remember Louis, he wasn't for nothing the best at it. Keep your faces still and serious, this should be all, the *courante*, a serious and dignified attempt at dancing on your behalf. Play the period, show the pomp. You'll have the opportunity to let go and show more of your own stunts, tricks and flavors, especially with arm movements, in the *bourrée*, should you want to. This one, however, is all about being pensive and in control. Still, don't forget to also use small bouncing steps: *Et notterez qu'il fault saulter les pas de la Courante*, as Thoinot Arbeau said in 1589. *Orchesographie*, what a nice name for a treatise of dance that was!"

They all marched dutifully *en ronde* and *en ligne* in the courante along the trajectories I had defined for them, peeking at their neighbors to make sure they were doing the same mistakes. All in all, a pretty considerate bunch, but let's see at the real party with all the booze and the other dissipations and carryings-on within touch.

I thought then of my father dying of cancer six years earlier. How he might have enjoyed knowing me in the neighborhood of France, the country of his ancestors and of his own for the whole of his childhood and youth, choreographing the old French dances. He had that remote pleasure in those things that one has in knowing that the local museum stores interesting stuff that sometime, perhaps in retirement, one would get to see at one's heart's will. Just that many times we don't get to those times of the retirement, or not much of them is made available to us — just what had happened to him — before all is done and over with and the ledger is closed with a clap in front of our nose after what many times remains just a curt forewarning notice is nailed to the doors of the cathedral or of the poor country church, wherever we are, because the time of the return to the *néant* is not prearranged for anyone, except for those who leave it all by their own sad fiat.

22 - Monte Carlo, 1985

The ladies went tiptoeing and hopping lightly along their designated path in the *courante* and feigned disinterest, their backs now to the gentlemen. Everything worked nicely, most of them sensed the music properly, I thought, didn't try to overdo it, allowing a bit of breezing and wafting in their moves, letting you know that they graciously skittered and fluttered over the parqueted floor from one place to another, no rushing, letting the wristbands sway only a bit in the air, an exercise of some restrained dignity.

The men, in turn, and I hope to God for the benefit of the species that most of them were gentle, just went about their business, the nose tips up, unruffled by the seemingly unfavorable breeze blowing in their sails from the other side of the floor over the sex divide, according to the thin storyline of the dance.

There were ten couples in the *courante*. The leading couple was a semi-professional pair of Russian immigrants who were at the time trying to get a foot in the door of the international ballroom circuit, both from what was once St. Petersburg, now Leningrad, but I figured with no real connections with the Kirov, even though they pretended to have been once there in the Vaganova's school in their incipient teenage years, whenever that might have been in time, how far back, it was only a matter of guessing. However, they were good at dropping names such as Nureyev, Dudinskaya, Soloviev, Baryshnikov as proof of their familiarity with the local gods and icons of the place. Honestly speaking, especially at this semi-amateurish level where we were with this party and its dances, one had to recognize in their bodies a certain quality of line, even though what good taste Vaganova's might have managed to instill in *them* was really doubtful. Once in the West these two had seemingly assumed that everything here must be strident or loud, Amerikan-ish, and that without being noticed in that respect, there was no chance for them in this marketplace. I knew real Kirov people first-hand, had danced with them in NYC, and Mischa Baryshnikov was one of them, thus I took this pair with some serious grain of salt, but they were good enough in this peculiar setting, enough for others to peek at them for some vague guidance and imitation.

Then there was the rich Swedish couple, not so young any more, probably approaching their fifties, though having seen the world over and danced in many corners of it, including in some nasty ones, if one listened to them over quiet vodkas churning their stories about brawls in some remote harbors in which, wonder of wonders, she was always the target of unwanted attentions and he the rescuing hero. They were decked out each and every time as for a parade, so getting in full togs for this particular party was probably a non-event for them. They knew well how to move on their toes, without major shocks and trepidations to the floor as in the case of others, he with his hand around her thin nimble waist, she with a bit of exaggerated lashing of the head, purposing to flutter her blonde mane through the air for obvious spectacular effect, as long it was, no doubt, and gold-shiny.

I was to find later that in their younger years, she had been a high-class call girl in Paris while they were both students at Sorbonne, with her income from those carnal proceedings making up the main of their day-to-day budget. Looking at that powerful, muscular, Amazonian body, I could easily believe that and more, as though reading about those actresses that another Swede had had in his control and in their turn had held him in their nets while making his many movies, some of them great. Double-edge swords they had played with each other, no doubt.

And this other couple, both French, both from the Alps, well-heeled *montagnards* from Haute-Savoie, climbing seriously each year Mont Blanc they were proud to belong to their province, the Matterhorn and some such, here mostly for the azurean sea and the view from the *falaise* where the Oceanographic Museum sits, happy to see this many people around them after the months of isolation in the mountains during their climbs. One could look at them and have the feeling that at any time they could leave civilization for rough nature, that their backpacks were just behind the door of the room in which they danced happily at that very moment.

They were very impetuous and impatient, this French couple, and I had to frown at them several times from the sides in order to tame them down during the *bouré* and to avoid this way that they step on the heels of other couples in front of them in the line formation — but their sincere enthusiasm, which others couldn't have bought for the world, made up for such slips.

***

The bomb had been hidden — as detailed by later police reports — under the proscenium, right in front of the small chamber orchestra hired for the day and at the time ending the *sarabande*, which was to have been the close of the pre-classical prelude to the party, ushering in the program segment in which the rock orchestra should have taken over. They had stood in waiting, the rock punks — as many of those in attendance thought about them, indeed while enjoying, in previous parties or shows throughout the *Côte d'Azur*, dancing to *their* kind of music — right behind the stage, and were strewn all over by fragments of bone, flesh and unmentionables of what had been the solid presence in this world, the incarnation of eight chamber musicians, five men and three women, as well as by pieces of their instruments, a combination of which went through the tall, thin, Japanese panels placed as a background on the stage on which at the end of the party the *duc* and Gala-Zoë were supposed to sit under small ducal thrones with simulated baldaquins over them as its sovereigns and receive the thunderous clapping of the by-then well-dined-and-wined audience, in a carefully planned climax.

As luck would have it, the back of the proscenium was chiefly in steel-reinforced concrete, and the explosives had been planted at the foot of it, most probably right before the start of the party; this way, all the power of the blast went, deflected, mainly toward the back of the side tunnel in which the orchestra was playing on the raised level of the stage, instead of blowing, pushing and crushing everything forward into the main tunnel, in which most of the party crowd was located, the majority of them still on the sides, as the direct attendance at the period dancing had been sparse, except for those already present at the rehearsal. People simply didn't want to embarrass themselves while dancing in an unfamiliar style. The concurrence of all these haphazard circumstances made it happen that there were no victims in the crowd proper.

At the time, Yvonne had been in one of the nine pairs in the *sarabande* taking the center of the floor, with each of the ladies revolving on delicate steps around her gentleman, the men arranged in a circle which they rotated slowly about itself, while moving on along it as the great wheel in a fairground. She had been tacitly passing visual pointers to the others for the whole duration of this pre-classical segment of the party, her fingers sending them with just well-disguised short curvings of the knuckles or flicks of the tips to a slightly-changed direction or freezing them on the spot, her eyes doing the same or expressing approval or discontent, her nose nodding in agreement with what she saw in the rolling-on of the dance in comparison with her plan, laid out for them during the rehearsal.

Her character for the party had been Hermes: wings were transparent-tape-affixed to her ankles, a short tunic like a gladiator's was tightened at her waist by a belt, dropping to just above knee level, her shoulders were free, and she had the caduceus, the kerikeyon, imprinted on both of her shoulders. Hands and legs were bare, no tights nor anything else, letting her pink-and-white-marmoreally-dappled skin breathe freely and show tight muscles underneath, rounded and well-defined around the knees and calves, the recognizable spindly structure of her legs generously displayed above white Roman sandals. Not for nothing had her ballet colleagues in NYC called her 'Towers.'

When a piece of shrapnel hit, right beside her, one of the dancers in one thigh, the Italian woman dropped to the floor in a faint. Upon seeing everything and everyone on the stage blown to bits, Yvonne had a moment's hesitation, which could have meant her end right then and there, had the explosion been setup in two stages. When she next realized she was in mortal danger, she threw herself to the ground, prone, trying to face away from the destruction and covering her head with her hands, as she had seen people doing when preparing for nuclear blasts in newsreels or movies of the fifties.

Looking tentatively backward, she saw there was nothing left in the place in which the stage had sat with the full chamber orchestra on it, just the empty dark side tunnel with what seemed a huge crater at its junction with the main tunnel, right behind the formerly-existing concrete wall of the proscenium, which had been blown off to a large extent too, as she could detect from her position. The lights had gone off everywhere except at a considerable distance from the stage, and a picture of horrible destruction lay around her. Her partner, a Scot, Dauvit Broun, had been thrown by a lick of the blast five or six meters away from her. His face seemed OK, but was streaked by soot and scratches. She thought she herself couldn't have looked too spectacular at that time, even though all limbs were in the expected places, as she gladly had it confirmed for herself by some quick tapping with the open hand, the rediscovery of the relief of familiar places filling her with the unequalled joy of survival. This was shortly thereafter tempered by the sight of mayhem and destruction around her, people trying to get out of the tunnel to the surface levels of the *duc*'s mansion, crawling bloodied on hands and feet or just running away, some of them knocked out or down by the *souffle* of the explosion as though a kamikaze had come on the wings of an ill wind and dropped and pierced himself into the *duc*'s subterranean properties with all the engine power he had had at hand on board his Zero, throttle fully open while plunging to the death of his own and others with a keen eye fixated on the target.

She looked around, no one about her seemed in any major danger, so she decided to take off at a fast clip, following those who had gone for the exits already, among cries and shouts and calls for police and ambulances. The duc had hired five guards-de-corps for the occasion, three of them former wrestlers and the other two boxers, all now at in-the-wall phones simultaneously talking to the police and urging them to come as soon as possible. By the time she got out into the street, police cars were already coming up to the gates of the mansion, blocking them with straddling vehicles, semi-automatic guns at the ready, the heavily armed and helmeted cops red-faced with stress and the smell of potential battle.

But there was no battle to be had, not an open one and not on that night, as the Italian Red Brigades, later reported by the police as having been the perpetrators, seemingly with some local help, had already decamped the area, apparently leaving no traces of any kind, just a blue-lettered white-paper manifesto in French glued to the imitation of a Doric column close to the stage, urging the killing of the '*aristocrate rats*' and promising further reprisals to the eventual survivors of this particular attack 'for playing the game of the capitalists pigs and even enjoying themselves while at it.'

Yvonne continued to run, clothes cut, face, arms and feet bruised and covered by soot, until she got well away from the area, which by now was already heavily cordoned off, then picked up or, properly said, jumped the first incoming taxi that took her to the villa up the serpentines on the slopes of Mont Agel where she stayed on that particular occasion, owned by the family of one of Gérald's local business associates.

"Your mother has been calling you for half an hour," Rejeanne, the lady of the house, told her.

"I couldn't sleep, so I was watching the TV. Then, I heard about an explosion in Monte Carlo in the news about one hour ago and I called," her mother said, barely breathing over the line. "Is this at the place where you were? That was my impression from the TV news reports — huge mansion, party, and so on, looked similar to me. Lloyd Robertson is right now all over it. Guess they've brought him from home as well."

"Yes, Ma, unfortunately, in this case, right instinct. I was right there. Huge blow, there are victims, I won't tell you more, I want you to have a good night's sleep. I'm sane and sound, that's important for you now. We two can't do anything more. Please go back to bed."

"But — but what could have been? Gas leak? A bomb?"

"Any of the above would be right with me for now. Probably a bomb, as it was too focused in the area of the stage to be gas-related."

"Stage? Then you must have been on it?"

"Thankfully, not this time. As a matter of fact, I wasn't

scheduled to appear with anything on the stage. I was in front of it, and somehow it didn't blow full-power toward us, but toward the back of the stage. Ma, now, you'll have to forgive me, I need to take a shower and go to bed. Please do the same, even though this might be morning in Calgary." Her mother was in Yvonne grandparents' home then.

"What kind of mother you think I am, to be able to catch even a wink of sleep right now? Anyway, I'll let you go. Let us hope God will receive the souls of those poor victims and accommodate them in his heavens."

"Same here. Take good care of you, Ma."

"You too. God, when I'm thinking you were this close! ... Bye."

Yvonne didn't want to contribute to her mother worrying, but she was happy herself. This had been a very close call.

23 - Montreal, 1985

Nimbly the squirrel ran — a big piece of food held in its long incisors — along one of the anthracite-black power cables suspended on old wooden poles in front of the town house, then suddenly jumped and disappeared into the crown of one of the acacias lining the sidewalk of Ash Avenue in Montreal, the crown, rich in foliage at this time of June, helping the disappearance with the green passivity and flutter of its leaves.

Had she been able herself to abscond in a similar fashion, Yvonne definitely would have attempted the feat without thinking twice.

As this didn't seem to be available, she contemplated it only from the remote stance of the amateur philosopher fighting her inner demons, only to decide at the very last moment that the time for action wasn't yet come, not something that would give her peace of mind, on the contrary making her confront head-on her lack of real resources fit to the situation.

A situation that hadn't improved at all since the bombing, at least this was what her discontinuous contacts with the *duc* — he still telegraphed her now and then at the offices of an auction house that could not betray him, or so he thought, as it was too involved in liquidating some of his assets — led her to believe.

The *duc* himself had gone underground, and that wasn't a surprise. Discovering to have been tailed by the Red Brigades for close to two years before the date of the hit, he didn't want to pursue his existence out in the open, not now. He realized he had been like a partridge, helpless prey to hidden hunters.

The best *she* could do was come back to Montreal, put some

serious water between her and any hitmen. There hadn't been any reported attacks by the Brigades in North America by that time, thus that should be a good bet and move, she initially thought. Still, soon after, she was reminded that Mafia, for one, had been quite successful in transplanting itself from the Old Continent to the New one, and had even flourished in the process.

Things had been tight for her lately, financially speaking, so it was no big surprise it had been Montreal where she had gone: more connections, a reasonable short-term rent that was easier to find until a new job materialized, the French flavor she still liked, even though not necessarily preferred, thinking back at her late father and her own friends.

She called her mother in Calgary. She was doing that lately from phone booths, just in case her lines might be tapped as the *duc* had reminded her in his messages, which he now sent in code.

"Oh, hi, Yvonne, glad you called. How has your day been?"

"Just milling around with nothing to mill. All this uncertainty bothers me a lot, and I can't do too much about it, nor can I think about my work the way I should." She avoided the word 'fear' in her talks to her mother, to avoid scaring her even more about the whole thing.

"I'd rather go to the States, however no one has really invited me, not even for a week, not to speak of months, which is really what I'd need right now."

"Your business has become too competitive, Yvonne. Had I known it would grow this way, I wouldn't have taken you to all those ballet classes. You people are too mean to each other."

***

On a day like all others, she went to the emergency ward of the Montreal General Hospital, alarmed there might be something wrong with her, now that no one was calling to tell or ask her anything, as many in the city had learned that it was she who was the ballerina who had been at Monte Carlo when the explosion happened and, she soon realized, the majority of those knowing her wanted to keep the distance from her, as well as the most cowardly option, she thought, that of pretending never having known her. Fear pervades everything, she had quickly learned, also that in the first round it takes out the people whom you talk to in your day-to-day life. People would rather do just business with you, if they have any, and forget about talking, when you seem to be under attack.

"Age?" asked the emergency receptionist, a slim, compact Filipino lady who didn't look at her while talking, her face, crammed with features and wrinkles, touching her radio from which news of the upcoming weather changes were broadcast to all and sundry by someone with a tight, strangulated voice, issued as though from a remote, sonorous oasis to listeners in a dumb desert. "You hear that? We should be getting a shower. This is Montreal again to you. We can't miss a rain, or we'd be dead," she said, penning the "33" having been issued by Yvonne.

"Place of residence?" was a preface to the questioner's standing up and making a circular round with a determined clipped walk through the appalingly small room provided only with a window, even that looking into an crowded waiting area lined with metal-plasticky chairs. "You know, I need take care of these varicose veins from time to time, and just sitting doesn't help," she excused herself, after sitting back at the minute desk provided with more telephones than a NYC police precinct would have, including a red one, on which a dirty-white old label said "911". "370 Ash Avenue, Apartment 6" was duly recorded in the lined ledger, now the writer was rubbing her hands alternatedly one over the other, as though applying a cream, which she hadn't done — that is, not yet.

"So what bothers you, ma'am?" For a moment, with so much European experience of late, Yvonne thought she had just heard the regal form of address, and laughed to herself as to her own mental confusion. Right after, she realized she couldn't tell the woman she had come to the hospital just to see more people around her on that Saturday evening, that would have been, perhaps, shameful, first to herself, and, worst, dicey to be taken as a serious reason to be seen by any of the doctors. And, on this night, she craved professional attention as a token given to her self-value, torn to shreds by the events in Monaco, where a dozen of people, half of which she had known — true, only in passing — had disappeared in a flash from the face of the earth, only yards away from her, as though they had never existed or as if they were as expendable as paper napkins.

"Oh, I have some terrible headaches lately, and they come together with stomach aches, and today they seem to be particularly bad, I don't know," she half-moaned the half-truths to the receptionist.

"Not that I want to give medical advice, ma'am, but have you tried any pills, are you currently on medication?" the woman said.

"I have, but they don't seem to have any effect anymore." Truth was, she had never enjoyed gobbling up pills, very rarely, if ever, did she go to it as a solution. She had been taught by several of her ballet teachers 'don't rely too much on artificial stuff, that can damage you, you know,' and that advice seemed to keep her in good stead, very rarely was she sick, and when in that condition, she preferred to take herself through the motions of recovery by what she thought to be more natural means: going on fasts, heading to a hot bath for a sauna, drinking medicinal teas, running — on grass, whenever possible, to protect her joints — in order to drive away the sickness by sweating, doing stretching or Yoga exercises on mats, and the like.

"Well, we never are what we were, aren't we?" cracked the woman, all-knowing, and for this, skepticism, well-hidden opprobrium, or whatever it was, Yvonne felt a need to slap her, to push her and the *it-all* of her away and aside from herself. This feeling came revulsing over her, as though confronting face-to-face an early incarnation of death, or a new Cassandra.

"The doctor will be soon with you soon, ma'am, please take a seat" — this directed her back to the waiting area, and Yvonne felt good that she hadn't told *this* woman about her fears. Who knew who might she be, behind those creases in her face?

A quarter of an hour later, she was made to lay down on a bed-on-wheels in a separate consultation room, all with no windows, just white walls and doors to it, and a doctor came in indeed, but only after another hour. "Hail to the Canadian health care system," Yvonne thought, "have the Red Brigades decided to terminate me by

Our Lives as Kites

making me wait? That's an interesting supposition and one not to neglect, not too removed from Chinese water torture, thus all the more steeped in tradition and to be feared."

The doctor seemed to be a South American of Chinese heritage, and his pronounciation was very similar to a Latino's. He was average in height, and, as one would expect in an emergency ward, not exceedingly concerned with appearances as after reading her patient's form prepared by the receptionist, came up close to the bed on which she was lying, and putting his right palm on her forehead, demanded "Show me where your pain is."

"Which pain?" Yvonne asked.

"I see here you've indicated head and stomach pains. Where exactly do they occur, if and when they do occur?"

She felt a tinge of professional reservation in his tone, but remained firm in wanting to play the serious patient's role to the hilt; that's why she had come here for, not just for what for her, in her situation, was peanuts — an interview with the peculiar Filipino lady at the desk.

How to proceed was another matter, and she had to quickly gather her wits, and establish a line of defense on a ridge in some imaginary mental field. Not the most difficult thing, but she couldn't totally improvise, there had to be a tiny-bitsy dose of truth in her story, she told herself, to be believable in the least, she couldn't play Scheherazade with a chance at not being soon a head shorter, without some core in her story hitting on real facts, at least tangentially. This had to be marginally better than school stories sold when arriving late for class. What could that be? She didn't want to tell the real story behind her coming back to Canada, the-Red-Brigades-and–the-circle-of-fear, or whatever name someone might have wanted to call it, or the doctor might send her to a mental asylum, and fast. Canada was so far from Europe, she told herself while vacillating, that stories coming from over the Pond back home didn't quite hold the record for believability.

The doctor seemed a bit upset at her taking too much time to respond.

"Difficulties understanding my question, miss?

"Pains. Where exactly do they occur? Show me, please. On

your body, touch the areas."

"Oh, thank you very much, doctor," she sneaked in a diversion, "for calling me a miss. I'm thirty-five year old, as my file has already probably told you, and my *missi*ness, if ever there was one, was gone a long time ago," she cracked, just a bit corrosively.

"Now, to answer your question, here you are," and she first took his left hand, his closest to her, with her right one, and touched it, before he was able to react and become defensive, to the presumptive areas, somewhere on the sides of her head, level with, but right behind her forehead. "Feel it? See?" she said, lilting as a baby, as if pain were anything material and visible, and talking with such determination and conviction that there couldn't have been any doubt to anyone that such was the case. The doctor was even more surprised when he then had his hand carried to her stomach and abdominals and felt there the metal quality of a ballerina, the results of decades of training and physical exercise, nothing flabby. He gently, but firmly, extracted his hand and moved it himself to palpate the areas of interest in his own manner.

"Does local massage temporarily relieve you of any of these symptoms?" he asked.

"Not really. By the way, I also tried acupuncture; didn't seem to provide any consistent relief."

"How are you then able to go past them, to cope? Any medication that we *could* consider as successful?"

"Only temporarily, I'd say. Tylenol seems to work, aspirin too, in terms of reducing the pain, even though I can't say I have any fever. However, it's all back after a day or two, and this is why I am here today, I am going through one of these bouts and I decided I need something that would work more long-term. I don't want to get addicted to some of the stronger pain-killing stuff, say morphine."

"Morphine? Are you using any?" He suddenly seemed worried.

"Not yet, but I have to tell you, the mind wonders when one has the pain that I sometimes have."

"We'll find something better for you than that. I'll be sending you to a neurologist and to an internist, let's see what they tell us." He took a seat on the edge of a chair at the melamine-covered corner table, took out a pad from his white coat's breast pocket, and wrote out two referrals to Drs. Whittingham and Clauzelle. They both carried his name, Dr. Edmund Chow-Sequiras, in black and glossy-as-lacquer italics, at the top. Yvonne, losing for a flash her patient's focus on herself, wondered if Sequiras had come along on his mother's or father's side.

"Now, they both have offices in this hospital, however I'd suggest you go to their private offices. You may find they have more time for you then," the young doctor added half seriously, half ironically, immediately continuing with a tone of light worry in his voice on the tail end of that, "Less crowding, I mean, it's only natural, you know what I mean," as though he had given the keys to the house by saying too much in an unguarded moment, his ears and the higher reaches of his cheeks suddenly a bit red, the countenance flustered.

Yvonne thought she was again being confronted with her power of extracting the truth — or, she iterated on the notion for a moment, some more or less remote or buried replica of it — from others without even asking for it, at the most unexpected moments, as well facing the double-edged sword of the accompanying embarrassment to which that lead for both parties.

It came, she suddenly realized, part and parcel with the notion of being a "dancer" which others had or learned to have about her. That was what she had declared at the reception desk, that was how the doctor consequently looked at her, as though the word, "dancer," said "discretion" in and by itself, just as "reporter" or "housewife" might have conjured "she will talk about this — she's professionally inclined toward it or just bored and in need to talk, to open up to neighbours or visitors." The accepted social convention seemed to be — everyone knew, or presumed to know it — that a dancer didn't talk, as she was wont to express herself in more corporeal ways, also, most probably, that she was satisfied with it that way and didn't need words to further decorate a dish to stimulate the appetite of others.

24 - 1985

She sensed there was in the air this flitting of dirty pollen of time lost, the malodorous acquiescence and presence so unpleasant to digest, so smelling of death, at times. The yellow death coming just a quantum faster, still hopefully many miles afar, at those moments, as though relaxing its grip only in our forgetfulness. Many times, she had felt driven to a wall, Yvonne really had, for the last several months. Whether these months had been two or five seemed to have lost importance to her in such day-to-day doings.

Even the familiar reflex of going to the ballet class had been absent lately. "What for," she asked herself sometimes, "there are no casting offers in sight," at least not hidden, as it were, after any corners along an invisible and perhaps non-existing way twisting and inching towards what could have been termed hope. She knew the trap of laziness of body and spirit, but somehow didn't feel up to facing it anymore, not now and not tomorrow and perhaps not the day after that.

***

I am walking in a long tunnel now — yes, I know this is a dream, but it's part of me too, can't break it apart from here, from the core of me as being here and now. I entered it at the beginning of the sleep, but I am all in and of it now, part and parcel, as it were. And it looks as though I am at Vaganova's school, in the museum, those great dancers all on the dark walls, walls so respectful of the dust of time. Of course, no Nureyev anywhere yet, he's a defector even in my dream. That'll have to wait for other times. Nijinski, Pavlova, the great Marius Ivanovich himself. But why do I stop at Kschessinskaya, at her of them all, the brunette Polish beauty with a long straight nose? Especially as she's insufferable here, the way she shows in this picture of her I have, no doubt one of those days when she played the princes and dukes in her life on her fingers and adorned herself to profusion with the real jewels given to her by the two Romanov grand dukes competing for fathering her child, no doubt one of the days when she wanted you to feel she had been already the future tsar's lover, that you yourself were nobody, even if you were Pavlova dancing with her in the same ballet.

But suddenly Her Serene Highness reaches from the sepia-colored picture and extends to me of all things an orange, and I feel I have to take it and at least show the beginning of a curtsy, for I feel that one can't easily refuse gifts from such personages, especially when they hang on a wall, flat with it for most of your time with them. I'm moving away to a corner, finding with difficulty a dustbin in Vaganova's museum. I start peeling at the orange, after making sure the guards aren't watching me. It peels regularly and easily enough, but when all the rind is removed, what I am left with in my hands is a hard, suddenly heavy ball-like earth globe and the language written over it seems none of this world, as though I am being prepared for an alchemy session showing me the hidden places of sacred minerals and what one can do out of them in one's life with enough knowledge. Will I have the patience for it?

Curiosity killed the cat, and I strain open the globe with my fingers and with something like a nail cutter that I happen to have — the happy logistics of dreams — in my purse. The ball's upper surface seems to be itself a thick metallic crust or cover, hinged at some points on the core underneath, which seems to weigh more by the second. Still, I manage to hold the whole of it aloft. It would be a shame to drop it on this hard ground, granite-like rock that surrounds me, as it might crack right then and there, and whatever secrets carried in it probably at least in part for me, would be forever lost. There are tall and low structures all around me, like pillars and mounds set in the obscurity of the dream through which I'm still navigating.

Someone closes in, it's a man and he cries out to me, "Don't open it and especially don't break it!" So I stop from mangling the surface of the ball and I turn toward him, "Why not? Do you know what it contains, then?" "No," he tells me, but it's the end of your dreams if you open it up." Surely I stop, but his face I don't like, doesn't look trustworthy to me; he isn't looking into my eyes as he talks to me, but avoids them. He is tall and slim, dressed in shiny blackish tights and a white long-sleeved bouffant shirt. I make out an aquiline nose, deep furrows on his cheeks and brow in the darkness around us, eyes deeply set in their orbs and shadowed by them.

"Who are you?" I ask him.

"I'm the dark angel of dance."

"Dark? Is there another one, then? Like Odille and Odette?"

"Oh, yes, there *is* another," he kind of reluctantly agrees, "the white angel, but that one never shows up when you need him." He is dismissive.

I'm taking another look at him — I *know* I'm of two minds — and open the ball. There's just a small piece of domino there, jade-like. It has written on it just "The library of dance," and on my reading it, the dark angel has already disappeared from view, I realize.

I'm out of the dream now, sweating in my bed. There must, there must, be a way to stay in dance, one just for me.

25 - *Body and Soul* I, 1987

No one but she could diagnose the problem. It seemed to be, for the uninformed viewer, most of it, or perhaps the entirety of it, a lack of sync between the synthesized music and the entrance of the first dancers on the stage, something that snowballed, in a sneaky manner, into a serious mess within just several beats, quite obvious to most of those present in the rehearsal hall as a rupture of some kind in the flow of the ballet and thus doubly scarring to her nerves, as it was she who was the choreographer in charge of the show in the works.

A forest of small pyramids, all white, in plastic, lay about the stage, temporary guides for the dancers, indicative, together with some lines in chalk on the black-painted wooden floor, of some of the main intended paths as marked in her motional diagrams, as cones in a driver's course would be, and several of them were turned over, a sign that some of her charges were still lacking control or focus, or were putting impetuousness before precision, a major *gaffe*, as she had learned from cool Mr. B in New York City. The diagrams sat unrolled in apparent disarray on a desk standing skewed in the corner, as old papyruses would — awating grander plans and poetry for the Pharaoh.

The dancers had to execute a rush of serpentine movements, crossing each other sometimes at elbow's distance, and there was no telling what would happen until they got it into their systems — the set trajectories of their bodies moving over the floor, and the appropriate calibrated energy to be injected into it all at any given strobe in time — with bumping each other the major risk, some of them already displaying on their bodies the traces of such unhappy encounters, in bruises on the outside of their upper arms, or in dark

Marius Hancu

purple she knew hidden by their tops on their ribs. The movements had to come in swooshes and spurts of energy as the music was pitched uncomfortably higher, while more volume gradually and sometimes surprisingly pushed out of the loudspeakers too. There was drama in the screeching intensity with which they had to suddenly turn at some imaginary crossroads marked by some of the cones, and Yvonne had encouraged the dancers not to avoid sliding on the floor at such short direction changes. "Losing balance and 'skating' a bit — she made air quotes sign — looks good if you don't mess up too much, say by falling or bumping into others head-first like a train," she argued, shouting out at them, hoarse voice and all.

She decided she needed some height in order to have a better view of the action, while still being close to the dancers, so she took a cafeteria table, yanked the oilcloth off it, clambered, or, in fact, jumped over the edge of it, crouch-pushed from legs and arms up and away from the surface of the table and stood up over them all.

"Please replace the cones along the chalk lines, everyone," she asked, raising her voice to be heard through the subdued jabbering among the dancers and the shuffling of ballet shoes over the floor. "We need to restore some order to this place, as it's begun to look like an untended stable."

After five minutes, the markers again in their places, she told them, "Listen, guys, while running around, I want you to keep sighting your designated partners, so the public would see you all looking for your loved ones among your crowd, searching for them. I don't want you to just run ahead on automatic pilot, without looking left and right. I need the drama of searching in your eyes. Crowd them and the rest of your faces with longing, desire, whatever, just don't behave like robots. All the same, you're entitled to look now and then at others, sexually spying on them, checking them out. You're tied and you aren't tied to your designated halves, hope the message is understood. Everything right? Take your places, then, please. Second part, first movement, all right?" She nodded to the audio guy to start the tape, pointing right away to the ceiling with her forefinger that she wanted more output from the loudspeaker, then making a short horizontal slash of the air with the palm down when that was reached to her satisfaction. After ten bars, she pushed her hand straight ahead, finger pointed, as if lancing someone — "Go!"

From four corners of the room the dancers came, from two of them, in one diagonal, the men, in white, from the other two the women, in red, one after the other. They ran in four spirals converging in the same point, the center of the stage, which was supposed to crowd them in something similar, perhaps, to some, to one moment in Béjart's *mise-en-scène* for *Sacre du Printemps.* Then, when they had converged, they would immediately separate with the pulsing-in-pulsing-out motion of a heart, out and away diverging in four spiralate strings again, most of them now however in pairs, hand-in-hand, mostly heterosexual couples, but not all of them, and some singles interspersed here and there. The tempo of music accelerated with the start of the pulsing out, and slowed toward its end. The four trajectories spiraling out didn't however end in the corners of the room but threw all the players out at different points on its periphery, where they disappeared, except those facing the proscenium and the public, who froze in caressing and adoring stances, gazing towards undefined points in space as if transported by the prospect of the future, its hopes and its pleasures within.

Then the lights dimmed, the music slowed to a virtual stop, and all the dancers discreetly filed toward the periphery of the stage.

They all emerged, separate again, the heart had another half-cycle and they emerged paired up once more.

Three full cycles — that was all Yvonne had thought it necessary to drill into the consciousness of the viewers the eternal searching for partners, the pairing; she thought that in art themes should always be powerfully issued. Burning the spectators by overexposure was a small risk she was quite willing to take to carry them along on the journey, and she intended to offer no excuses for it. She had also had the music rewritten just to show more recognizable themes.

***

The chalk is here, written in the heart too, and I feel it rasping over what they call the inner cockles of it, as a file. John and Laura are set to emerge the first from the corners. *I know* whatever is wrong there happens during the crowding in the center, in the helter-skelter of finding the exact partner and emerging in the designated pairs. For heavens', it so simple! Everyone should follow the small marks in chalk on the floor. What is it they do to mess it?

It must be something in the pairing, the music is at its peak then, and one can easily lose focus, crowded from all sides by other people reorganizing and repositioning themselves while running — jogging in effect, as things are still not that fast — also, to boot, the sound sharp banging in your ears.

Still, there's something much deeper that bothers the heck out of me, and I haven't told them anything, as I may seem undecisive, should I open my sweet mouth before finding a solution to this one — it's the feeling that there's too much of a mechanism and straining about it and not enough sentiment, and I don't want to be called just an ordinary amanuensis of the hieratic priest of teamwork, Mr. B, that's how some have called him, God keep him in his airs and graces.

There's this too with many of these and other dancers — their classical training, it shows — they're too disciplined and perhaps rigid-looking to the modern viewer, a bit programmed in their motions, too wooden in their embedded care for *attitude* to let off enough of their own steam. I need to take care of it somehow, inject a healthy dose of natural in their moves. Rethink them from scratch, even.

***

There was some method in her locating the problem though. She watched the dancers' feet and carefully listened to the sharpening music, she knew those tripping had to fall out of sync with it some time during a sequence of critical beats, overmatched by it. Everything had to start from the base, from the feet. She suddenly became aware the music was just a huge *swoosh* at the time of the trouble occuring, no local rhythm to it — *no damn beat in it, but this is how I wanted it* — just the overall progression, the feeling of an absorbing black hole in full suction mode.

***

It must be this, the lack of beat, of punch, of clear tempi, the amorphousness in the music, this gets them into trouble, as there's no compass anymore to hang on to it. Still, I don't want it changed, I've already bothered John no end about it and, in fact, the music is fine now, it's just difficult to sync with it at that particular time. I'd better think about something else, no doubt. Give them other reference points to look at a parallel music or sound tape, running independently of the main one, heard only by them. OK, feasible, but I don't want them loaded with headphones or gear like that. A light signal, glimmering on-off on the intended beat? That would give them a good enough clue. Right, a strobed light would do fine, I think, flashing right above our group, high enough not to be visible even from the seats closest to the stage, strong enough to be distinguished by the boys and girls, still, weak enough not to create any shadows on them. That could be it — a hidden lantern.

***

One hour and twenty minutes later, the lights manager has bricolaged an improvisation: a gray lamp, hung above the dancers, a long cable leading to a nifty push-button switch in her hand, while she was still standing on the cafeteria table. "You barely need to touch it and it's going to switch off and on. You should be fine," he said. Now, with everything literally in her hands, she tried the switch several times, then spoke up.

"Come on, everyone, break's over. Let's get into it once again. Now, please listen carefully. We'll use this lamp for syncing. For the time being, just manual mode, thus pray I'll be right and that my fingers are still fast enough. Putting in a second track with music to sync the light will definitely take some time, so I'll try to fix our mess this way for now. So, please run forward, or better, move in general on the approximate beats or strobes of the light. Approximate, as I don't want us to look too regimented. Thus allow yourselves some tolerance with respect to your neighbours, don't strike or step too strictly with the music, at the same time as them.

"And think again through Auden's words 'Body and soul (Not-Me and Me) can have no independent existence, yet they are distinct, and an attempt to make one into the other destroys,' the motto for this piece. You hear me? *Destroys.* That's what we want to show, this unity inside the human being, sought after all our lives, which we can't escape either all our lives, which in the end is still a fight of opposites. We would on some days, if we could, live and play just for and through our body, on others just for the, ethereal or not, pleasures of the soul, just for imagination. But we can't. This seeking and escaping is all we want to show, the recovery, the loss of oneness. Seeking, escaping, oneness in one and in the couple, it's all. Our flow and movement should tell ebb and flow, flow and ebb, you know, attraction and rejection, loss that is. The very short happiness of oneness, of meeting the match.

"OK, enough pep talk on my part, let's get going. Sync with the light, everyone. And on!"

The music rolled out of the loudspeakers. Keenly she observed them, oh, yes, and waited for any signs of confusion. However, there was no more bumping, the whole of it much smoother, focused and hotter on the part of the dancers.

***

I might have just moved Pavlov's dog to react … Heavens, great to be past this snag. Still, there doesn't seem to be enough visual contact and searching between them. It's as though I had to go among them to provoke some real eye and hand holding as they do in kindergarden to pair kids up. Good to have three weeks still till the premiere. They need to visibly search for partners and, when finding one, to lock in on them — caught you! I mean, visible for the parties of interest, and those, modesty makes me play this tack, are only the spectactors, and we really need to snag their interest or this will be a short run. The eyes, the arms, the facing of the body, its momentary tilt while in motion, must all show that — and — Passion! Burn! Told and re-told them that *maintes fois* but they must be thinking of tonight's tumble in the hay with Miss Margaret or Mr. Faust, or whomever, I don't know.

The props, that crowd of huge eggs breaking up on the stage right at the beginning, to reveal yolks and egg whites, function well enough, can't complain, I mean they open gracefully and gradually enough, as flowers would, as I had wanted. A lunar lake with crackling eggs. Still, something must be done about the lights, there must be some graduation in the way the dancers assume their final colors, the women the red, the men the white. The drift from the yellow of yolks to the red which is carried most of the time by women on their tight, thin body suits — they do look like divers, that critic whom I invited at the rehearsals, Rebecca Dubbs, was right — isn't helped by the illumination. Having those yolks and whites as long light-colored bands of ultralight transparent silk fluttering up from the broken shells while initially covering the people hidden in the egg, as well as the fans blowing them up, should make this all easy, they just need to point the lights to them and gradually change colors in a very limited area of each egg, as the dancers emerge. They probably need to use more focus and some filters, I don't think or pretend to know myself what exactly they need, but I've already told Jacques to look into it for tomorrow and it's his job to deal with, together with the set director. I told them the drift of it, 'What I want is eggs, eggs, eggs, followed by bands, bands, bands, then people, people, people, and nothing too damn strictly synchronized or time-regimented, we want some spread on those events — an egg cracking here and bursting forth its precious contents, another, doing the same a bit later in some other place, and so on and so forth — otherwise it gets all too mechanical and we're starting to feel as though dropped into a world of robots, definitely not something we have in mind. Now, how they take care of the lights in this transition is only their cup of tea and I won't try to stick my oar in, but I need my effect.'

Marius Hancu

***

Two hours later, Antonella Boeru, the stage director for the production, a Romanian recently arrived to the North-American shores, and this, she said, after dodging bullets on the border to Yugoslavia over the ploughed no-man's land, from her loving, generous fellow-citizens doing the coward thing for Ceausescu, sat at a huge table in an open-area office behind the stage and played absent-mindedly with her own model stage sets, in front of Jacques, the light manager. They were alone, Yvonne having left them to their own devices with what was her unmistakeable harbinger of trouble "you need to focus, guys."

"I wish I knew what she wanted," she issued, sighing, chin propped in.

"I think I do. She wants something less obvious during that initial scene, nothing too striking," Jacques dared to advance, still mouse-like. New to the team, this Romanian, so Jacques had decided to play carefully, not to hurt any sensitivities. Can't show oneself too clever.

"But we're already there, to my mind."

"Not to her, and that's all that counts. I know her, she won't let herself be convinced when she feels there's something wrong somewhere. She just hangs on to it and to you like a bulldog, and something has to give up, and that's usually you, I'll tell you. That's her sixth sense, she argues."

"Fine, I think I can deal with that. I've never argued for her giving up on anything, just for telling us what exactly she wants."

"Well, she has this idea that you must be empowered to do things your way, thus she won't give you too detailed pointers, not to straitlace you, that is."

"Fine, it's good to have some give-and-take, still, I wouldn't mind more of a framework, you know what I mean, within which we can play," Antonella said, looking a bit unsure of herself and of the whole situation. This is a new, another continent, for her. Something she might say wouldn't be understood the same way as in the old country.

***

Yvonne, she was flying once again. High, and the thoughts were with it too. The eternal separation intervening at death, souls who couldn't survive without their bodies — forget the religions — except in others, in their fragmented, kaleidoscopic, but not entire, broken and broken-edged, and worst of all, again time-limited, images of you.

***

They come in terribly disjunct sets, and if one believes religion, or poetry for that matter, most of the time it is only the soul who is immortal, the shelf time of any body out there terribly finite and of course, this is elementary math now, much shorter, always making its owner unhappy with his or her contract.

For what we know, they are put together or, maybe in a more fortunate expression, grown together by parents and society, and for the duration of a lifetime, they manage to tolerate each other and shack up. Is this a sexual, perhaps even an incestuous relationship? If only they weren't so unlearned, undecided or secretive about it, the philosophers or the theologians.

To start with the duet, the one's body and soul and to move to the quartet, those of the couple. They emerge from the eggs as the primary pair, run through childhood and adolescence to young adulthood and there in that sexual crowding in the centre of the stage the messy quartet, the double pair, two souls, two bodies, emerges, with its own attractions and rejections, conflicts much more than squared, perhaps cubed, or whatever power is left in algebra to show unexpected branching and multiplication in infinite trees, sometime happy, sometime cancerous, of self and of each other destructive. You have the nuclear adjective at its most potent as this is the stark, fecundation's fundamental pair, still nuclear in its potential boilovers and blowups.

26 - Meeting Sarah, 1987

"The things you can discover at a party!" Yvonne thought. It was at a private National School alumni party in Toronto where she was apprised that Sarah Pritchett was available for work as assistant choreographer, or just as assistant, period.

"Hi, Yvonne," said Laura Larossa, approaching with that spectacular red-headed beam of hers that could only mean she wanted something, and took her aside. "I've heard you've set up shop and that you may need some help. Congratulations, by the way."

"Thanks. Part-time only for now, you know. Need to keep expenses under control until taking off, as it were. Office skills at a minimum. Anyone in mind?"

"You may remember Sarah Pritchett from school. She was, if memory serves, one class up from you. Seems to know Laban notation and similar stuff. Of course, office skills, otherwise I wouldn't have approached you."

"Notation? That would be great, as I'm not too good at it myself and I definitely need some way to document my stuff. Also, having someone with a bit of common background, as the School, could help a lot. Anything you could tell me about her? Something I should know upfront? Just between us, I don't know her too well from school, even though, of course, I remember her."

"First, as you can see, she's not here at the party." Laura smiled, stating the obvious. "So I can't put in touch with each other immediately. Well, I think she's right now out in the boonies, perhaps not so figuratively speaking, in a dentist's office as it's in the suburbs, also part-time, and would take anything that would bring her back in touch with dancing. She knew that you and I were

Our Lives as Kites

friends during your American period, so she asked me to inquire. Wonderful girl, lots of energy."

"Any unmentionable hangups that you want to share with me?" Yvonne laughed, but there was something on her face, a shadow, a concern, that told Laura that she was serious.

"Not into drugs, as far as I know, and that's recent. Probably into men, just like most of us the not married ones," came back the answer, Laura's face again just as beaming as at the beginning. "She was corps for a bit at the National, as you know, even at the time you were still here. Never went higher. Afterward, I guess, mostly odd office jobs, none to do with ballet, far as I know. Ah, even a projectionist's assistant."

"So, she doesn't mind getting her hands dirty, I guess. Right?" Yvonne wanted something more committed from Laura, but there seemed to be nothing warmer forthcoming, so, she thought, "that'll have to do for the time being".

The arrangement with Laura was for Sarah to call Yvonne later in the week, in order for them to have a first talk with each other, as Yvonne, at least, didn't remember the two of them ever trading more than several words in passing, most probably just quips, if any, in all those years at School. Being together at parties with Sarah — that, Yvonne didn't remember. Different circles, she guessed. Sure enough, the talk did happen the next but one day and the voice at the other end of the line seemed, to Yvonne, really anxious, as though Sarah was really talking about her dream job.

"Yes, I'd love to work for a choreographer, and I mean in *any* capacity. Most of the work I was involved in outside dancing hasn't been interesting to me, not something I like to do while having some fun too. And enjoying myself at work is important to me. So much the better," Sarah said, and Yvonne wasn't sure she liked being placed in a hot spot by such play on collegiality, " if the boss would be someone like you, with some common background like the School and the National and so on. I'd love to be considered a candidate for the job."

"I'd have to warn you in advance that it, I mean the job, might not be great in everything. It might be, at times, a bit tedious or menial, as a lot of it would be in essence just secretarial stuff, setting up appointments, manning — sorry for the sexist term — the telephone lines, typing business letters," Yvonne said, treading the water carefully, ever the scrupulous in this respect, not willing to create in anyone any unwarranted expectations that could come back later to haunt the relationship, to haunt her. "However, yes, it's all about dancing and ballet, as this is where I'm for the time being."

"And by the way, are you used to typing from dictation, including recorded? Many times, I'm just flashing out bits of scripts or just brainstorming scenarios on my dictaphone or cassette recorder."

"Ah, that'd be easy." Sarah's voice perked up over the phone. "I've been doing lots of such stuff for doctors. Many times, these days, at the end of a patient's visit, they dictate diagnosis and comments this way."

"Only trouble is, my commentary might seem illogical or inconsequential at times, as I'm just rambling or blabbing away in search of ideas. Still, I want them written down, so I can make a further iteration on them later on, with a fresher mind or in times of dryness when there's nothing clear in sight in my mind. I really think good ideas don't just pop out all the time, and one should be careful to have them down," Yvonne felt the need to explain herself. "I might be travelling, or I might be playing with my kites."

"Your kites?"

"Oh, sorry to freak you out. How careless of me!" Yvonne said. "From childhood, I've had this fascination for playing with kites that must surely seem strange to others, especially now that I am an adult. I've got quite a collection, started by my father. It helps me relax and feel a connection with nature that is lost in today's world. Anyway, the thing is I get great ideas this way. Nothing like clear dancing motions, nothing definite, nothing that will tell me have a *pirouette* here or a *pas de bourré* here; more like those vague, loosely-contoured, ideas, or feel of ideas, that I need to start working on a piece from scratch."

Whatever jingles with you, dear, but that's a bit out there in some remote branches. But let me get the darn job first. She seems quite deep about it, Yvonne. Or that's just to impress the audience. Can't tell yet. We'll need to keep a watch on this natural algebra or whatever that is, in case the job happens.

"And, not to spook you, I mean more than I've already done it, but sometimes I'm also having it, I mean the dictating thing, in the morning, when waking up from one dream or another. Matter of keeping in touch with inner me. You might think I suffer of logorrhea by now," said Yvonne and laughed.

"Something else about the way I'm doing things these days. I travel a lot; as you know, a choreographer is kind of a gypsy. You have to show up where they want you and when then need you. Many times on short notice for some fixes or say teaching a new soloist in the cast a role. Not that I would complain. Now, I might on occasion be able to bring this person, I mean the assistant, with me, if the producing side allows it and covers the expense. However, in general she would stay at our base in Canada to keep in touch with the world and keep up a stable front for the all-important me." There was an ironical tone right at the end. "And, not to forget, there would also be the collecting-slash-clipping of newspaper comments about my shows. For the quote, portfolio, unquote, you know. If favorable, of course," she laughed.

***

Yvonne was alone at home in the shower now, the small side window half-open to let the steam, musing on the latest talks with Sarah; one could have called them job interviews just to confirm business had been transacted and advances made, but she didn't, not to herself. She would have done so only on being convinced this was a viable candidate, and she hadn't reached that stage in the proceedings with Sarah, not at all. She couldn't point out exactly why, but this lack of conviction she felt floating around in herself was not something to be swept away under the carpet just for the sake of convenience. Yvonne didn't like cats and their hiding of own dirt was, to her, one of their least pleasant habits and proverbially so — even though she smiled about it. She trusted her instincts and in this case they hadn't reached a unanimous decision. It was like a balled-up hedgehog of a matter, difficult to grasp from any direction.

"I don't think we two see life in the same colors or through the same glasses. Plainly speaking, she sways too much to the-glass-is-half-empty side for me to be fully comfortable with her," Yvonne said to herself. "Boredom, that's a deadly sickness. If she brings it around with her everywhere she goes in, well, one should just say pass. But perhaps I'm wrong, perhaps things would be different if she gets something touching on dancing.

"How strange this is, to live in the same place with someone for several years, for hours a day, only to later on find that the contact has been flaky, that I can't take anything from it now, anything, that is, that'd help or swing my decision.

"Should this be boredom about life, that's a *bouillabaisse* whose taste I won't have the patience to sample. Contagious stuff, could drag another down. If it's just about previous work, what I do may be just what she needs to get into a good swing of things and — how do they say it in HR jargon? — right, perform! and really help me. One exception here: dancing burnout from the years with the School and the National. Quite common, unfortunately, and there's nothing I could do about that. If she's touched by it, we better keep each other at a respectful pole's distance."

"So, Sarah," Yvonne asked two days later over the phone, "when did you learn Laban, I mean notation? Laura told me something about your knowing it."

"That's right. Mind, I have it somewhere in the back of my mind, would have to dig it out, spruce it up. Several years ago, I was still with the National in the corps, and they brought in a specialist who, for three weeks or so, gave those of us who wanted classes on it. You must have been in the States already at the time. Never used it on any real ballets though, but I didn't get at the time the feeling it'd be a big deal to work with it. They made us then use it in several small class projects. Now that I've got the basics, so …"

"Ah, Yvonne, now that you're asking. Yes, 'course I know Sarah." Nicholaus Hermanthaler was talking from the West Coast, several days later. "She danced for me corps in *Swan Lake*, I think she made even *pas de quatre* on one occasion, as I thought she had some very nifty *pointe* work. Ah, so dancing quality isn't of concern to you on this occasion? Just work habits slash mentality? Fine then, I see now what you're looking slash fishing for. Can't say I remember her ever being late. Important bit, isn't it? Yet, neither do I remember her asking for more rehearsal time or staying late. So, basically, clocking in, clocking out, right on the beat. OK, so I worked with her toward the end of her career. Everybody's fed up a bit with *le sacre métier* by then, present persons excluded, of course. She just did the job. None too enthusiastically. I remember her costumes fitting her very well, and remember asking her on one occasion how she always managed that. Good relations with the costumiers always help, she said. Thus, I figure she must have keen eyes for costumes and as such might help you in this respect on new shows or on refurbishing old ones, say if anyone in the cast isn't quite up to the snuff, in fit, colors, you know the drill.

"Oh, this might be irrelevant in your context, but women and women, you never know, this is a negative reaction sometimes, you know," he laughed.

"What are you talking about? Spell it out, if you don't mind," Yvonne demanded.

"OK, then, here you have it: she's terribly jealous. One night, I entered one of the men's dressing rooms at the National, and one of the dancers, and I won't tell you who that was even if you were to pay me a million, was complaining that Sarah was dragging him through a tough time. Yes, I remember well, he said dragging. And the other two were, like, come on, you didn't know she's so jealous? On which planet do you live, Mister? And the guy who was now the butt of the jokes said: she just popped up at our home one evening and created a big scene with my wife, if you can imagine that. Good thing my kids weren't at home, especially as they are big enough to understand stuff like this."

27 - *Body and Soul* II, cca 1987

JOHN MARCUSE: I still remember being paired up by Yvonne with Joanne Skeen for *Body and Soul*, two years ago or thereabouts. After the first *barre* class where she met all of us, she told everybody on the cast that pairs and pairing were to be a big thing in that piece and that we had better get used to the idea and to our respective partners. She then gave us the pairings, which she seemingly had eyed and thought about and done during the previous week, while attending other shows of the company as well as classes.

JOANNE SKEEN: Yeah, and some of us then thought, why not, that might involve even some more intimate knowledge and some laughed that could mean even sex. Now, I can tell you now that in the end I really got to know John better, but in unusual and unexpected ways. Not that I didn't know him before: we were in the same dance company, when all was said and done; nothing unusual to it. We all knew each other some way or another, many were involved, shorter or longer term, with someone from the company, but Yvonne wanted us to get sort of 'mood- and physically-synced,' those were her words, by spending meaningful time together during rehearsal, and I mean just for setup, just to get in the skin of the characters. She was supposed to provide the definition of "meaningful" to us, and, dear me, it was to be an original one.

ANN DICKSTRA: So, next time, at the first rehearsal, she brought in twenty five copies of a book with Auden's complete poems and told us to be prepared to read from it to each other. What we'd read was supposed to be our choice, but it had to be longer poems, at least two pages in length, she said, in order for the right mood to set in, to settle and coalesce in each of us. And that we should switch from one to the other in the pair after each page, in order to shuffle the meaning and the involvement between us as in a baton passing in track.

ARMAND DEFERRE: And, no, it wasn't only for half an hour that we would to do this, it'd be a full hour, count on it, she said. And what would be next off, someone asked. Well, she said, *barre* work in couples, for one thing. Yoga work, again in pairs, for another. And there's more to come. She was to direct it all, she said, and I'll tell you, when it came on, it was nothing fast. A lot of supported stances, on both sides, which the ladies found a bit strange, as we're normally the supporting party. No, she wanted each of us to feel the weight of the other, the tension in her or his muscles, his or her flexibility at the moment, his or her apparent insecurity about a move or, worse, about themselves, there and then. And, this part, we needed to do it in complete quiet, to listen to our partner's exhaling and inhaling, to weigh and time our support on it, as though she was the lost petal and I was the wind carrying her a-flutter, or the other way round, you get me.

LOUISE FINGERMANN: And there was no music in any of this, but it came in soon enough — Bach and Handel; a lot of them — in other parts of the 'unification,' that's how she called all of this. I think now of Kubrick's *Barry Lyndon*, same measured flow to it, that's exactly how it felt at the time.

JOHN MARCUSE: But the strangest bit must have appeared the notion of playing chess with each other, especially as many of us hadn't moved a chess piece in years, and many others didn't know how to play at all. Mind you, we're not mental intellectuals, but physical ones. I, at least, sometimes, think of me as a laborer. (Catcalls from the others "Yes, you are one, John.") You too, don't worry. But in the end, we got to that too, and you could see the what, the twenty, thirty pairs of us, sitting akimbo on the parquet floor — wow, I still feel the pain in my butt — of the rehearsal hall, moving small pieces of plastic and challenging each other with "check" or "mate." "Those who don't know have to teach the others," was Yvonne's short reply to our initial backing off and rearing up in the face of this challenge.

LOUISE FINGERMANN: No, that wasn't the strangest thing. That was to come when she asked us to prepare for a rehearsal by

Marius Hancu

running in circles, again in pairs, for half an hour on the stage. We had to hold the hand of the other; this might have been the toughest part. Imagine running several miles, it must have been six or seven, while holding someone's hand. "Comes with unification, body and soul coming together, as Auden wanted it, man and wife coming together, as I see it, she told us."

ANDY DONGARRA: The body and soul being paired during the life was a big thing for her. It was as though at birth they were separate, floating around with no aim, like separate balloons or what, until education and experience and simply growing-up put these two entities together — don't laugh at me, it was her who said "entities," I'm not into those words — and now they were one in the same vase, she said. And it was the same with man and wife, life put them together, some fumbling through chance again, but in the end the fit is found and kept up for decades, if it's a true fit, or otherwise time finds it out and dismisses it, and another one is tried out, if we're lucky or we're left to loneliness. And all this "unification," I mean strands in it, must have come to her from Stanislavski, or Stella Adler, or Brando who was her star pupil, "Method Acting" or something like that, immersion. Now, if any of you laughers have seen "A Streetcar Named Desire," I mean the movie, you know that at least for Marlon it darn worked.

LOUISE FINGERMANN: Still, now that I've mentioned the running, I'll have to say that about her, she was running herself the full monty with us.

JOHN MARCUSE: And damned if she was any tired by the end of half an hour. I mean, no breathing any harder, no sweating — at all.

LOUISE FINGERMANN: Well, that's no big news, she was known for this from times when she was active as ballerina. Partners said it — no sweat from her. Big plus for any partner, as all of us know. You don't get messed up by the other, you're not his or her occasional towel. I, for me, I know I can't offer this advantage and I'll use this opportunity to apologize to all present, heh, heh.

ANDY DONGARRA: You serious? Most of us do it, I mean the sweating. Why do they keep those towels in the sides in performances? Natural urge of the body, or secretion, to call it straight. But yeah, Yvonne was that way in those rehearsals. No sign whatsoever of being tired at any time. Gosh.

JOHN MARKOFF: And yes, it was at roughly at that time, that in theatre, not in ballet, in Leningrad, I mean old Saint Petersburg, Russia, they brought Lev Dodin in back from the cold, or was it Siberia, into directing, and I've heard he too was into a lot of immersing into the role and long rehearsals. So, here you are, different strings to different folks, but Yvonne was into something both old — as Stanislavski was what, turn of the century, way back — and new.

ANN DICKSTRA: Still, us is us, I mean dancers, but the thing to watch for me in all that was her secretary cum assistant, her amanuensis, what was her name?

JOHN MARKOFF: I think it was Sarah.

ANN DICKSTRA: That's right. Sarah. I mean, she had been a dancer herself, back in Yvonne's times, certainly less distinguished and all, still, a dancer. And it was a sight, I mean her face, watching what her boss, Yvonne, was getting into. It was as though what she was watching were the travails of a fool, who was doing things not to be comprehended, and for no practical purpose. She must have meant, like we all did at the beginning, I mean, chess and running? What for, Yvonne? But we got our answer in the act, the performance itself, the feel, the energy and the smoothness in it all, and mostly the being-into-it, while she seemingly was left with just the writing down of everything, without, I thought from her face, the best of understanding or effort.

JOHN MARKOFF: Nah, Ann, you ladies are too tough on each other. Fact is, at times Yvonne looks to me to be a great choreographer, at times bordering on genius. You think I should take a hike on this genius thing. Fine. Anyway, any times you have a person like her, it's bound to face some lack of understanding from her peers. This talk here is just proof of our initial, or even current, misunderstanding of her. So, why fry Sarah more for it than what we should ourselves deserve? All right, I see where you are coming from: she's her day-to-day assistant, she should be familiar with her manner of doing things and thoughts, and so on and so forth. Yeah, that's right, but you know that? Familiarity doesn't necessarily breed understanding, as you may be bumping against your inner limits or on your old thought reflexes.

AURORA PARASCHIV: Surely, those two were and still are — as they are yet together, as far as I know — as fire to water. I remember Yvonne having somehow clambered up under the lights at center-stage, during the rehearsals of *Body and Soul*, on some perch up there known only to the techies, only to see the effect from above of the light strobe she had arranged with the light-master to sync us, all this while Sarah was sitting quiet on a stool underneath, taking notes, but so cold to the progress so obvious to all of us after that move.

JOHN MARKOFF: I'm older than most of you guys, so perhaps Yvonne tells me more. Once, she mentioned to me that at the beginning of the eighties, eighty-three, eighty-four, she kind of bottomed out and then gradually figured out the only way to keep the light on in her life, some fullness to it, and I think I'm close to her words here, was to go into choreography. I'll tell you, when you think that way, you're doing things with some swing, you feel at times that you're the arrow in the bow. *And, just for myself, I can still remember what she read to us from Auden's* No, Plato, no *on the first day of rehearsals.*

ANN DICKSTRA: Also in the mix seems to have been that close brush she had with death in Monte Carlo. Red Brigades blowing up a society ball where she was arranging a dance.

28 - *Shakespeare's Triangle* I, London, 1988

She had been dreaming a lot about Patrick lately, and there seemed to be in her soul a tear, a cut that was only getting larger, as though there were a crazy surgeon at work with scalpel and bone-crushing apparatus taking, one could have said, no heed whatsoever of his patient's moans, so one afternoon, upset with it all, she threw away the letter she had intended to write to him, and, lounging on her settee, decided instead to go Shakespeare for the rest of that day — her small modest pain must be in there somewhere, catalogued and covered in tome and verse, and its replication in that mirror of old might feel like relief, even though not really being so. And, sure enough, there it was from the very beginning all laid out under the serene light of time past and written down, as though great Will had got a detailed order from her:

From fairest creatures we desire increase,
That thereby beauty's rose might never die

and had kindly answered, with a reverence even. Days later, she enclosed the quote in several lines, something like "how interesting, I've just found this," nothing more explicatory than that — fluff, she thought to herself, but one need keep up appearances — and mailed it to Patrick, thinking that nothing could ever be more explicit than this. No reference to this particular message was ever made by him.

Now, weeks, months in fact, later, lo and behold, there was this British gig. They would like it to be ready two months from now, a tour in France coming up, so she must really step it up as there's the time involved in getting across the Pond from Canada for final choreography with the dancers, rehearsals and so on. When warned they wanted "if at all possible, a British theme," she flashed back the answer, as though ruminating over the thought at all of her meals, "Why not Shakespeare? There's nothing more English than him," and they said, "Wonderful, but kindly not Romeo and Juliet, there have recently been two, the classical with Nureyev and Fonteyn by MacMillan, and the more modern with Donn and Farrell, by Béjart, not to speak of Zeffirelli's film, with Olivia Hussey and Leonard Whiting, but anything else might be a reasonable play with us." Still, they mentioned they wanted this to be for three or four soloists and twenty minutes, both at the most, and that'd be stretching things, kind of. She called back within two days with the title, *Shakespeare's Triangle*, and said two males, one a younger one, the other more experienced, plus a female, preferably experienced — experienced, to me, she added, means preferably principals — would be everything required, plus corps, of course. To revolve around Shakespeare's imaginary love life as shown in the Sonnets — that is, nothing to do with Anne Hathaway of the second-best bed and with their three children. Ah, they said, and she felt a question mark was raised trans-continentally, and potentially hanging dangerously, that would conceivably be both hetero and homosexual love, wouldn't it. Yes, she said, I think we're on the same page, that's not only my reading, some of your own resident experts cleared the ground all right in that direction. Fine, the person at the other end of the line, a producer, Shirley Eckersley, said, I guess the public, even here, and perhaps more so in France, is somehow more used to *that* idea in ballet these days, we're in the eighties now, what with many prominent dancers known to be dabbling both ways. Just nothing too graphic on the, you know, and she came up with it directly, especially on the *other* side. Right, she said, that was my view too, don't worry. She might need some large-scale screens and projectors, to show short clips from the Sonnets. Not a given yet, she'd have to think more about it. Also, "Could you by all means also hire a voice actor, able to invisibly — that is from off-the-scene — read Shakespeare to provide a more human and a more specific touch to the dancing development?" That was seen as a bit tricky, as they needed to hire outside, but British theatres are so rich in

Our Lives as Kites

unutilised Shakesperean talent, and I personally know a great 'male voice,' so you can count on that, Shirley concluded.

This would be Shakespeare, S. in short, as is the wont of many of the commentators of the Sonnets, in his thirties, facing middle age and unsure and perhaps dealing with wobbly love interests, himself representing what in this day and age would be labelled diminishing capital, let's not say perishable goods, drawn and pulled and wrenched and having his soul quartered between two polar points, the Youth, most probably male, his former and still strong love, and his latest love interest, the Dark Lady.

This would also be in fact several spatial domains, parts of the virtual space Yvonne had in mind now, at the beginning of the work, meaning S.'s potential zones of craft-related, social and amorous interests where he would work, roam and play the odds in love — and mix all of the above, S. being who he was — say, for one of them, the Globe and the spectators crowding it, say, for the other, the court and its dances and partying (though no one really says anything about him being involved in any high-level amorous or other intrigue — and that, in itself, was good proof, in those times, that he kept his head), say, otherwise, inns with rough partying going on long into the night.

Another part of the space would, as she saw things then, be occupied by one or two large screens, showing flashes (never more than three lines at a time, what with the short attention span these days, also old speech and the competition of other events and the whole motion and the dancing on the stage) of the Sonnets, during breaks in dancing or in parallel with it. Finding a place for them that would not take spectators' minds from the dancing would be highly advisable. If not, better not to have them at all, she'd be left with the voice recitations interjecting from off-stage. Shouldn't be too many either, to be kept strictly as surprises, also as illuminating beacons, if not lighthouses.

The music, then. Wouldn't be a bad idea, not at all in fact, to use Zeffirelli's style, something longing, sounding period-ish, making you to yearn with S. stationed at sea, as it were, in love doldrums. Also danceable, as Mr. B would have said; something to which she could imagine several steps initially, to start off the blocks, and a full choreography a bit later.

S. would be the idealist — or the sucker in this day and age; the Youth and the Dark Lady would be both brash or elegant, in turns, in exploiting him. He would be playing for huge stakes and knowing it, but without backing off even a slight edge of light, carrying his heart on his sleeve; they — they would be playing double, getting involved even, the offense and sickness of it all, with each other, playing pennies, cynical and unaffected. The depth is with the Master, "this is elementary, my friend," she'd say to an imaginary critic, "just read his work," and the losses couldn't be otherwise. The tricky part would be, no doubt, to suggest, to put forward, this depth on his part. It may take a great dancer with good acting. She was thinking carrying significance in facial expression here, not just in motion and gesture, and many good dancers she knew couldn't master that, they were dead as a post in this respect, only interested in their legs and hands and in their exposure.

Yvonne soon realized she wanted to do something classical, perhaps in Balanchine's reading of the term. Still, beside, say, *grands tours* and *piquets penchés* she wanted to enter some modern stances and linking steps. Walking, and the manner of walking, regarding and the manner of regarding, each other and around, posing, had to be important points, as she wanted to suggest at least part of the decorum of the times with that. So much more as she had in mind nothing in terms of period costumes, everything had to be simple, just hints at historical time, there would be only full-body tights for the men and airy long-to-the-ankle white skirts, thin white tights for the women. Big change in store, though, in terms of neck and wrist wear, to produce a whiff of the period: the ladies would have both ruff collars — some closed, cartwheel-like, but nothing hanging, please, won't be even safe, some open — and ruffed cuffs, with nothing in terms of sleeves, that is bare arms, while the men would have to wear mainly black ruff collars. The men would also wear black, brown and burgundy, thus mainly darker, jerkins over the tights, cut at the shoulders, showing Renaissance shirts, belted. She was of two minds whether to ask the males to wear rucked cuffs, but she knew she wanted some of the men to wear cascading front ruffles.

No miming, just dancing, that was another early decision.

The dancing, playing zones, those could be organized on two levels, stories, or be flat.

In the two-levels scheme, there would be on the right a look at the back at the Globe, with spectators looking in toward back right of stage, looking in, that is, toward an imaginary stage of the Globe, Shakesperean or other play going on, from the second level of a structure, mainly at forty-five degrees, with their backs to us, faces partly showing. On the left, there would be the Royal Court, or any aristocratic court for that matter, as we have no idea how high S. went in his love queries, a flat surface showing a large dancing area, not more populated with furniture than what Ashton has in *Marguerite and Armand*, that is a large *salon*. This would be the place for social dances and interaction. We need space, space, there. The Globe, in fact its gallery, would be rougher, spectators bumping each other for a seat. If this set is what is chosen, she thought to have Will climbing up and down a wooden spiral staircase styled for the period (or were the stairs at that time in metal, by any chance?). The advantage of this setting would be more three-dimensionality in dealing with the space, always an advantage when showing motion. However, Shakespeare clambering that staircase, whatever its shape, would be less than elegant, or better said, more difficult to choreograph to anything catching and holding the attention of the viewers, and that was a major concern for Yvonne. True, there could have been a center transitional area between the two zones, and the stairs, whatever their shape, could have been placed more toward the right.

In the other version, the totally flat one, the Globe would be just the spectators standing facing back right, possibly with no physical structures to signify the court and the theather. This would be more abstract and pure, she thought, but drier, perhaps.

S. would move between the two zones, flirt, beg, go up to or accost his lovers, bring them into the main center area for tête-à-têtes, whether confrontations or exchanges of adoration, where they would really engage spatially and emotionally, dancing or otherwise, just walking, prowling around each other, throwing heavy or challenging looks, jealousy, desire, one and all. They would be dancing in couples, S. with the Youth, S. with the Dark Lady, the Youth with the Dark Lady, there being however only one big scene of conflict in which all three of them, in the third act, would show up at the same time, with everything up for grabs and accusations and enticements flowing galore, but of course figuratively, from and for each of them, all come in the open trying or pretending to cut the Gordian knot, only to find everybody was at some loss. While they're in a pas-de-deux, the third could be sometimes present, in a visual second plane, throwing them irritated or dismissive or amused looks from the side; more or, on the contrary, less confident in being able oneself to couple or pair any of the other two for the time being, but not giving up — we're dealing with three strong-minded or at least stubborn characters here, to make things clear. The third would be the third wheel to the cart for the time being, the odd one, trying to dismiss what the currently-constituted couple is showing off, trying to upstage them in dignity or moves, trying to replace one of the other two in the combination, trying to get in. So, in the end the dancing would have to implement this dialectics or whatever philosophy of the proverbial *ménage à trois.*

The bits, the projected flashes from the Sonnets would, of course, not have any direct connection with the actual dancing, it would be part of the identification process, projecting the main character as being great Will and not just any middle-aged man fighting centrifugal forces of conflicting, waning or emerging amours. Perhaps some of the words could be somehow sync-ed with some of the poses or expressions at the time, but that couldn't be guaranteed for any continuity as neither time nor rhythm are the same in dancing and in poetry. And this isn't under any circumstances following the Sonnets' verse and rhyme, but their general flow and mood, if, pray God, we get there, Yvonne thought.

Going back to the music, a Pavane should do just great for the slower, sadder or even tragic parts — perhaps I'll arrange for some duels or some such, they had them in spades then, no doubt, and he had them in Romeo and Juliet and elsewhere, Yvonne thought — a Galliard or a Minuet when things were boiling over in passion and angst, side leaps, *trabucchetti,* for the men, and sly feints, *seguido fintos,* for the ladies, and a Canary would be just the thing for the push-and-pull mesh of jealousy and attraction. Whenever she wanted solemnity, a Courante might serve fine her purpose just as well.

Big question mark right here. Most of the center-side pas-de-deux are going to be modern in style, even though movements could be derived from period dancing (still have to think about those, mind you). Some of these may have to run in parallel. Any ideas how to achieve that? She needs to brainstorm, won't be easy. Perhaps the music and the lights will fade out for the courtly left-side, and fade in on the center part. Or, perhaps, she may have to freeze the action in the left side, really freeze the dancers in place as white blocks of chalk, and switch the center action on, take it to some completion, and resume again with left or right tableaux. Or just totally empty the left side of any dancers and continue in the center with the main characters.

"Let's get a nice magic and cardinal number, four, for the sections. It could rhyme with *The Four Seasons*, even though Vivaldi isn't my choice, at least not yet, for the music," she said to herself. There could be a section on S. and the Youth, another on S. and the Dark Lady, another one on estrangement, the Lady and the Youth strumming the strings of love for each other now, and the last one, where S. brings the castaways — well, he had to show some dignity at some time or another and flick them away from him as insignificant flies — back to him again, and if not reconciliation, tolerance is espoused, Master Time fingered as the real and common arch-enemy of each and all, the one and only god who really doesn't allow us the final repair of our errors and sins against ourselves and others. The pas-de-trois left for the end, the wintry winter of the soul and old age frowning and sneering at him, still, a spiritual theme rising up hopeful and shining, but thin, delicate and frail, in music, toward the future, probing, doubting, sounding off, endeavoring to find, and there would unashamedly be a Christian bent to this: What's left of us, God, pray, first, at the end of life, and second, at the end of time?

In tune with this division, it's only reasonable and symmetrical to have four, again, four musical themes, also four background hues in the lights, which one would take for the effulgent sky.

Marius Hancu

Four, and this is how she saw those sections before starting work on the detailed choreography, most of which would be finalized anyway over in London.

The first act starts on a slow, dignified, processional pavane taking place on left stage, coming in on a circular path; ten pairs or thereabouts.

S. and the Youth are already at center stage, facing each other diametrically opposed on a circle that will be their initial trajectory, frozen, knees half-flexed, arms to the sides, horizontally, in a *plié à la seconde*. Their sights are on each other and are not, most of the time, taken in by what's happening on the left, in fact they are absent to it. It may be that their love is past its peak, but it's still there and still strong, especially on the elder's, S.'s, side. There's still intensity in their looks to each other, still desire, but things seem gradually to fade on the Youth's side, losing visual focus on his partner, directing less of his motion toward him, more independent in motion, as things progress.

The whole center stage dancing is not baroque or Elizabethan at all, but a mixture of classical and modern in styles and moves, sometimes in counterpoint with the period music to the left, sometimes in sync with it. They float and are grounded in their own world. They are of their own time, but their issues are of all time, their sins of the same tree. Say, the one-*up*-one-*up*-one-two-three-*up* sequence of the pavane, with *up* showing a short stop accompanied by an eventual rise to a *demi-pointe* on the toes and balls of the foot could be replicated by the two men in their facing *pliés* with a lift toward the left on the first tempo, lift toward the right on the next, high leg raise in a *developpé* to the left again on three tempi, than down to ground, repeat. Or they could change their initial stances and stand with the side to each other, athwart, riding the large circle, and move with high knee military-like motions on the first two tempi, followed by a one-turn pirouette on the next three.

Once again, they could start back to back in the center, move with pavane-like steps as in a duel for several steps, then turn around simultaneously, stand in place and raise their right hands slowly as aiming in a simulated duel, the conflict boiling in them, the arms recoiling under impact — mind you, should swords be seen as more contemporary, the gestures would be of the *en garde* salute. No victims this time, no real weapons, of course, just miming, no one drops to the ground, they would advance to center in the pavane steps, turn back to back and iterate this one for more imprint in the eyes of the viewers.

Then, say, in the second act, the dance in the group on the left could be a hearty galliard, while in the center S. and the Dark Lady would do their own pas-de-deux, he with, say, *entrechat six* jumps instead and during the *trabucchetti*, the side leaps, and she would do some work on pointes, say, *piqués de côte*, during the feigned sequence, *seguito finto*, of the ladies.

She then wrote down some choice morsels from the Sonnets to eventually be used in voice-overs and put them into her file:

1
From fairest creatures we desire increase,
That thereby beauty's rose might never die

12
When I do count the clock that tells the time,
And see the brave day sunk in hideous night;
When I behold the violet past prime,
And sable curls, all silvered o'er with white;

Then of thy beauty do I question make,
That thou among the wastes of time must go

14
Not from the stars do I my judgement pluck;
And yet methinks I have astronomy
But from thine eyes my knowledge I derive

40
Take all my loves, my love, yea take them all;
What hast thou then more than thou hadst before?

Marius Hancu

No love, my love, that thou mayst true love call;
All mine was thine, before thou hadst this more.
And yet, love knows it is a greater grief
To bear love's wrong, than hate's known injury.

74
When thou reviewest this, thou dost review
The very part was consecrate to thee:
The earth can have but earth, which is his due;
My spirit is thine, the better part of me
    The worth of that is that which it contains,
    And that is this, and this with thee remains

84
I think good thoughts, whilst others write good words,
And like unlettered clerk still cry 'Amen'
But that is in my thought, whose love to you,
Though words come hindmost, holds his rank before

118
    But thence I learn and find the lesson true,
    Drugs poison him that so fell sick of you.

130
My mistress' eyes are nothing like the sun;
Coral is far more red, than her lips red:
If snow be white, why then her breasts are dun;
If hairs be wires, black wires grow on her head.

I grant I never saw a goddess go,--
My mistress, when she walks, treads on the ground:
    And yet by heaven, I think my love as rare,
    As any she belied with false compare.

144
Two loves I have of comfort and despair,
Which like two spirits do suggest me still:

The better angel is a man right fair,
The worser spirit a woman colour'd ill.
To win me soon to hell, my female evil,
Tempteth my better angel from my side,
And would corrupt my saint to be a devil,
Wooing his purity with her foul pride.

These should be enough, she thought.

29 - *Shakespeare's Triangle* II, London, 1988

The pull on the string out here in Blackheath, in London, had been so strong, as though there was no end of clouds all crowded in one small piece of the sky, drawing her bird away, snatching at it with enough nerve and power to possibly make her grip fail at any time and lose it to twisting winds. Twisting, that was the work most worrisome to her, as stress could suddenly build into the string in ways for which it hadn't been threaded by people down here. She had her thick construction work gloves on, leathered in the palms, or otherwise, as on other occasions, skin could be lost in a moment before she would realize it, before the burning would develop, before the blood would have time to show up in a pink rush on her hands. There seemed to be a tunnel in the sky that was taking in her kite on this day, as it advanced or retreated in the same direction, not too much side wobbling. This helped, as she didn't have to move around too much, just to stay steady in place and reel out and reel in the line. She was fighting the wind the way, at times, at home, thinking about it, she thought about Papa Hemingway's old fisherman Santiago fighting with the beast of a fish for days on end, somewhere out in Cuban waters. When the wind was really heavy, she rolled the string all around her midriff, around her three-quarter length oilskin jacket with solid-thick zippers, two or three times she looped it, as anchoring it on herself, giving it her full weight, while leaving enough play to the hand in order to adjust for the shorter-term moods transpiring from up above.

The day had been humid, the leaves of the trees shone with drops of water, the Thames high, and the sky was covered with a dense low network of ashen-mauve clouds, heavy and dark, so she wasn't the least surprised with the opposition she was facing in trying to

Our Lives as Kites

guide her oh-so remote prisoner around. It seemed to have become instead the prey of forces of another realm and recovering it, she thought, might prove to be a matter of resilience and patience, and a couple of challenging hours.

The tunnel in the sky showed intent and greediness and she left for home with the feeling that there was to be some definite resistance in some corners down here to be dealt with. It was just a matter of opening her eyes and the eyes of her mind to the latest happenings, in order to grasp the pull of things and the most dangerous waves that might rise any time.

***

At night, she had a problem in going to sleep, what with the hotel bed, the mattress of a different consistency and hardness, the sheets of a different feel and starchiness, and with the new surroundings, the traffic noise seeping now in and then through the closed and yellow-curtained windows. Some driver or other dropping his weight on the brakes in what she could only imagine as a desperate attempt to avoid another vehicle, perhaps having been asleep at the wheel for a fraction of a second at the end of a long day at work. Groups of noisy youths rushing around in open cars going to parties and showing off full intent and the expendable energy of the age about it.

When she finally went over to Morpheus, it was, of all people, Tabitha Clark of old who was there to welcome her unctuously at the entrance of a large English country manor, one of those she had probably recently read about as being inhabited by rock stars more than the old posh countenances. She was of generous body these days, Tabitha, or so it seemed, all covered in silks and tulles, throwing inviting arms and hands to the side — in the old-balletish *à la seconde* stance that seemed so off even in those undefined circumstances of the dream — and forward to lead in the visitor, as in showing a museum to children there for the first time, as in a *Open, Sesame.* She, Yvonne, would feel the discomfort of showmanship even in her bed on her awakening, as things had been pressed to her hands, unwanted gifts or even tips, the purpose of which had to be tied with the intent of showing off.

Somewhere in the background, there was the vague silhouette of her mother, somehow reproachful, as though in the course of saying, "I told you to keep in touch with Tabitha, I knew what some families can do for their progeny and, what, some others still, unfortunately, can't."

And back behind somewhere in time alloted to the same night, unconsciously gone through and slept over in the consequence, this chess match with Patrick. They hadn't been at it for real for quite a while, the chess, and one of the reasons was mirrored, and she felt it ironical, in the dream. The pouty face of Patrick, puffy from holding face in hands for minutes at a time, which was eternity for his kind of patience, in the hope of helpful ideas, after a loss, and him losing to her too frequently for his amusement. And even in the dream, that's what had happened: with a sweep to the side he knocked down all the pieces, kings, queens, pawns, rooks, knights and bishops, sending them all tumbling to an invisible floor where they fell with the non-noise of the dream in the non-space of a local black hole, and light-blueish a puffy cloud had deus-ex-machinaed in there, into which Patrick, turning a white-togaed back to her, had sought refuge behind a tall pedestal of a statue, none other than a profile of Henry James's — it must have been her recent dropping into *The Ambassadors* as in a bath of syntax.

30 - *Shakespeare's Triangle* III, London, 1988

"Come in, come in," Tabitha was saying, with large, smooth, welcoming gestures. "There's a *huge* place for you in my attention and love, we're *old* friends, aren't we all, the Nationals? Not that all of us have been *that* lucky, but look, life is out there for those willing to take up what chances show up in their path. And I think you and I have been so — I mean willing. At least, I know for myself, I was," she babbled.

"Including those chances, no doubt, as your husband, twenty years older, one foot smaller than yourself, put in your way by your parents as by happenstance," Yvonne took it up to herself, later during the party, after reviewing the actual details, or should we say circumstances. "Money goes to money and clings to it, Alberta money to London money, no doubt. Why should the young flowers of the good families get into losing propositions? But hey, perhaps nature was, at the time of his begetting, generous for him, and he might hide some well-hanging parts in substantial operating condition. And wouldn't that be a miracle!"

There was no manor in the countryside, but a huge two-storey suite, with a spiralated white-balustered inner staircase covered in mahoganied parquet in a fashionable apartment building, in the Kensington area.

Tabitha had showed up at the opening gala. "I just hope she did't crash in here, but paid up the entrance fee," Yvonne had thought to herself, while exchanging perfunctory kisses for old-time's sake.

She soon discovered she shouldn't have been worried, the family was one of Royal Ballet's silver sponsors by now, so they paid their dues some ample way, no doubt, which she didn't want to get the details of, moving to the ladies' room just at the time her old *barre* colleague had started to give out the details under her breath. It was Tabitha who had learned about the show from the glossy circulars sent to the sponsors by the administration, and she came by with that very circular letter, bubbling and sipping the bubbly. "Look at your name here, *Shakespeare's Triangle*, choreographed by promising young Canadian choreographer Yvonne Fillon'! You have arrived, dear. Still 'young,' see, it's in writing. And in London, of all places. Look at us, both colonials. Am I not lucky to get to see you again in such *lo-ve-ly* circumstances! But how! Next time around, you'll be 'consecrated,' or even 'famous.' As to 'young,' I'm not so sure, what with the ballet commentators and the ad copy writers here, they are a pretty nasty bunch, and then time passes for all of us, doesn't it?" she warned nicely.

Then, navigating among guests at her party and tugging her in her wake, Tabitha introduced to Yvonne her two daughters, soon to be debs. Medium height, well maintained, still far from the weighty efflorescence of their mom.

"Have you young ladies done any ballet, like your mother?" she dared the question.

"No, no," demured the oldest, and the other one just nodded in quiet blonde confirmation of that answer.

"No, my girls are too good for ballet, sorry. That might have been fine for you and me," she chuckled to her after the girls left, "but these are other times, less anally-constricted ones," she passed *sotto voce*, "and I don't want them tortured like we were."

"But the beauty of it, the ideal, that doesn't count?"

"Well, it may count for you, I see you're still in that damn business, and what could I do for you, if you enjoy torture?" to which she swigged a small glass of vodka to go with her salmon *hors d'oeuvres* served by a cheery maid in a clean, crisp, black-and white-apron, and suddenly her neck and face caught more color and her speech perhaps more ardor. "For them, knowing waltz and other social dances, and especially *other graces* and going to balls, is more important that making love to the *barre*, that's how I think about it and they don't seem any unhappy. They never asked me to go to a ballet class, and I wasn't fool enough to suggest it. Nothing like my mother in that way, I can tell you. Now, naturally, we all admire your show and so on, but that's your and your own artists' business and tribulations, we don't want to go into that kitchen. Not me, at least. I lost my adolescence to the *barre* and perhaps even my virginity, with all those extensions. Even though if I think well, that might have been John Marsell, but I rather believe the ground was already furrowed," she chuckled. "So, thanks but no thanks, no ballet training for my girls."

***

It was this, Patrick's coming to see her at the Royal Ballet — in her temporary office, assigned to her as a visiting choreographer — to take place on another night following that party at Tabitha's.

And it was to be this way as Yvonne had refused his offers of going out in London together — her mind hadn't warmed up to the thought, that is to say nor did her mind nor her heart feel it as being romantic, just *passé*, history. She had what she wanted, or so she thought right at this time, and didn't want to turn back to her own past thoughts when this certitude hadn't been there, recollecting all those circuitous days, the deadends, the threads broken in the air — that would have brought the taste of lemon into her mouth and acid on her brain.

When she did have time to think of men it was mostly George these days; his bear-like approach to love, the massivity and the playfulness of it all, his equable nature, he, so difficult to make swerve from his set tracks, his tendency not to rush into changing train of thought just for the sake of it or for showing off, all this seemed to agree with her just fine, left her more comfortable, as well as confident, at the end of the day.

She didn't like at all the idea of serving Patrick with an opportunity on a platter to take a more contemporary pass at herself. So, when during the party at Tabitha's — where he had been as by chance invited, a coincidence which seemed to Yvonne as though Tabitha knew something about them and wanted to favor something like a reunion, at least in order to have something to report on to her other social contacts — he had tried to get in close, with a lateral sweet-hug around the shoulder, tightening Yvonne to him, and when, in a fast continuation of that, he had moved his right hand lower, around the side of her midriff, she had flashed at him with raised eyebrows and had taken a quick *coupé*, a slide to the side, away from him, unobservable to others, but surely felt by his hand and his awaiting body, and even worse, by his attendant and awaiting mind, if one based impression on the change of look on his face, from the jovial to the disappointed and the edgy, like blinds collapsing while one's trying carefully and calmly to obturate an intemperate sun. She hadn't quick-elbowed his ribs, that would have meant contact, and contact, even though negatively intended, can change things from one moment to the next, or at least the perception on the side of one of the parties, she thought.

"Still, it seems that something more practical is running through the high corridors — as Lorca would've said — of old Patrick's mind," the thought came to her, after two minutes together in that office, of handing of flowers, of renewed congratulations on the show and especially on her choreography. "Let's see what that is." She placed a glass of water in front of him, for old times' sake. She didn't want him to become dry in the mouth for the wrong reasons. He sat and was now fiddling uncomfortably with his perch on the chair. It came out in the end, after several minutes of small talk, him still fidgeting, as:

"You've thrown us a beautiful challenge, Yvonne. Yes, the gauntlet is down there."

"Excuse me, 'us' being who?"

"Lead male dancers. Everywhere, I mean, and it's not complimenting to curry favor with you. That, I hope, I'll always have, at least a tiny bit, in some remote cockle of your heart, shall we say."

She didn't encourage him.

He continued, "It's a wonderful part you have in here. So much temptation, so much inner fight, so much of time's passing. And such contrasts with the Dark Lady and the young fellow, the Youth. This is just to speak of the main lines. It was a great choice, Shakespeare, for something to be put on in England, we'll always resonate to *him*. Still, I've no doubts it should work everywhere. He's still huge. But I certainly didn't expect this to come from the

Sonnets' side, no, sir. I could've bet on any of the tragedies or comedies. Been there, done that. The love for and of the *Sonnets*. I didn't know you had this much of the first, thus thank you for letting in us, me, on you," he laughed. "Why not, the *Sonnets*, but then, it hasn't been done before, haven't checked; anyway, not this way. And the dancing's great, some great sequences and *pas-de-deux*. I could see it a bit differently at times, a little bit edgier, a touch sharper. But perhaps I should be more modest and careful for now. Let's get first where I have to get in this all." Then, again after a longish suspense in the conversation, it suddenly came:

"Now that you know how I like it, *love it*, would you, Yvonne, put in a word?"

"To whom?" She didn't quite see the follow up, not yet.

"Well, you know, to *them*," and he pointed desperately toward the wall. She got it, immediately after observing the physical direction of his pointing, that he meant the powers-to-be at the Royal.

"Ah, but *for what*?" She already guessed it, but she wanted him to make the effort of the extra step, of putting himself out in front of her. Also, she didn't want to put words in his mouth. "He is, in the end, a man. Let him deal with it," she told herself.

"Come on ... Come here," and he made a sign for them to approach heads, to which she complied. That, confidences, she could still allow him.

"You know," he pointed to himself, in the same effort to discretion, "in your S., in your *Shakespeare*," he released it to her ear. On retreat from this intimacy, his face was injected, a rarity with him, and his thirty-something temples showed tensed blood vessels. This was something he really wanted, she could see that, not just acting in order to get back into her graces again. It was him and the business side of his art and he wanted to open a path.

"Ah, you mean *that*?" Now that she had it confirmed, she had to think about it, but she had on already the most neutral and non-committal countenance, as she truly didn't want to sound too encouraging or too disappointing to him. It seemed, on the face of it, the situation, as a tough nut to crack, whether she decided to help him get the part or not.

She knew perfectly well that Patrick had been lately only on an guest artist, on an on-and-off basis with the Royal, after leaving them years ago for New York, a principal here at the time, just as she herself had done at a different time, she a soloist then, but in Canada. The journeys of life, trying for the fleetingly great, for the seemingly absolute, for fame, why not say that.

The Brits might not have said too much at the time of his leaving, but — Yvonne was thinking now, looking at his still young face, more mature, and now riddled a bit with concern, at his long blonde hair, caught at the back of this neck with a black string, the entirety of him releasing the old bright charm out of that pair of green eyes — any company in that situation can't feel too happy about losing a star in full ascent like a flower from a bouquet lost while riding in *bateau mouche* on the Seine, even though he had promised to keep in touch and tour with them on an invited basis, "should the circumstances allow it."

She knew that those, well, circumstances, didn't quite materialize while he was happy as a sparrow and busy in New York, yet that they had done so much more in recent years when he had to start to move around and show up with companies all over the world, while his attraction as a top dancer was probably, just somewhat, on the wane. Probably fading, that is, in the natural change under time; probably, as she hadn't seem him dance in over four years. Without telling him, so as to avoid untenable promises, she wanted to help, definitely not because of their intimate past — this, for one thing, she said to herself, and wanted to stick to it — but because she had once held him in high regards in her dancer's eyes and, not least, because she remembered her own lean years at the end of her own soloist track, packing and moving to Monte-Carlo and other operas and ballets in a roving fashion, without really finding a place to fit in for long, simply because she had been herself in transition to a painful place in her career as a dancer for reasons that had simply to be associated with cruel Father Time, as she liked to call it.

"I'll try to see what can be done about it," she said, deliberately impersonally. She knew already that the part was performed in an informal rotation by two dancers at the beginning of their thirties, John Danville and Frank-Leonard Sheen, Danville being the more brilliant one, Sheen the steadier, both of them technically marvellous. She expected opposition — how open, that remained to be seen, but such things are never really open in ballet companies, that she knew too — as they had been faithful to the Royal Ballet, never leaving the company since the end of their teens.

Later that day, Yvonne called Judie Anderson, the ballet writer. A former dancer, also married to a dancer. She knew Judie wasn't on the rumour circuit. After moving around in circles, she delicately issued the fathoming question, "Ah, by the way, since we're talking common acquaintances, have you seen Patrick dancing, I mean lately?"

"Patrick, Patrick Donovan? But of course, it was only three months ago that I saw him in *Giselle*. Sweet Patrick, him of the huge calves, long arms and fiery eyes, and of a retinue of admirers! Splendid form, still, perhaps losing a bit of height in his *grands jetés* and *Bournonville jetés*, perhaps it was only my eyes, a bit of *ballon*. Buth then, not even Nureyev or Bruhn escaped that. No one under the sun does, do they? He's always had great taste, perhaps too much, when I think of it, having been more corrosive, or decisive, with more edge, if you want, in his dancing of course, at times, might have helped his style. Mannerisms, here and there, some have talked about it in so many words. Coming after Nureyev, that fierce, animal presence, I think that's understandable, everyone would lose in that direction, in that edge, at least from what we see and understand now in terms of other leading men still around or coming up. Don't know that much about Russians, but Baryshnikov is out here and Soloviev did himself in, if you can think, thirty-seven or something, full bloom, or perhaps he sensed the beginning of the slope down and didn't want to get there. Be great forever, Soloviev might have thought, at that dacha, with the shotgun in front of him. But those, sorry for the digresssion, I mean Patrick's, long arms seem to have gotten ever more expressive and he seems to be better at managing time, timing himself better, letting more meaning into his gestures and his face. I think we're lucky to still have him around. Still a great *porteur*, by the way. Ladies, I mean his partners, and I, for one, strictly mean those on stage, love him."

"Doing many shows, still?"

"I'd be careful about the wording. I'd use the term 'irregularly.'

However, still a good show to catch and those in the know, I mean the old-timers, adore him, making full house. We terribly missed him here during his escape to brash America. Now that the prodigal, and penitent, may I add, son is home, we enjoy seeing him onstage, whenever shown, and he's been lucky to brighten our days with his, I guess, not cheaply gained, I mean sweat of the brow, expertise, in Mr B's work. Even in, er, what did I say? Ah, yes, *Prodigal Son* it was. Ha, ha."

"But you were saying he's not cast too frequently, weren't you?"

"You could say that. Indeed, you could."

Two days later, she took the producer, Shirley Eckersley, the same person who had originally placed the inquiry about the ballet itself to her in Canada, out to a coffee shop close to the ballet theater, on the Strand, feeling more comfortable than in the house. However, the ground didn't seem sound at all, from the first side inquiry about Patrick in S.'s role.

"You know, Yvonne," Shirley looked into her eyes, didn't evade the exchange, over the smell and the steam of the coffee, "I can't tell you the reason, sorry, but I'm very skeptical something could be done about it all, or even that something ought to. I'm sure it's been already looked into; I mean what with Patrick's accomplishments, definitely has. I suppose it's just some unfortunate circumstances, old histories. Had Patrick gained such support for other ballets, from such insiders as you are on this one, not to speak of an author," she laughed, "that might have been *considered*. But not, unfortunately, in this case, I don't believe so, knowing what I know. I don't think it's even being too late to the train, it's different. But I'll go and try to talk to some of the powers to be. Please keep this strictly between you and I, even for Patrick, we don't like to disappoint people, or to create unwarranted waves, as this is a delicate sea to navigate, as you very well know." She never mentioned who those in charge, or higher ups, might have been, but Yvonne wasn't surprised, common practice in the business — it was plain old "tell 'them' on a need to know basis, don't show them any of the ropes." And she wasn't a local, so she couldn't have asked for more, not if she wanted to keep her own relationships in fine and dandy order. She would remain in London for three more weeks, in order to make sure the first series of the show were fully successful, as in contract — and her deepest desires, of course. However, no feedback to her reconnaissance ever came from Shirley, and she had to accept it at face value.

Years later, Yvonne was to know that everything had been, at the source, an old indiscretion Patrick had once committed with the wife of the director assigned to her piece, Julian Roberts.

31 - 1986

It seemed to Yvonne that from the men in her life, the one that happened to come to her mind the most lately was George, and those apparitions by themselves at times spurted sparks as spectacular as Christmas-tree fireworks. She didn't try to put any special interpretations to it all, but those were patterns of which only the blind or dull in feeling, she thought, slightly furrowing her forehead under her page-short curled locks, could have been heedless.

The nature of their sex, in which she felt expanding under his enthusiasm and corporeal — including sexual — dimensions as a hot-air balloon in the most-filled-of-desire directions, physically and consciousness-wise, was the definite lead-in and background to those apparitions. During it, she felt not only touched everywhere, and in places reached by no one else, places that acutely pinged in response, but also felt held up there on some inexperienced, high plateaus, in a high-wire act, as though a conductor had ordered a note be kept high up in the space of sounds for some terrifically long duration, and had not dropped his baton, until her ears started to strum and her breathing was galloping for air. It was the proverbial size, but in all respects, and not something to neglect had to be the feeling, the perception of his body under her hands, her own impossibility of somehow hugging, girdling, really fully grasping him in any diagonal, so big and thick he was in muscle and plain size. She felt rather being a vine climbing up a huge sequoia, modestly trying to enter its existence, to register with it.

One of the lessons she had to grapple with was to use lots of helping oils in the doing, and to only gradually accept his presence in herself, as her body, bones, muscles, skin and membranes, distended itself to the mythic realities of his. Calling into effect his full range of digital play and magic during the prelude was most helpful too, so much so that her center felt it was flying ahead as a wheel-less piano. And his sport had taught him a great deal about touching as massage. Taking their time, that seemed to be the name of the game. Yet, her body was getting so excited while doing just that, that primeval hot squirtings, eruptions, took place from deep within herself, things unheard with other men, especially in so preliminary a phase of the contact. "I think we've discovered geysers in myself," she laughed at George.

The sex with Patrick was, by comparison, all rapid fire and somehow just scratching the surface, not that she didn't enjoy it.

She had tried to think up a ballet with beings such as George, and had a hard time with it, when she realized how difficult would be to assemble a group of people his size. She would have to go to some international athletics meets and hire some of the discus or hammer throwers, no doubt. How they would move on stage would be another matter, but she hoped perhaps the public won't have the same expectations from some of these Antaen figures as from ordinary dancers, it would be as though producing something for a family of elephants. Grace in power and weight would be grace redefined. Perhaps she might try it, but for the time being she was fond of having the man all to herself, as she thought — and she couldn't have pointed out the reasons for thinking so — that George was much more monogamous in spirit than her.

She liked him on other points too, thinking, well, this is why people called the Pacific the Pacific. Difficult to upset in any shape and form, perhaps because he had been trained to store up any drop of mental and physical energy for those long throws of a two-kilogram object, or because those rippling masses on him were perhaps by themselves a becalming influence by their own inertia. And no, Patrick didn't have this equanimity, there was a much shorter fuse and what one could, no doubt, call impatience. Even when talking, he, Patrick, switched focus without taking time to stay too long on a subject, and mirroring that feature of character in sex, he did the same in his exploring of points and zones on and inside her body.

"This need for patience, this might well be just me changing," she thought with some remorse. "From execution, to thinking, all still in dance, when that execution wasn't believed by the powers-to-be as something which I could be trusted with any more. When dancing yourself, you need your reflexes to be sharp as a razor. Talk choreography, and the balance changes to vision and thought. I think I can agree with this."

To herself, she had never accepted the alleged diminution of her physical prowess, still thought gradual retirement from active dancing of mature dancers a clever move on behalf of the dancing society at large to make room for the new generations of dancers. In class or at rehearsals, she was still very much into demonstrating everything full-bore herself and that brought at times with it some pains and aches, as she wasn't so warmed up and flexible at any time as the active dancers usually are, they, who go through several re-warm-ups a day, but was sitting and watching others, or just reflecting at or critiquing what they were doing, for hours at a time.

***

Today it's a Sunday and George is taking her to the Varsity Stadium. He wants to put her through a real workout, he said, not the wishy-washy stuff she's used to doing day in day out in her sport. Rubbing it in with ballet as sport, is he too. She was willing, wanted to see him up close by in his element. He hasn't ever expressed an opinion on her dancing or choreographing, just sitting through the rehearsals, at times plainly and admiringly open-mouthed at her "moves and stuff," as he refers to them when they talk about it.

She's watched panels of patchy yellow as splattered and splashed by a Pollocky painter during her dream the whole night, and she's thinking right now that any change from that can't be but a relief for her inner tableaux, framed or not framed they be. "I'm in urgent need of a better gallery, or else I'll turn and toss again for several nights to come."

32 - *The Metamorphosis* I, 1992

The last reading of the skies, both from the radio and out the window, was propitious: I should be able to raise my kites that afternoon without fighting the winds too much. So there I was, carrying the six-foot Jeremiah on my shoulders, barely able to walk in and around inside the Montreal metro cars. Went past the colonnades at the entrance in McGill, took to the left field, the students now on vacation as it was June, put the kite down on the ground, sat myself on the dry uncut grass.

I looked around with relief, practically no one to bother my concentration with the repetitious, thickheaded questions of the curious bystander: what's it made of; aren't you afraid of being electrocuted; do you have to pay any taxes for it, the vehicle, that is, and for it, the activity, that is, in this province; is it an expensive hobby to carry on in this day and age; are all kites made in China these days, that's what I heard; do you lose many of them to the sky master; why would you use such bright colors, don't you feel them too strident, you might trouble the Maker up there with them; and so on and so forth. I had on a pair of sneakers, just in case I'd have to run around a lot, something unavoidable at times if you still wanted to recover your kite from the grip of the sky and you had to allow it some play to get into softer air territory.

Two hours later, Jeremiah's face, while descending under bumps of breeze, looked for a flash to me like a beetle, and it was then that it came to me: Kafka *had* a beetle, or whatever coleopteron that was, in *The Metamorphosis*. I had liked the novella — or was it a short story? — written by Kafka before WWI — 1912, in fact, I've recently found — and, if I remembered well, one of his only books published before his death: amazing economy of words and of fireworks in terms of figures of speech, though still so sharp on my feelings from the first read, like a knife with no handle to grasp on, on which you cut yourself peeling ordinary apples and then you exclaim "How foolish of me" and you become angry, first at your choice of knife, then at your lack of thinking in not having placed a rag or something around the base of it, to protect yourself during the damn work. "Stupid, fool! How could I," you're crying out, but the experience and the memory of it stays with you for several days in the cut and the intermittent bleeding and the tasting of your blood, which you need to suck on at times, when nothing better is at hand.

Would I want to do it? I saw myself going at it only in a tragicomic reading, which would have allowed for some humor, however dark, and eased in with it some miming, as in a ultra-dark *Nutcracker*. Otherwise, I would not be confident to be able to remain faithful to the original in any dance interpretation. Of course, there was always the possibility of providing every single audience member a copy of a short libretto right before the beginning of the show, but even so, it's difficult to assume they'd read it at all, even if the ushers decreed out loud "Reading time now, please, everyone!" Even so, even with miming, it would be difficult to believe dancing — on account of its intrinsic nature and not for any details of the story at hand — could suggest to the finest detail the nature of the way things happening in that family both before and after Gregor Samsa's overnight metamorphosis, the dirty dentelle of relationships. It should be clear with anyone thinking about it that, when a reason is somehow provided or intuited, an easier justification for a certain manner of dancing exists, and spectators are more comfortable with it. I wouldn't like them, the public, to think this is in some manner or other an 'abstract, dear, you know, it is damn abstract' ballet with no support in a clear sequence of events. And I think the reference to *The Nutcracker* will be in order, as in that work, too, facts must be suggested or hinted at by some 'theatricality,' including in props and costumes, and not by dance alone. I mean, one can do 'pure ballet' only when reasonable to do so. I far prefer to be seen as original in dancing based on known motives than in hiding the story behind the dance.

There would be three parts to it, as in the original. Nabokov, for one, made a lot of this number, and I suspect there might be something to it.

Big question mark: how to show Gregor in his beetleness slash beetledom slash some undefined vermineness (some translators make him a 'vermin,' others still an 'insect') in which he falls after his sudden metamorphosis? The multitude of legs should be restricted to six, out of which two should be artificially coming out of his 'back' between his formerly-human legs and arms, now all legs. The dancer should wear something rigid on his back, as a convex, oval, shell-like, exoskeleton they call it, covering him from knees to neck, and should crawl most of the time on the new legs; not an easily-to-dismiss feat. He should be able to wallow or swing, at times, on his 'armour-like' back placed on the floor; thus the need to have something convex enough for the shell. Golden brown should be a good color for the shell. Should we want him to crawl upon the walls and the ceiling, as he does in Kafka, that might not be so easy without some tricks, perhaps magnetic things attached to his legs, which would retain, clamp, him to iron-made walls. Another way would be to provide a net of barely-visible rungs all around his room, on the ceiling too, which he would grasp at while crawling about. His bottom part should look as described by Kafka: 'brown belly, slightly domed and divided by arches into stiff sections.'

The first part should show us the happy Samsa family before the catastrophe, the stress on Gregor and the short happy times together. Everybody but Gregor sits at the table in the living or sitting room, father as usual idling away the time carefully poring through the newspaper. Gregor himself? He's out there in the real, mean, business world, paying back his father's debt by working as a travelling salesman. So, he's to be shown running from the left to the right of the scene, then back the other way round, in front of their house open to us in cross section, with the suitcase of samples hanging heavy on his arm, getting him out of balance. He runs to the right, to the left, opens his suitcase in front of some prospective customer right out in the street for décor simplification, gets rejected — most of the time, goes on to his next sale visit, and so on. He's short of breath, the poor fellow, stopping center stage at times for just a second to look forlorn to the horizon, at life coming at him, and now and then, just barely, with flimsy hope, toward the inside of the house, where he wishes he could be.

During some of his runs, he's chased at a trot by the chief clerk of the company he works for, who drives him around to his work as a proper slave owner would, as well as by his minions. Between some of the runs, Gregor gets into his house, would dearly love to have a drink of water and some respite, but father demands first the money Gregor's earned for them — imperious 'give it to me' gesture here. The sweet younger sister plays the violin — and she wants money too. Payments to them in large notes are mimed. Then they rush him out of the home back to work. His runs are high-kneed ones, his hands are flying around him, he looks like an uprooted windmill, neck bent under the daily strain of work. The sister takes breaks in her room in her violin playing and beauty-making and does some dancing; short, modest, pirouettes, skips in a circle, whirling in *chaînés* and quick moving to the side in *piqués de côté* around the penny furniture in the room, basically just a small table, a single bed and a commode with a mirror. The elders peer at her admiringly from Gregor's room, the one in the middle, through the just-open door to her room. They, the old fogies, the father claiming a back illness, the mother an asthma problem, take a ridiculous-looking *pas de deux* now and then around their own room or in the living room in a polonaise. The rooms, arranged in a semicircle, communicate with each other and are open on the spectators' side to allow their view, of course. The elder Samsa reads newspapers busily at all times of the day, and while reading them, makes gestures at the articles, as in "Listen to this now, can you really believe it?" He makes dancing, better said hopping, rounds of the rooms he's in, now and then, with a stick in his hand for support and holding a hand to his back. He's bending himself to one side, then to the other, in a ridiculous minuet by himself.

A short parade should be reserved for the happy family coming from left to right, probably going to a picnic on some occasion. They are coming along, all aligned behind Gregor, the proud support of the family these days and for some years now, sliding ahead slowly and happily, on the long steps of a waltz — no turns, please, this is still a modest, controlled, knowing-their-place family. Then, in the middle of the stage, his sister rejoins Gregor, and both of them, brother and sister, hand in hand, skip for several steps ahead in *Bournonville jetés* and hop forwards in *emboîtés*, showing off a bit the energy of the youth of the family and their apparent love for each other. The family caravan could eventually be made even to go round the house, in what would be a 'merry outing,' with the parents happily but heavily and painfully, it seems, following their progeny.

In one of his short visits home, Gregor enters his sister's room and watches in rapture her violin playing, immobile and in silence. Soon enough, he has to leave for work, and does that by stepping back with *grands* and *petits jetés en arrière*, in a circle, bent all the time in half-reverence, showing reserve and modesty, his appreciation for his sister's talent. He exits while inaudibly dancing backwards and carefully closes the door after himself. Alternately, he could do that in hops toward the back in *arabesque sautillé en arrière*, changing at times the support leg.

This preamble isn't really in the book as a separate scene, but gleams through in Gregor's reminiscences and in Kafka's commentary about the family's past, interspersed here and there. This gleaming made me feel it should be important to visually establish in the ballet a historical background for the life of his family. After this introduction, I mean, we could get to the earth-shattering experience of Gregor's metamorphosis into a huge insect — human-size for the sake of clarity, and of course for fidelity to the original text.

We'd show it happen on a dawn of a morning, as in the book, however we'll insist on a change of light and of music. If before the misfortune everything were in natural colors, of course brighter for the day, after the change we'd have all the lights filtered in a light, spectral mauve that would create a strange atmosphere throughout those parts. Not only that, but the music would switch from joyous, jumpy preclassical to moody, anxious modern. I'm thinking of parts of 'Wozzeck' by Alban Berg, physically scratching music, paining at times, though with ridiculous powers to clinch viewers' attention and focus it on the events at hand, for all its disarming lack of comfort.

I wanted the light and the music, as well as Gregor's costume, his motions and gradually altered voice — not that he would speak much in the ballet, but say from the nature of his moans — to throw us all into altogether another world, human only in part, coleopteral otherwise. This is where Gregor and his family are all now, mostly as a result of the unlucky change, but also coming from their updated and enriched sins against him in his new horrific state.

So, classical prettiness of motion would at this point give way to the rough and modern, allowing contortions, strange spatial articulations of the body, for both beetle and humans. The dancing steps or motions themselves should show the change. Only here and there, as in the final scene, would I allow snippets of 'classical' to get in the tussle at hand again.

I think there's no point in perhaps trying to make Gregor a beautiful beetle. On the contrary, we should get him as awful and naturalistic as the costume designer can go without loading up the soloist too much, weight-wise, I mean. Still, I don't want him to be made into a caricature. Everybody else around him is a caricature à la Švejk, no doubt — same period, don't forget, Hašek and Kafka, same city, Prague — but he's not one, Kafka makes him to think and act throughout the book as a very sincere person, full of good will, the salt of the earth, exploited by each and every canaille, by the more and by the less powerful, especially by those close to his heart. However, that beetle should move awkwardly, no doubt. Kafka goes to great lengths to describe the pain Gregor is in when moving, be it crawling on the floor and over the walls, changing sides from topside up to bottom-side up, hiding under a sheet, and so on, in that room that is the only space alloted to him until the end, for, once a beetle, he never succeeds in going past the doorways of that very room. The claustraphobia of being trapped in that armored body and shut in that room forever must be terrible, for he stays a human at heart, even though no one in touch with him in his awful new life really believes that or cares about it either. A great set of jaws is mandatory and should be designed in, as he at one time unlocks and opens a door by using them, when he finds that his hands have in fact disappeared for all practical purposes. He's become ridiculous on a human scale for even the most ordinary day-to-day routines: opening a door, getting out of bed, moving around, talking, eating. Nothing works for him anymore in the familiar universe, everything at last humiliates him, forbids itself to him.

We are on this fateful morning of the transmogrification. The new mauve-ish light of the dawn comes up, gradually focussing on his room. Of course, no one but Gregor is supposed to get up this early in the morning. The light is kept off for the time being in the other rooms. His alarm clock rings clanging throughout the house like a death knell, but the old Gregor is not there to respond. His newly-created body is laying flat in his bed, encased in his new armor, about which he doesn't have an idea yet. Three times he tries to sit up in bed — impossible. His former hands beat the air in an attempt to find where he is, as though in a bad dream; only slowly and gradually can he place them on this body, which, shocker, is hard as stone. This should be shown in a rhythmic motion, gradually amplified as he becomes more flexible and aware of his new body's capabilities. He lies on his back, which is quite convex, and, again rhythmically, he sways from right to left on it in an attempt to get out of bed. On the fifth attempt, he manages it and falls in rhythm with the music onto the floor. But he's succeeded — he's flat on his face and belly on the floor, the six legs moving agitatedly, trying to find something, anything to use for traction. How the two limbs in the middle, between the former pairs of legs and arms, manage to move, is another matter, which will be solved by the special-effects guy together with the costume designer. I don't care, but there should be some activity in them, they can't just be immobile — not credible. To the end, he won't recover his nimbleness again. This is a slow-reacting huge beetle we're dealing with, nothing too youthful or energetic. His human age doesn't come into account, it has become immaterial.

Poor Gregor still doesn't have a clue on what has happened to him, but he knows he's late for work. The neighborhood church tolls six in the morning, and we see the father, mother and sister all striding with long sneaky steps to Gregor's doors on both sides (he's in the room between theirs) and pound them twice (the parents from the living room on the left, where they are at their breakfast, the sister from her room to the right of Gregor's room), then all of them turning in ridiculous sync toward the church and accusingly fingerpointing to its pealing the hour, like, "What are you doing,

Gregor, about it?" How strange this day looks to them, when Gregor hasn't taken a sick day at work for fifteen straight years! Then we see the parents go to the breakfast table, where, in nervous excitement, they play for a while a sequence of musical chairs around the table, while the sister does the same in sync in her room — watch the timing, the music is crucial here — she, on her side, swapping nervously positions from her bed to her chair in front of the dresser, all three of them going through the movements with bent knees and heavy padded treads, this interrupted at intervals to go one or all to Gregor's door to pound it and to point again toward the clock, signaling procrastination and neglect of duties on his part. They press themselves against his doors, trying to hear the noises issuing from Gregor's room. After three or four appeals, there's a response from his room, but that is nothing human-sounding, perhaps a loud clicking of some sort. We should provide Gregor with a device producing that strange voice under his direct control or sync some artificially taped sounds with his apparent replies — he's raising his head and one of his many feet, asking for patience.

Not surprisingly, Gregor's honorable and profitable company can't tolerate his missing even a few hours of his work, so when he wasn't seen by the office assistant in the station at five in the morning, the chief clerk, no less, and two minions are sent after him and they come toward Samsa family's house in parade steps that are similar in style to their running after Gregor during the first part — high-stepping steps, in the manner of brass band drum majorettes, but much slower and purposeful this time, the chief clerk at the front of the formation, the other two one step behind, behaving slavishly all the way through. They want to put an end right now to what they see as skiver behavior by one of their employees, without allowing Gregor even one morning of respite. So they climb the stairs to the family's first floor, still in marching style, and once inside, dismissively and semi-militarily salute the parents, mime asking questions and wondering about Gregor's intentions for the day and his future with the company, and not shying away from threatening him with dismissal for bad conduct. They, the clerks, go in turns and knock at his door, and the sounds we hear on the knocks are queerly similar to Beethoven's destiny's knocking, 'pa-pa-pa-paaah!' It must be clear they seriously go after him.

Then, in a counterpointed scheme, the two groups, the family and the inspecting party, take turns at the musical chairs dance scheme in the living room, at parading through the flat and at pounding Gregor's door from the kitchen side. The family shuffles, the clerks walk militaristically. From time to time, they show up in full formation and pound the door, all six of them, the sister from her side, one upon each's of Beethoven's beats, to make the farce more farcical. Then, in exasperation, upon finding that Gregor apparently either doesn't want to open the door or can't do so, the mother sends the sister and the maid for the doctor and the locksmith, respectively, each appropriately mimed.

While everybody else moves around the flat doing of course nothing but being concerned with his becoming a lazybones, Gregor has gradually approached the door of the living room, going slowly at it, at half or one quarter of the speed of everybody else. His crawling can, again, be counterpointed to everybody else's motion. We should have him go in long circles and spirals around the room, as though still disoriented within his new body, as though lost in a labyrinth to which he has not clue. He is finally able to grab the key with his huge mandibles, move it around in the lock and unlock the door with a loud click. He's somehow now rearing up on his back legs to signal to the full assemblage outside his good intentions of returning to work, without realizing the effect his very appearance might have on them. So, when he finally manages to open the door, the first and most shocked is the chief clerk, the closest to him at the time, to whom Gregor has been wanting to submit a message of his good will for his bosses at the office. But whatever he articulates is ghastly sounding and his whole twitching body is nightmarishly menacing to them, such that the men from his office all scurry away. The trio moves as a unit in awful sync as they change their mind and try to come back twice in an up-and-down climbing of the stairs, but each time they are frightened at the renewed sight of the hideous human-sized insect and finally disappear cowardly in the adjoining streets.

Of course, his father has by now seen Gregor in his new look, and the father's the only one who's not scared by him — how could he be? He has tyrannized Gregor all this life, perhaps forcing him to grow this shell as a form of defense, as some of the commentators see it, (but not Kafka, who doesn't provide any explanations for it) — and threatens him vehemently, now that Gregor's most probably no longer a source of income for the foreseeable future, now that he's not able to pay the father's own debts, pushing him back aggressively into his room, in the process crushing some of his feet against the frame of the door. So, Gregor finally finds himself back in his room, bleeding now in his coleopteran fashion, while his father's dancing a hopping, awkward, victorious, menacing dance of domination, "Now I showed him!" over in the living room, also while his mother's wallowing on the floor in her tears and praying, mostly in fear of their son, not anymore in concern for his well-being. The tide has turned for Gregor and his family and the church bell ominously tolls outside.

I think we'd better go on now straight into an outline of the dances for the second act, so we'd know from the get go what the major pieces are and what work must be done there.

To start with, there would be the feeding and hiding piece. Grete, Gregor's sister, still has sympathy for him, even in his new state. He was her highest supporter toward getting her to study music at the conservatory in the near future — she's seventeen now — he even thought of paying from his own pocket for those studies. However, she can't hide her definite nausea and revulsion at the sight of him in his new form, even without ever expressing that to him, and it doesn't take long for Gregor to get it. This then becomes a carefully choreographed, I mean this figuratively, piece. As he for months hasn't been able to leave the room, she has decided she needs to bring some food in there. Now, whenever his sister's coming in, what he does is crawl and hide under a couch in his room. A warning routine is established between them: his sister knocks; Gregor gets under the couch; he covers himself with the sheet so she won't see him even by mistake; she comes in and leaves his food on a plate or something. Grete's approach to the door to check up on him through a crack in it should, I'm thinking now, be done in small side-bouncing jumps, similar to *coupés*, from a flexed-knee stance, flat sole to flat sole, as from a *à la seconde pliée* to another *à la seconde pliée,* but not quite so open, or perhaps similar to *piqués de côte*, without the *pointe* work, of course. We'll have to decide on the final choice during rehearsals. She should have this routine of placing, while approaching the door and several meters away of it, both her hands as in a mimed hearing horn to an ear, and of putting her head against the door as for helping her to better hear, in order to realize if he is moving around at the time, which would prohibit her entry, as she doesn't want to see him. He, in his turn, should retreat under the couch face down, as a beetle would, but at the very last moment, would turn himself on his back in order to be able to draw the sheet over himself. I want him to zig-zag through the room, to show disorientation and panic at the thought of her seeing him if he weren't to move fast enough; say move two-three feet one way, then two, three feet at an angle from that, say sixty degrees or so, and so on, as drifting.

Then there'd be the sequence of Gregor's crawling over the walls and ceiling in between meals. I think I mentioned previously how this could be done technically: clamps, holes, hidden rungs, or other stuff still to be found. My concern here is his specific kind of motion, his hitches and shuffles, his detailed crawling, how to make that idiosyncratic walk, thus visually memorable by itself. Patterns are important, I think, in order to impress the sight. So, which patterns should we have here? How about a hitch on one side, the one damaged against the frame of the door by his unthinking and callous father when pushing him back into his room? So, that side would make shorter steps and stay lower, the other would be more energetic and get higher. This would, of course, lead to a drift to a side, toward the side with less power and traction; he'd go in small arcs, commas if you want. I want a strange, rhythmic, but sober and sad, music to that sequence, something that would show how far he is, physically speaking, from us over here on this side of the animal-human divide. The overall effect should be, perhaps, one of pity over a damaged animal, whose survival for that very reason in a rough world is doubtful.

Then there would be that furniture-moving scene where the mother for the second time really sees Gregor up close in his beetle-like reincarnation and loses consciousness on account of it. The mother, smallish, asthmatic, weak, sickly, and totally dominated by her husband. I'd have her advance in small stuttered steps, toes out, as from a première stance to another, or a bit à la Chaplin, coughing frequently, or holding her handkerchief at her mouth to prevent that, sometimes obviously gasping for air like fish on dry land, convulsively. Quite often, she sneaks a look toward her husband for approval, as though asking, "Am I doing well, Sir, am I doing what you want?" and you can bet on that "Sir" being there, the old-fashioned way. The daughter's explaining to her they need to remove the furniture from Gregor's room in order to allow him more freedom to roam around, crawling, as she's seen the tracks left in beetlish adhesive secretions by Gregor everywhere, and he seems to need more space. Funny thing is, she's never asked Gregor about it, and, in point of fact, he wouldn't like his room left empty as a cave, with none of his former human possessions and mementos. Still, she is able to convince her mother, and so they get the chest of drawers, that contained his fretsaw and other tools, out of his room, after much difficulty, then his writing desk, at which he's worked for years, since infant school. So, Gregor asks himself, "What could I save from my former possessions?" His sight is caught by a picture of a lady in a fur boa, to which he had once affixed the wooden frame he made during his fretsaw work, thus very dear to him. So, while the women were in the living room, taking a break after having pushed out the writing desk too from his room, he quickly crawls up on that wall, to keep that possession out of their grabby hands. And in that position, totally exposed, is he surprised by his mother and sister who come back too soon for him to have gotten away in time from their line of sight. The mother cries out and swoons away. His sister heavily admonishes Gregor, runs for drugs in the living room and Gregor follows her, even though in his state of awkwardness he's not able to really provide any help. The sister runs back to his room to administer whatever medicine she found to their mother, and at this time, the father comes home and surprises Gregor out of his room, a situation in which Gregor definitely shouldn't have been, in his father's view, and in the living room.

Now, let's get back to motion, or choreography, whatever. Those furniture pieces should be in fact quite light, and placed on casters, so they would be able to slide and whirl around easily, even when so pushed by those two slight-framed women. There should be a game of "furniture ping-pong," following the music, where the mother and the sister push each piece from one to another over the floor, both in Gregor's room, and from one room to another. They catch it and push it back as in not being able to grab it properly. In the breaks, they hold their hips and the small of the back in pain, and wipe their brows — in delayed mirror movie images of one another. On the other side, Gregor, when running to save that picture, should zig-zag over the whole room from one modest remaining thing to another, to show he doesn't know what to save first from his possessions. Also, when the women create all that hubbub, he should move in place under that couch and the sheet in extreme agitation, smallish multiple legs bouncing off the floor with each perceived noise, his beetle head shuddering on each shout or bang. He's increasingly bothered by human noise.

So now, we're getting to the scene with the apple bombardment, where the father, totally estranged from his son, wants to push him back out of sight in his room. He father is back from his new employment at the banking institute, spic and span in his new uniform. He looks totally changed from the layabout he was during the time when Gregor's income was a given. He only sees an insect in Gregor these days, deserving of being eliminated. A cat-and-mouse cruel game is danced first, where he runs Gregor all left and right over the room, until Gregor loses breath, not a big surprise in his present condition. We should provide a small bowl with fruits on the sideboard in the dining room. Gregor's father takes several apples or some other fruits from the bowl, fills his pockets with them, and then with an baseball pitcher's exaggerated windup aims at Gregor, trying to hit him back into his room. For each of the incoming projectiles, Gregor should try a feint, zig-zagging to the left, then to the right, here and there trying to bunt some of them with his front legs. This is a dance of hit-and-miss. Several of the projectiles miss the target, but finally one lodges onto his back, probably into a crevice. Under the shock, Gregor should start up as though some major center had been hit. He faints, is pushed back into his room, and only the imploring intervention of the women of the house saves Gregor from immediate extinction at the hands of his own father.

33 - *The Metamorphosis* II, 1992

"The show that the Stuttgart Ballet has brought to us in the Badische Staatstheater's Großes Haus at Ettlinger Tor, choreographed by the new star of international choreography, Miss Yvonne Fillon, has been marvellous."

Thus Karl Ambreuser, the local dance critic, prepares himself to buzz with excitement in tomorrow's edition of the *Karslruher Zeitung*, reading the draft of his upcoming review to his wife.

"As the show is on for only three more days in our wonderful city, each and all are warmly advised to use the opportunity to see at work a splendid young troupe in wonderful sets and original *mise-en-scène*, in a choreography that engenders an excitement perhaps not equaling in intensity, but definitely challenging in illuminated concept, the presence, several years ago, of Mr. Nureyev in our city with the same company. This is all the more surprising as just two decades ago, not a thought was given to a woman conceiving such dancing, except for Martha Graham. How things change, and we with them. 'Let them ladies dance, not make dance!' was the refrain those days. Thinking back about last night's show though, it is for us mostly a happy 'Et in Arcadia ego.'

"Miss Fillon, for one, publicly subscribes to age-old tenets of Diaghilev's and of *Les Ballets Russes*, that a symbiosis and a synthesis between all arts, between all senses, should, first and foremost, come through in a live performance, be it of theatre or of ballet. It wasn't then a surprise that challenges should arise to our excited perception and mind from all quarters. But the mix was a potent, inebriating, yet exhilarating poison to the senses. As Tristans we were in a tragic show strangely drawing us in, in which we were witnesses and actors thereof, waiting for our Isoldas and leading

Marius Hancu

them in adventure at the same time.

"A good first question could have been: Why Kafka, of all authors?

"We know Miss Fillon's answer would have been 'He's simple and direct, goes to the core without much ado and pretension. Like a surgeon's knife. Also, to what corners of human nature he turns to! One is even afraid to look there on a comfortable, peaceable, good-natured, day. Then, he's so fundamental, so existential — and I'm trying here to use the word without its philosophical connotations, if that's at all possible with how much coin has been minted on it — that one wonders, why not? Just because others haven't tried him in ballets, this is no real reason not to, on the contrary. So, here you have the challenge.' We know, because we asked her, and this was her answer.

"When asked point blank, Miss Fillon told us 'she isn't "Stanislawski" nor is she "Method"' in her approach to teaching her dancers the acting part of the role, but that she might take and use things from each. Says she: 'It's really unconceivable that a contemporary ballet dancer wouldn't have at least sympathy for Stanislawski's Method of Physical Acting, when the main principle that system's proposing is having our own bodies for the most faithful and available instruments. This is indeed basic for any ballet dancer, something we're taught into irrespective of method or master — the body as the lone instrument we possess and that we have of necessity to rely on. Now, we might well not use other sides of his teachings, as they are indeed so varied and contradictory at times, as varied are our own influences too. Nor, on the other side, could we neglect Method Acting, as it helps, with its focus on previous experience and psychological motivation, reach deeper into ourselves. However, its farthest reaches are, to my view, too much for the ballet dancer, as she or he must at all times keep a control and awareness of his own body reactions, as we can't just let go and be full-frenzy-"interiorized," as it were, as perhaps theater or cinema actors may go at times.'"

"Karl, you don't want to go there, dear, this is too theoretical, all this method and stuff, you don't want to lose your readership. This is good only for you critics," his wife clamors from the kitchen, as he's resonantly reading his copy, wandering through their house on Wolfartsweier Straße.

"So then." He judiciously skips some matching paras. "When we turn our sight to what the third act of *Metamorphosis* revealed to us, the amount of impressions forced upon our senses from so many angles was staggering. It was, first, that surreal light, dimmer and dimmer, descending on Gregor's room, him gradually sliding into other worlds, into nevermore perhaps, ever more separated in light and in feel from his family, his crawling and shuffling about his room — now practically a prison cell — growing so much scarcer and more awkward by the hour, his idiosyncrasies, that raising of his head from under his shell, that crawling biased to a side as a result of his being hurt by his own father, so much deadened. Gregor, ever more animal in nature, his dialogue with his family, most of all, with his beloved sister, reduced to a naught. At this stage, he is present especially by what he is *not* doing.

"One of the most impressive things in this third section is the counterpointing and counterbalancing between two groups: the Samsa family (that is, the father, the mother and the sister, as Gregor, by now, has been excluded from family interaction for all intents and purposes) and the tenants the family has been forced to take in as a result of Gregor's not working any more. Just like two choirs who respond to each other roam they" — "Great phrase, Karl," comes from the kitchen — "about the apartment in accusations and recriminations until the father takes up again a productive job and the tenants are evicted. Each of the groups is endowed by the choreographer with a common set of steps to argue their inner alliance, still, within that common motional wave of the group there are small wavelets of the individual, his or her small steps, who proclaims the diminished individuality to which they still cling and which they still pretend to have — Gregor's sister showing off her budding coquettry with bursts of *bourré suivi* or *piqués de côté*, their father showcasing his new uniform of a bank employee, flashing long militarish parade steps, the mother — dragging both of them down, hanging on their arms when out in the park for a promenade, with her lack of energy and her disappointment — shuffling clean-the-floor steps. Then, still in the family group, there's also the motif, the refrain, of gestures of removing themselves from any touch with the pariah of the family, Gregor. Each of them three has rejection gestures and patterns of their own, still all are pushing away from him with open palms as though they there are Pharaoh's guards on some Egyptian frieze. The lights treat and follow each group wonderfully different, giving them compound personality this way too. To enforce commonality, the three tenants aren't very far from military uniforms in their dress, nor are they from mimicking each other at each turn. There's a wonderful play at group and individual personality that Miss Fillon has injected into the mix. It's very clear they move and think as a group. If you want, both Stanislawski and Strassberg at work."

"Still in those theoretical dead waters, Karl? Get out of that bog, please."

"But it's nothing of the kind, Karin," he says, while already crossing out that very last sentence and having a quick swig of vodka for a well-deserved compensation, still fighting what seemed to be a losing intra-family battle on issues of principle.

"Listen, Karl, I'm gonna tell you what I felt during that show, and you may want to take it with any amount of salt you wish. And, by the way, I swapped notes with Helga Riedlinger and she was rhyming, last time I checked. Wanna listen for a minute to the vulgus, *Schatzi*?"

"Why not, go ahead, Karin."

"We kind of agreed, Helga and I — that she has two winds blowing in there, your Miss Fillon, and the funny thing is they don't cancel each other out. That's a tall order for anyone, we think, so good for her. The first one, it's something to got with nature, like a deep belief in something about it. Deep and strong enough, that is, to bring it over in our perverted, vicious, scheming, urban view of things, without being embarrassed about it, and still survive."

"Stop right here. Any arguments for that? Watch your step, you're in the line of fire," he guffawed over the two rooms in between them.

"Couldn't care less, Karl. I'll serve you now my and Helga's observation and if you don't think there's something real to it, you can forget it next thing, which you're going to do anyway. You *never* think others might, even for a tiny second, be right, do you?"

"Wow, that's a tall accusation, Madam. But go ahead with your perceptions of the show, that's the point of order now. Have them out. Out, out on that billiards table, and be ready for them to be knocked about deftly with my cue stick."

"Well, those dancers in this show are made to believe in their bodies, there's no doubt about that. You talk your Stanislawski, I'm talking nature. The way they act, the way they look around, now and then, it's as though there's a direct conduit from somewhere up in the air, in the sky, in the moon perhaps, that's coming down a ladder or a pipe into their souls and makes them believe in their muscles and ligaments, in the support available there. It's as though there's an altar to a godless nature, and to it they pray. Those tendons and muscles, those skeletons, aren't foreign to them, they aren't afraid of them, they go at it with them. Still, it's as though by going back on that ladder, they can be back to the nature and refill themselves. What fuel, I have no idea, but there's a give and take with Mother Nature, their bodies as intermediaries, no doubt. They're made to dance as part of a larger thing than that stage, definitely larger than themselves."

"I'm not sure I saw all this pan-Mother-Nature thing, but I've got to say they surely went confident into their steps, as if there was no perceived limitation in their bodies. Now, how about the second one?"

"Well, how discreet can you be?"

"What do you mean? About yourself saying something on that second issue?"

"No, dummy, it's about Helga and the *way* she got to her information. Pledge not to say a word, serious?"

"OK, you have it. Go ahead."

"Helga had an intimate rendezvous with one of the dancers from Stuttgart."

"Not a *première*, knowing Helga."

"Don't be a bad boy; we women too have the right to go after the better endowed in the other sex. Endowed as in overall-body-like, not just in the dirty appendices you have right now on your mind. Well, point is, the guy seems to have been more loquacious than your usual post-coital male, present persons surely excepted."

"So what did he say?"

"Well, twittered something to the effect that your Miss Fillon asked the troupe to imagine that they dance as though they were on a fragile balance beam between dreams and the real world. Also, that if they don't have their own dreams, they might as well buy some, plug them in and assess ownership. But don't worry, she told them several of her own, just in case that would prod them into the right direction. Those, I can't tell you, as other activities seem to have taken their due in the right course of time in the end part of the rendezvous, as you might, or you might not, sorry, imagine, and reporting was affected."

"What you're telling me is just another version of Method Acting, or some Stanislawski, *mein Schatz*, if you haven't yet realized. This lady seems set to sell old coins as freshly out of the mint. Anyway, the outcome is quite dazzling, on this I think we can agree, can't we, *Schatzi*?"

"On that, yes, I'll give you my vote on *that*."

34 - Sarah's Call

" ... so, Mom, it's only now that I can talk to you today, 'been busy the whole day, running errands for Yvonne at her studio for her new show with Kafka's piece.

"What errands, you're asking? The whole kaboodle, you know. First, there had to to be some new tape bought and brought in for the audio. Like — for the Nagras. I can't tell why we had to go short on it plumb this morning, eye-zaktlo when they needed new copies of tracks for some of the dancers to take home and roll on them the whole night — rehearsal sleep immersion, I guess, some call it, visualization, others — to get into the role. Would that also require waterbeds or something else, I don't know. Yvonne's an intensity fiend, and that's what she would like them to do. What's left of it when they go home and they get to their respective and dear squeezes, I can't be bothered to imagine, but it must help somewhere or somehow, at least some of them are swearing by it. Go figure: people don't sleep these days or nights anymore, I guess. I mean, not with those with whom they should be sleeping with in the first place, but with those headphones, on. And damn the sex. Sorry, Mom.

"And that's not all. Some of the tapes have been made in the rehearsal hall, with Yvonne's voice coming over the music, her pointers and instructions, outbursts, all, so they can dream about them too. Again, some like it, as the torture is the name of the game for them too, not only for her, which one should know by now it is.

"Not for me. You know me. I've always wanted to go home and make *tabula rasa* about work. Have a tea, once; have a drink, now — no sweat, Mom, not too much. Perhaps that's the side that let me down, perhaps that's where I've lost ground to guys like Yvonne,

Marius Hancu

who butter their bread with work. Even as a child, I wasn't dreaming about the *barre*, wasn't sleeping with it in my arms. OK, in my dreams.

"Can't complain: no such thing as burnout in my quarters. Still, can't go out and see my name posted anywhere. 'Assistants' aren't part of the cast. They might be mentioned, that is to say flashed, on a good day, at the trail end of a long movie, when everybody's scooting out of the theatre, but not on a one-page ballet poster, no, ma'am. That's how it is I'm looking forward to some movies made with Yvonne's ballets. God's beneficent and in His infinite wisdom should know about my frustrations, so there's hope one day I'm gonna get there. In small print, no doubt.

"So-oh, that's how it is these days: me, doing the scout work — pardon my French — for Yvonne and her studio and office.

"But this dream last night freaked me out to the back teeth. Hear me out, will you, Mom? I know you don't like to talk dreams, but humor me on this one. So, it's as if I'm on this long truck-trek and as it is there's no driver in my truck, it goes by itself. It's only me, on the passenger side in the cabin, and this means there's no way I can ask for directions, nor about our destination. But I know, 'coz I see it with my own eyes, this is a tightly serpentined course, and the grade is so totally high, so I'm huffing and puffing in short order just by looking ahead of me at it. There's several trucks, couldn't tell how many. All that puffing away of heavy diesel fumes, it dims the sight in front of me and soon enough I need to put a hanky over my mouth to be able to go on and not lose my breathing and the pitiful remainders of thought I can still produce and contemplate under the circumstances. It's as though this is *Wages of fear* and Yves Montand has jumped off of the cabin and left me with the nitro all to meself.

"So, finally now we are in fact at that darned target point on the map. All trucks pull up one after the other in a large semicircular graveled place, the air full of the burning diesel and of the dull engine noise, just that I'm the only one opening a cabin door and striding forward to what it must be a castle as it has many doors and gates and tall, thick, walls of stone. And when I look back over my shoulder, there's not a sliver of a thin soul to show up in any of the cabins either, not that I can see inside them, as though the window glass is all tinted. It's as if I've come alone here to these undefined boonies and for what I don't quite know. It stands to reason something is crooked, but then, in some layers there's something like a voice that squeaks up that it all can't be but a dream. Only question is, how forgettable, if painful at this flick of time? Would this gonna be long-run, another small voice inside's croaking thinly.

"But I won't be stopped and go on making the rounds to each of the doors, banging on them in sequence, until one cracks open just a tiny bit, and two eyes look at me, one, then the other, as the crack is too narrow to let them both look out at the same time, and I can't tell whose they are, but they do seem to have a familiar twinkle to them, this definitely I know. Alas, I am not allowed in, the door closes with no, zilch, words of question to me after the eyes have taken my measure.

"Then, just after turning back and leaving, the recognition flashes: those were Yvonne's eyes, there's no doubt about that. So, I'm tracing my steps back to the door and start banging, harder this time, on it, crying out loud 'Yvonne, let me in! I know you and you know me!' But this time, the door remains closed for several long minutes, so in the end I decide I'd better leave, as there's no hope for me behind those doors.

"What'd you say, Mom? What did I do then, you're asking?

"What could I have done? I just went back to my truck, the one I came on, or a lookalike, far as I can tell, as all were the same, and no drivers in any of them either, and waited and waited in the cabin, hours like, in the dream, I think now, looking back at it, with the hope of perhaps having one of them castle doors open for me. Never happened. Woke up a bit later. But the advantage on *their* side, I mean for those inside the castle, was that they were not alone — I could hear them chirping behind the doors — like I was in the trucks, which was the worse I've ever felt, worse then going to the shrink, as then there was someone to talk to, I mean the shrink. Right, you have to pay for schmoozing, the sweet talking. Nothing good, or reasonably good, is free anymore.

"How do I feel after such dreams? Well, Mom, truly like a schmuck, no doubt about that either. I mean, can't get away from

Marius Hancu

Yvonne, the goodie-goodie, not even in my dreams. No life having all its marbles, this, not if you ask me.

"'least I wasn't in the same class with her at the National School, even though same age, or close. Managed, it seems, to squeak me in elementary school one year earlier than everybody else, didn't you? Ri--ight. Point to make: your daughter's better than everybody's else's. There's, still, that minor point that life has its own time for deciding on such things, and it's really much later that the chickens come home to roost and be counted. So, less play at an appropriate age, where did that lead to, one might ask, mightn't one? Any hidden responsibility out there? I don't hear any claims to that, no, I really don't. I know, that's Monday morning quarterbacking, but I need to score a point here and there, at least, and perhaps, most importantly, with you, needn't I? Have a more balanced ledger of sorts.

"Now, wasn't it a shocker for me at thirteen or whatever to see that my growth wasn't to be any closer to your height, reasons unknown? Wonder if there's an actual father of smaller dimensions than Mr. Pritchett, whose name I'm carrying with honor nor blemish? Another surprise was the blooming of my globose parts, which were to prove successful with the stronger sex, yet not on the ballet stage, the latter having most probably to do with my breasts being centrifuged in pirouettes toward the *porteur noble*, making, well, and pardon my French again, contact unavoidable and at times undesirable.

"The situation became even less bearable whenever I had to show up in a group, something which helped straight comparison. Like, I remember being cast in the *pas de quatre* of the little swans in *Swan Lake* for the National. They had needed a replacement for one night, and I knew the part, even though just a student. The old story, the way Yvonne herself got her big break with the National in *Don Quixote*. I was just sixteen, but there were people out there, and that trickled down to me through those channels that always exist, who said there was more activity and lively bouncing on my front, though, naturally, supported by the bustier of my tutu, during those *coupés* and *pas de chat* and *petits battements en chassé arabesque*, than on any of the three other swans, even though they were adult members of the corps and we moved all together in the so-tightly-knit fashion of that dance that guarantees the whole bunch falling on their faces at the smallest hesitation on the part of one. I don't have to tell *you*, mother, the good and the bad sides of such remarks for my multiple egos. Launching heavy, rolling, balls into bowling pins. One never knows the final outcome. Still, one can't have everything in this world, I told myself.

"However, things being as they are, do I really have to find reasons for me not really being at Yvonne's perch? This is a question to myself and to you, Mother.

"But I'll tell you another one, just for the record to be measured, perhaps, at the last hour. And that's about levels. Levels seen in everything. I was told, and so I began to tell myself, which of course is the worse, not to dig too deep, not to find games behind games, pits inside pits, leaves behind trees, birds behind sky. There or behind clouds. Not to let yourself caught dreaming in plain daylight. Not to let yourself spin out the dreams of the night. That always, a story is what it reveals to you in the first grasp of intuition, that first impressions are king. Or queen, whatever. You sure had a short fuse in those times, Mother, so perhaps that's not surprising. Why complicate education when straight answers carried one to enough closeness to the truth? Why fumble into the imaginary, why rummage, you said, in it? It doesn't pay, you said, time's short even for the real."

Sarah's mother had been dead going on ten years.

35 - Toronto, 1986

Patrick wasn't arrayed in anything striking. By his own standards, this was a modest display: white jeans, gray long-sleeved V-neck with the sleeves pulled one third up his forearms that should have been covered by his blondish downy hair if he hadn't depilated himself thoroughly for years. On this occasion, his forearms displayed generously displayed bronzed skin. As the season at the New York City Ballet was finished, he had allowed himself generous exposure to the sun on Martha's Vineyard and Long Island beaches, cold as the Atlantic's waters were for any reasonable amount of swimming.

Getting off the plane in Toronto, he seemed nervous and distracted, enough to force a stewardess to trot daintily on her medium-high heels after him, her first-class passenger, with one of his hand luggage pieces.

In fact, he had this feeling that he and Yvonne had stretched this imaginary piece of fine thread suspended between them to its limit. The point seemed to be that both of them wanted children. However, he wanted them outside anything conventional, while she could see them only within a marriage. Last time they had been together, three months earlier, in New York City, the sex had been great, but this issue had raised its ugly, shard-like head and couldn't be removed, for in truth there hadn't been enough give and take on either side. They really were, both of them, deeply entrenched in what they wanted or didn't want.

He wondered to himself why he was in Toronto, of all places, what curse dangled over his head, as a dirty cloud, for him to go to the place that could not be reasonably expected to bring to himself the most amount of pleasure — if sex wasn't to be involved, and most probably it wouldn't be.

The existence of the danger word — love — in his vocabulary had been questioned, angrily or sarcastically poked at, by many women before. Still, it was Yvonne who was careful to throw just enough light on it so that the point was out of any dispute between them. That was that, was the understanding, and there should be no more talking about it between them.

His hotel was somewhere in the Harbourfront, a long way from Pearson. He had opened his thin book with Lorca's poetry he used to carry on all travels, and thoughts wafted through any tall corridors or green backgrounds the poet offered to his señores, when they were interrupted by the driver's heavily Russian-accented voice: "Excuse-me, sir, aren't you Patrick Donovan, the ballet dancer, please?"

"Wow," he answered, interrupting his dreaming and transposing himself in the limited confines of a taxi in the heat of June, claiming miles for its own in Toronto, Canada. "How do you know about ballet and me?"

"Well, sir, when you have children you will learn many," said the driver. "My girl is only twelve, yet she's in a ballet school, doing well, we parents think. So I bought for her many cassettes and watched some of your shows, made in England, I think so."

"Yes, in terms of legal recordings, I have made some of those with the National Ballet. I'm less sure of the pirated ones," he said to himself under his breath. "How does your daughter like them?"

"Oh, sir, she's very fond about you, just telling us, I'm going to be a ballerina and dance with Patrick Donovan."

"If she's already twelve, there's some remote chance I'll still be around then. If she's good looking, we may make a special effort toward that. However, very few of us get into those Nureyev-like late, let's not call them protracted, years," Patrick quipped to his thoughts, dropping back to his reading. He didn't want to get into a close inspection of his future plans, which, at any age past thirty, any ballet dancer would be loath to get involved in.

Long trucks passed whooshing late-morning hot air by and around them and inside through the window partly open on the driver's side. The driver — now Patrick recalled from the sequence

Marius Hancu

of arranging his luggage in the trunk of his vehicle — wasn't too tall and kept his thinness in good stead. "Good omens for a light ballerina, thank God for us guys in the business," Donovan rattled off internally, while watching the driver's I.D. just above the front window, which portrayed a much younger version of the owner, still with the same long hair at the back. "That's where the romantic side is coming from, no doubt. That's how we still get ballerinas, for if it were just for the crew-cut fathers, there may not be much of a hope left," he mentioned, throwing back his own blond mane, freely flowing on this day. Verse and boring traffic, it all made for some dozing, especially with the driver silent for now.

"There's a limit to where we can go this way. I once hoped you'd understand it," Yvonne had told him in March, in New York. "Honestly, that hope isn't anymore with me. I heard, well, I know, you have several children, I've never asked you about it — in what, ten years, isn't it close to that? — nor have you given me any details. Why would you want another one outside of marriage, with me? Honestly, I don't like the names such children are called out there in the world, and what pain the lack of a permanently present father takes them through. Think school, think sports, hockey, baseball, basketball, everybody would show up with their parents. Well, to say the truth, they would parade and preen for these parents in front of those other kids with divorced or runaway relatives, as Patrick Donovan would be by that time too. And no, take your hand from there, ple—eeze, I want you to listen to me seriously for once. Will you? Come on, stop it!" she cried, pushing away his right hand that was trying to play with her clitoris while both of them were pretending to watch a John Dean movie on TV, propped up on their bed pillows at three in the morning in his apartment. "There comes a time when one is supposed to pay their dues to the society. I bet you'd rather not ever hear such frank talk and I recognize 'ever' is a loaded word, which no matter fully applies to you. However, I'm still going to tell you something. I won't have a child with you, just to sue you for child support later — something that, most probably, knowing the merchandise, I'll say you wouldn't pay anyway if it comes to that — in order to be able to feed or educate that poor child."

"That's what I like about you girls, waiting until three a.m. in order to start claims on rights and wrongs, instead of going at it during reasonable times. I mean, totally inopportune."

"Sorry, you don't listen until this late time in the night; your focus isn't there for such issues," Yvonne told him. "Not only that," and reserved this for herself, "but I know your tricks: once I mentioned the subject, you'd be running away. Here, at least, I have you a prisoner. The bed might not be the best place for rational thinking and talking, but it's better than nothing."

***

So, what is love, Yvonne? I'm asking myself, this March in New York City. I have no idea where Patrick is, so I can think.

We are in this labyrinth which doesn't end. We might come back in the same place only it's thirty-five years later, and we the parties don't even recognize ourselves, but there's the original recording in our personal history which is still around, witness to a fact which no one can deny now, even though we ourselves are just shells ready to be emptied out into the wide sea.

The love is the labyrinth and each and every step done along the way in it, forward and backward, at the times of confidence and at the other times of loss of direction, is the feeling for which one can't compensate just by being there, with no soul, because it's a scheme in which you need to pay in order to get the rewards, minimal as they might be, even the rejection wall. Even the rejection wall, in order to be presented to you by the gods of love, you must show involvement, how much I wouldn't be able to tell you, but my modest guess after being in the brine up to my neck, is it's a lot.

And no one could tell me things are of a different nature, as I have my guesses that go through the glass of windows, through the bronze of bells, through the time of days and the days of time, round and round.

There's only one thing better than really and truly finding the other person. It's the feeling of waiting for them and having the hope.

He keeps me hanging out there on a limb, Patrick does. There were those times, nine, ten years ago, at the beginning, when there was hope, now I know it's all a dead end with him, not what I wanted and especially, not what I want now, at this leaf of my life.

I must have been then twenty-four. Met him after one of Royal Ballet's shows in Toronto. He, two years younger — that might still be an issue with him, not that, of course, has he ever-ever mentioned it with me — the bright star promoted to principal at nineteen, bright, brash, boastful, eyes wide open, ready for anything, ready to grab and grasp anything within reach, and I was one of the twigs extending there and then. In Toronto, I was still 'corps' then with the National Ballet.

Took me a while to realize he's a 'man of property' in Galsworthy's sense, a material boy in today's world, very territorial, never relinquishing anything caught in his widely-cast net. Even more, he was of property even in this dancing, never going out too much on a limb, never stepping out to that remote edge which could take one down into the chasm. This was sweet comfort to his female dancing partners, who wouldn't have liked, most of them, to be launched up away in a lift as Fonteyn had been by Nureyev, in a show, never to be caught — whether in anger, lack of control or acute awareness of the moment, we will never know.

At the time we first met, Patrick was already a great porteur of flashy elegance, supported by those huge thighs and calves of his, still with everything anchored in amazingly slim hips. More rounded than fibrous in their appearance, his muscles were, and sometimes he tended to gain weight outside his optimal range — but then a dancer is never too light. At those times, he got in his own way in terms of explosiveness and jumping ability, *détente* — never outstanding items with him. The arms were very long and, some mentioned, with a bit of prejudice, 'as those of a black.' Anyway, they moved gracefully, still manly, endowed with thick upper arms, covering large expanses in their wake and gripping ballerinas' midriffs and lifting or launching them in a firm flash.

Part of his stage well-crafted or perhaps more well-managed mystery or persona was the idea of never taking on really evil characters. "No slimeballs for me, please!" he'd say, and the casting directors not only knew about it, throughout his career, but complied, on account that they had on their hands a terrifically built Prince for their unavoidable fair tales, blond, flowingly long-haired, radiating charm out of a pair of green eyes staring and sparkling straight at you. All of which made for marketable materiel, which, the management said and the critics agreed, shouldn't be polluted by negative connotations. When I take into account his natural instincts the way I know them now, I'm still of two minds whether he hasn't missed some of his best parts this way ... OK, so if this is tongue in cheek, I can take my lumps, still I don't think I'm out to do him any character assassination.

As with all my men, for him too, it really took me a while, that is years, to make the separation between shell and reality. Nothing to be proud about, just between us. I think I need a pair of huge goggles to help me out. Noble dancing — Patrick wasn't that, not a Bruhn, but represented it well enough to be believable. Other noble stuff — let's leave that for some other time, OK?

And I wonder where it all started. It may have been back in England, with his parents, feeling cornered as immigrants and grappling with the need to pierce at all costs through the thick dross around them. Hundreds of couples of ballet parents trying to serve success up on the platter to their prodigies. Also, their old-time connections with Vaganova's school and system giving them a feel of innate superiority, which was definitely a fearsome and decisive thing to have in ballet terms, but what a heavy burden this feeling of superiority might have been in terms of molding a fair character in a youth.

One thing that I liked in him was being so talkative and extroverted. The first reaction to this ebullience, much more Russian than English in nature, I always thought, was one of being mesmerized, which was OK, even though you felt you relinquished some of your own will and independence in the process. The next, and the more positive one, in fact, was one of being carried away with him on this wave of optimism and I-don't-care-ness, *j'm'en fou-nnes*, a thing that, all in all, made you be more resilient to the stuff around us. Not a bad thing at all to have around you. So I had ample reason for being caught in that soo fine spider mesh.

Marius Hancu

***

Patrick was out of the taxi in front of the Harbourfront hotel. The doorman took his luggage and passed it to a busboy. It was just the essentials, as he wasn't scheduled for any shows that time in Toronto, thus no need to be spectacular. "So," Patrick thought, "I guess this means I need to tip both of them, no doubts here."

The view from the wall-to-wall balcony window of his room over the lake was full of calm and light on the day, still he didn't have time for it. Something had registered with him, of course: Yvonne wasn't present at the airport, nor were any welcome messages or small gifts making their presence felt in his hotel room, as he was expecting in their best days.

The ground was moving in their relationship and he felt it right now as he looked at himself in the washroom mirror. No doubt looking good, but concerned, he could tell. Perhaps he should shave again. "Let's do it, it's a long time since this morning, what with the early rise for the flight" he pointed out to himself. Yvonne didn't like a beard brushing hard over her face, this he knew, so he shouldn't punt on that.

He'd gone to the Museum of Modern Art in New York and bought several large impressionist posters, as she loved to visit the place for those lilies of Monet covering huge walls. He took them out of the special long tubular handbag, bought at MOMA also, and arrayed them on the table, as he really wanted to make a good impression from the start. He knew they were beautiful, the only question was how honey she was going to be. He intended to take them straight away with him to her studio, where he was to pick her up for their agreed-on lunch together. Another bad omen — she didn't seem to be taking any days off during his visit.

Her studio was down west on Bloor, quite a distance past Spadina, in quarters where the artists had their cheap digs. It seemed her building had formerly been a large textile plant; the third floor hosted her current professional home. Large windows all around, concrete walls thinly painted. Her major investment had been to cover the floor with something less hard, more uniform too, in order to reduce the punishment felt by the feet and the ankles at impact, and to install long wooden *barres* along all four sides of the rehearsal room. Two locker rooms, one for men, one for women, each having its own shower, doubled up as dressing rooms with vertical mirrors installed on the inside of the locker doors, where the crowding became considerable right before class, with everyone trying to look their best under the circumstances. Two small rooms, placed right beside the elevator shaft, thus providing no light, but constant clanging, were dedicated to Yvonne and Sara's respective offices. Spartan quarters, these; still Patrick didn't flinch a muscle. This is what the god of dance usually provided, all over the world, to the most daring of his servants, those who tried to strike it on their own, especially in their beginning years. And these were the lucky ones still being able to continue their craft. Patrick had never been on his own in terms of ballet, always under the umbrella of some or other outfit caring for his welfare; thus he knew to appreciate Yvonne sticking to her guns on a treacherous road.

The elevator registered its usual halting clang and he stepped out of it. Two backpacked girls made way for his exit, practically jumping out of their shoes when they seemingly recognized him — most probably because of his mane of blond hair and his sharp green eyes — then stepped right in and the machine moved down to take them out into the world.

Yvonne's name was on the door closest to him.

He only had to knock and he would see her again. A bit of unusual emotion flooded him, a rarity, still he went on with a firm knock and instantly recognized her voice, a bit on the high side, a bit as that of a child, as usual, ringing from inside, "Come in!" He pushed the door open and got a glimpse of her at her desk, in front of an Macintosh computer.

"Here you are! Hi! Welcome to the Big T!" He had gotten words that he was looking for; however her expression was a little tense, her mouth hadn't fully opened, the lips still a bit tight, the cheeks still a bit strained. She was clothed in a pair of faded-gray jeans, tight over the ankles and throughout, the muscular roundness of the legs as well as their length, starting from narrow, relatively high hips, easy to reconnoiter. The extremely tight midriff, caught in the

Marius Hancu

belt, gave way to her firm, still not rich, upper contours, from an orange apache tank top, tucked into the jeans. She rose from her desk, the back very firm, a bit overextended, as though challenging him, with those longish strides ballerinas have for a given, toes pointing out, heels carried in, and offered — was it reluctantly, or so it seemed to him? — her cheek for a kiss.

He caught her around the shoulders with a one-arm hug, brought her to him, and she complied, but there didn't seem to be reciprocity. They touched shortly. He had hoped for a mouth kiss, but it didn't come.

"So, how's your day, very busy?" He realized, by the isolated tolling of a church bell somewhere nearby, that by then they had moved into the time domain of the noon.

"In fact, it is, even though today I only have classes with junior dancers, no show rehearsals."

"Anyone promising?"

"The girls who just left are quite good. From the National Ballet School, fifteen years old, or so I think, coming to me to convey more personality, or so they're saying."

"I'm sure this must have been a good idea," he laughed at her, the mouth a bit sneery.

"If by this you mean that *I myself* have personality, this I may have to agree," she laughed. "Whether I'll be successful in bringing it out in them is an open question, but sure am trying. But let's not idle here, let's go out for lunch. I think you may be hungry after your flight and the waiting in the airports."

"Food is something which I'll never deny to my body, in reasonable amounts," he acceded, smiling.

"So let's do that. May I ask Sarah, my assistant, to join us? I don't think you know her. I don't like to leave her eating alone from some bag here."

"I thought this lunch was for us two, not for others. I'm not coming here every day. But if you insist on being charitable ... "

"Please, let's take her with us. We'll have time for ourselves tonight," said Yvonne, and Patrick wanted to take this as coquetry or sexual innuendo, but it felt more as reserve and he didn't like it. He didn't reply, just let it pass. "Also, she's very well connected, you never know when this'll come to help you," she went on. "OK, let me call her." She knocked on the door of the other office, "Sarah, are you coming to lunch?" "Yes, right away," the answer came, and in ten seconds Sarah was out, as already prepared for the event.

"Sarah, this is Patrick Donovan. Patrick, this is Sarah Pritchett, my assistant."

They shook hands, and Sarah said, "It's an honor to meet you, Mr. Donovan," to which Patrick quickly replied "The honor is all mine, and please call me Patrick." He noticed her face flushing and her eyes widening.

"You know, Patrick," said Yvonne, "Sarah's been dancing until three or four years ago, now she helps me in terms of both choreography and office tasks." While waiting to catch a taxi, Yvonne updated them on the plan, "OK, ladies and gentlemen, the choice has been made and it's Yorkville for today. Now, both of you, with your rich social life, even though Patrick isn't a local, know Yorkville inside out, which is considerably more than can be said for yours truly. Still, the place where we're going for lunch is, at least I hope, new for all of us. It's a Romanian restaurant. Those Romanians who are getting away from Ceausescu's talons are few and far between, and quite poor, so it is a surprise to see how well this particular one is doing. Perhaps it's just the menu, which I'm sure Patrick will appreciate at least in part, as he'll probably recognize his parental *blinis*, well, at least a modified version of them — perhaps it's something else, but more about this later. Also, rumor has it that the wines are better than the Russian ones."

"Well, I'm sure you've chosen the right spot, Yvonne," Patrick said, extending his vowels a bit as usual — was it gallantry, slowing down the rhythm for the ladies to get all intentions, was it something from his Russian background, Yvonnes still couldn't tell that — while exchanging a quick smile with Sarah, more for politeness' sake. Still, he had had already time to scope her and her smallness was nicely compensated by richness where it counted — generous, globular breasts. "That might have been a problem, but only in terms of dancing, no doubt," he sneered to himself. Ink-jet hair, caught in a ponytail made up for a face that was a bit on the dull, expressionless side, the more as it was anchored by a nose which

Marius Hancu

was just crooked enough to create an unbalance toward the less undesirable in those parts of her figure — he detected more sources of reservation on the part of potential, or mostly past, as he could gather, casting directors. Otherwise, nice, smooth skin on the forearms and the face, seemingly never exposed to the sun. And she held his look.

It took them a quarter of an hour to get to Yorkville, on account of Bloor being surprisingly busy for this lunch hour.

The restaurant, *Doina*, didn't have a terrace; however, like many of the restaurants in the area, was able to keep the windows overlooking the street wide open during the summer, so they looked for a table at the street window. As this wasn't one of the main Yorkville thoroughfares, the traffic was tolerable and Sarah said they shouldn't expect to be disturbed too much by it.

"I think I'd better chose a round table, so none of us three would feel disfavored," thought Yvonne and quickly found one.

36 - Toronto, 1986

In the subtle play of choosing their seats at the restaurant table, in which neither of them wanted to seem indecorously rushing, nor to lose ground to the others, Patrick was left with the seat facing the window, and by delaying his own choice, he had been most chivalrous in not forcing the ladies to expose themselves to the crude light of a June afternoon.

Both women were now partly facing away from the street, shadows being shared by their faces with the relatively low-ceilinged room. The setting looked as though Patrick were on trial for something or another and they were the master judges.

Narrow beams crossed the restaurant hall in a network of tremulous light tiptoeing delicately through, supported by the air of the room, much cooler than outside.

The waiter, a thirty-something tall thin man, with a haunted, pained face, came around, placed the tall menu cards in front of them carefully, even a bit over-ceremoniously, then asked with reserve in his definitely raspy East-European accent if he could bring them something to drink. It was orange juice for the company, as though, on what promised to still be a hot day, no one wanted to take the risk of hard drinks.

"So, what would you like to order?" asked Patrick.

"Look, Patrick, this is my territory, so if you don't mind, all ordering goes through me and I take care of the bill," said Yvonne on a stern tone.

Patrick decided not to push things any further for gallantry's sake, as this promised perhaps to bring more involvement on her part for the common good of them both. "Why not, let her feel the gamble in the whole plot," he said to himself, and loud "You're

Marius Hancu

putting me in a rough corner, Yvonne."

"Well, you put me in the same corner in New York, so this is just payback, should you want to talk about it." She laughed.

"No, as a matter of fact, I don't want to even mention it any more, I don't want any trouble, *milady*." He opened his arms, threw them to the sides in the air, as in a mock surrender and laughed at both women, muscles on his chest rippling under the yellow short-sleeved polo tightened by the move, teeth flashing uniform and quite large the white of terribly healthy and in-shape people. Sarah seemed to shudder for a moment, as under a quick draft of cold air rushing by, and turned her sight and even her face a bit off to the side, as though in a reflex move meant to protect it from a waterfall.

"Waiter, we could use some guidance here, if you don't mind. What would you recommend from this impressive collection on the menu?" Yvonne asked with a bit of sarcasm the garcon, who happened to be in the neighborhood, having served a round of dishes at another table and moving toward the kitchen.

"Right away, madam, sorry," he replied, and two minutes later was indeed back from the kitchen.

"My suggestion is to start with the borsht with *perishoare*, that is meat balls."

"Borsht, why do I know this name?" laughed Patrick.

"Take good care of this gentleman, he has some Russian blood in his veins and thus knows quite well some of the stuff in your parts of the world," said Yvonne to the waiter.

"We'll try to do our best," he replied, however his face didn't reveal any special pleasure in having to serve what he might have perceived as a perennial historical opponent and sometime ally. Then he continued, "For the second dish, I'd recommend *sarmale*, which are similar to what the gentleman may call *blinis*, cu *mamaliga*, something like the Italian *pollenta*, a paste made of corn flour. As for *mititei*, small fried sausages — I guarantee, absolutely delicious with a glass of beer — while for the beer, I'd suggest German Löwenbräu.

After some consultation with the others, Yvonne came back to him "We'll take your suggestions. Make it three, please. Except for the beer we will take red wine. How about this Cabernet Sauvignon?

Is it any good?"

"Yes, this 1980 Murfatlar is excellent, I think."

"Then you have an order. We'll decide on the dessert later on."

"Thank you, madam."

The waiter gone, they faced the more daunting prospect of conversing with each other.

"So, Patrick, have you ever danced in Toronto?" Sarah took the initiative, seeing after a minute or two of procrastination that the silence lay suspended in the air.

"Indeed I did, as a matter of fact I remember meeting Yvonne at the beginning of my first show here. I was with the Royal Ballet then."

"He's kind enough not to mention it's already ten years since," Yvonne added, and there was a long look at Patrick as though reproaching him the passed time — personal gains and losses in the balance. As well, she told herself they were just as unmarried as back then.

***

I would have done the world for you then, Patrick. Still, not making you a baby, not even then. Not outside of the conjugal yoke. I'm not sure, if this idea is coming from my parents, family or what. Still, as things stand, it's rooted down deep in me and I can't help thinking that a fatherless child is quite unhappy. Didn't want to bring about unhappiness and cold or want. Scold me for it, do whatever you feel like, that's where I still am.

And, Patrick Donovan, I *didn't* want to anchor you in one place or pinion you. Didn't want that for me either. Hot ice together, I'd have liked to have melt, still together, in a single miniature iceberg, out in the world. Nevertheless, this may be this art, business, whatever, we're in, so transient, so fickle, that each of us wants a place to burn at the time they can still do it, with a reasonable flame out there and what.

I still have in my senses the smell and the expansive, all-encompassing feel of your skin when, naked, I wrapped myself

Marius Hancu

around your hips for the first time, the throbbing, the hot, sweet explosion and dissolving. It must have been three in the morning at my place, after your last show in Toronto in that series. I didn't want to go to your hotel with all your company around, and you didn't want to come to my place, then in Beaches — too far, you said. So for two days we only had lunch together with your touring gang around us and touched hands or thighs under the table, waiting for the perhaps-perhaps. The taxi driver didn't know what happened along the way to my home, me jumping and easing into and sitting in your lap and crying all the time, but that was just happiness in waiting for it to happen.

And how short all that was, with your taking off the next day for London. You laughed it off, "We'll see each other soon, don't worry," but oceans being what they are, that proved to be a chimera. I still keep my calendars for all my years since highschool, and there are several years in the last ten where there's no notice of rendezvous between the two of us. Empty, you know, no recordings, total blackout.

The talk from you was flowing and flourished: freedom, no shackles, meeting other people, the works. Hm, now that I think about it, I think "the works" came in my speech with experience — let's not mention age or cynicism here — I don't think I'd ever have used it in those years when I first met you. I won't ever tell you that, but that part never comes easily, not to me, getting to know other people any time soon after reaching that intimacy with someone. Wouldn't know why, as I see other people changing love partners left and right, but perhaps that's just sex. Still, even in "just sex," getting to someone else's membranes is not something that I, for one, can do on the spot, no questions asked, especially with this AIDS making the rounds of male ballet dancers. The number of my one-night-stands is ridiculously minuscule. Go figure — still, I'm in show business.

And, yes, Patrick, I *hope* for heavens you're still hetero — for my own good and yours — for I *know* the question, asked upfront, will so very rarely elicit the truthful answer.

Single. Single. Single. I cherish the independence, on some days, but you should know by now this label I won't carry for the rest of my life, as you seem to intend for yourself.

That child would be the utterly temporary act of possession, sour proof of your not wanting involvement. So, no deal, fair prince. Instead of an itinerant one, which is nothing more than a fly, I'd like to have one that cares about his kingdom, a bee, for a change.

Words. As though I were able to put into words the emptiness I feel with each of your departures for remote shores.

The moving, the word of it. The caring, the word of it.

***

The borsht having revived energies, the conversation established itself on a surer footing.

"Tell me what project you two are involved at this time," Patrick found himself asking. For politeness' sake, with two women at the table, subjects that spelled at least some threadbare commonality were flagging themselves aggressively to the attention.

"There's a show coming up for the Stuttgart Ballet, basically Ariadne and the minotaur, you know, the Theseus story. Then there's another with them, on Kafka, which is much more hush-hush, as we barely discussed the first premises. We're just finalizing, for the first, the choreography design, before jumping up on a plane and staging it at their place. Costume and stage design is their cup of tea," mentioned Yvonne.

"Yes, but could I tell about the design, Yvonne?" asked Sarah.

"Go ahead. I know many bad things about Patrick, but I think I know he's a discreet chap." Yvonne laughed agreeably.

"All right. It's just that Yvonne and the stage designer in Stuttgart, Walter Lindtke, a very imaginative fellow, if one considers the color prints he sent us of the stage designs, agreed to think of the labyrinth as today's oppressing city, through which one is supposed to find his or her way out."

"Oh, you shouldn't have told me *that*," laughingly chastised Patrick. "Now, each time I go around London, I'll get depressed. Perhaps Dickensian, those stage designs? I mean Oliver Twist-ish and stuff, you know?"

"Perhaps. Just a bit. It's still a modern city, less chimneys, this isn't Mary Poppins, you know," Yvonne said.

"So, how does your modern hero, your Theseus, find his way out of the maze? Is he guided by radio dispatch by Ariadne, instead of the thread?" he joked.

"I don't want to deal with such technical details in my ballets, and you know that, Patrick, don't you?" Yvonne said. "I want to keep things on a more abstract level, so it's going to be just a wandering, roaming about, with no props such as the one you more than graciously suggested. Radio, what an idea!"

"He's marked as 'gliding with long strides along the street'," you know, Sarah added, "so all we care is for him to glide reliably, gloriously and beautifully enough. Whether he finds the exit may still be a question better left to the philosophers at the end of the ballet, don't you think, Yvonne?"

"Well, this is my last card, and I'll tell no one at this time, including you two, how I'm going to play it," she said, smiling dismissively. "Although I have something clear in my head, it may well be decided right at the spot of the crime, in Stuttgart that is, depending on how I'm going to feel about their male star, Desinger, mainly about him projecting energy, and not just a pale flicker, right at the end of it."

"Wow, then I don't envy that guy," Donovan laughed, "I wouldn't be sleeping well right now, if I were him, but be running track."

"Well, don't worry," Sarah chimed in, "he's fully updated on the demands of the role, he may be doing exactly that while we speak." Her eyes and Patrick crossed for a moment, and flickered laughter at each other.

The second dish, the *sarmalutze in foi de vitza* and the *mititei* came in and was dutifully studied for a moment by everyone at the table.

"Smells good, I have to say," Patrick acquiesced.

"Cheers!" They clinked glasses of the newly-opened Cabernet.

"Ah, that's a solid wine, pretty well tannined, I'd say" Yvonne said, after rolling it in her mouth for a moment.

"Seems right to me too, no complaints here," said Sarah, placing the glass on the table and clicking her tongue.

Patrick looked at her and felt amused by the sound and the way this petite woman, seemingly a right ball of energy, with the roundness of her breasts going into a state of tremulous excitement with each of her laughs, had just generated it. However, he didn't linger in his looking at her, as he felt Yvonne's eyes stationed for a moment on his, perhaps telegraphing something that he didn't catch, still forbidding enough to stop him in his tracks.

"So, how's your hotel?" Sarah asked, and from the instant tension in Yvonne's eyes, one could say she hadn't liked the question one iota.

"You mean, *The Spring Harbourfront*? I still have to see it, I came straight to your offices from the airport. It should be fine, in point of fact I like the Toronto hotels: on average more space in general than what we have — I mean, we *had*, during my years there — in London, perhaps, and cleaner than the ones in the Big Apple — where I live now — that also are unpleasantly expensive.

"But these *mititei*, they are delicious! And the meat is so well done. I also liked the *blinis*, or whatever they call them in Romanian." He looked agreeably around the restaurant, walls covered with folk table cloths and napkins, a big picture of Nadia Comaneci in a corner receiving the ten in Montreal ten years ago. "A nice place, and I like the music too. What is the name of that piece?"

"It's *Ciocarlia*, the Lark, sir," the answer came from the violinist.

"And when you go next to MOMA in New York, you may want to have a look at Brancusi's sculptures, and then you've closed a Romanian circle indeed," Sarah pointed out.

"Oh, I know his birds," Patrick said. "They seem to have been a subject of a censorship trial in the twenties, when brought over to the US. The Americans, ever the prudes. Same happened to Henry Miller and Burroughs, not that I liked 'Naked Lunch.'"

"Oh, come on, Patrick, coming from a Brit making his living in the Big Apple, that doesn't fit well — not showing respect for your hosts," sneered Yvonne. Patrick just raised his shoulders in powerlessness as in "What can I do?" but didn't articulate it.

"Something tells me those same redneck Yanks fighting Henry

Marius Hancu

Miller wouldn't have allowed Mr. B. in the US if things had been as they wanted, and then Patrick would be out of a job today. Not everyone's the same in the US, definitely not. Didn't you guys go to *Studio 54?*" Sarah asked hotly.

"Yeah, good point, but Studio 54 is another planet altogether, even in New York City," said Patrick.

"Even for you? I thought that would be your world?" Yvonne's eyes drilled him, even though her mouth was relaxed and tempting.

"I can't say I don't enjoy it. Now, if that means I'm of a different species, of a different planet, so be it, I'll go with it, I guess." He lifted his hands in annoyance, as in "What can I do with you, Yvonne?" Silently again, but irritation was brewing in him, Sarah could tell by the veins in his neck. If Yvonne saw it, she didn't react.

"Interested in any dessert?" she asked.

"Not for me, Yvonne, thank you," said Sarah.

"Same for me," Patrick said. "I'd rather go in some fruit shop later in the afternoon, to make some provisions for my stay, but that'd be it."

"Then, ladies and gentlemen, let's decamp."

After paying the bill, they found themselves outside, under a hot summer sun, intent on burning everything under its rays.

"So, when am I going to see you today?" Patrick asked Yvonne, with Sarah looking on.

"I'll give you a call at your hotel after five. I hope to be done with the work by then. We two are going to take a taxi to work; you should enjoy this sunny afternoon around downtown or go walk the Harbourfront, it should be great to be out in the open today."

"I'll take your second suggestion then." Here he turned to Sarah "It's been a real pleasure to meet and talk to you, Sarah. Hope to see you sometime soon."

"Likewise." They shook hands, and Sarah felt an unusual pressure from one of his fingers in the center of her palm. Was that intentional? She raised her head to look at him from her smallness and because of the sun, had to use her palm to shadow her eyes. She had a double take at him all right, squinting up, and left within the next minute with Yvonne — she, a bit red-faced after his fleeting kiss on her cheek, as though shamed of not being able to control her natural reactions — in a taxi that had just pulled over to them.

With just a light handbag for a load, he decided he'd take a walk for the benefit of the digestion and perhaps some thinking. There were two and a half hours until Yvonne was to call him at the hotel, so time aplenty, he thought. Taking off Yorkville toward Bloor through Avenue Road, he felt himself already breathing better on account of the wider street. Space, this he liked. "Give me avenues," he said to himself, "and I'll be on them." He considered University Avenue as a choice for going toward Harbourfront, he recalled it being much wider than that pitiful Yonge, and thus switched toward Queen's Park. Ten visits or so to Toronto over close the same number of years had made him knowledgeable enough of the downtown area to strike ahead on his own feet.

He looked back at the lunch just over, and had to recognize things didn't look good with Yvonne. She had seemed detached, very formal and indifferent at times. He was trying to figure out what magic buttons he could still have recourse to, but there weren't too many but old devil sex, and as to that the evening, or the night, at the latest, will tell the story. Certainly on her side, there didn't seem to be any noticeable intent of making the first step toward more enthusiasm between them.

He passed the grey back of Hart House, the pink stone of Queen's Park, and University Avenue opened down south, just what he needed to get to Harbourfront. A swoosh of energy came onto him and he threw a *saut de basque*, something like a triple Axel, arms closed to first position at the beginning, to spin up, then casting and opening them away, to brake the rotation right before landing. The ankle felt fine, the thighs and the knee took in well the landing, the footfall was catlike. He was ravished, the rush took over and he triple-jumped again lightly, as concrete wasn't good for one's body, then skipped with high-knees, arms pumping up and down.

***

Calm down, Patrick. This isn't good on your joints and you're thirty-two. Not exactly the age where an accidental injury would be a cinch to heal.

But I can't stop this flow.

Keep it in yourself for later times, the energy.

Eh, hop, another pirouette, this one *accroupi*, really low, tucked to the ground on one knee.

OK, people are beginning to stare, I'm going to pull the plug on the show, fellows; don't worry, no threat to anyone's rat race, for heaven's sake.

But look, there's no one around, just your wish of being looked at, you, slave of vanity, you.

Hey, I haven't come here to practice my jumps, not even virtually. Think about the woman. That's your pain. Don't get carried away by anything else.

My mind is bobbing up and down on an unquiet river. Wish it weren't, but it is.

Three levels down, I feel the rush of blood coming and washing through veins and arteries through that sex we had several years ago, in Palma de Mallorca, in the penthouse of a hotel with open windows, windswept by the breeze.

And, up here, I know, wish it were today. But it isn't, and something tells me it just won't happen again, not that way. It's as though back in time with Mr. B., hoping that something great will be made, choreographed for a male dancer — slim hope for that, what with him busy with his female icons, LeClerc, Tallchief, Farrell, and his May-December stories. Nureyev didn't get a part with him, and it was slim pickings for Baryshnikov too, at the end of the line. It's that and he didn't want male stars perhaps shoving him out of competition for straight sex and love for his ladies. So, how could what I'm doing in NYC be different from what it is now for me, just five, six, years down the line, even if Mr. B. hasn't been around for two years now.

Damn and damn again. Now that I think back about it, this is coming crystal clear in focus: Yvonne won't stay. This is over and done with. Just mushing around, whiling away our time.

Perhaps I should have stayed with Manuela. Never asked too much, her, never this "when are you coming back?" When I was there, I was welcome, end of story.

Yvonne always wants the world. What marriage, I ask you? Even with a prenuptial agreement, you never know, if something happens, you're up in the air, hung out to dry, especially with the courts they have here in North America, and I hear the Canadian ones are even more pro-women. So there.

But if *she* leaves me, I'll damn get back at her, so help me God.

***

It's six o'clock and they finally are together alone in her apartment on Prince Arthur. He looks around, a pretty crowded space, made all white by the later afternoon sun sneaking in through pale curtains.

"Do you feel comfortable with this much stuff around you?"

"You mean, thrown around me?" Yvonne asks. "It doesn't bother me at all. I'm keeping the focus on the job, not on the outside details."

"Fine, but still, it'd bother me."

"I think we found and agreed a long time ago we're not compatible in everything, Patrick, didn't we? Or so I thought."

"Right, agreed, don't worry. Still, I wonder how it doesn't bother you. That power of focus, it must be something out of this world," he says lightly, not to irritate her too much.

"Well, you might not believe it, but some people tell me that's the secret of my success, so why should I, of all people, discount that? They might just be right. Try choreography sometime soon, to see for yourself." She's just pressed the inferiority button, he's just two years younger, still hasn't authored any ballets, while for her the one in Stuttgart will be her fifth. If he's feeling it, he isn't saying anything, not necessarily out of recoiling from it, but aware that just one extra word can derail his purpose for tonight and for the whole Toronto trip.

"What wine do you keep in here?" he finds himself asking, just to get into neutral waters and smooth along toward his purpose.

"I've got an Australian Pinot Noir, if you don't mind it. Try the cupboard to the right of the sink in the kitchen, bottom shelf."

Marius Hancu

The bottle is there, dusty, in a cluster of several ones, perhaps one of the perennial loves of the hostess. Still, he doesn't remember Yvonne drinking on the sneak. It might be just for visitors like him. He might have competition. *Now that's a thought, Patrick.* Not one he's comfortable with, but then, he's not alone either when going places, so here you are, the pay back — and the independence he's been himself suggesting.

He takes out two bulky crystal glasses from another cupboard, pours out the wine in them, looks for some mineral water, finds it and pours it in some water glasses, to have around to cut the taste of the wine, in case of overkill of the taste buds.

But where is she? He hears the noise of the water in the bathroom, sounds like a shower, he knocks on the door. "The wine's here! May I come in with it?"

"No, please keep out!" sounds the voice from inside.

"All right, all right!" He backs off to the dining room, sits back at the table and starts drinking his wine. "If she doesn't want to drink it now with me, she can just as well drink it herself later alone, or I'll keep company with a re-order."

In fact, truth be told, she's just inserting a deep-seated diaphragm, not to risk anything, should it come to sex tonight. Months later only, will Patrick know he's been deprived of any chances at offspring on this occasion, but for other reasons — she will abort the undesirable pregnancy. The diaphragm will not have been enough.

37 – Sarah, Toronto, 1986

The thought hadn't been present — and I'm trying to be honest here — until he mentioned the name of his hotel. It suddenly broke in and found its way through clouds of indecision, spurred by some pointed looks at my breasts and at my face, though short and rushed, as forced by circumstances, during the restaurant lunch. Not indifferent, and given the opportunity, ready to act upon, those looks told me.

There was the unavoidable thing, the potential treason to Yvonne involved. There were, however, movements in the air at that very same time that made me think everything was a thing of the past between them, with what looked like Yvonne not really fawning over him or actively seeking his ardor any more, and with both of them too sarcastic for making good jam — as my grandma would have said.

As to myself, the arrow hadn't been in the bow for quite a while, and at thirty-four I was every bit as anxious as I ever had been to get back into the fray. Some clock ticking? Perhaps, if I were to call reality by its name, however it mainly was that rush, which I hadn't felt for quite sometime, just not knowing which hand to use first to help myself from the honey fate had generously plopped on the table right in front of me in the shape of this gorgeous-looking male examplary, looking ready for the taking, at least for short term installments.

So when, the next day, I saw Yvonne come in the studio — and if not 'frustrated,' then I don't know what the proper word is, 'coz she was fuming against everyone and everything — I knew something was cooking. She might have gambled high and the ensuing score on her face didn't seem anything to brag about. Then I overheard her through the open doors calling and fixing a business appointment at seven at night with one of the private sponsors of her company.

By lunchtime, I had decided the chance was there and I'd better act. So I placed a call to Mr. Donovan's room at his hotel, and, would you believe it, he was in.

I said, Remember me, how are you doing today? Keeping busy in Toronto? And he said, Certainly I remember you, and not exactly busy, I went out on the lake this morning, hired a small motorboat, just the thing for this great weather you are enjoying here right now. Oh, don't worry, said I, it's not like that all the time in Toronto, you're just a spoiled visitor. And, among the heavy schedule you have, would you have time for a coffee together? Pause of ten seconds here, then he, and very slowly and quietly on the line, asked, Why not make it drinks on the rocks somewhere in Harbourfront tonight? Would that be too much of a stretch, he said? Not at all, I said, people travel, one should use whatever moments available, otherwise life's gone and no reports can be made thereof, as though it never passed by the interested parties. So that was agreed and the rest was small talk about details, exact time and space and some such.

I left Yvonne's studio earlier than usual, first, to create some distance and avoid spiritual interference of the last moment. I wanted to fly free in my own air and not borrow anyone else's, I mean not too much in any case. I also wished to go home and change into something less functional and more breezy from the duck suits I wear at work during summer. Suffice it to say, those two hours also were a buffer in many ways.

There was this light black silk miniskirt I had, and put on; a burgundy shoulder-cut short-sleeved vest to go with it and that with thick dark lipstick opened me like a black tulip and offered me out. Right under the neck, a small half-moonish silver pendant. The hair turned up in a high roll, with long geisha-style pins in, black too, and with its natural shine, as I still wasn't using anything on it. Carving the air. The breasts cupped in the highest firmest bra I had, I thought. That was I of that night. And the thoughts. And the expectation and uncertainty. How would such a man switch on a dime between two women, if he would? Perhaps with some violence and roughness, with some sour taste still in his mouth. But the caveats were too weak in comparison with the excitement. I trotted out of the house.

There was the fact that I had to go to his hotel, meet him in front of the reception desk before going to the designated bar somewhere else, still on the Harbourfront. Surely the whole move of going to his haunts, instead of what could be seen as surrendering by asking him straight to come to mine, looked in some respects a good opening gambit, but only time could tell.

Having decided that I wanted to take a taxi right up to the hotel, so as not to be intercepted by undesirable gazes, I pulled up there just fifteen minutes later, after some attempts from the hack driver to get at me with some smooth talking. He might have thought I was one of those top-of-the-line call-girls, à la 'Scent of a Woman," visited by Al Pacino, just this time going out herself on a rampage for a kill. Maybe my lipstick was too indicative, maybe the skirt too mini, maybe the roll of the hair or the sticks in it too high, maybe the bra bumped up the essentials too much; anyway, he tried it, useless of course. Not that he had any come on, this wasn't a bad sign to have that someone in the other species, for now someone probably on its lower rungs, reacted to my props, was hooked.

The summer sun was mild by the time I entered the hotel lobby, five minutes late, perhaps. He was already there, Patrick was. Orange polo this time, with the straight, tall carriage and the blond hair he reminded you of Balanchine's "Apollo," which he had danced several times, replacing Peter Martins. The three Muses weren't there with him this time, and I certainly didn't mind the lack of competition.

He seemed nervous. "Oh, here you are!" he said. Probably made nervous by my being late a bit. We shook hands. He again pressed his middle finger into my palm while doing it, smiling jokingly. Was this now our coded signal? Wouldn't have minded a bit.

"Thank you for answering my invitation." It was nice of him to phrase things this way, as it was me, if I recalled correctly, who had instigated movement toward this date. However, as I didn't enjoy being seen as the pushy sort, I let him take the initiative. He then took my right hand in both of his and added "It's a joy to look at you tonight. You are very sexy," and kept my hand for a moment longer than one would have thought the norm, whatever that might have been.

"Thank you" I said, looking up toward his face as we were close by — the privilege of petites like me. The shine in his hair, and the joking green of his eyes, seemed fascinating to me; the pecs didn't look so bad either under the cottony polo, nothing like a bodybuilder's, in his case everything was compact and slim, not bulky or rotund, the very long arms sinewy, no hair on them at all — total depilation at work, most probably. The pores in his face were quite visible, not a very smooth front in that respect, and the lineaments of it were rich from close by, nothing round, soft or pudgy about it, but marked and muscled underneath, already starting to show extra lines and ridges at the corners of the eyes, especially when smiling. His hands were dry, and I was grateful for that, as I don't feel comfortable making contact with anything wet..

"I suggest we go to the bar at 'The Ferris Wheel,' I heard good news about it, plushy, quiet, nice private booths," he said.

"Fine with me."

"OK, then, shall we?" and we set off by foot as it wasn't much of a walk anyway, three blocks or so. At the exit from the hotel, he held the door for me with one hand and when with the other guided me out, he placed its fingers firmly but gently right at the low of my back and he certainly knew where to put it, as I instantly tingled all over. Or was it just me not having been close to a man this swell for quite some time?

I dared to ask, just to clarify the waters, "So, did you meet Yvonne today?"

He looked at me, there was a short pause, his eyes narrower just a tiny bit, but looked straight at me, didn't shrink from it, and said, "Yvonne and I decided last night there wouldn't be any other meetings between us two while I am in Toronto," and made a gesture as of "let's pass this subject over" and I didn't have, on my side, any desire to reopen the matter, or the wound, as it were.

We followed the narrow promenade along the shore. The weather continued to be great, there was just the usual wet breeze around the lake, however nothing like the stickiness you're sometimes getting in the city from the car exhaust and other stuff like this.

"So, are you from Toronto?" the question came.

"No, not born here, but in Vancouver, in B.C., on the West Coast."

"I know Vancouver. We were with the Royal Ballet there too."

"Why do I have the impression from press clippings and so on that you enjoyed your time with the Royal?"

"That is basically true. They opened everything for me. Still, after eight years with them I felt I needed a change of atmosphere, both city and work, that is, and went to Paris, at the Opéra. A good time, with Nureyev around as a director, but he and, to a more modest scale, myself, had our difficulties with the French system. Not too open to foreigners, they much more prefer to work with the local breed and two or three choreographers had a hold on the repertory. There's no big surprise to me that Béjart had to go to other countries. How about yourself, where did you study ballet?"

"National Ballet School, in Toronto. Just like Yvonne, but she was a local by then, while my family was still in Vancouver." On mentioning her name, his face twitched a bit, and I realized a pretty large chasm had been opened somewhere out there, and that I'd better not go close by it.

"Why do I have the impression we're already there?" he laughed and pointed to the restaurant's name showing up on the façade of the building right in front of us, neon tubes over the silvery metallic cover of the walls. The place wasn't too crowded, so we had the choice of an indoor private booth or of an outdoor table. I wasn't wrong that both of us wanted intimacy, so inside we remained, after a short conclave.

Old-style violet plush everywhere. We sat ourselves one beside the other, on the sides of a corner sofa.

"Amazing construction you have in your hair with those pins or whatnot they are. Can I touch it?" he asked.

"You are allowed access if you proceed carefully and don't tread on the flowers."

He extended his arm and touched delicately with his fingers the pins, then the hair, went around in weightlessness for two or three rounds of delicate inspection, then lowered his hand on the back of my neck and started rubbing it with two fingers, just with the topmost fleshy part of his fingers, in fact parallel with the spine, up and down.

"Hey, this wasn't part of the contract," I moaned, eyes closed by now, pressing my neck against his hand, vertebra by vertebra. And purring can't have been too far, when suddenly the question came — "Good evening! What can I get you?" This was the waiter, and I recoiled back a little, but Patrick didn't retire his hand. The place was dark, so no one, except the waiter, perhaps, could have seen my blush flag being flown high on my face.

"How about yourself, dear?" he asked.

"A Dubonnet for me, please."

"OK, a Dubonnet for the lady and a vodka Martini for me. Both on the rocks, please. Also, two glasses of Perrier."

The waiter having left, this seemingly was the right moment for him to advance toward the corner, and ask me "Why don't you move closer too?" which I did, so now I was within his full reach. He extended his right arm, placed it around my shoulders and intently started to dispense focused massage on my right shoulder, deep, deep to the bone. I was close to crying from the pressure, but he touched one of the pleasure points on the back of the shoulder and scribed it with his index finger in round circulations, so the heat rushed up again. I moved my left hand over his thigh, grabbed hard at it, very firm muscles twitching under my grip. Then of a sudden I just bumped into a huge peak. I moved my hand away, but he put his hand above it and guided it back in place, all the while staring mischievously into my eyes.

The waiter came, progress being thus inhibited for a while, for I really wanted to clink glasses with Patrick before going any further into this.

This was a strong Dubonnet, and it kicked in immediately, as I hadn't eaten for several hours now. Blue flashes started to pass my inner eyes, the skin felt distended as the surface of a soap balloon, ready to blast, and I imagined for several deep gulps of air and of the saliva of my mouth the huge peak disrobed and all in me down there, working me out to screaming.

Only that Patrick wanted to talk now, of all things. You never know with men, what the alcohol opens them up to, sex or gravitas.

"Do you know Mr. B's 'Agon'?" he asked.

"I might have seen a bit of it on television, with Diana Adams, I think."

"Right, she danced it in the fifties with the black guy, Arthur Mitchell, the first black principal in major ballet. Anyway, you're lucky, as for many years it was unofficially banned in commercial broadcasts, as it showed a black dancing with a white girl."

"Exactly that. It was made for them by Mr. B in the late fifties. Remember how skinny, needle-like, both of them were? Amazing. Very accurate dancing they had. My point is that they want me to do it next."

"And? Wouldn't you like it?"

"I wonder if I'm not too big for it."

I saw his point. There was a lot of flexibility involved in the original 'Agon' and the comparison with Adams and Mitchell might have worried him. However, I didn't want to put any stops on our budding connection, so I tried my best to stay encouraging, even though I wasn't fully convinced.

"I'd say you should try it."

"And what happens if I'm messing it up with the critics? They might say I'm not able to do what a black dancer has done before. I mean, among them, not openly, of course. But enough to condemn me to the ash heap of history, as it were. Also, even if I dance it well, as it would be with a white partner, the contrast might not be striking enough to capture the original contrast, fascination, or whatever you call it, of black versus white skin."

"Perhaps your main concern should be if you yourself like it and would like to dance it at all."

"You know, you ladies think the same — Yvonne told me the same," he said, and probably seeing a shadow passing over my face, kind of straightened himself up "but we won't talk about her tonight."

"And by the way, your vodka's getting warm, and other things are getting cold, too" he said and replaced my hand in the same place where it had been right at the beginning of this diversion. Just as

Marius Hancu

well, there was no need for insistence on his part, as I was fascinated by the unseen presence as by a coiled serpent and wanted by my free will to help it regain consistence and striking power. My fingers grabbed cravingly and tested and there seemed to exist major reason for interest on the uptake.

38 – Sarah's Dream, 1988-89

There's flow, watery, jasmin-scented air moving closely tucked in sheets of neverminding leafs lost from the orchards, sidelong light coming in through my windows, open for the occasion, and done for is the sight of me in the mirrors all around the house and — and waves, waves, waves, appear unabashedly carrying everything caught in their crests, this strange spume gathering force.

I'm prey now to a silence rounding the space as it covers the corners, it takes my breath, it, the silence, and there's no defense that I can quickly assemble off of nooks and cranies.

"You should, you should." Words burn me up high to awareness, still not close enough to the surface, something's fighting back in me, holding me down, I surely can't tell who I am, nor where I am, compass lost — and this terrific winds of jasmined air don't cease. It feel un-whole, as though parts of me are doled out in the remote corners of some — *this*, perhaps, of them all — city, to defaced beggars. Were those body, were those soul, these parts?

***

The letter "A" flashed shortly through the sky, then went to hang from a rafter, as though a famous player, Lafleur or Gretzky, had his jersey retired in the National Hockey League. It apparently waited for company, for it remained relatively agitated, a-flutter in the secret winds, roughing up waters.

Sarah saw herself at a table, tearing out, separating stamps from a philatelic sheet, no knives, just fingers pulling away on each side of it, until some of the small perforations started to crack open.

The small noise didn't call anyone's attention, for there was but herself in that frame.

On one of these stamps there was the figure of a dancer, and, skewed, the view in the dream opened up, and there was Patrick pirouetting in the small stamp frame, all the time looking at her, as though she was, in that virtual space, the only spectator present, or available, or even noteworthy. She didn't know how to extend a hand and touch him, and applaud she tried and couldn't either, the sound was totally off and whatever she called to him, it was lost on the border between worlds. Then it was as though she had been taken away to a meadow with a copse of trees where her view radically changed and it was now all a white sky extending its whiteness to the horizon, and all around her there were small hills, rolling one to another, sometimes their flow interrupted by patches of woods, through which her sight wasn't able to penetrate, and on each and every hill there was another person — both men and women they were — and all were standing out there pointing at her. Even later on, remote from the dream, she couldn't tell if their pointing had accusation or the shock of surprise in them, as their faces didn't have any expression or meaning.

And in the dream she felt guilty of missing or lacking something, and all those people witnessing it, and felt an urgency to change things, but what was there to change, — she was given no hint, not at that time.

Being barred access to that knowledge, this was what stayed with her from that dream as a true hole localized somewhere in herself, an untold story grabbing at her with its lack of words, which she knew they had to be, or otherwise everyone else there wouldn't have come out pointing so insistently to her. It was like the entire world knew that she was missing something, but the links of communication had broken down, one way or another, and they couldn't tell her in soft or hard words, in silence or in cries, what that was.

Then all this was fading and she felt as though a deeper sleep had set in over her, so that no memory was left to be reeled in as a fisherman's catch. The recollection simply didn't operate — waters too profound to fathom, would she later on conclude, disappointed.

This must have taken a long time, for when it was over, it averred itself that she was now in a room on the walls of which were displayed multiple copies of oil paintings, all showing her mother, teeth set, looking at her. It wasn't Mother's best day, no doubt, because her forehead was furrowed with concern and she looked intently at Sarah, as though, again, trying to tell things that she would need to know if she were to be protected from untold threats.

"You should, you should," her mother told her now and seemed to look out the window of the tall building in which she stood, as though looking to a ground quite remote and much lower, as though finding herself in some medievalish donjon with something happening right then on the other side of the moats, in the field reaching the outskirts of this huge architectural contraption. Was it a citadel, what it was — she couldn't tell.

In the dream, her mother was as she remembered her since Sarah was young, a tall, imperious woman, the long black hair dropping straight as an arrow behind her shoulders, the main feature of that which only Sarah saw and called her beauty. The pair of smallish, a bit unclear, eyes, didn't have the gift of enthusing anyone else, especially when one considers they were placed above a nose which dropped faster from its middle than it had done first from her forehead, an aquiline feature that typecasted her for 'the reserved,' or 'the rational, but semi-ugly,' characters, as the critics said. The critics, for she had been an actress and sparring with them was one of her perpetual pleasures and vagaries.

And this next is the part of the dream, Sarah mentioned later, where *the idea* was suggested to her by forces unknown. And this is how, she later argued to whomever was there to listen to her recounting this peculiar dream, that she claimed to have passed through her sleeping mind on that fateful night.

Her mother having retired to the remote places from where she had come in this younger version of herself, that inner sky came back to a white, but there were no hills this time, only a large flat field covered in pebbles, and in the middle of it, there was this labyrinth, as they sometimes have in the movies and lose people in them. This one was made all in snow, and she still knows there was nothing white or pure about that snow. It was all dirty and flecks of

Marius Hancu

soot were coming through the air from all sides, not too hard, but not pleasant either — there was this carrying wind blowing over everything.

And in the corners of the labyrinth there were four people, and seemingly they had to go out through the maze and reach another corner than the one from which they had just started. Even though they didn't seem to have Ariadne's threads with them to guide them through, nor similar implements, still they carried small sheets of paper, so one was prone to think of them as maps or some such. And they went ahead, and looked at the maps, went on, and looked again. And this was going now for two hours straight now and none of the four was in any way closer to the corners, they all waded through it at a slower and slower pace, and they seemed to be definitely lost, from what she could tell. And then she zoomed in — that dream allowed her to do so — to their maps and what she saw annoyed and worried her no end, as the instructions clearly didn't lead to any of the exits, but were meant to obfuscate them. Who would have done that to those poor souls, *that* she couldn't tell, but it was right there, the malicious or the criminal intent, for they could have spent their entire lives in there with no chance to see the life outside the maze.

And she couldn't have stayed put, nor quiet, even if that was a dream and something told her she didn't have to believe what her eyes, or mind's eyes, told her to be true, about the dire straits in which the four journeymen were in.

So she went to the large map placed outside the maze and studied it for something like five minutes, which must have been a lot of heart beats for the poor souls within the labyrinth. And light was made in her mind and she cried out to all four to halt their progression for she had news for them. Then, she took them one at a time and navigated them through the maze with her voice until they were out at another corner from the one they had started off in, and the four lived to see another day.

That, she later said, was when she realized she should never trust her first reaction, the convenient one, and let people do what they mistakenly thought they had to do, but better ask them to do, if she could at all convince them, what she herself thought — relying on her own determined thinking — believe it was right for the situation. You might just be the only person having the key to a situation and all others could be in the wrong. Act your belief, if you have one. And that "You should," she construed, was only a hint and empowerment that she needed to have in order to act on her own, to believe her own, where others thought otherwise. That Patrick had danced in that very dream only to herself could only have strengthened that belief — it was always the smaller lever that moved the mountains, she said.

39 - *The Puzzle* I, Berlin, 1991

The invitation had initially come in the late eighties, right after the fall of the Berlin Wall, from a pro-unification outfit that wanted to promote access to Western art. At the time of the original contact, they wanted something new, modern, with some play on the unification motif. Then, after the Wall had been over and done with, they contacted Yvonne again. They had acquired a large grant from some pan-European organization commisioning a modern piece, on the only requirement that in the cast there should be dancers from at least fifteen countries — most of them European, though they would accept one American and one Canadian among them. So the logistics, the syncing of so many people for a single event — the expectation was they might get lots of international TV exposure — became a major issue.

Through one of Nureyev's protégés at the National Ballet of Canada, Menelaus Seferis, a choreographer himself, thus competition in one way or another, who was, however, a sweet and helpful man, Yvonne got to know a communication whiz at Mitel in Ottawa, Steve Underhill. The moment Underhill heard about the commission, he gloated: "Oh, you should talk this over with someone at Thinking Machines in Massachussetts. What you're trying to do touches on stuff that they're using in their massively-parallel computers. Daniel Hillis himself, the founder, may be interested."

She got to Hillis, but he suggested she talk to Alicia Thompson. "A brainstorming session with her could take you along much farther in your project."

"The Puzzle," the production, was supposed to be centered on a kaleidoscope with a soul, in fact, a great many of them, tens, hundreds of souls, perhaps.

Yvonne described it to Menelaus Seferis, before it ever saw the stage: "You know, with a real kaleidoscope, you turn it or shake it once *et voilà*, a new configuration, a new stem, arises. You twist it again, you get another geometrical layout.

"Lifeless geometry, you'd say. Where's the soul? Only on the outside, that agent of change — your hand. Still you wouldn't be able to tell in advance what each shake would pop up. There's crystalline coolness, randomness, lack of control, small chaos, that takes care of that.

"Now, assume you pepper your chunks or slivers of glass down on a huge table. Next, assume this table is the stage — the place of all adventure for people like us and, to boot, for our audiences.

"Even more, give a living soul and body to each of the slivers. Then, go to the extreme and make them human, your brothers and sisters — dancers.

"OK, so I've translated most of it into a play in *our* realm. Still, something's missing: the agent, the shake. What to do about it?

"Well, do you want to go democratic or dictatorial?

"So, you want democracy? Fine. We'll equip each of these dancers with a soul and consciousness of their own — the egotistical, the altruistic, the whole shebang of human variety in personal history or education. All of them contemporaries — or perhaps plus or minus two or three generations.

"Put them together. Now, you had better expect conflict, love, alliance, fight, wars, all colliding and combining for an average lifespan of seventy years, if they're lucky.

"Shake and stir — no, you don't need anyone to do that to them. It's enough just to put them together, then Adam and Eve, Cain and Abel, the stories will *all* emerge.

"It won't take you long to tell me that on a stage all this will appear awfully amorphous, that there won't be symmetry, aesthetics, beauty. And you're right, society looks that way. In a democracy, everyone pulls the way their damn free will, personal history, disappointments in love, and perhaps intelligence all tell them how to react, under the spur of the moment. The symmetry is mostly in teamwork — when our humans fight one another for a trophy in rhythmic gymnastic, or in Scottish military precision. Don't forget to add the fifes!

"You want some order, a common pull or motive? Stalin or Hitler would do just fine for the purpose. However, we would honestly have to count them as external shakers, the oppression strong enough to cover everyone, roughly the equivalent of telling everyone what and how to breathe, roughly the equivalent of putting a sky over your stage."

Here, she cut her own flow — torrent, as it were, the way it was coming to Seferis at the other end of the phone line — and told him: "Mene, I must leave you now. I really need to go out and meet that wonderful costume worker I'm working with in Toronto. She may have some input, you know. All these people, fifty or so of them, must be really lightly and compactly dressed, or utter confusion could ensue on the premises if one snatches somebody else's stuff. I think Béjart with his costumes for *Le sacre du printemps* was onto something. There won't be any scarfs flapping around, no belts, no jewelry, this much I can tell you right here and now. Bye for now."

"Don't burn your candle at both ends on this one, Yvonne," he interjected. "It could be quite a while to put everything together for this gig. But hang on to it, seems a great idea."

Yvonne laughed to herself: pretty much everybody knew how many flops Seferis had had, along with his admittedly memorable hits. Honest to John, this is just par for the course in this business. Still, he was someone with whom everybody liked to talk, as there wasn't even one evil fingernail in his once athletic constitution, now a bit rundown by women and famous men — he was definitely bi — and red wine, together with his great grills and barbecues.

The dream she had the night after that phone call was like no other she had had for the previous five years. There was this huge gate adjacent to the city, the unknown city itself a citadel with a seemingly square layout, surrounded by a crenelated wall, then by reeking, fetid water on the outside, standards flying high on the donjon. She in a party of defenders up on the walls.

The sky in that dream was busy with travelling clouds, whirling and twirling around apparent centres of force. The people in the citadel underneath watched the clouds with terribly anxiety, eyes telescoping their motions in the sky, their feet following in step each of their undulations and gyrations in the wind, as though in a trance. They, up above on the walls, didn't talk to each other more than the people of the city, all their attention caught in this collective watching of the threatening clouds.

A rainbow then appeared — however, a very unusual one, its colors separated, each on a different cloud, the colors all moving around in the sky with the clouds, the sky itself a huge kaleidoscope playing with the colors of the rainbow.

Suddenly, at the horizon, a huge light arose and expanded, red-hot, then faded away, and all those people submissively and simplemindedly, having had until then eyes only for the skies, stopped watching the heavens above, and instead, looked around and started to talk to each other, as though re-discovering their neighbors. Once this happened, it was as if the sky had lost any significance to them.

She had woken up without knowing which part of the dream, if any, had been enjoyable. It was more like awe, the condensed feeling left with her. However, the colors and the switch in the overall concern of the inhabitants of the city in the dream were to stay with her for a long time.

Yvonne lived in Toronto's St. Clair area at the time. A cramped apartment, its kitchen-slash-dining-room-slash-living-room glass door opening to a small balcony, barren of flowers at any time of the year, demonstrating to any onlookers the busy schedule of its current inhabitants. Nearby a patchy park, peppered with straggly trees, their leaves corroded by acid rain and other side-effects of modern civilization. The bedroom window looked on Rosehill Ave, where the traffic wasn't heavy enough to bother those on the tenth floor, especially someone coming in exhausted as she did from rehearsals or classes.

One of the bedrooms was transformed into an office; a large draftsman's table on trestles, a platform as it were, plain, not lacquered, with wide paper sheets laid out on it, ready to receive her markings, sketches and write-outs for her choreographies. She didn't use any of the current standard notations; she had a personal set of

Marius Hancu

signs, the significance of which was hidden to anyone but herself: arrows, curves, rectangles, trapezes, circles, ovals, wide swaths as an entranceway swept up for visitors. Some of it was in color, those necessary to separate one format from another, as tin soldiers would be separated on a game board.

Menelaus Seferis got to see once some of these sheets at the National Ballet, crossed himself the way the Eastern Orthodox Christians do at their size, intricacy and undecipherability, then asked her, "Is anyone else able to understand them?"

"I don't worry too much about posterity," she answered. "I make them to help my own memory, nothing else, so why should I bother about readability?"

"Of course. I was just twitting you. It's just funny how much they look like Apollinaire's *Calligrammes*, the way you write here and there your notes, scribbling them around your icons or symbols, your marching or take off orders, whatever they are."

"Well, thanks. I know *Calligrammes*, but believe me, there's nothing decorative in my notes here, while I'm sure your sweet Guillaume makes a conscious effort 'to make beautiful,' which is nothing to be condemned. On the contrary, it's nice to find stanzas or lines floating here and there, as people do in Chagall. By the way, I have some ideas about Chagall, but that would be for some other time."

She had thought about something to make dancers show up in apparent weightlessness, to be able to dance Chagall. Still, there was real work to do on the engineering side of it to have something at all operational, also to have something the mechanical details of which would be well-enough hidden from the spectator — really critical, to her mind, to achieve *the fly diaphanous*.

40 - *The Puzzle* II, Berlin, 1991

This hadn't been the kind of rehearsal Yvonne had intended, not by a long shot; on the contrary, it was, plainly speaking, turning into a total loss. Two plastic mineral water bottles lay on the floor near her, emptied, another had been just opened, stray witnesses to the strain wafting through the crowded and perhaps already loaded air of the rehearsal hall in Berlin. No inkling could have been found on her face, except for the eyebrows a tiny amount ever closer to each other and the darker and harder light accepted, simmered, filtered out, and projected back into surrounding space by that pair of large blue eyes. Only she could have told there was sweat beading up behind her ears, as per her wont in times intense, also that her bra was already wet at the back, but she wasn't into holding this knowledge layered up in her awareness, but pushed it down and definitely did not share it with others. Still, she was happy wearing on this particular day a bright yellow cotton polo shirt that breathed well, which also absorbed any by-products of stress, for a decent end-of-the-day.

In fact, this rehearsal had been designated as first of a series of three aiming to prepare the world-wide premiere of her new ballet "Random Reconstruction — The Puzzle," which was supposed to take place in not more than a week on one of the largest open-air stages of Europe, an oblique, however well-meaning, homage to the fall of the Berlin Wall just two years before. "World-wide" really meant world-wide proper in this case — the presence of a partial complement of facilities to be used several years later by Seiji Ozawa to synchronously conduct five choruses located around the world during the opening ceremonies of the Nagano 1998 Olympics.

As the third rehearsal was, as expected, to be full-dress, hundreds

Marius Hancu

of leotards, sweatshirts, tights, ballet shoes and slippers — no tutus, as this was supposed to be something really in the manner called "modern" for lack of a better word, although "contemporary," Yvonne felt, would have fitted the bill just fine — were in storage at the Deutsche Staats Oper, the temporary seat for this ad-hoc ensemble of dancers and support people, where the dancers limbered up everyday in class previous to rehearsals prudently scheduled at two in the afternoon. Noonish would have meant a crime, to be long vilified as an affront, by the German trade unions willy-nilly involved on the technical side, as would have happened also in most of the siesta-loving European countries.

It was during that first rehearsal, when after half an hour, in fact immediately after the first ensemble motions, that Yvonne realized no one was in sync with what she had expected from them. They, the fifty or so dancers, had received their marching orders in e-mail and-slash-or fax, one month in advance. It just happened that very few dancers lived and danced in the same city or knew each other, so practicing in pairs or small groups had been impossible. The only thing they could do, and the more experienced ones, had been doing, was to perform sessions of mental visualization based on the scripts received, as well as solo practicing, with no recourse to a rehearsal companion able to provide commentary or even partnering at any time, unless they found someone able and willing to do that for free. Yvonne called this *in vitro dancing*, having, most probably, caught the term from one of her biologist friends.

The floor of the rehearsal stage at Staats Oper Unter den Linden was marked with a taped grid, a set of eight parallel lines perpendicular to another set of eight parallel equidistant lines. Other obliquely-set lines indicated diagonal routes, future trajectories of walking, running, moving.

"Hello, everyone." Yvonne requested the dancers' attention over the audio system, speaking into a microphone in one of the corners of the room. She was perched on a five-foot tall pedestal. "Please, each of you, take up your initial position, *one*, on the grid." Several minutes later, after some milling around, they seemed to be ready. A table had been brought in close to her, just in case she wanted to climb on it for a better view of the proceedings.

"Please take your required stance for the initial position. Ready for the music, are we? Now, ready, set — go on three. One, two, *three!*" She signaled to the music director to start the tape. This was supposed to be a digitally synthesized Vivaldi, his "Four Seasons."

Barely five bars had issued from the loudspeakers when she cried out "Cut, cut! What is this, everyone? Don't you know your original stances as part of the scenarios? Let's go back to that, with no music. Stance, please! Freeze, now!" She was perplexed, as no one was oriented the way they should have been in her recollection. With all the corps watching, she started to talk over their heads with some of the individual dancers.

"Ariana" — she was Greek, blonde, red tights, white leotard, average size, slim — "you should be in the two-three square of the grid, that is two horizontal, three vertical, at the beginning, crouched, facing west. I don't think you are in that place, or are you?"

"No, if I remember well my script said 'start in the seven-two point of the grid. That is where I am now, facing north of grid, standing, raised arms in fifth position *en haut*.' I don't have my script with me, but I could go right now to the dressing room and find it in my bag, if you don't mind my leaving for a moment."

"Keep your place, please," Yvonne said, and she mumbled to herself, "perhaps she's short of memory; let me take someone else."

"Jason" — that was Jason Trimble, from Edinburgh, Scotland, a massive six-foot-tall man endowed with huge thighs clamped in minute knees, with a pair of thin arms and an Afro crown of curly hair as though teleported straight from *Jesus Christ Superstar* — "Jason, could you tell me where you should be right at the outset?"

His reply was cautious but firm. "Five-seven in the grid. Pirouetting — if my memory doesn't fail me."

Yvonne knew there should have been one dancer in motion at the beginning, intended to attract the focus of the crowd while all the others assumed static stances. But it couldn't have been Jason. Also, according to her own script, he should have been at two-two in the grid.

"OK, people, please hold on to your positions until Ariana and Jason rush to me their own scenarios. Quickly, you two, please!"

Ariana rushed to the dressing room, which promised to take some time. Yet soon Jason seemed to have quickly found his scenario in a backpack on a side of the stage, in a crowd of similar personal effects. He was the first to come to Yvonne's podium with his printed copy.

"Look here, please, second page. Isn't it five-seven in the grid. Pirouetting?"

"Lemme, lemme see. You're damned right it is. Let me wait for Ariana." The Greek dancer arrived after three minutes or so, panting, after climbing over the abrupt stairs leading to the ladies' dressing rooms in the basement.

One look was enough for Yvonne to realize Ariana's scenario was also totally off. The general text regarding the scenes, general flow, seemed to correspond with the diagrams, but did not marry with hers.

Yvonne cried, "Sarah, where is Sarah?" Her assistant had been quietly sitting on a plastic-frame chair in a corner, with a full copy of the original documents, text and diagrams in front of her.

"I'm here, Yvonne," she said. She had gone around the podium, in order to be in front of Yvonne. "What has happened?"

"Well, haven't you witnessed what happened?" Yvonne asked with a lower voice to avoid further agitating the dancers — it was very important to keep them all mentally prepared for the final show. "They don't seem to have received the proper diagrams and descriptions. Everybody has prepared something else than what I expect them to do. Did you yourself send those attachments?" She looked at her closely. This would have been the first case of crass negligence on the part of Sarah. They had been working together on and off the better part of five years now, pretty much from the beginnings of Yvonne's becoming a choreographer. Thirty-nine now, the same as Yvonne, Sarah had been in this case the nexus between this large group of dancers and Yvonne.

"Yes, it was me. Still, for the soul of me, I can't understand what happened. Perhaps it's just here and there, missing file names, don't know," she said in a low voice herself, half hissing under her breath.

"OK, everyone." Yvonne addressed the corps in a louder vice. "Let's see where we are, as we've got to deal with some confusion. I'm sorry, but we'll have to do some detective work to see which role each of you has mentally prepared for, based on what you received in your correspondence. Perhaps we can do some repositioning to make up for the errors with the least changes in your assignments."

Yvonne had realized there seemed to be double trouble.

First, right at the beginning, she had individually cast the fifty-odd dancers to a certain position in the grid, expecting them to dance a given part starting off from there. And, based on the first tests, they weren't in those positions. Where each particular dancer was specifically involved was critical. Her grapevine had told her that Jason Trimble was too heavy for the complex pirouetting required at the startup. She had paired Serge Polyakoff from Paris, of the Ballet National de l'Opéra, especially with that role, as he was known as the fastest and lightest turner of the group, long arms, his general thinness and sharpness helping a lot. He had worked with Nureyev during the latter's tenure as director of l'Opéra in Paris and Nureyev had always cast him in such roles. Yvonne knew you could distrust Rudi's relationships but not his professionalism.

Second, the dancers were in the wrong scenarios. Again, *who* was doing *what* was critical. As things were at the moment, she found that neither the initial positions nor the assigned scenarios had reached the intended dancers, nor were they paired with each other. She took a sip of water from the bottle and a deep breath, then continued in as settled a voice as she could.

"Hello, everyone. Please, all of you, take a seat on the floor, wherever, this is going to take some time. I think today's rehearsal will be dedicated to finding your proper initial places in the grid." She wasn't sure how long it would take to solve the mess, but she knew they couldn't leave for the day without a palpably good start and, once she had determined that, the way she was, she was all ready to go again, all purposeful intent, like a capable drill-sergeant leading his company around enemy fire with all his art, once there was an objective.

"OK, who's now at zero-zero in the grid, please tell me."

"It's me."

"Hi, Li Na." Yvonne personally knew most of the dancers, the selection and casting having been her own work. She had their files and this one she had recognized with ease. A Chinese-American girl, shaved in the head, à la Dalai Lama, tanned-skinned, perhaps a Tibetan Buddhist herself.

"Well, by rights you should have been at five-five but let's forget about that for a moment. I'm more interested in what you have been rehearsing, let's see if we can stick with that for you. Please, show me the moves for the first several bars of your script, perhaps we can leave you at least your dancing."

The girl stood crouched toward North, face glued to the knees, arms behind the head, clasped. She started raising her head and spine, keeping the legs down close to the floor, and suddenly threw her arms into the air with open palms, as though in desperation, head pushing toward the sky. Then she started gradually to stand up just from the legs now, keeping the torso and the arms in the same raised position. Still a moment later, when the legs were extended to three quarters, she dropped one arm to her hip, clapping the hip with its open palm that remained in place after contact, pointing with the other toward the sky, and started to move around it as a vertical axle, knees a bit bent.

"OK, I know what you mean," said Yvonne. "Let me have a look at my notes. OK, OK, I've found you. *It's not* the role I had in mind for you, but stick with it for the time being." It wasn't one of the critical ones, and Li Na was versatile enough, she knew she could count on that. "However, in order to execute it, you'll need to re-locate yourself at seven-five in the grid. Please move over there and sit down on the floor or grab a stool from the sides.

"OK, everyone, we'll have to go through this for each and every one of you and that is fifty-eight dancers. I think this will take me about three hours, assuming three minutes for each of you, which might be too short to be real, but … You see, some of you might — luckily for them — still be reassigned their original roles exactly per my casting, as they may be too related to your particular talents in my mind, and I don't want to dismiss or miss any of that. For those reassigned today, this will take a bit of learning, but you are to be coached by the dancers who got your roles in the first place by mistake, they themselves needing to be taught by others. Thus, there would be some coaching for you during the uptake. I'll tell you who is who, don't worry. This also depends on the degree to which the rest of you can perform some non-optimally-assigned dancing.

"Sarah, could you bring me that chair over there? Thanks. I'll need it." Sarah's face was blotched all red-white and she didn't look back at her. *Naturally, embarassed, so should she be.*

"OK, people, let's get back to our muttons.

"Serge Polyakoff, where are you?" She found him in a corner with her blue gaze, darker and more focused for the occasion, he still being, at this very instant, deep in talk to a sweet Italian, who tapped him gently on his arm to signify he was to move upfront for talking to Yvonne, which he did presently, all in a short run. "I need you to start with that pirouette at the beginning in point six-two, as I have it here. Jason, we'll need you to relinquish that role and — sorry to you both — coach Serge for it, while Serge will coach you in what he's been training at home, back in Paris, however, not for four-five where he initially was positioned, but for three-six, the right position in the old, initial, script, I mean yours, Jason, sorry for the confusion. You two can leave right away for the group rehearsal hall. Lucky enough we have three of them reserved, ask the porter. Come back tomorrow at the second ensemble rehearsal with your respective roles learned. Go along. I don't have time to get into any fine print, you're professionals. Bye now, see you later.

"OK, class, I'm talking zero-one now, next in queue. Who's currently located there?"

"It's me. Hi, I'm Adriano Marchetti of Milano." Long gray tights, same gray for the Apache T-shirt, a wiry thin body underneath, high cheekbones under a closely cropped brown crown of hair, intense black eyes contoured by a pair of thick brows.

"Could you show me the beginning of your scenario?"

She found it was exactly what Li Na has just demonstrated and confirmed to do, only starting toward the south. There were several replicas of that sub-scenario spread over the grid, thus this wasn't strange per se. "Fine. I know now. You'll keep your role, but you need to go to six-five and sit there, please. And, please, we need your face shaved for the final rehearsal. That is a must, sorry. Thank you." The Italian had already smiled and nodded. Everyone was buzzing, however all seemed to have remained patient.

"Next, (zero, three). Who is it?"

"Hi, Alexandra Panova of Kiev, Ukraine."

Tall, rounded to the minimalist contours in which roundness was acceptable in the ballet world, definitely a magnet for the male audience, and perhaps for some of the other half too, with sparkling blue eyes, telling of passion quick to flame. Yvonne knew. *She's one of my stars, let's be careful here she gets what she deserves if we want this to have some echo with the public.* Then, louder, "What do you have for us, Sasha?"

Alexandra quickly danced something of a replica of what Li Na and Adriano Marchetto had, however, oriented toward the West in the starting position.

"No, no," Yvonne said. This is hopeless, it seems that none of the principals have been assigned their own scenarios. I'm going to kill Sarah tonight. The stress in this interior thought must have been strong enough to be somehow felt by Sarah, who turned her face toward her in what was perhaps an advance request for pity, or just the indifference of someone who sees herself lost.

"No. Class, who has got this script?" and she went through the dancing and mimicking, or pantomiming, of the first seven bars of Alexandra's script, just to give them an idea. She was supposed to project the silhouette of a woman standing, head bowed, arms clasped together in what seemed to be deep praying, then dropping into an *arabesque penché*. "Who has this part, please?"

"Just a moment, please, coming, coming." Someone was bumpily coming from the back, talking to her along the way, "But I *want* this role, I really worked for it in my private rehearsals."

Yvonne looked at the incoming dancer, judging her quickly while she was proceeding. "No, she's too plain, no sparkle, can't do for this one." By the time Nancy Bermann of Israel was in front she had lost the role, and no one knowing Yvonne was really surprised with the quickness and the irremediableness of the decision.

"I'm sorry, clerical error." That was a nifty bureaucratic swing, ready to throw in the face of people when one needed a break. She looked at Sarah to place the blame more personally, but hidden and guarded enough to restrict this quick regard exchange to between them. "I cast Alexandra in this role and I'm going to stick to it.

Please swap and teach each other your new roles. Your new positions are — just a moment — they are: Nancy, three-three; Alexandra four-five. Please step into the small rehearsal rooms right away and thank you for the understanding. Don't forget to write down your positions and to swap the diagrams for your scenarios between you."

They left, and Yvonne, looking at their backs, realized Nancy Bermann was still mumbling about the reassignment. Still, she knew, that with Alexandra pushing her, Nancy would have to release that part to the other dancer. Whether the other was decidedly more beautiful and sparkling than herself was probably thoroughly disappointing, but then, it wasn't the first time in Nancy's life that things hadn't gone her way. And she looked at her rival, Alexandra, "This girl, she's not a prima ballerina assoluta, she must have had some rejections to her life too. So what, there's place for all of us in this ballet corps and I'll make the best of it." And armed with this, one can call it only appropriate, set of principles, Nancy accompanied the lovely Ukrainean to a small exit located at the back of the stage.

***

Serge Poliakoff and Jason Trimble were by this time already in the rehearsal room 2, which had a view over Unter den Linden. The light came haltingly on this clouded day through a set of old-style windows, witnesses perhaps, in their narrowness, to the time of the large inter-war renovation of 1928, a time with other architectural ideas floating around, most probably stressing solidity and stability over quality of light, from what the two dancers felt and exchanged. The parquet was properly waxed, with something that didn't make it too slick for one to slide or, even worse, fall.

For the time being they were alone, still they could have company, as well as interference, coming in at any time, so they started immediately, having shaken hands and offered short introductions of themselves on the way over.

"First, let's swap diagrams," said Serge, "I, perhaps it's only me, need to have something hard to rely on and point to at home, while thinking about the piece and digesting it by myself, when trying to find a link in the chain that might still be missing for me then."

Jason took his notes received by e-mail from Sarah out of this shoulder bag, Serge found his in his duffel. They both put them on the floor, sat down on it — "not many tables or chairs in these places, are there?" asked Jason — and pushed them to slide over the floor to the other.

"Here you are. Done," said Serge. "OK, do you want me to start showing you what I learned about the piece that was mine and now it's yours?" He laughed.

"Go ahead. I'm all eyes and ears, figuratively, of course, but let's first slip this cassette with the music in." Luckily, a small audio system with two loudspeakers belied the bareness of the room. Having been first in on this occasion had its advantages, they could set themselves to be masters of the music in that room. "The newcomers would have to more or less follow our choices," Jason said. "Which is always a good thing, so let's keep control over the newcomers, OK? "he conveyed *sotto voce* to the French dancer.

Serge was now up, standing in his tan stretch-cottony maillot and tights just under the knees, bare footed, "even though," he said, "Yvonne wants us to use those awful green slippers she had made for us for this show by the shoemaker here. Superlight, she says, and, more importantly, fitting the roughness of the floor to have in the final show, and I know the Germans are definitely good in terms of comfortable shoes, I know that from my Salamanders," while the Scot preferred to watch him still sitting on the floor for the time being, craning his neck looking up, following his motions.

The cassette, Jason saw it on the label, had been recorded three years before by a smaller formation of the Berliner Philarmoniker with Karajan directing and Anne-Sophie Mutter playing the violin solo, on the occasion of opening the Chamber Music Hall of the Philarmonie. He didn't know then, but would see in the coming years the video of the same recording, with Mutter in full glory, in a deep red dress, décolletée — as she never liked anything between herself and the violin — rimmed by black above the bosom, the old conductor – just two years before his death — playing the harpsichord and directing. He felt it was intense, especially on the side of Mutter playing serious as a Valkyrie, but also of the Philarmoniker themselves, perhaps feeling one of their last occasions to achieve glory with Karajan, as a great horse, a Bucephalus, would feel the last occasion to be ridden by his Alexander and rear up all the more under him.

The attack of the strings in the Allegro of "The Spring" was acute, the pain of new life breaking forth from under the load of winter, dullness and universal death. Jason remembered the part that Serge would have to be dancing now and didn't envy him, as he had to slightly bounce and rotate in a *grande pirouette sautillée* with the working leg extended at ninety degrees up to hip level *in plié developé à la seconde* for many long beats, at the beginning and again later on, the ballet soloist carrying the first break from under the ice, the rest of the dancers consonant more with the orchestra's part, the tension now growing, the expectation of new warmth, the trepidation. And he didn't know yet, but Yvonne will tell them during rehearsal, that for her this rush breaking forth, this is what breaking the Wall had been all about, the new spring for Europe and for the world.

Serge was in "The Spiral," from which the dancing of "The Spring" began. The cold of winter — all dancers crowded and huddling, each with hands extended over the neighbors, as though to conserve energy against the elements. The music starts, that poignant rush of the soloist on the violin, followed by the strings desperately wanting an exit from the winter. And on the cry of the violin the man at the center of the huddle frees himself from the crowd and starts pirouetting, and the others detach themselves each from the crowd and start running with small steps along spirals, arms still along the hips — the fear, the cold, still there — the heads gradually facing up toward the sun, opening up to life. And this was what Serge was trying to show Jason now.

"You see, from Yvonne's commentary, which I hope still applies," he laughed, "this run of yours should be in a spiral, each one of you behind the other, while I'm turning. And those small steps should come in rhythm with the attacks of the strings, here lost and slow, here rushing, but always kept small as though the energy comes only now in the bodies, with the spring rushing into the village, or city, or whatever this place is.

"I'm shuffling my feet on the floor, you see, I think she wants the shuffling to show this apparent lack of energy at this particular time beat in the seasons. And from shuffling, see, I can – here accelerate — here, slow down — more with the music. See the arms, lost along the body, there's no tension, no energy in them, the whole movement is legs shuffling, knees a bit bent to show tethered, limited running. The face should be still, blank, lighting up as the goings on of the spring, the music, grow."

"It's tough," said Jason, "I think the violin tries to imitate the lark, rising and falling in the sky, joy with it, and those breaks are going to be tough to have in dance. Not sure if you catch me."

"I think I do, man, I think I do. I thought about it myself back home," Serge told him, at the end of another shuffling rush through the spiral. "It's tough because she doesn't allow you to pump your arms; for what I see, the arms are a pretty inanimate object in that whole movement, except on the comings back."

Those were the intervals during which all dancers, having arrived on the "outs" of the spiral, away from the center, came dancing back country-style but just barely, nothing heavy, as the music suggested, two-by-two, male-female pairs, arms linked at the elbows, skipping back lightly toward the center, with no huddling this time, only to start another shuffling advancement along another spiral. Out on the spiral; in along the radii, coming back to the center.

"Now, let's get on with your pirouettes" said Jason, "I think you should be going forever something like those thirty-two *fouettés* Odile has to do in 'Swan Lake,' batting from the knee with the free leg, and opening and closing time and time again the arms around her, to help continue the motion, you get me?" He whirled around on semi-pointe several times, Serge having to control his own smiling, as really those huge thighs of Jason's wouldn't have been able to turn for the length of time required in the Allegro, even with the breaks available during the rushings-in of the corps toward the center, when Serge was supposed to just walk around in the center, taking in the dancing of the others.

"Wait a minute, I'll start the tape in a minute. It's just four minutes or so, this Allegro," Serge said, noticing that two other pairs, two men, and a male with a girl, had entered the rehearsal hall, positioning themselves in the other corners of the room, far from the audio system. The replay took off again, and he started his own ideas of pirouettes. Lighter weight and more talent made for much more facility, that much would have been simply obvious for anyone watching – Yvonne had been in the right to stick to him for the pirouettes, this part with so much gyration in it.

41 - *The Puzzle* III, Berlin, 1991

[*The immortal soul of Yvonne discoursing*]: So, here we are in the middle of Berlin, with nothing to show for a beginning, and a lot to adapt and fix. With calm, levelness, steadiness — all difficult aims for the time being. For what disturbances bring into the life of a man — or woman, as one should say and write in this over-illuminated age — if not lack of direction and hesitation, a tack which many a time is lost, thoughts looking for a home, the askance and askew looking for a view, the toll looking for a bell. And the saddest thing for us dwelling in the forever world is to see the short-term interest — one could not use such an exalted term as 'ideals' for them — taking over the actions, for how could one otherwise qualify whatever Sarah Pritchett did in times leading toward this day. Still, perhaps her everlasting soul is just that, plenty of envy, uncensored lust, desire to grab from others, and we shouldn't be surprised by it. The important thing for us with Yvonne was, will remain, to think and project ahead of us, lay the groundwork for good, let the good take care of the bad in the due course of time, as it doubtless will.

***

Yvonne had, by this time, finished reassigning the roles.

"OK, everyone, we see each other tomorrow at two in the afternoon, same place. I'd be very grateful if you could try out the new roles with the previous owners of them. And, by the way, I'll show up at class and in the rehearsal halls tomorrow morning so I'll be able to make on-the-fly corrections or give you commentary or help."

It was already quite late in the day, around seven, when she finally left the building of the Staatsoper Unter den Linden.

Things were starting to fall in place, but what a downer of a day! She still couldn't fathom how in the world Sarah had been able to mess up the whole thing, messed it up twice in effect — first, the initial positions, second, the assignment of scenarios themselves. She would have to talk that over with her but now just wasn't the right time, she needed to keep her own energy level up, and any such discussions, which easily could get bogged down in contrary assertions, recriminations, negativism, were bound not to help in that respect. For now, she simply had to take the long-term interest of the show to heart and push ahead, past be damned.

She decided to lock herself tight in the hotel room — room service, no calls accepted or returned, 'Do Not Disturb' hanging on the doorknob. Luckily, just a five-minute taxi ride — a Turkish driver — had been enough to take her from the Oper to the hotel, located on a quiet side street. It had seemed expensive, but it might be worth it now. She ordered the only chicken on the room service list, went famished through it, realizing in the process how worn-out she was, the natural consequence of such a dog-day — under the aegis of Sirius, W.H. Auden would have claimed — forced herself not to imbibe any alcohol, took in some hydration with fruit juices from the fridge in the room, then lay down in the bath tub to soak and get in some extra energy from the hot water, enough to make her relax. She looked for all the world as Cleopatra with a towel turbaned around her head, she laughed benevolently to herself in the bathroom mirror. "I signed up for this," she said to herself, "so let's not complain too much or be queasy about stress." She preferred to play the drill sergeant to herself and others around performances and it seemed, this time, it was just the thing, with already one rehearsal lost to Sarah's confusion — and she left something suspicious floating around with so many dancers taken out of action by some easy-to-avoid clerical error. But tomorrow was another day and she looked forward to a change in the winds of fate.

Throughout the commotion, there were several things to be happy about, though. All dancers had landed in Berlin on time and had punctually shown up for the rehearsal, a thing to appreciate under any circumstances involving a crowd of sixty or so aficionados *de la vie bohème*. Then, the costumes were all ready, as were the shoes too — these German craftsmen were a treasure, several adjustments were still needed for some of the dancers, a tuck here, a 'give' there. It was coming up on nine o'clock at night, only perhaps one, maximum two hours left before the sleep would take her away, thus she decided to mentally review the cast, now that everybody was there where they should have been months ago. These were top notch, young pros, able to switch tack on-the-fly, so she expected everyone to be tuned in by the time of the live performance.

Still, this had been, to a large extent, a lost day. Even more, most of the visualization and other training the dancers had done by themselves was mainly off, as it applied to the wrong scenarios. "Darn, Sarah, what did you do? As though you're not vested in this show!" she scolded ragged the probable culprit in her fancy. "Did she have the blues and thus only muddled though the job?" Sarah had acted as a rank beginner, throwing everyone for a loop.

While on the way to the hotel, she had to listen again to Vivaldi's music in its entirety. Too many times, "The Seasons" had been divided for her during that very day into snippets, bars, morsels. She wanted resonance restored in herself, she wanted to have its sounds and vibrations from one end to another, unexpurgated, continuous, for there weren't any interruptions to it in her ballet, nor were there any cuts to the original music. She wanted to cleanse herself of interruptions, and of the piece-meal feel, as it left dangerous territory to have in your mental image about a piece of music.

She was aware that in the Tiergarten Park, at the time of the show, there might be fifty thousand people, and she was concerned about the notes at the end of the spectrum — very high or very low. How were they to propagate in that environment over such distances, with trees and buildings thrown into the combination? With several giant screens, visibility should be OK from all angles, still, the details on which she wanted to work the next day might well be nigh-invisible to remote spectators. However, this was the pact with the devil she knew every performer in a large-scale arena was confronted with.

Ariana and Serge Poliakoff are among the first to arrive on the premises of Oper Unter den Linden for the second day of the rehearsals. Ariana's blonde hair radiates above a set of black tights and a green T-shirt; Serge is resplendent in white tights and a red T-shirt. The attentive observer has most probably already noticed them stepping out of the same taxi bringing both to the Oper. If that same observer were learned in physiognomy, and of the expressive type, he or she would readily contend that both share marks of a short sleep — one reason why at this very moment they share something else, a large thermos full of Turkish coffee, brought just in case.

It is eight thirty in the morning, a Tuesday, and the sun comes in benevolently through tall windows in the hall where the ballet class was given for warm-up, limbering up and general maintenance of the week to the dancers of the resident company, as well as to visiting dancers from all over the world. Yvonne had it arranged — and paid for it — to make such classes available to all the dancers involved in Saturday's show, yet the sheer number, close to sixty, promises to make this a serious logistical issue, as the class is usually given in a hall that definitely won't be able to accommodate such an extra influx without some special arrangements.

"Ladies and gentlemen," Anneliese Grantsch, the ballet mistress, tells everyone over the loudspeakers in a very pleasant, but German-accented, English, "taking into account that at times we may reach ninety for the total number of participants to the class, we'll divide the class into three groups, each of which will come by rotation into this hall, where we have the *barres*. We are, of course, aware that all of you would like to have your bodies passed on the rack on these traditional instruments of torture and," she chuckles, "support for all of us. Things being this way, we'll work in three twenty-minute installments, or should I say rounds, the first of which should start in three minutes from now. Please, only thirty of you should remain at the *barres*, here, this is the limit, we don't want to get too familiar with each other this early in the morning." Here she laughs. "The others should divide equally into rehearsal rooms one and two. Now, fortunately we've distributed the sound feed in all three rooms, thus everybody will hear my splendid voice carrying the commands of the routine and hopefully that'll help in terms of getting into the local rhythm. After twenty minutes, we'll have a five-minute break, during which those in rehearsal room one will come here and those in here will step out to rehearsal room one. After another twenty minutes, the same will be done with those originally located in rehearsal room two. OK, let's get going, only thirty please remain at the *barres* here. Thank you for your cooperation and see you soon, but by installments, if you don't mind."

Anneliese, many of them know already, is a former star of the East German ballet, and, now they realize, a very glib one. She has been able to successfully make the transition into the ballet mistress role at the Oper, as nothing compromising has been yet discovered in her Stasi files. Others, who have been quickly and decisively retired from all positions of real interest, have not been so fortunate. Still, there are rumors that she was a beneficiary of the steroid treatment so much in vogue with the GDR women swimmers — women carrying door-wide shoulders — rumors aided by the palpable reality of a considerably bigger Anneliese in her last active year, a reality that is said to have led to complaints from her porteurs at the time, hit, one after another, by hernia and, finally, to her retirement.

Yvonne has already showed up herself for class, yet this isn't her territory and she knows it, thus she takes her time. She prefers to have her dancers properly limbered up today before approaching them in earnest. She moves to a place in rehearsal room one, having left most of her stuff in the ladies' lockers. She's decided to go through this routine as she does most of the days of the week, to be sharper during the day, but she knows her best must be available during the afternoon at the full rehearsal of her own ballet.

For the time being, she just motions to them in recognition here and there, instead of a fully articulated "Good morning!" which might be felt as too intrusive.

Sarah has shown up too. She has a concerned look, and "She'd better," Yvonne tells herself, "'course we're in big trouble just because of her." She fathoms there's a need for an open explanation between them, but views herself as still too edgy on the matter, still moving toward a decision. It's not there yet, she doesn't feel up to it yet, especially not after a night of uneven sleep. This is funny, somehow: Sarah is wearing a business suit, navy blue, and high heels, not the usual grey stretch-polyester pants she brings around for rehearsals. Not that she ever gets into the physical side of it anymore, that is in class.

"*Grands battements*, everyone," Anneliese's voice is heard in the loudspeakers, several minutes later. Series of ten, each leg, alternate."

"Can I hold on to you a bit, Yvonne?" someone asks her from a side. She turns. Oh, but it's Sonia Tourelle of Nice, in fact of Nice and Monte Carlo, she's freelancing between the two places. Sonia does *grands battements* at the moment and places a hand on Yvonne's shoulder for two explosive series, in need of stability, as they are without a *barre* in this room.

"OK, now we can switch roles, I'll play the *barre* for you," she laughs.

"And what do you know, I'll take you up on your offer." Yvonne does herself a triplicate series of the same, changing hand for support on Sonia's shoulder. "That was nice. Thank you very much. Can I help you with something else?"

"No, I'm fine, I'll just do some *pliés* and some stretching on the floor."

Sonia's dressed as a gymnast today: mediterranean-blue athletic briefs, a midriff top tank and a pair of pink ankle warmers.

The Berlin weather continues outside in a glorious fashion. The sun drenching the parquet makes some of the dancers squint, so one of them goes over and turns down the angle of the horizontal window blinds a bit.

"Change of hall, everyone," Anneliese's voice resounds over the loudspeakers, so Yvonne and Sonia move to the room with the *barres*.

"OK, everyone, eight per barre, please," Anneliese tells them, making sure to flip the microphone off, so it wouldn't be heard in the other two rooms.

"Now that you're already warmed up, we'll start with some

stretches in *développé* on the *barre*. Right foot on the *barre*, please, and on, press, release, gradually dee-eeper, please. Yes, that's it, Nadia. Switch to the other leg. Don't rush your stretching, Alex.

"Let's get to the *pliés* now, please. Gradually lower, bob down, until you feel it you know where," and she pointed to the lower part of her buttocks, smiling, joking like an older Puck. She's in an orange leotard, no skirt, Anneliese, well muscled, fibres showing up from the capri leggings, as well. For a flash, she thinks back of the times in Karl-Marx-Stadt of the GDR when she was practicing her ballet moves right on the edge of the municipal swimming pool, with everyone bathing, so people were turning heads, where does this girl think she is, but were all quieting down, once the poses, jumps and pirouettes were more daring, enough to have her in the water at the smallest mistake, as on a balance beam in gymnastics.

"Now the *petits* and *grands battements*, then some *dégagés* and *rond de jambes*, please."

"God, this is definitely some New York City Ballet class right in front of our eyes," Yvonne hears clacking right behind at the *barre*; she turns a bit, and it's John Torres, of Puerto Rico. They met during her best years in New York City. She knows she's still in great shape and she's proud her *barre* work still gets accolades. John is half Hispanic, half Navajo, an explosive dancer, if ever there was one. He partnered her once, at a gala given at the Metropolitan Museum, on a cold winter Saturday evening.

The room is square, on a corner, and the corner sides of this old, but probably entirely rebuilt after the last war, building have some tall wide windows, their light partly cut in thin slices by the blinds.

***

Four hours later, everyone is warmed up and focused, awaiting the first attacks of the violins and of the harpsichord — it must be the old maestro himself there — in the "Spring," and the whole corps springs into the first steps of dance. The voice of the soloist violin rises as a lark of a sweet spring morning under a mild sun on a translucent sky, dew still on the leaves, and is responded by another lark at some distance, on one of the first violins, both challenging the sky in spurts of freedom and vital energy. Serge and Alexandra, the soloists for this part, are diametrically opposite on the scene, with a wide swath cut in the circle of the corps to allow them movement, and they rush, both at the end of their long independent pirouettes with *fouetté* of the entrance, with small guarded steps to each other, as though not yet daring to take in the new circumstances, the arms free to the sides as wings, stopping at several steps away from each other, then rush away again, the fundamental natural attraction fighting at this time of the year with the individual freedom allowed and told by the season. Everybody's in the full swing of the first allegro of the "Spring," and Yvonne likes what she sees. Most of her dancers seem to already have a reasonable grasp of their parts already, at least for this segment, and there's a certain sense of extra focus in the air, no doubt caused by the lost day.

Her plan is they should all have, at the real show, different colors and touches of color to their costumes — coming at the end of the day, from the German tailors associated with the Staatsoper — to enhance the original idea of the kaleidoscope in each of its human fragments, its slivers of human glass, as she doesn't want any uniformity, nothing that would show up as regimentation, as a copycat. "There's no company here in this show, there's no village here, there's a community only in variety, one of individuals, and that's it, I'm going to push variety in everything," she boasted to the sponsors about her ideas right upfront, so they wouldn't be boiling in their own juices later on for facing too large a hit in surprise. "It may be that, to some of you, Vivaldi sounds like a nice social or courtly dance *à la campagne*; well, it's not my idea here. We may have small or even larger groups that will dance along the same motif at one time, that is similar steps or moves, but I'm going to allow differences in their execution — take a deep breath for a poetical thing to follow, ladies and gentlemen — as the sea doesn't force all the water drops in a wave to behave the same, even though there's, no doubt, some liquid cohesiveness and tension at work there." The costumes are all urban, contemporary, nothing country, still, all light, to allow easy movement. No long skirts or long coats, nothing heavy or rustic. She made no bones about it: "Not a

Gisellle, this."

She has laid it out so that each musical movement and several of the sub-movements, if time allows it without major stops in the music, should have a match in a different starting pattern on the grid for the people, as a 'stella' would show up in a real kaleidoscope. "Mind you, your focussed spotlights should tapered off and on during intermissions — sync that, please, with the music director and his tape playback — so we allow the dancers to rearrange themselves in a bit of a shadow and discretion, you know," she instructed Johannes, the local light master, during the morning, and he's supposed to get around to doing it even during this very rehearsal.

They are now rehearsing the Largo in "The Winter," the orchestra fully in pizzicatto, with Serge in center stage, in the deep loneliness of the season and of the threat of old age, a threat because he's still shown as the young man that is is in real life. Around him four groups, equal in size, of about ten, that will never reach him during the whole motion, even though slowly approaching him in their spiralate motion, each of them moving around itself and around the stage as a leaf carried by the wind. It's a large trefoil, it all, moving with a slow, dignified, breath of motion. One group is a circle, all holding their arms on the neighbors' shoulders, perhaps à la Zorba, rotating around its axis and around the scene with long, elastic, relaxed steps. Another one is made up of two lines of five dancers each, all holding, left and right, their neighbors' waists in a relaxed grip, with full extension of the arms, thus not too close to each other, in similar rotation to the other group. The third is a square of three by three, all separate, sliding around, as though skating, part of it in pointes in *pas de bourrée couru* and in *croisés*, part of it in barely raised toes, *relevé*, partly stepping and gliding in *glissades*, moving as a whole without any contact — and she knows this is difficult, giving them special attention. The fourth group is five couples dancing around in slow waltz, soles to the ground, a slow dance of old age, again covering the whole surface around the center stage. While all this goes on around him, Serge — the only one all in white — walks around, arms to the side, palms down, thus more in dejection than in acceptance of any help offered by others, moving them in desolate *ports de bras*, body bending to the front and to the back in *cambrés en fondu* and *en rond* and sideways, the legs in wide, yet tired, sweeping steps, here cutting into full lunges and falls, there stopping quietly in *arabesques* of last effort and energy.

Just a bit later, they need to rehearse the first part, the *allegro non molto* in "The Winter." She's left it for later, only too aware of the difficulties of tempo they might face. To some of the audience, she guardedly hopes, some of the poses should strike a certain similarity with sports, and in that, flash off some modern connections. The corps ladies will be moving most of the time in what in Yoga they call a balancing dancer's pose, bouncing in order to advance, *arabesque sautillé* that is, while the men will counter hopping from a martial arts pose, again standing only on one leg, the other being raised and held immobile in front as for a kick strike to the head of the opponent, or in the frozen stance of a cobra ready to pounce, basically in a *développé croisé devant*. And, on that sublimely controlled staccatto held by the orchestra violins, they would have to advance in two circles, the women on the inside, going clockwise, the men on the outside, going anticlockwise, twelve in each, most of the time bouncing in these stances, in stubborn advancement, in a rhythmical background for the soloist in the center, those hieratic stances suggesting perhaps an old Egyptian frieze, archers after archers behind the pharaoh. At times, they would have to change the support leg, interrupting with *coupés* the old motion. In center, Alexandra and Serge would have what she hopes would be one of the great *pas de deux* of the show, full of supported and independent *pirouettes*, scissored *entrechat-six* in sync for both of them, full scale circling and jumping in *grand jettés en manège* round the stage for him, alternating with long series of damnedly spinning *fouettés ronde de jambe* for her, all in the great passion flowing from the solo violin.

Final, 1991

Wet, steamed, and, for the most part, submerged in the water of the tub, the water mildly hot as she usually wanted it at this stage of her cleansing, she was alone in the bathroom of her ballet studio on Bloor Street West.

By this time of the late afternoon, everyone must have already left for their homes. To make the circumstances even more propitious for an undisturbed bath, she didn't have any class on late Fridays, not now, in the hot summer of that year, with the lull caused by the kids leaving for their vacation or, for those not physically leaving, letting their minds leave and stray from anything strenuous, anything that could be related to something that somehow or other could have been labeled as 'work' and thus boredom-inducing.

At this time, the clanging of the elevator door, the only noise left in a building now even more deserted for the weekend, had no difficulty reaching her. A former textile factory, now refurbished for studios and offices for people in the arts, its hallways still retained that concrete-like bareness, and the impersonal, rough wall painting couldn't help but imprint this state on the viewer. Also, most of the studios kept the large windows of the former destination, metal mullions rudely reclaiming a stark expression over the expanses of glass. Yet it didn't count on this occasion, as the sun was still strong enough to penetrate the thin white opaque paint covering the bathroom windows. Still, some angles were too dark for her taste, even at this time of day, thus she had the lights on.

The familiar winter-time hum of the radiators was missing, the quiet even more intense now. As well, the neighbor above, a sniveling — whenever met in the elevator or on the staircase — massive, but not tall, bearded painter, didn't seem to have any models in for that day, thus his bed, or perhaps his floor — Yvonne had never peeked into his place, so this uncertainty had to be left unresolved — wasn't creaking with the vigorous post-séance sex he seemed to administer, gift, or perhaps require as a bonus, the sound of which sometimes created snickers among her own pupils, especially the younger ones, though they never asked for explanations, for they knew that the request would have been taken by their mistress as a definite sign of a break in their own concentration, at all times something seriously frowned upon.

With radiators switched off the building's water circuit at this time of year, the boiler seemed to be easily doing its duty, her hot water piping hot at the spout. From it, with many iterations, she produced the mixture of right temperature, just what she wanted for full-immersion, soaking in it for what at times was approaching the half hour.

She had recently bought an old-fashioned heavy-crystal bottle of water scent, musk in fact, and this was her first experiment with it lavishly poured into the tub water. Its effects were spectacularly frothy, large-bubbling frothy, and she played with the bubbles, poking at them with her nails, which were sharp, going at it slowly, in random patterns, skimming the surface. She laughed at herself being so childish in doing this, enjoying the youth there was in her, its being still in her. It was as though the scales of time had become a softer skin, that skin of an instant belonging to those bubbles, as though the roughness of those dragon scales melted into smooth feeble surfaces, so when touching it, the time, its touching, didn't take you of a sudden to heavy bleeding. And there was also, and always around in her mind, sometimes hidden but never quite lost, never quite dry, the timid hope that from these plays, via channels and connections unknown of the spirit, would emerge the higher, more adult, games of ballet, those in which motion and body would replace bubbles, in which sentences and sequences of turns, extensions, lifts, stops and rushes of steps would replace the water in which she was right then and there and the foam, would replace their minuscule waves and motions, a fluidity turning into another. And the Mediterranean was in a small replica there, and her own swimming and dipping around the boat with the girl years ago. The sun and the azure and the half of the world underneath them, water and earth, as though eons back behind in time at the scale of her own existence, still so much in front of the eyes of the mind, conscious and unconscious.

The Muzak in the hallways of the building was trickling in now, a sure sign that the janitor had already come on this afternoon, as he sometimes did, so as to finish his job earlier and leave for his own slice of the common weekend. He always liked to listen to music while he trundled away bins, large and small, metal and plastic, from rooms and storage areas on each floor to the back courtyard, where the municipal trucks were supposed to come to pick up the garbage on Monday mornings. However, she wasn't hearing the familiar bumping and clattering noises and the groans accompanying his heaving, pushing, and unloading; all she detected was the louder music.

She was again letting her mind hover above that latest alphabet of motions and stances, all Egyptian- and Indian-inspired, which working through her imagination, tensing and flexing it, somehow was succeeding to float in front of her eyes for so long these days. She wanted to frame and code such an alphabet for herself first, give it some finiteness and closure in her own innermost mind boxes, before thinking of any definite work sprouting from and with it, before asking anyone to adjust their limbs and their rhythms to it in what in the beginning would seem strange ways. She had looked at friezes of old, Pharaonic-time art in several museums, at pictures in albums in libraries or bookstores, some of which she had acquired, at Yoga and Kama Sutra books. Palms at, for our times, strange angles to the wrists, fingers and toes out of alignment with the normal extensions of the body, turnings and rotations on planes different from the contemporary ones, rhythms, accents and stresses that seemed out of sync to the modern eye and ear.

Once the alphabet were in her possession, or at least the lion's share of it, she would grow the feeling she wanted in large swipes, concatenations and sequences of it, as carrying the blues, the joys, and the pains and the wants would be much easier then; it would come ingenerate as breathing does, and it should come that way. Then, she would be the carriage driver, the horse whisperer, the tamer and the liberator at once, getting the ghostly stallions out of hiding in clear thought and muddled unconscious.

The elevator doors clanged open and closed and she heard a shuffle of steps through the poor insulation of the building, on one of the hallways, on some floor; otherwise crystalline silence.

Yvonne dipped for a moment her head under the water that was already high enough, ready to spill from the tub. Fully supine, fully submerged now. She needed a final rinse of her head, so she twisted, plowed and snatched her head with energy through the water, going with the hands through it, matter of getting rid of any remaining soap before drying herself up.

Innocuous, outside the bathroom, in a corner of the hallway, to the right of the door, on a tall small-surfaced four-legged wooden table covered with a red-dentelle table cloth, this General Electric white-plastic-shelled hair dryer, already plugged into a wall socket located right underneath the table top, but switched off for now, which Yvonne liked to use, standing, once out of the bathroom. It certainly was a bulky item, and she had intended for some time now to buy a new, portable one, to be used everywhere, when traveling, in this place, and at home too.

Raising her head from the water, face in her hands, she pushed from her legs and sat up a bit higher, her back against the inclined wall of the tub opposite the taps, and continued rinsing her hair. A light, subdued, muffled click was heard in what must have been the lock of the entrance door of the studio. This must be Jolion, the caretaker — too old; as well, he didn't enter the bathroom at any time anyway — no reason to be concerned. There was still soap in her eyes and the air in the room was dense with steam, so she could barely make out the wall in front of her. Still, she could tell, this was more of a tiptoeing than a shuffling to this tread on the floor of the passageway outside the bathroom. Seemingly coming closer. Still not anxious, she continued to splash and scoop with her cupped hands water on her face and top of her head and to pass her fingers through the strands of her hair. She came back to the thought: what could an old, withered, and sometimes wobbly-from-work janitor do to her, worst case? But she cried out, just in case, "Is that you, Jolion, out there?" It echoed sharply on the tiled walls around her

Marius Hancu

and on the hard, concrete, structure of the building, but its resonance was suddenly broken by the door opening outward, suddenly creating more space for her just-uttered cry to travel and to lose itself.

Only a high-speed camera, with several hundred frames per second, if that, would have been able to make sense of the events that followed. An all-in-white silhouette, thin arms still bare to above the elbow, a visual blob of moderate size for Yvonne at the beginning, had sneaked into the bathroom from the hallway and was now momentarily standing past the door frame, the feet in pink sandals on the wet floor, the face hidden under a huge pair of orange-tinted skiing goggles in a terrifying sight, the hair drawn back, a baseball cap low above the brow. In the same motion, the hair dryer appeared in the right hand. A shout followed: "That's for you, happy one, take it!" which was hard enough to awake all senses in Yvonne and to not think during that instance about who the person was. Stunned, but with eyes open as for eternity, followed she the electrical implement being lobbed toward what to her seemed a mountain of water in which she herself was, a target impossible to miss. In a reflex motion, a leg thrust from the water kicked with its wet toes the device. On impact, a first electrical discharge appeared to have taken place. Reversed in its trajectory, the hair drier went, of all places, back to its original holder. Hugely surprised, hands that first had the intention to bunt it back or away, found in the muddle of thinking and reacting, grasped it for several thousandths of a second too long and a massive discharge followed, filling the room as though lightning had struck with the shaking and the smoke of burning human hair and flesh.

Epilogue, 1995

"They could have my brain in a bottle, *in vitro* I think they call it, picking its vibrations. Of a dance, of course. That's the next step I guess," Yvonne said. "For the time being, I'm allowed to do this from this wheelchair. Glad the hands and the sight are still in place. And George, whenever he has the time to come over to rehearsals, to push me around. Not that I can't do it myself. Just letting me focus on dance and not on anything of my silly movement around the place.

"Crazy women. She, for doing it — but she paid for it with her life. I, for going on, partly paralyzed then.

"George it is. George?"

Acknowledgments

I would like to warmly acknowledge the following individuals, groups and companies:

- Cheryl Perkins, for an outstanding review of my manuscript.

- Sonia Dumitrescu, an exceptional ballerina and ballet teacher, for an introduction to the modern ballet in never-to-be-forgotten live shows, as well as for many illuminating conversations on the burning passion of those possessed by this great art.

- Liana Macri, for help in spreading the word about the book.

- Many of the members of the *alt.usage.english* newsgroup on the Usenet, for help in mining the riches of the English language and of many literature works. Especially, but not only: Charles Bellemare (CDB), Donna Richoux, Professor John Lawler, Don Phillipson, John Dean, Robert Lieblich, Peter Duncanson, Frank ess, Ross Howard, Mike Lyle, Cheryl Perkins, Jerry Friedman, Mark Brader, Eric Walker, David (the Omrud), Iain Archer, James Silverton, Ray OHara, Lars Eighner, Raymond S. Wise, John Varela, Irwell, Robin Bignall, James Hogg, Stephen Calder, Cece, Isabelle Cecchini, Leslie Danks, Athel Cornish-Bowden, Derek Turner, UC, Tony Cooper, Adrian Bailey, Peter Moylan, Skitt, Horace LaBadie, Nick Spalding, Django Cat, Harvey Van Sickle, Pat Durkin, Harrison Hill, R H Draney, Ian Jackson, Laura Spira, Katy Jennison, Roland Hutchinson, Glenn Knickerbocker, Snidely,

John Holmes, Aokay (David G. Bryce), Evan Kirshenbaum, Carmen L. Abruzzi, Stan Brown, Joe Fineman, Don Aitken, John O'Flaherty, Alan Jones, Charles Riggs, Martin Ambuhl, Maria Conlon, Jonathan Morton, Arcadian Rises, Mike Barnes, Prai Jei, Steve MacGregor, Bob Cunningham, Guy Barry, Matthew Huntbach, J. J.Lodder, R J Valentine, Lewis, Whiskers, GordonD. Sorry if I missed anyone. You have all been great.

- My critique partners, especially: Clarksvill, Cheeno, Mooderino, Toddkonrad, Sky.

- Many of the members of the *www.dance.net* site. Especially, but not only: maureensiobhan; Christine Killian Dunham, from The Dance Center in Pocono Pines, Pennsylvania; Ashwini.

- Curtis Brown Ltd., for kindly allowing me to use the quotation from "Body and Soul" from W.H. Auden's *The English Auden: Poems, essays and dramatic writings*, ed. Edward Mendelson © 1977.

- William Shakespeare, for quoting his sonnets.

The errors are all mine.

Comments and suggestions are welcome at kitescomments@gmail.com. I would especially appreciate feedback from the dancing community. However, I am sorry I cannot commit to providing replies to everyone.

Works consulted

The American Ballet Theater Dance Dictionary (online): http://www.abt.org/education/dictionary/index.html, which I recommend to anyone not having a background in ballet and dancing who wants to have video presentations of the various poses and steps. Youtube is great too in this respect.
  Gretchen Ward Warren, *Classical Ballet Technique*, University of South Florida Press, Tampa, 1989.
  Geneviève Guillot, Germaine Prudhommeau, *Grammaire de la danse classique*, Librairie Hachette, Paris, 1969.
  Gail Grant, *Technical Manual and Dictionary of Classical Ballet*, 3rd edition, Dover Publications, Inc., 1982.
  Julie Kavanagh, *Nureyev*, Pantheon Books, New York, 2007.

Made in the USA
Lexington, KY
09 June 2013